The Holts: An American Dynasty

AWAKENING

IT IS A TIME OF INFINITE PROMISE AND UN-IMAGINABLE TERROR . . . AND FROM THE SHADOWS OF PREJUDICE AND WAR, ONLY A FEW—THE STRONG, THE BRAVE, THE LUCKY —WILL EMERGE TO BECOME A PART OF THE GREAT AMERICAN CENTURY.

India Blackstone—An artist both talented and rebellious, a pioneer political activist and feminist, she has chosen a way of life that makes her anathema to some, an inspiration to others. But for a woman of her time, independence of mind and spirit does not come without cost . . . and she's about to discover how high the price can be.

Sally Holt—Fun-loving, flirtatious, at ease in New York's high society, she always knows the right dress to wear and the right thing to say. Loved by nearly every man she meets, she wants only one . . . and he may be lost to her forever. Ultimately she will have to make a choice—which could lead back to a place she thought she had left behind forever.

Frank Blake—Drifting through life and across the country, he is a spiritual nomad, searching for the one cause he can seize with a passion. His fierce political radicalism and his fiery love of India Blackstone are the two constants in his life—neither of which is strong enough to stem the powerful urge to wander.

Roger Stiller—A New York artist with little talent and no scruples, his short-lived love affair with India will lead to scandal, bitterness, vicious rumors, and finally to vengeance. His rising influence and power in the city's artistic circles could prove devastating to India's reputation and her career.

Juergen von Appen—Handsome, charming, well-educated, he is the one man capable of winning Sally Holt's heart. But Germany is his homeland, and when the guns of war begin to sound and American blood begins to spill, he will have to decide . . . between his love for Sally and his loyalty to his country.

Robin Cochrane—A British soldier and casualty of war, he has lost his leg in the bloody killing fields of Europe. As a hospital volunteer, Sally Holt nurses him back to health . . . only to risk breaking the heart of an already broken man.

Jerry Rhodes—A forty-year-old bachelor banker and Wall Street hotshot, he offers India—as she approaches middle age—not only financial security but an opportunity to bear a child. It's a chance she will take . . . even though he may ask for her soul in return.

David Rhodes—The fruit of a star-crossed marriage of convenience, he will bear witness to a moment of absolute horror and tragedy that neither he nor his mother will ever forget. He will seek sanctuary on the open road, only to find that the past is mere prelude to the kind of pain a cruel world can inflict.

THE HOLTS: AN AMERICAN DYNASTY
VOLUME TEN

AWAKENING

DANA FULLER ROSS

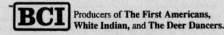

BCI Producers of **The First Americans,**
White Indian, and **The Deer Dancers.**

Book Creations Inc., Canaan, NY • Lyle Kenyon Engel, Founder

BANTAM BOOKS
NEW YORK • TORONTO • LONDON • SYDNEY • AUCKLAND

AWAKENING

A Bantam Book / published by arrangement with
Book Creations Inc.

Bantam edition / November 1995

Excerpt from "Joe Hill's Will," which appears on page 139, is
reprinted courtesy of Industrial Workers of the World.

Produced by Book Creations Inc.
Lyle Kenyon Engel, Founder

ISBN 0-553-56904-X

Published simultaneously in the United States and Canada

Bantam Books are published by Bantam Books, a division of Bantam
Doubleday Dell Publishing Group, Inc. Its trademark, consisting of the
words "Bantam Books" and the portrayal of a rooster, is Registered in
U.S. Patent and Trademark Office and in other countries. Marca
Registrada. Bantam Books, 1540 Broadway, New York, New York
10036.

PRINTED IN THE UNITED STATES OF AMERICA

OPM   0 9 8 7 6 5 4 3 2 1

AWAKENING

THE HOLTS *An American Dynasty*

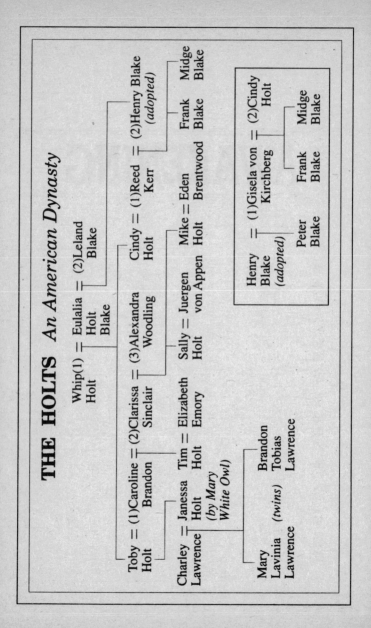

THE BLAKES, THE BLACKSTONES, AND THE BRENTWOODS

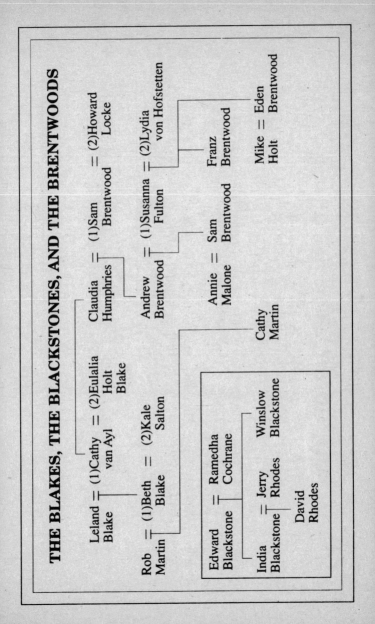

PART ONE

1900–1915

I

Greenwich Village

India Blackstone pushed up the creaking sash and leaned her elbows on the windowsill to survey her kingdom. The air of Tenth Street in the first April of this new century was laden with the smells of cooking cabbage, cheap red wine, Mrs. Dunagin's potted geraniums on the second-floor balcony, cats, and when the wind was right, faulty drains.

India loved it all. It was a heady mixture combined with the odor of linseed oil and turpentine from her studio, the biggest room of her three-room apartment. She leaned farther out and watched a courting couple kissing brazenly under a lamppost. It was no wonder her mother had not liked this part of New York City, or that her conservative and overprotective father had harrumphed and gone away in a temper. But India was in her element here. She felt as if she had suddenly sprouted wings, and Greenwich Village was the right place to try them out. She wrote her parents dutiful letters, and they wrote back disapproving ones, but she didn't go home to Oklahoma. She knew that if she went back there, she was sure to land in the net of a good marriage to a nice boy, and possibly the chance to paint on Sunday afternoons if the nice boy and inevitable children didn't require her attention.

Now she had a contract to produce an illustration every month for *The Gentlewoman's Handbook,* providing her with enough money to afford a third-floor apartment with a kitchen, a north-facing skylight, and the background coo of pigeons. The bathroom was down the hall—and was occupied from ten to twelve every morning by Daisy, a Floradora Girl who took pains with herself—but it did boast an actual tub, which India enjoyed when she could find it empty.

There were strange, cheap restaurants to explore, and entertainment ranging from Broadway plays to socialist lecturers and soapbox oratory on street corners. Mrs. Dunagin was here in the ground-floor apartment to screen her callers, and the postman, who was in love with her, brought her other people's mail just so she would have to stop him and give it back.

He was down there now, waving a handful of letters at her. She smiled, waved for him to wait, and clattered down the stairs, dodging Mrs. Dunagin's cat, Max, and Mrs. Dunagin herself, who popped out her door.

"You've got yer apron on again!" the landlady called. India had once gone out hatless in a paint-stained pinafore, and now Mrs. Dunagin considered it her duty to preserve her from sartorial faux pas.

"I'm just going for the mail," India called. She flung open the front door of the building in time to see another familiar figure striding up Tenth Street, one she didn't get to see every day. She blinked, but he didn't vanish.

"Three for you today, Miss Blackstone." The postman held out the letters with the air of presenting her with a rose.

"Thank you, Mr. Verner," India said, staring past him and only glancing at what he gave her. She caught, peripherally, the return addresses: her parents, a young family friend in Oregon, and Frank Blake. She transferred her gaze from the envelope, posted from New Mexico, to peer over the postman's shoulder at Frank himself.

"What are you doing here?"

"Bringing your mail," Mr. Verner protested.

"I wrote you I was coming," Frank said in Mr. Verner's ear. The postman jumped and glared at him as India tore open Frank's letter.

"So you did," she said, reading. "It says so right here."

"Is this man bothering you?" Mr. Verner straightened his uniform jacket.

India looked up dubiously.

"It's all right, son. She knows me," Frank said, clapping the postman on the shoulder and pointing him toward the street again. Frank shook his head at India. "Femme fatale. You attract them like flies to overripe persimmons."

"You're always charming," India said. "I suppose you might as well come up."

Frank followed her up the stairs, whistling, and tipped his disreputable cap to Mrs. Dunagin.

"This is Mr. Blake, an old friend of my family's," India said, obliged to introduce him. "You'll make me a scandal," she hissed at him as they reached the third floor, but he wasn't listening. He tipped his cap again to Daisy, who had emerged from the bathroom in a silk wrapper and a cloud of gold ringlets.

"Get in here!" India pulled him into her apartment and shut the door.

He looked around him with interest while India wondered if a man you had made love to four months ago could really be considered your past or was merely an inconvenient manifestation of the present. She knew she loved Frank and had seen no other way to acquire an experience that society reserved for the marriage she was unwilling to make. She had no doubt that Frank loved her, too, in his footloose way.

He hadn't changed. His sandy-blond hair, now bare of the disgraceful cap, drooped in a careless wave over one eye and was getting too long around his collar. He was handsomer than he had any right to be, and muscular, and he looked at the moment like a bum. His trousers were as bedraggled as his cap, and he wore a pullover sweater instead of a jacket. On his feet were heavy boots, workman's boots. The only sign of respectability was his gold signet ring, the emblem of the military school from which he had never graduated.

Frank inspected her apartment with a grin. Nice young ladies from good families didn't run away to paint in New York in an apartment with a brass bed in the parlor, her father had told him.

India grinned back at him, glad to see him in spite of herself. Nice young ladies didn't sleep with men in the barn, either, but she thought it had been worth it, and only a fool would marry Frank. "I'm not in the gutter yet, despite predictions," she informed him. "I have a job."

"I saw the wee lassie." Frank picked up a copy of *The Gentlewoman's Handbook* from the table by the bed, which doubled as a sofa, and flipped it open to the monthly short story: "The Lass of Loch Lomond." Opposite the title page, a maiden in a plaid gown gazed with naive desire at a young man whose kilt and plaid cloak were rippled by a bracing wind.

India snatched it away. "They made me," she muttered. "My father liked it, though. He's a romantic. It halfway resigned him to my staying here."

"How long did you sell yourself for?" Frank asked.

"I knew I shouldn't have let you in," she said. "The others I've done for them are different. Here." She took him into the studio, where the latest was on the easel. A blond girl sat under a scuppernong arbor with a cat at her feet. The grape leaves framed a face of sylvan beauty, a little country Diana.

"Nice," Frank said noncommittally.

"I convinced Maxim that I'm not the Lass of Loch Lomond type, and he saw my work before he hired me, so he ought to know it."

"Maxim?"

"The art editor."

"Mr. Maxim?"

"No, Maxim Fontarel. Things are fairly casual there."

Frank lifted his eyebrows, and India made a face at him. "I'm a disgrace. My father has said so."

"Not in anyone's terms but your father's. Poor old man, and mine, too. The world's full of them, trying to keep their children on the straight and narrow and convinced the nation's going to hell in a handbasket." He smiled, turning her other canvases away from the wall and looking at them without asking. She didn't protest.

A few he recognized as having been done before India moved to New York, but the rest were all her magazine work. "Where are the things you used to do?"

"I haven't done any since I got here. But I will. I just need time."

"Do these take that long?" Frank gestured at the girl under the arbor.

"I have two more commissions with other magazines, and there might be a chance to do murals in some nob's hallways. Just scut work, filling in the master's designs, but it pays."

Frank gave her a startled glance over his shoulder. "Are you that broke?"

"I don't want to ask Father for any more money. It gives him privileges I'm not willing to accord anymore."

"Mine wouldn't send me any if I asked him for it," Frank said.

India didn't doubt it. He looked as if he had jumped out of a boxcar, and he probably had. Compared to Frank, she was a dilettante at bohemia. She thought he was far too proud of it, too.

"What are you doing now?" she asked, but Frank didn't answer. Probably, she thought, because he didn't know. She looked at him thoughtfully, wiping her hands on the paint-splattered apron, then brushing her hair off her forehead and striping her brow with yellow ocher and cerise. She was tall, nearly as tall as Frank, with heavy black hair; her skin was too dark to be fashionable—the legacy of a mother who had been the daughter of a Rajput noblewoman and a British officer. India's angular bones and ranginess had come from her English father. She didn't look anything like the girls she painted for *The Gentlewoman's Handbook,* but somehow the men she painted into the scenery for them always looked like Frank.

"I'll make you tea," she said abruptly and went to light the gas ring in the kitchen, which opened off the parlor at the opposite end from the studio. Frank followed her into the parlor, stepping between the bed and an overstuffed reading chair with a fringed hassock. Something that looked like a balalaika hung on the wall.

"Are you getting musical?" he inquired.

"No, that belongs to Mike's friend Pyotr," India said over her shoulder. "He left it here because when he gets drunk, he pawns it."

"No wonder you don't have time to paint."

She turned, the teapot in her hands. "I paint all the time, damn you."

He smiled at her. "At least one of us has a plan."

She poured tea. "Then why are you here?"

"To see you, sweet." Frank looked at her over his cup and put it to his lips.

You'll be gone in two weeks, she thought. *I'll make a bet with myself.* Aloud, she said, "You can't stay here. Mrs. Dunagin would die."

"I'm staying with old Mike," he said. Mike Holt, his cousin, was married to Eden, and the two of them were anything *but* old and staid. "At least until the whirlwind begins tomorrow. Sally's coming out for a visit. Sixteenth birthday present."

"Oh, goodness, I had a letter from her. I didn't even open it. That must be what it was about." India laughed. "I'm not certain that New York is ready for Sally."

"She's a terror. Mike will have to beat his disreputable friends off with a stick, and Eden's planning a huge party. She'll stuff me into a tailcoat if I don't take to my heels."

"You'll hurt her feelings," India said gravely, and Frank looked shamefaced. Sally Holt was his cousin Mike's little sister, the baby of the family and its acknowledged beauty. Everyone in the family except Sally was in trepidation of launching her into adulthood, but everyone adored her.

"I shall have to have a decent dress made," India said. "Oh, bother." She took off her apron and considered the black gabardine skirt and shirtwaist under it.

"Take Sally with you."

"I suppose I could. I never know what's in style. It will make Mother happy if I tell her I've been to a proper party."

"It will be excruciatingly correct," Frank said. "Bankers and tycoons of all stripes, and only upper-crust poets and anarchists. Mike promised Aunt Alexandra, or she wasn't going to let Sally come."

And how have we ended up where we are? India thought. *What's wrong with us that we can't do the proper thing?* A couple of Frank's cousins had an odd kick in their gallop—Mike made moving pictures—but nothing like Frank. And what about herself? Her parents were old friends of the Holts and the Blakes; she had the same sort of upbringing. So what was askew with her that she wasn't willing to put aside art for a family, as Frank's mother had done, or find a husband and take up his interests, like Mike's Eden? *I won't,* she thought stubbornly. *Can't, don't, shan't, won't,* like Kipling's Bandar-log.

"You're looking particularly mule-headed," Frank said, misinterpreting her train of thought. "If you want me to go to Sally's shindig, I will." He stood up and put his arms around her waist from behind, talking into her hair. "The last time I saw you, I was afraid your father would find out and horsewhip me. I still am. For God's sake, your parents are friends of my mother's."

"Then what are you doing here?"

He turned her around, smiling gleefully. "I don't really know. But I'd be delighted to have your company for dinner tonight."

"Do you have any money?" India asked suspiciously.

"I do." Frank produced a bankroll from his pocket. "We'll go get Mike and Eden, and I'll get cleaned up. You can put on a frilly dress."

"I don't have a frilly dress," India said.

"Then put a darn bow in your hair," Frank said. "Loosen up, woman. It's spring!" He kissed her quickly, then let go of her as if he thought that might not have been a good idea.

He ended up spending the night with her. After insisting on taking India and Mike and Eden to the Madison Square Club for dinner and spending nearly all the money he had, he saw India home and went upstairs for a cup of tea, tiptoeing past Mrs. Dunagin's door. What India had suspected might happen pretty much did.

But it seemed worth it to her. After all, having a man up to your room was barely considered fast in the Village, although her mother would not have seen it that way. When India turned comfortably in the brass bed in the parlor and bumped into Frank's warm flanks, she decided that on the whole it was an improvement on the barn in New Mexico, where they had made love the last time.

In the morning they went with Mike and Eden to meet Sally's train, and neither one of them remarked on the matter of why Frank had not returned to their place, although India supposed they probably wanted to. The air was balmy, and all the women on the street had on their new Easter hats, like walking flowerpots. She could smell roasted peanuts in the air. It seemed as if the new century stretched ahead with nothing but delight in store.

Sally Holt descended from her Pullman car and put her sooty veil back over her hat brim to take a deep breath of the hitherto forbidden city, dangerous and exciting. She danced down the steps and flung gloved arms around her brother, around Eden, and around Frank and India indiscriminately.

"I want to go to the opera," she said. "And I want to see the Statue of Liberty. And I want to go shopping. Mama gave me money for a new wardrobe." She beamed at them out of china-blue eyes, her face framed in rose-gold curls that not even the soot of a four-day railroad journey seemed to have dimmed. She had been escorted, of course, by an elderly family connection, a Senator Levering, who was bringing his granddaughter to New York for her debut. He tipped his hat at Mike and Eden, and the girls parted with kisses in the air and the promise to keep in touch.

"We'll have to invite her," Sally said blithely to Eden, "but what a tiresome girl. She knit mittens for the poor all the blessed way across the country and never looked out the window."

"A little of that would do you no harm, Miss Gadabout," Mike said, hefting her carpetbag and waving a porter over to take charge of her steamer trunk. "If Mother gave you money for a new wardrobe, what's all this?"

"Oh, just the clothes I couldn't do without." She smiled at India and tucked an arm through hers. "And I want to know what you've been painting. I liked those Indians that floated in the air like angels over the Christmas nativity."

"I'm afraid I haven't been doing anything very interesting," India said, embarrassed. "Just pretty girls for magazines."

"I've never seen an artist's studio." Sally seemed to regard it as she would a trip to some mysterious enclave, a joss house or a Gypsy caravan.

"You can have tea with me tomorrow," India said, suddenly eager to show off her three rooms and her independence to her wide-eyed cousin. "Frank can bring you. But he doesn't get tea," she added. "He can fetch you again afterward. We haven't had a visit in a long time."

"Girl talk," Sally said happily.

"Frank will be glad to fetch you afterward," Frank said.

When Sally arrived at India's apartment the next day, she seemed suitably impressed with the balalaika, with the cat that India had painted on the wall so that it seemed to sit on a little table by the window, and with the cheerful litter in the studio. The air smelled like linseed oil; the open window let in a drift of feathers from the nests on the sill. Sally could hear the pigeons cooing.

"The cat on the wall was supposed to frighten them off," India explained. "Like rubber snakes in the garden. But it doesn't work very well." She clapped her hands at the sill. "Shoo!" The pigeons flapped up indignantly and settled down again, preening ruffled feathers.

Sally laughed. "Maybe you should just feed them and let them stay. They make a nice noise."

"I know someone who eats them," India chuckled. "Maybe I should just do that."

Sally looked around her, fascinated. In the clear north light that spilled through the skylight and windows, the studio seemed to float above the roof, magical and mysterious. Even the pigeons seemed to strike her as exotic. The girl under the scuppernong arbor was still on the easel, and several of her sisters sat propped against the faded wallpaper. Their backgrounds were rosy or golden, dawn just spilling into turquoise sky.

"They're beautiful," Sally said, picking her way through the jumble of open paint boxes and smeared rags. "I don't remember anything like these."

"I wasn't doing magazine work in Taos. These have to earn their keep."

"You actually get paid money for them," Sally said with a sigh. "Is it exciting?"

"It is when there's enough to pay the rent." India smiled, aware that she was showing off a bit and enjoying it. "It can be a little too exciting when there's not."

Sally peered curiously at the faces. "Who are they?"

"Professional models, when I can afford them. Friends when I can't. People I see on the street and remember."

"Self-portraits?" Sally said. "You're always available."

"Heavens no. Not for this kind of work. I'm not the right type. I painted myself a few times in Taos."

"These are prettier," Sally said. "I don't mean prettier than you, but the pictures themselves are prettier."

"I know." India wondered if Frank had primed the child. She wouldn't put it past him to use Sally's naïveté to embarrass her about doing illustrations.

"Frank says you ought to be showing your work in galleries," Sally said, confirming this suspicion.

"Let's have tea." India bustled into the kitchen. It was postage-stamp-sized, too small for Sally to follow comfortably. India kept her back to Sally while she put the kettle on the gas ring and made toast.

"I don't see why galleries wouldn't show these," Sally said, undaunted. "All my friends have framed ones like these from their favorite magazines."

India relented. "Honey, these aren't the kind of art that the galleries show, not in New York, for goodness' sake. They'd laugh their heads off at me if I came in with these. I keep trying to get time to do the kind of thing I was doing in Taos, but I guess I got sidetracked." She smiled and turned around with a plate of toast that she had trimmed into little triangles and spread with goose pâté. A china teapot with a dragon painted around it steamed with green tea. "I'll tell you a secret, one that Frank doesn't know and doesn't need to. I'm having too much fun to worry about doing serious art. Just being here and getting *paid* for my work—earning my own living—is enough for now. I'll have time for serious art later. If I tried to support myself with that now, I'd have to go home."

"Oh, no!" Sally said, mock horrified.

India laughed. "Precisely." Frank could sneer all he wanted to about "selling herself." *He* was male. He could go anywhere, do anything. He had no idea what a heady freedom she had achieved with her small rebellion and her magazine art, no understanding that for now it was enough for her, the freedom she'd never had before—to explore the Village, to make odd friends, to eat sardines and drink coffee at three in the morning while finishing a commission that was overdue. All of it was wonderful. She had no urge yet to beat her head against the masculine domain of serious art when she was welcome here.

Sally bit into the toast, ravenous for food and stories. "Tell me what it's like living here."

Oh, dear, I'm a bad influence, India thought. "It's—exciting," she said, choosing her words carefully. "It can be a little frightening. All sorts of odd people live here. You have to realize they're only odd, not dangerous."

"My mother says women who live in places like Greenwich Village are fast," Sally said, sounding a little wistful. India was glad she wasn't Sally's mother.

"Well, they have different rules, maybe. And fewer privileges." India poured them tea, admiring the sinuous way the thin smoke coiled out of the pot while the dragon twisted his toes around the outside. "I don't think you need to worry about a dull visit."

"Oh, I'm not," Sally said. "I want to see absolutely everything there is to see. I want to go riding in Central Park. I want to go to the theater. I want to do it all."

"All" proved to consist of a great many other things as well that Sally thought up as she went along. Over the next few weeks she and India did most of them, with Frank and Mike and Eden. India, whose energy was of a different, more focused sort, found herself scrambling to keep up with Sally. They spent a day at the beach, for which Sally produced a very daring bathing costume that her mother didn't know about, with no sleeves at all and a knee-length skirt with no bloomers, only stockings underneath. It had white sailor braid down the front in elaborate curlicues and a matching tam-o'-shanter with a white cloth rose. They rented bicycles, and after Sally taught India to ride one, they wobbled triumphantly through Central Park, where they also rode horseback, which both girls were good at, having grown up in western ranching country. They went to the theater and saw Olga Nethersole in *Sappho*, because the New York *Journal* said it was so improper that no one should go to it, and then they wished they hadn't, or at least Mike and Eden did, since the *Journal* for once had not been exaggerating.

Eden and Mike had moved from their first apartment in the Chelsea Hotel to a more staid middle-class neighborhood on Sixty-ninth Street. They had a brownstone house with a room for dancing, which pleased Sally. It had been intended as the music room and wasn't really big enough for a ballroom, but when they moved all the furniture out and rolled up the rug, it served as one for a modest number of dancers.

Eden invited the Levering granddaughter to the party. Eden's grandmother and Mike's parents had offered the names of old friends, so Eden could also invite their daughters and granddaughters. Frank promised to appear in a tailcoat, and Eden and Sally took India shopping.

They sat in Mme. Miznetsky's salon and approved or rejected the gowns passing by on vacant-faced models. "No more big sleeves," Mme. Miznetsky said. "All is here, in the front." She tapped the pouter-pigeonlike froth of lace and satin that fell from the model's bosom. Then she studied India. "For you, deep colors. Claret. Emerald."

India looked at Sally.

"Claret," Sally said firmly. "You have a nice dress in green. I saw it at Christmas, if you haven't been painting in it or something."

"Claret, then," said Mme. Miznetsky. She chucked Sally under the chin. "And let this one put your hair up for you."

India did just that, although she was not entirely comfortable with the result when Sally did her hair before Eden's party.

"I feel like the country cousin," she said dismally to Sally as they were dressing. "In Paw's old work boots and Maw's sunbonnet. I'll never learn how to dress."

"If I had the nerve to go live by myself in my own studio," Sally stated, "I wouldn't care how I dressed."

India chortled.

"Well—I suppose I would," Sally said, admiring her new cerulean blue gown. It had a tiny waist and lace dripping off the shoulders. She held on to the bedpost while India pulled her stays tight. "I just mean—well, you don't seem to be afraid of anything."

"And what are you afraid of?" India inquired. Sally struck her as fearless.

"Oh, goodness, not doing things right, I suppose," Sally said. "Not having what I want. That sounds fearfully selfish, but I'm just going to die when I have to go back to Oregon. I hate Oregon. I loved it when we lived in Washington, while Dad was a senator. New York is even better. I'd live here with Mike if I could. Oh, India, it's such heaven, the parties and the theater!"

"Not to mention the dozen or so young men who have called since you've been here."

"Oh, they're fun, too," Sally said blithely. "I'm a terrible flirt, and Mama worries about me, but I know just how far I can go. I'm too young to get serious about a boy. These boys are just practice."

India sighed. "I don't suppose you could teach me to flirt."

"Well, for goodness' sakes, how old are you?" Sally asked.

"I'm twenty," India said, embarrassed.

"And you can't flirt?"

"It never seems to work," India said. "One boy thought we were engaged, and I had an awful time with him. And I let another one kiss me, and he tried to rape me."

"Not Frank?" Sally said, shocked.

And how do you know about Frank? "Certainly not," India said, equally shocked. She remembered that she wasn't in Greenwich Village and that Sally was only sixteen. "And I shouldn't have told you that. It isn't suitable."

"It's all right to tell *me* that," Sally said. "But you can't tell anyone else, or they'll think you're fast."

"I'm aware of that. I didn't go to finishing school for nothing." They chortled in secret, shared amusement.

The party was a great success. A rehearsal, Sally said— she had decided then and there, between her first waltz and the second, that she was going to come out in New York.

"And how are you going to talk Dad into that?" Mike inquired. "It'll cost the earth, even for a quiet sort of debut, and Dad's pretty well planted in Portland, like an old madrone tree. He'd probably rather be dead than do the New York social whirl."

"Mama wouldn't," said Sally, who had no intention of having a quiet sort of debut anyway.

A few weeks later she went home to work on them, and the spring air that had seemed so bracing suddenly became muggy New York summer. Without Sally to chivy her out of her studio, India went back to painting, and Frank, as she had predicted, went who knew where. She heard from Mike that he had gone west again and was working in the oil fields. It was certainly for the best, India thought. Now she would get some work done. The claret-colored dress was covered with a sheet and hung in the back of the wardrobe. As a treat, India gave it occasional outings to the theater, but it whispered rather too strongly to her of Frank Blake.

A few months later India heard that Frank had been home to Washington for Christmas and was on speaking terms with his father. He had left at New Year's and now was working in a settlement house in Chicago, teaching immigrants to read. India's father wrote that he had come through Oklahoma and worked punching cows for him for a while, but then he had gone on. A terrible shame, and a great sorrow to his father, and what did a young man like that, who had had all the advantages, *want*? India couldn't tell him.

She wasn't entirely sure what *she* wanted, either, when it came to Frank Blake. Maybe it would be better to forget all about him and take up with someone not afflicted with a wandering foot. But what would she do with this hypothetical man if she found him? She didn't want to get married, although having discovered sex with Frank, she was disinclined to be a nun. What was the matter with her that she felt that way? Respectable girls didn't let boys kiss them until they were engaged—at least all the books on behavior *said* they didn't. India privately doubted that, but she was sure they didn't sleep with them in a barn. Still, she couldn't have waited until she got married if she wasn't going to get married.

When she had first taken the notion in her head, India had gone to Sally's older sister, Janessa, the doctor, and demanded to know about contraception. Janessa, who had made a lot of trouble for herself by advocating contraception for married women, was horrified at the notion of India's requiring it herself and the illicit activities that the request implied. She had given in when India made it clear that she intended to do as she pleased with or without it. Janessa had demanded to know who was taking advantage of her in this immoral fashion, and India had replied that it was quite her own idea. At Sally's party Janessa had pressed India's hand and inquired earnestly if she was "all right."

India didn't think Janessa had figured it out about Frank, unless of course Mike had said something to her. She suspected that the fishy eye Janessa was giving Frank Blake had more to do with his other shortcomings.

"You are breaking your mother's heart," India had informed him as they danced. "I have it on good authority from nearly everyone in your family."

"Nice that they're keeping track." Frank's eyes crinkled half shut, and she thought he was amused. He was dangerously handsome in his tailcoat, and she had noted the attendant mothers watching him warily. She had no doubt that their daughters had been instructed to dance no more than once with Frank Blake.

And what was she doing still dancing with him, so to speak? Waiting like Penelope for a footloose Ulysses with no prospects and doubtful fidelity. She was perfectly certain that Frank knew other women in those other cities and that whatever he felt for her wouldn't stop him from having relations with them. *If I want a man, maybe I should go look for one*, she thought irritably, but she hadn't the faintest idea how to do it. Maybe if Sally came back to New York for her debut, India could ride on Sally's coattails. There were always plenty of men around Sally.

Sally got her way about the New York debut and wrote, bubbling over with it, to India:

> *Father looks like a Frenchman on the way to the guillotine at the thought, but we are all coming, and he is prepared to do his duty and discuss world affairs with all the other bored fathers while Mama and I sink blissfully into an orgy of champagne suppers and new clothes. I pointed out to him that I am his last child, and after this there is only my wedding to be dealt with. Then he'll be off the hook and can go back to Portland and the ranch and take root in his hayfield and discuss manure with old Bert Givens down the road. But he didn't seem encouraged.*

It wouldn't be long before a wedding happened, India thought. Sally would probably be married off the same season as her debut, and then she would be a young New York matron—no doubt part of her plan in coming out here—and have what she wanted. India couldn't fault anyone who knew her own desires quite so clearly as Sally did.

She arrived with the daffodils in the spring of 1902, and India found herself routed out of her comfortable Village nest and martyred again to the New York social scene, but it was hard to complain when she was so glad to see Sally. India had never had a close friend—unless she counted Frank. Other people found her odd or stiff or "unwomanly." Sally found her admirable and courageous. It was flattering. And for some reason, the life that women were expected to lead, ordinarily so incomprehensible to India, made sense when Sally embodied it.

"Oh, you're wonderful," Sally said, inspecting India's apartment, now repainted in a pale brick color with gold vines trailing up the walls. The windows were covered with Gypsy scarves instead of curtains, and the balalaika had been joined by a set of panpipes, a dancing Indian god, and a hookah. A handful of daffodils was crammed into an empty chutney jar. "When I have my own house, I want a room just like it."

India laughed. "You could have themes. One room to entertain the vicar, one room to be a radical, one to be a bluestocking." Despite her butterfly exterior, Sally read constantly. It came as a surprise to her beaux, but they wrote it off as an endearing quirk.

"Certainly," Sally said. "Maybe without cockroaches, though." She picked up her skirts a little.

"Oh, they're awful." India made a dash at the kitchen floor to stomp on one, and when it scuttled under the baseboard, she stamped her foot in annoyance. "You can see the bohemian life has its drawbacks. I've put roach powder *everywhere*, but there are always one or two. I don't think the men below me clean house until there aren't any unused plates left. But I'm not making quite enough money to move. Rents are high in New York."

"Father wants my portrait done," Sally said. "I told him we should hire you. Make sure you stick him for a big fee."

"That wouldn't seem to show family feeling," India commented. "I'd do it for free."

"Don't you dare! We aren't actually related, so it's all right. Courtesy cousins can take advantage of each other with impunity. Only blood relatives are supposed to do things for free."

"You're too young to be a cynic," India said.

Sally laughed. "I'm not one really. I can't quite manage it. Life's too nice."

India inspected her. "You look as if that's true. I don't know how you got prettier, but you did." India felt only a mild disappointment that she didn't look as good.

"That's what being back in New York does," Sally declared. "I've just been dying on the vine in Portland. Mother wants to marry me off to some nice farm boy who'll run the Madrona." She put the back of her hand to her forehead to indicate anguish, like pictures in an elocution book. "It's not my fault I'm the youngest. I told Tim I felt it should go to the eldest son. He didn't thank me." Tim was her elder brother, between Janessa and Mike. Tim ran a newspaper in San Francisco and had no desire to be a farmer. None of them did, it seemed.

India wondered what would happen to the ranch when Toby and Alexandra were gone. It had been in the family since the 1840s, when Toby's father had gone west with a wagon train on the Oregon Trail, and it would be a shame for it to go to outsiders. Still, she couldn't see Sally willingly taking it on, with or without the nice farm boy.

"So you didn't fall in love with anyone while you were home," India said.

"I've had two proposals. Does that count?"

India chuckled. "Only for them."

"I am *not* going to fall in love with anybody in Portland. I am determined. And I haven't even come out yet. Who wants to miss all those parties?"

"Then what have you been doing?"

Sally made a face. "Watching hay grow. Getting 'finished' at Miss Potter's School in Portland. You know what that's like. Your mother made you do it, too."

"We read improving literature."

"We practiced deportment," Sally said. She picked up the dictionary that India kept to crack nuts on and balanced it on her head.

India laughed. "We painted in watercolors."

"We learned conversational French." Sally flopped down lengthwise on India's brass bed and kicked her kid boots off. She put the dictionary on her stomach. "Can you say 'Pardon me, but can you direct me to the police station?' in three languages? I can."

"They were afraid you might need to know," India commented.

"I am *extremely* well behaved! All the old ladies in Portland have said so to my mother."

"Maybe the old ladies in Portland don't know you well enough," India suggested, sitting on the edge of the bed.

Sally chuckled. "I am completely finished and am now prepared to dazzle the populace with my accomplishments."

India grinned. "I expect you will." Sally *had* grown up, she thought, despite her joking. She looked surer of herself and less awestruck at the wonders of New York. New York had better watch out.

Sally sat up again and rested her elbows on the dictionary, cocking her head thoughtfully at India. "And what have *you* been doing? Your letters don't sound to me like a woman who has *told all*."

"I've told you all there is," India said.

"What about men?" Sally asked. "What about the one who eats pigeons? Or the one with the balalaika? And whose hookah is that? Do you *smoke* it?"

"Pyotr brought that," India said. "The one with the balalaika. He's a friend of Mike's. I tried to smoke it once and nearly died, so I've decided it's purely decoration. And there aren't any men."

"You don't sound like there aren't."

"I don't mean there aren't any *men*. I mean there aren't any men. Just men I know."

"That's crystal clear," Sally said.

India stood up and paced while she tried to untangle her explanation. Sally was older now; it didn't seem so important to pretend to demure saintliness. "I know a lot of men," she said. "Friends. I'm afraid to try to be anything else. I told you I don't know how to flirt. I tried a couple of times, and I don't think I've gotten any better at it. I get sidetracked. I get to working, and I don't come out for a while. The ones who're interested seem to give up. Even the postman has gone on to another infatuation. He gives all his extra mail to the druggist's sister across the street now."

Sally crossed her feet at the ankles, stretching her toes like a cat. She pushed a couple of errant pins back into her gold pompadour. "What about Frank?"

India went to the windows and twitched one of the Gypsy scarves until the drape suited her. "I had a letter a while ago. Frank's not . . ." She shrugged.

Sally gave India a puzzled look. "Not here, for one thing. Where has he got to these days?"

"He's in Chicago."

"Is that why you don't see any men here?"

"Certainly not," India said briskly.

Sally looked worried, as if she couldn't tell whether India was really happy with things the way they were. "I see your pictures in all the magazines," she said. "Every time I find one, I get excited and show it to all my friends. We think of the nasty smudges we scribbled in watercolor class and are green with envy."

India smiled, relieved to be off the subject of Frank. "Do you really want me to do your portrait?" She could see it, hung over the mantel in the front parlor at the Madrona, weighted with a big gold frame.

"Nobody else. When you're famous, it will be a family heirloom. Make it huge, so my grandchildren will have to carry it around with them forever, and it will be a permanent nuisance. There's immortality for you."

India chuckled, but she was flattered in spite of herself. "All right. See what your father thinks of the notion."

Toby Holt proposed a fee somewhat smaller than the extravagant sum that Sally suggested but larger than what India would have had the nerve to charge him. He inspected her domicile with raised eyebrows.

"No wonder your father's upset," Toby commented.

India didn't answer. She was mixing paint while Sally perched on the model's stool in the studio.

"I suppose you think it's none of my business."

"Well . . ." India began uncertainly. While she might have been flip and irritated with her own father, she found it harder to do with Sally's. "Father thinks I'm on the road to perdition. I find that insulting."

Toby smiled. "You can take care of yourself? Resent the implication that you can't?"

"Precisely," India said.

"I won't argue with you. You strike me as a very competent young woman. But it's an imperfect world. Women are vulnerable to . . . to blandishments and deceit. And to gossip, even if they're perfectly upright."

"Then perhaps we ought to change that," India said.

"You have your work cut out for you if you're going to change human nature." Toby was avuncular. "Don't you want to marry and raise children, once you get all this out of your system?"

"Father," Sally said, "there are more things than that in the world for a woman to do. This is the twentieth century."

"That was quite sufficient for your mother," Toby said, "and I do not feel that she has led a confined life."

"India's going to be famous," Sally said. "You can't be famous while you're burping babies."

"I am not unenlightened," Toby said, "but I have always believed motherhood to be the more valuable contribution."

"That's because he's never had to be one," Sally said after her father had departed, promising to call for her in the afternoon. "Of course I *do* want babies," she admitted to India after a moment's thought. "It does seem valuable, being a mother."

"Everyone seems to think so. Even the feminists," India said. "I have no idea what kind of mother I'd make. I'm afraid I'd get wrapped up in a picture and forget the poor thing for hours on end, until it starved."

"That's why babies have such particularly piercing wails," Sally said.

"Well, you need a husband to have babies," India said, and then, to change the subject before Frank's name came up, she added, "I don't suppose you'd let me paint you again. *Life* is running a series on 'The American Girl.' You're just right." She appraised Sally's Botticelli profile and rose-gold pompadour.

"Really?" Sally bounced excitedly on the stool. "I've always wanted to be a model ever since I read *Trilby*."

"This is *Life*," India said through the number-two brush she held in her teeth. "Quite respectable. But I'll pay you model's wages."

"You don't have to do that."

"I'd have to pay a model."

"I never earned any money of my own before."

"You'll make just about enough to buy a new pair of gloves." Maybe less, India thought. Heaven only knew what Sally's gloves cost.

In the weeks before her debut, Sally spent endless hours with her mother, and sometimes Eden, buying gloves and hats and tea gowns, evening gowns and walking costumes and calling costumes, petticoats, corsets, corset covers, waists, stockings, walking shoes, dancing slippers—everything essential to the proper coming out of a young lady of eighteen. Certainly no old gowns would do, and anything bought in Portland was deemed too country for words. They browsed amid a sea of silks and supercilious saleswomen, conferred behind fans and shopping lists. What could be worn again? What could only be worn, as Toby said, for tea with Mrs. Astor? Fashion in 1902 decreed the new straight-front corset and the "kangaroo bend," in which opulent bosoms and bottoms stuck out fore and aft over flattened stomachs. The models looked like pretty pigeons, in iridescent taupe and mauve. Collars for daytime were high, up under the chin and stiffened with bone. Necklines for evening plunged and were accented with chokers and ropes of pearls. Hats were huge and covered with feathers and foliage, even bunches of grapes, and sat on elaborate pompadours, held down by hatpins.

Sally modeled her purchases for the family over tea and wore them with Alexandra and Eden on the endless proper calls on other debutantes and, more importantly, on the dowagers whose word was law in the universe of society. Riding down Fifth Avenue in the elegant barouche her parents had rented for the season, Sally silently blessed even those old ladies. Life was charmed.

When she wasn't shopping or making calls or going to other girls' parties, she took a streetcar to India's studio and sat on the high stool while India painted her. The portrait of Sally finished and much admired by the family, India was now working on her commission for *Life*.

Sally peered curiously over India's shoulder when she was allowed to. Fascinating to see oneself on an easel, she thought, like a mirror that had stopped moving when one was in the perfect pose. Marvelous to have one's face in a magazine. And wouldn't that make some other countenances turn green?

"When do you sleep?" India asked her.

"Who needs sleep? We will all go to Saratoga and collapse on the verandah to get our health back when the season's over. I can wait till then."

India mixed paint on her palette. "You talked your father into that?"

"No, Eden's taking me. She says if she has to spend another summer in New York it will curdle her disposition and she'll be cross for the rest of her life. Imagine Eden being cross. But Mike won't leave his moving pictures, and she wants company. Isn't it amazing how when you want something, it just falls into your hand?"

"It falls into yours."

"I suppose it does," Sally said. She thought India sounded a little annoyed about it. "I don't do things to people to make it happen. The stars just seem to line up right. It's all right to enjoy what comes, isn't it?"

"Do you mean, should you suffer on principle?" India asked.

"I know I've lived a sheltered life." Sally looked thoughtful. "It won't feed the children in the tenements if I don't go to Saratoga. It might if I took up a collection, though. Could I do that?"

"To make up for being lucky?"

Sally grinned. "Maybe. It's probably a good thing to let God know you're appreciative."

"Hop back up on the stool so the world can appreciate you," India said.

Sally was wearing a white waist with a lace bertha, and a yellow rose stuck jauntily behind one ear. The skylight bathed her face in buttery yellow light, and her expression was both demure and devilish. The high-boned collar accentuated her slender neck so that she looked like a rose herself, gold petals nodding on a pale stalk.

"Everyone's coming for my party, even Gran and Tim. And Janessa, of course." Like Mike, Sally's oldest sister lived in New York. "Aunt Cindy and Uncle Henry and Midge, too. Midge is coming out in Washington this season. Frank had better come." She looked at India as if she were in charge of him.

"I came out in London," India said, not taking the bait. "Because all Mother's and Father's family are there. It was very strange, not knowing anyone but the family. And they do some things differently there. I had to be presented to the Queen, poor woman. She looked so old and tired."

Sally decided India wasn't going to talk about Frank. Maybe India would meet someone suitable at the party. Sally envisioned a dashing dark-haired man, a gentleman artist with a suitable income and a tolerant frame of mind. Or possibly a dashing banker who would appreciate an artistic wife. All India had to do was fall in love. It couldn't be that hard. Sally herself was confidently awaiting the experience.

As it happened, Sally was the one who met the banker when the night of the big event finally arrived. His name was Stephen Overstreet, and he did something on Wall Street that Sally didn't quite comprehend. He was educated and debonair and could do the cakewalk and the two-step. Sally danced with him just one dance more than was respectable. Everyone could tell he had fallen head over heels for her.

"Well, there you are," Mike said to Toby. "You won't even get her back to Portland."

The rest of the family concurred. As she swept by on Mr. Overstreet's arm, Sally saw them watching her, a gallery of nodding heads like the front row at the theater: her parents; her older sister, Janessa, who was really a half-sister and middle-aged; her brother, Tim, who owned the San Francisco *Clarion*; her aunt Cindy, Toby's sister; Peter Blake, who made automobiles in San Francisco; her cousin Midge, practicing for her own debut; and Frank, who had appeared from nowhere and told her that he personally knew three fellows who had the new illustration from *Life* pinned up on their walls.

They were all watching Frank, too, who was dancing with India and looking nearly as debonair as Mr. Overstreet in his evening clothes, except that his shoulders were too big for them. When that song was over, he claimed a dance with Sally and admired her dance card. "Good thing I got my bid in early."

"Oh, I'm the honoree," Sally said. "Everyone has to dance with me."

"I'll bet it's just as full at other girls' parties." He swept her into his arms, and they whirled down the floor. Toby and Alexandra had rented a ballroom at the Astoria for the evening, since Mike and Eden's house would never have held half the guests. Senator Holt, retired, was still famous, and the guest list reflected the huge number of friends he had.

Sally giggled. Frank was a cousin she had grown up with and therefore struck her more like an extra brother than a possible beau. "Yesterday I went to three parties in a row—a luncheon, a boating party, and a dance. I made sure that Midge got invitations for all this week, while she's here."

Frank looked at her from under a raised eyebrow. "Midge wasn't sure you'd want her intruding."

"Oh, she only said that because I was an awful brat when we were babies."

"But you've improved?"

"Well, I hope so," Sally said. "There's nothing more tedious than people who go on being dreadful in the same old way. I'm practicing up new ways." She gave him a wicked grin. "What have you been doing for the last two years? India never says."

"I take it being a Nosy Parker is one of your new ways," Frank said.

Sally exploded into laughter with an undignified and charming snort. "I just like to know things."

"You know too much already," Frank said. "However, I will tell you. I've been working at a settlement house. It seems to serve a purpose. I get the feeling that I'm *doing* something there, and Miss Addams, who runs it, is a corker. But to be honest, I'm getting an itchy foot again."

Don't you come here and upset India again, just when she's getting successful, Sally thought, but there was no point in telling Frank that. It would probably just make him do it. *He* didn't want to marry India, Sally thought, but he would probably have a fit if someone else did.

"Men have all the fun," Sally said.

"You look pretty chipper to me," Frank commented, admiring the froth of French lace and satin in dusty rose that fell from her bosom, the tiny waist trimmed with rosebuds, and the dog collar of pearls, her coming-out gift. Her expression of blissful excitement matched the swelling music of their waltz.

"Oh, I am," Sally conceded. "I can't think of anything I want that I don't have. Except maybe a glass of champagne." She beamed at him expectantly as the music stopped, and he went to fetch it.

When Frank returned, he found Sally surrounded by a cherubic eighteen-year-old whose collar appeared to be much too tight every time he looked at Sally, a bachelor senator with a house on Fifth Avenue and a cottage at Newport, and Mr. Overstreet. Frank handed Sally her champagne and grinned at her. "I'll come back for the wedding," he said.

II

Juergen

After the uproar surrounding Sally's coming-out died down, Toby and Alexandra went back to Portland, leaving Sally with Mike and Eden for a while. After all, there would be more parties and other girls' debuts, and it wouldn't be fair to make Sally miss them.

Frank drifted away. When India asked him, snappishly, what he was looking for, he said he was looking for himself and sounded depressed about it.

"We'll all be excited if you find anything," India snarled. But she kissed him good-bye and lent him train fare, knowing full well that he would probably give it to some starving hobo and then ride in a boxcar himself.

India decided to attend to business, and over the next few years she did so with a furious concentration that earned her not only money but the novel pleasure of spare time. The New York art world—the world of serious art, of new schools and astounding new ways of looking at life and painting it—beckoned her, and she wistfully thought of how easily she could be absorbed by it. She had friends who lived in that world—mostly men, though, she was coming to realize. The women all seemed to be the models or the wives or the lovers of artists. Even Mike's friend Pyotr called her pretty lady, made advances to her for form's sake, but never seemed interested in what she was painting.

"It's just like being back in Taos," she said irritably to Sally at one of the gallery openings that constituted most of

27

her social life. Sally's social life, on the other hand, included four or five parties a week—all reported in the *New York Times*—and the occasional weekend at Newport, but she trotted happily to galleries with India, peered at incomprehensible paintings, and nibbled away at soggy hors d'oeuvres with every evidence of enjoyment.

Now Sally made a face, chuckled, and said, drawing the words out sarcastically, "Just like Taos?" Taos was in the middle of the New Mexican desert. It did not have what could be considered a chic nightlife. Or any nightlife at all, unless you were a coyote.

"Just like Taos," India said. "If you want anyone to notice you, you'd better wear pants."

"Well, they would notice," Sally chuckled. "The police might, too." It might be 1907, but it was still possible for a woman to be arrested if the police thought she was inciting a riot by her clothing, or anything else.

"You needn't take me so literally," India said. "You're just trying to jolly me along. I don't feel like it tonight. All the artists in Taos were men. They treated me like someone's pet kitten. 'Look, she's trying to paint. Isn't that cute?' I thought New York would be different. I thought the twentieth century would be different. It all looks just like it did. And these sandwiches are horrid." She made a face and dropped a triangle of thin bread and cucumber into a wastebasket. A brass spittoon set next to it had seen some use. India pulled her skirts around her ankles disgustedly.

"It's just a club," Sally said tolerantly. "Men have clubs. They feel awkward when women want to get in. They don't know what to do with them, and they can't cuss and tell jokes."

"Is that why when I asked the fellow who runs this place what sort of art he was looking for, he looked me up and down in the most offensive fashion, and said, 'Male'?"

"Well, of course he looked you up and down," Sally commented. "You look smashing tonight. That's a compliment." She sighed, apparently worried. "I wish you knew one when you saw one, you prickly thing."

"You make excuses for them, Sally," India said. "As if they were children. It's not a compliment to leer at someone. And he told me to go away just because I was a woman."

"You complicate things for him, pretty lady," Pyotr said,

wandering by and overhearing India's complaint. "If he hangs a show by a lady, the other gallery owners will make fun. Also you will argue about how it is to be hung. Women are trouble."

"Pyotr, you're just sticking up for him. That's disgusting."

Pyotr shrugged. "You don't paint serious anyway. When you do, maybe I will stick up for *you.*"

India let her breath out in an aggravated sigh as Pyotr strolled off again. He'd been just about as annoying as any man that she still liked could possibly have been.

"India, honey." Sally sipped her tiny glass of sherry and looked at India speculatively. "Are you getting a little bitter because of that rat Frank Blake?"

"Frank Blake is the only man who *is* interested in what I'm painting."

"Well, maybe. But it does seem to me that you have an awful case against men lately. Isn't there anyone you—"

"Want to fall in love with? I don't notice *you* sending out wedding invitations." India was somewhat surprised by that. Everyone thought Sally would have married by now, including several of her overconfident suitors. But she hadn't. She had watched Senator Levering's granddaughter and two other girls she knew get married that first season, and thought two of them had made mistakes. She watched from afar as Consuelo Vanderbilt, in whose circles the Holts didn't move, was forced by her mother to marry the Duke of Marlborough, whom she didn't even like. No thank you, said Sally, and she kept on going to parties and attending literary afternoons and musicales. She cajoled her sister Janessa into getting her a volunteer position at Janessa's Cherry Street Women's Hospital. It was marginally fashionable for young ladies to do good, and since Sally's bluestocking sister was a doctor, no one thought it more than mildly odd. It had given her the chance to persuade Toby to let her stay in New York with Mike and Eden. Sally would have nursed wild pigs for that, India thought.

"Not being married doesn't mean I don't like men," Sally said cheerfully. "I just haven't found the right one. I like being courted, I truly do. You ought to try it, and maybe you wouldn't be so mean to the poor things. They're only doing what they know how to do. Let them make a fuss over you just for being a girl, instead of trying to make them treat you like a man. It's lots nicer."

India produced a snort of derision that made Sally grin.

"Now take that fellow over there." Sally pointed across the crowded gallery past a woman in a huge hat to a dark-haired man lounging by the door. He wore evening clothes with an elegant but slightly raffish air, and he bowed to each woman, young and old alike, as she came in through the door. "He has lovely manners, and he looks a bit wild. That Gypsy Davy look, you know. Just the kind you like."

"Is this how you plan to amuse yourself until you do find the right man, by picking them out for me?" India asked. She grinned, some of her irritation fading in the face of Sally's relentless cheerfulness and good sense. Sally wasn't stupid or easily tyrannized, but she knew what was what: A young woman was expected to marry. Sally just lived within the confines of that knowledge more easily than India.

"That's Pyotr he's talking to," Sally said. "Get him to introduce you."

"Never," India said. "Not while he's talking to Pyotr. Pyotr will say anything to embarrass me if he's in the mood." She watched the man at the door with more interest than she admitted, however. Did he know the owner, that toad, or was he simply a self-appointed doorkeeper because he happened to be standing there? She turned around to ask Sally what she thought, but Sally had vanished.

India browsed her way along the walls with a mental shrug. She was here to see art, not fluff her feathers like a silly hen and wait for men to notice her. The exhibit was hung with canvases that looked to India like superimposed photographs—strangely angular women and still lifes viewed from several directions at once. The gallery goers craned their necks sideways trying to make sense of a green woman whose eyes floated in the middle of one breast, and asked plaintively, "But what is it meant to be?"

India thought she knew. It was as if she could look at the woman from all angles simultaneously, including possibly from the inside. She wasn't sure about that, but the effect made her slightly seasick in a fashion that she found stimulating.

Gradually she lost herself in puzzling out the pictures' cryptic messages and found herself even able to return the gallery owner's smile when he crossed her path. The effort was a little tight-lipped, but she managed it.

"And what do you think of this work?" he inquired, rather obviously waiting for a shake of the head and a helpless *"What is it?"*

India pondered the canvas in front of her, two pears and a dog sitting on a table with a red cloth. The dog appeared to be looking in three directions at once, and the pears were both eaten and not. "Very powerful," she said slowly. She let her eyes slide along the walls of the crowded gallery. "Someone more familiar with the style should have hung the work, though."

She moved on, satisfied when the fact that she had actually managed to insult him registered in the owner's eyes.

Sally appeared again and took stock of her. "You look better. What have you done?"

"Been trouble," India said, mimicking Pyotr's accent. They giggled, eyes dancing under their enormous hat brims. Sally's was of crinkled blue velvet with a black ostrich feather drooping over one eye. India's was plainer, a tan straw with a rose.

"Well, I've found out who he is," Sally said. "His name is Roger Stiller, and he just came back from Paris, and he isn't engaged or married. Or even carrying on with his model, Pyotr says." *"Just now,"* Pyotr had also said, but Sally didn't see any point in adding that. Any man who took up with darling India wouldn't need to chase models.

"Oh, for goodness' sake!" India said. She bristled slightly, and Sally decided she had gone far enough for one night. No one could push India. And if anyone wanted Sally's opinion, India's single state was Frank Blake's fault; getting India happily settled was going to be a matter of outwaiting Frank.

Having made sure that Sally had said all she was going to say, India perversely let her eyes roam back to Roger Stiller. He was certainly good-looking, in a rakish way that produced a reaction in her that nobody but Frank had ever elicited. And if he had been to Paris, he wasn't likely to go anywhere else for a while. Maybe she could threaten Pyotr with murder if he said anything to embarrass her, and *then* let him introduce her. If Sally got married—and despite her protestations, she was bound to soon—Frank would be there, of course. It might be nice, in the charged emotional territory of a wedding, to have some other man by her side.

But somehow Sally didn't get married. It didn't seem to disturb her, and it wasn't for want of proposals, but she told India, "When I think of actually spending my *entire life* with any of them, and waking up next to their faces, as well as everything else, every blessed morning—well!"

"I'll fall in love when the right fellow comes along," she was still telling India in 1908. By then India and Roger Stiller had gone through the early stages of a romance and were embarking on a more serious arrangement. "I can get my excitement vicariously until then—all I have to do is watch you."

India laughed, but her eyes gleamed. Roger didn't leave her side for days on end except to vanish into his studio. He was beginning to be well thought of in New York artistic circles. He painted scenes of New York, the saloons and drunkards, sunsets over tenement roofs, pushcart vendors with their sleeves rolled up, factory girls eating their lunch on back stoops, caught in the narrow alleys. Social realism was what they called it. The Ashcan School was the term more sober and proper artists used, but even they could not deny that it had a power lacking in the society portraits by Sargent.

Roger was dark-haired and brooding, with a smile that lit his face like a candle when he used it. Frank had hated him on sight, but Frank was off again now with Bill Haywood and the newly formed Industrial Workers of the World. Frank had found his niche, it seemed: getting his head busted by Pinkerton cops for the rights of the workingman. That was the way Roger put it, and India knew from his tone and other comments he made that Roger had little tolerance for Frank or his politics. She had to admit that Roger had no reason to like him. Frank's first comment upon their meeting had been, "Moving in?" spoken with a raised eyebrow.

Roger hadn't quite moved in, but he and India were looking for a place that was big enough for both of them. Two studios was a problem. At last they found it, not far down Tenth Street from India's old apartment, three rooms (two with good light), a kitchen, and a bathroom—an extravagance, but India believed they could afford it. Her illustrations were selling well, and her pictures of Sally had started a fashion for that type of face. There was a spirit in India's American girl, who was becoming known as the Blackstone Girl, that the languishing maids of the nineties lacked.

Roger sold a picture to a rich bohemian, one of the many, mainly women, who wanted to be part of the art scene, and he and India moved in. They never even discussed the idea of marriage, which made them both scandalous and dashing. India knew couples who *were* married who pretended they weren't.

The apartment had to be christened, naturally, so they planned a party. They bought beer and cheap red wine and oysters, still smelling of brine, off a pushcart. India made a cassoulet of chicken and ham in their tiny kitchen. Over its arched doorway she had painted green vines adorned with trumpet flowers and the motto "Here with a loaf of bread beneath the bough."

Roger kissed the back of her neck as she bent over the narrow counter next to the postage-stamp-sized sink. " 'And wilderness were paradise enow.' How long until these people go home?" He stuck a corkscrew into the top of a wine bottle.

"They haven't even got here yet," India said. She leaned her head back against his chest and smiled at him, upside down while he opened the wine. The door knocker thumped. "Go and be nice, you antisocial wretch."

"Nice as pie." He snatched a sausage off the plate she was arranging and flung the door wide, sausage in one hand, the straw-covered bottle in the other. "Abandon all hope ye who enter here! Have a drink."

By ten the apartment was full. Some of the early arrivals had gone home, but latecomers were still straggling in, and a group at the center had settled in and might be there till dawn. In the middle of it was Sally, listening to Pyotr argue with a department-store magnate's daughter over whether the common laborer was nobler in his mind than the social worker of comfortable income who tried to make the laborer's life more pleasant—a subject about which neither of them had any concrete information.

Mike and Eden arrived a little after ten, wriggling their way with a guest they had brought through the smoke and the chatter to India in the kitchen. She was heating sausage rolls, a voluminous apron tied over the claret-colored dress, which was now eight years old, too full-skirted and out of style. The whole shape of women had changed this year. A new sheathlike corset eliminated the kangaroo bend, and hips were slim, outlined in flowing, floating fabrics. Skirts were shorter, up to the instep, and going higher. Nevertheless, India looked astounding, like a painting of a Gypsy.

The young man with Mike and Eden was blond and thoughtful looking, with a military school carriage and impeccable evening clothes. "This is Juergen von Appen," Eden said across the din. "He's attached to the consulate here."

"I am delighted to meet you," Juergen said. He bowed and kissed India's hand, which widened her eyes.

"His father is a second cousin once removed to Peter Blake's mother," Eden said. "Or something."

"Third cousin," Juergen said with a smile. "They knew each other fairly well, and he said I should make General Blake's acquaintance."

"General Blake not being available, he settled for us," Eden said. General Henry Blake was Frank's father. His first wife had been a German baroness and the talk of the family. Her son, Peter, made automobiles in San Francisco.

"Actually, Peter wrote to me," Juergen said, "with addresses of people he felt might be kind enough to take me under their wings." He spoke perfect diplomatic English, with an interesting accent.

"We're charmed you're here," India said. "Will you have a glass of wine? Or beer?"

"Beer, if you please." He rocked back on his heels and looked around. "You have a very charming home. I like your doorway."

Goodness, India thought, *he should liven up the party.*

Juergen took his glass of beer and melted into the middle of it as if he had spent his life in Greenwich Village and not, as India suspected, Heidelberg. There was a pale but noticeable scar just under his left ear. Well, that was diplomatic training for you, she thought.

The department-store heiress eyed him with patent interest and moved over on the sofa. He took the seat with a murmured thanks, but he wasn't really looking at her. He was looking at Sally, curled on the overstuffed hassock, feet tucked under her crepe de chine skirts. And Sally was looking back.

Oh, no, India thought. *Oh, no.*

Roger came into the kitchen for more wine. "You look like you just swallowed a bug," he said, kissing her ear. "Old Schultz and Anderson are in the studio arguing over whether the perfect female form is narrower in the waist than the bosom by more than ten inches. They're using your paints to demonstrate. I hope you don't mind."

"I do rather," India said. "Let them use yours."

"Too much mess to mix up oils. Let them piddle with the watercolors."

"Oh, never mind," India said. There would be more mess than that to clean up in the morning. She pointed at Juergen and Sally and said, "Look at that."

Roger raised his eyebrows. "Old Ironsides?" he said, laughing. "Little Miss Impervious? Oh, my!"

"Tell me about Oregon," Juergen was saying, his hands clasped around his knees. He had tried to give the sofa seat to Sally and take the hassock, but she had refused with a shake of her head. "I have never seen the West Coast of the States."

"It's very beautiful," Sally said, her expression impish. "If you like the country. It's bigger than the landscape out here somehow. Our family place is near Portland. It's called the Madrona, for the madrone trees. Dad was born there, and his father was one of the first white settlers in Oregon."

"Ah. The Wild West."

"I'm afraid Portland is awfully tame these days. From what I understand, in the beginning they spent more time fighting the Russians than they did Indians."

Pyotr gave her an elaborately aggrieved look. "Beautiful Sally, if the Americans had looked like you, we all would have fallen down in our tracks."

"You probably would have fallen down anyway," Sally said, noting the level in the wine bottle he had set at his feet.

"She doesn't love me anymore," Pyotr said wistfully to the heiress. "She is falling in love with a German with dueling scars."

Juergen looked bewildered, as if he was unsure whether

this was their normal style of conversation or Pyotr was prodding him.

"My father is attached to the Madrona by some kind of blood tie, I think," Sally said, ignoring Pyotr. "Since he left Washington, it's become harder and harder to pry him away from it. I think he's disappointed I didn't stay and marry a Portland boy to run the place."

Juergen smiled. "It is delightful that you did not. What do you raise on this—farm? ranch?"

"Ranch, mostly. I don't personally raise anything on it, mind you. But horses for the most part. Remounts for the cavalry are the mainstay. Mama raises fancy hunters and jumpers and sells them to Vanderbilts to ride in Central Park."

"A most unusual family. Michael tells me that your elder sister is a doctor and your elder brother owns a newspaper."

"Yes, and Mike makes moving pictures. I'm the boring one."

Juergen inspected her in the most polite way possible. There was no trace of a leer, but something warmer than that. "Never boring," he said softly.

Sally smiled, eyes down, preening a little. She looked as if she were made out of fresh flowers. He took note of the department-store heiress and inclined his head in her direction as well, scrupulously polite. "I have not yet met any boring American women."

"How long have you been in New York?" Sally asked him. "I could introduce you to heaps of them."

"I'm sure I shall meet them myself in the course of my diplomatic duties," Juergen said with a smile.

"How long have you been here?"

"Only long enough to write to your uncle, General Blake, and your cousin Peter. They were most gracious."

"Well, you would appeal to Uncle Henry," Sally said mischievously. "You look very well behaved."

Juergen smiled. "I am not at all sure that is a compliment, Miss Holt. I shall attempt to take it as such for my vanity's sake."

"I'm being bad," Sally said, not looking particularly penitent. "Have you seen much of the city?"

"Some of what the guidebooks have to show me. And

the interior of quite a number of stuffy offices. I should like to see more of it."

Sally wrinkled her nose. "Not of the musty offices, I trust. I understand that the diplomatic life is overprovided with those."

"I have," Juergen said with a sideways glance, "recently acquired a motorcar."

"Oh, glory!" Sally said. "I want one desperately, and my father is convinced I will break my neck. It's a Blake, I trust?"

Juergen laughed. "We Germans are very loyal to any family connection, however tenuous. Of course it's a Blake."

"I shall wheedle you to take me riding in it," Sally said.

"You needn't wheedle."

And that, thought India, was that. She supposed she should have known that when Sally fell in love, it would be with a thump like a wall falling down. Juergen left with Sally to escort her home, and India watched them go with some trepidation.

The flowers arrived at Mike and Eden's the next morning, a huge bouquet of two dozen red damask roses.

"Heavens, how German," Eden said, amused by such extravagance, but she was impressed. A note in a little envelope with the embassy crest was tucked into the flowers: It would give Herr von Appen great pleasure if Miss Holt would permit him to escort her to the theater on Thursday evening. He would call for her in his automobile at eight.

"An old-fashioned sort," Eden said. "No telephones for Herr von Appen."

Sally, eyes gleaming, got out a sheet of her best cream-colored notepaper and responded that Miss Holt would be delighted. By Thursday she had tried on every dress in her wardrobe in front of the mirror in her room, calling Eden in for frequent consultation. Mike was alarmed to find them rising like mermaids from a froth of silk and lace, with Sally muttering that none of these were right and she wished she had time to have something new made.

"Now see here," Mike said. "Dad'll skin me alive if I let you go off and marry some German."

"Who said I was going to marry him?" Sally said airily. "He's only taking me to the theater."

"You never tried on all your clothes and fussed like this for any of your other beaux," Mike said. "If this fellow's that important to you, I'm unnerved."

"Well . . ." She stood in front of the mirror in a wrapper, an evening gown of midnight blue held across the front of her. Her bare feet stuck out from under its hem. "I don't know him, Mike. I don't know what he'd like."

"He appears to like you," Mike said dryly. "That's what worries me."

"Pooh," Sally said. She put the midnight-blue dress down and picked up another of old rose with jet lace across the bosom. She swirled, dancing with it. "I haven't even begun to worry you."

Juergen took her to see the Irish National Theatre Company's production of *The Rising of the Moon*, but, given a quiz afterward, they most likely would have confessed that they had been eyeing each other far more often than the stage. Something about Juergen's slim shoulders next to hers felt right to Sally, as if this was the man she should be sitting beside from now on. She tried out that sensation, pretended they were in church, at the opera, at a board meeting of hospital volunteers. Each time it felt sensible to have him there, an accustomed sensation like a familiar room. Despite India's joking, Sally didn't want but one room in her house, and she knew already how it should be furnished.

When the play was over, Juergen helped her on with her evening cloak, letting his fingers linger against her throat just a moment longer than was respectable. His eyes gleamed, and he lowered his head in unspoken apology.

"I have enjoyed myself very much," he said, "but I should like to go some place that allows conversation. A late supper?"

"Oh, yes." Sally beamed. "Take me to Café Martin. We can talk and watch all the *other* people watching each other. Someone told me that a woman actually smoked in there last week. She was British, I think. There was a terrible to-do, and someone threatened to have her arrested."

"I can see you like excitement," Juergen said. "Is there a law against women smoking?"

"Yes, if you can believe it. The Sullivan Ordinance. The city passed it in January, as if they didn't have anything more important to cope with." She laughed as Juergen handed her into the Blake and tucked a fur robe around her knees. "Personally, I think smoking is hideously unladylike, and I wouldn't do it for worlds, but a city ordinance does seem excessive."

"You are a woman of much charm in your unwillingness to bend your sisters to your own notions of what is right." He cranked the Blake, and it roared into life. He climbed in beside her. "It is very refreshing."

"Well, goodness, my convictions are just my own. India, for instance, does things I wouldn't dream of—I wouldn't be surprised if *she* smoked—but I can't expect the whole world to be as conventional as my wonderful self, I suppose."

She made a joke of it, but Juergen touched her cheek with his finger before he put the Blake in gear and said, "If all American women were as wonderful as yourself, I might have fallen in love with one of them and never met *you*."

He slid the Blake into the traffic of automobiles and carriages, eyes on the road now, and he and Sally were silent as they drove. The Blake's roar and Juergen's need to concentrate on not running down hapless peddlers or enraging the crowd of carriage drivers by frightening their horses seemed to make conversation imprudent. Sally felt as if she were floating a few inches above the Blake's red leather seat, like the little silver Diana who adorned the hood, draperies floating behind her, bow strung to let fly.

After they arrived at Café Martin, Sally emerged from her coccoon of fur robe and evening cloak, and the maître d'hôtel led them to a table for two where the arch of a window would frame them decoratively for passersby. There they could easily have been one of India's illustrations, the handsome blond young man in evening dress and the ethereal beauty in old rose and jet lace. The maître d'hôtel never put ugly people in his windows.

"Oh, come," Juergen said. "This is no place to exchange life stories. Over there, please. The table by the palm tree."

The maître d' sighed and led them into the shadow of a monstrous potted palm.

"Much better," Juergen said. "Thank you." He transferred a bill into an expectant hand.

"Thank you. Most people are dying to sit in those windows, but they make me feel like a Pekingese at a dog show."

"I have much the same sensation at embassy events, when I am directed to be charming," Juergen said. "Something in one simply rebels." A waiter appeared, and Juergen ordered champagne and crab cakes, raising a questioning eyebrow at Sally, who nodded happily.

"The oysters are excellent tonight," the waiter informed him. Oysters were more fashionable.

"All the same, we will have crab cakes," Juergen said. He bent a reproving eye on the waiter, who scuttled off.

"Oh, bless you," Sally said. "I've tried and tried, but I hate oysters."

"I noticed," Juergen said. "At Miss Blackstone's party. I notice these things."

"You notice beautifully." Sally smiled at her hands in her lap.

"I find it easy to notice what you like," Juergen said. "But it is also a necessity of the diplomatic life, in a foreign country."

"Is it very different here?" Sally asked. "From Cologne? Or were you posted in Berlin?"

"Because Mother and the girls are in Cologne, I divided my time between the two."

"What is your family like? Are your sisters older or younger than you?" Sally had only a vague picture of them, feminine versions of Juergen, with a gray-haired mother who was possibly fat and rosy.

"A little younger. My mother is conservative, and they have had a very sheltered upbringing. I hope they will marry, but I am beginning to wonder. Maybe she has protected them too much."

"They have time yet." Sally had always felt that she had time, too, and now she knew how right she had been. She smiled wistfully at him when the champagne and crab cakes appeared. How would he like America, she thought, if he stayed here? How would his sisters like it? Eden had said that he was their only support. "Do your sisters go to diplomatic parties with you and practice being charming, too?" *I bet I could marry them off*, Sally thought.

"They have a social circle in Cologne, in which they are very comfortable. Twice a year Mother takes them to Berlin to shop. They are more comfortable at German parties with fewer foreigners."

"But not you?" Juergen seemed comfortable anywhere.

Juergen smiled. "Most definitely not me. Germany needs to become less insular, but sometimes I think we are taking a very long time to do it."

"My father says that change only happens as fast as the oldest generation dies out," Sally said. "That a person can absorb only so much change, and after that you have to wait for them to die before you can accomplish anything else. Poor man, he ought to know. He was a senator for six years."

"He didn't stand for reelection?"

"He lost." Sally chuckled. "He tried to shove along too much change on people who weren't dead yet. At the time I thought my life had ended. We had to go back to Oregon."

"You don't like Oregon?"

Sally grinned. "I liked Washington. I like New York."

"You would like Cologne," Juergen said. "It is very old and very beautiful. One day I will show it to you." He grinned back at her. It changed his whole face, took away the formality and left an expression younger and more reckless.

They sat and stared at each other across the table while the crab cakes got cold. When Sally came home, Mike and Eden knew that something irremediable had happened.

It didn't take long for news like that to spread among the scattered Holts and Blakes. Who was this fellow? They all wanted to know by the end of the year. India wrote them reassuring letters, and so did Mike and Sally's older sister, Janessa. And yet, as more than a year passed, India stayed uneasy about the relationship, and so did everyone else. There wasn't a thing wrong with Juergen. No one could say there was. He was cultured and charming, he came from a good family, and everyone liked him, even Frank. All India could say in his disfavor was that he was German. It was 1910 now, and relations between England and Germany had been dicey for some time. America tended to count herself in on England's side, whenever and whatever. The people with their noses to the wind, particularly Sally's brother Tim, said that something unpleasant was coming. And in any case, where would Sally and Juergen live?

It wasn't her business, Roger said to India. And where was his tea? Roger had made a sale a few months earlier to a Chicago bank with a president who wanted something to make the workingman feel understood—that was how he explained it to Roger—and had promised to recommend Roger's work to corporate fellows. In a frenzy of energy, Roger had done twelve canvases in as many weeks, some so fast India never even saw them. They prepared themselves to be rich.

India's work was still selling well, better than ever, and she was brooding over a piece for *Lane's Weekly* while she listened for the kettle and thought about Sally. She was looking stretched lately, fragile and a little wispy, not like herself. She had stopped living with Mike and Eden a month after meeting Juergen and had taken her own set of rooms. Toby was happy to go on supporting her, he had written India, as long as she didn't haul off and get married to a German as an alternative. India knew Toby wanted Sally to go home—he was getting old—but Sally stayed on, still not married to Juergen and occasionally going about with other eligible men, though not very often. Sally was twenty-four now, and old ladies who knew her mother were beginning to tut-tut about her, not married *yet*, such a pity.

Well, and look at me, India thought. *How did I get to be thirty?* It occurred to her to wonder for the first time what she had done with the last ten years. Hard to say, she thought. She looked at Roger's back as he paced in his studio, waving his arms occasionally at whoever it was he was talking to in his head. Most of the time India felt content. Any unease merely lurked around the edges, where she could conveniently ascribe it to worry about Sally. She hadn't seen Frank in over a year.

The kettle shrilled, and she made two cups of tea. Roger took his absently, still staring at his canvas, and India went back to stare at hers. She had let this one sit for over three months, not quite sure how she wanted to finish it. The girl in the picture sat on a park bench, pigeons at her feet. A tree behind her and another to the side leaned into each other, framing her, almost like scissors coming together. The grass was littered with the debris of battered trees and someone's sodden and abandoned hat. India called it *After the Storm*, and an observer couldn't be quite sure that those trees weren't going to come down all the way and catch her. She was reasonably sure that *Lane's* was going to want more than trees in the picture, an apologetic young man, perhaps, mending a quarrel with her, to give another metaphor to the storm. India was irrationally determined not to put him in. She liked the picture without him.

And then, of course, they would send it back. *Oh, let them,* she thought. *I have to assert myself once in a while.* She made some finishing touches, worked out the shadowy form of the young man she had nearly put in, and set it aside to dry. Tomorrow she would box it up and send it off. It would take a week or two at least before they rejected it, so she could assert herself for that long.

When Sally and Juergen wanted to quarrel, they went out in the motorcar to do it. It was well known at the consulate that he had an American lady friend and, he was given to understand by his superiors, disapproved of. Cultivating the wives and daughters of the influential was one thing—just one of the duties of handsome young attachés—but becoming serious about them, possibly marrying them, was another. There was nowhere in the city that Juergen felt was quite private enough to talk seriously with Sally.

"I don't know why you want to talk at all this afternoon," she said, her words clipped and muffled by the roar of the Blake's engine and the folds of the motoring veil tied over her hat and face. "We've been all through it."

"I know we have," he shouted back over the engine. "Let's try not to discuss it until we stop." He headed the automobile out of the city, where its noise was lost in the constant roar of other motorcars, streetcars, carriages, and the thunder of the el, and into the countryside, where it shattered the stillness and filled the fall air with gasoline fumes. It was one of those perfect fall days at the end of which a harvest moon would rise over some farmer's cornfield and float lazily in the air like a balloon.

So many things were in the air these days, Sally thought. Count Zeppelin's dirigible and now the Wright brothers' machine, which actually flew. She couldn't see the need for either of them in the sky with her hypothetical moon. After frightening two cows and a pig, Juergen pulled the Blake off the rutted country road into a meadow that bordered on a pond. A cow in the distance gave them a bucolic stare but no further show of interest. There was no fence, so they trudged across the meadow, the last of the summer's grasshoppers rocketing from under their feet, and spread a quilt and picnic hamper by the pond. Sally pulled her veil off and shook the dust out of it into the wind.

"That's better," Juergen said. "You always look as if you were in a birdcage in that thing."

She unpacked deviled eggs and cold chicken, and Juergen stuck a corkscrew into a bottle of wine. "It's very charming here," he observed. "Country scene with cow. I rather like the country."

"Just not *my* country, not on a permanent basis," Sally said as she put the chicken on a plate.

Juergen put the corkscrew down and looked at her, although she wasn't looking at him. "Dear heart, how can I? I have a country. I like America very much, but how can I forsake Germany for it? All my family are there. My mother, my sisters—"

"All mine are here!" Sally said, smacking the plate of chicken down onto the quilt. "You want *me* to leave here!"

"It is usual for wives to follow their husbands," Juergen said reasonably. "It is the husbands who have to make a living for the wives. And you could visit home anytime you wanted to."

Sally looked miserably at him. "I'd want to all the time, if your consulate's reaction to me is a measure of how your family would feel."

"I am not so besotted that I think everyone will love you because I do. Particularly not other women," Juergen said with a chuckle. "But they would behave themselves, and we needn't live with them. We would have children and be our own family."

"What if there is a war?" Sally said. "Tim says there's going to be one. Then what?"

"Oh, dear God, surely not with America. Americans have more sense."

"I don't know if anyone has any sense," Sally said morosely. "Juergen, what if there is a war?"

"Then we'll cross that bridge when we come to it."

"We may not be able to," Sally pointed out.

"My darling, I will do anything I can to persuade you you will be safe," Juergen said. "Any conditions you want to impose—"

"It's not being safe! It's being miserable, and lonesome,

and cut off. Juergen, I love you beyond anything, and I can't bear the idea of living in Germany!" She put her face in her hands and started to cry.

He looked helplessly at the cow, as if it might have some advice. "I can't be an American," he said gently. "I'm a German."

Sally scrubbed a napkin across her face. "Will you talk to my cousin Peter? At least talk to him? He's had a foot in both countries for years, what with his motorcar business and all, and he's coming to New York next week on business. Eden said to bring you to dinner. If you'll listen to him, I will, too."

"We are to gamble on what he'll say?" Juergen scooted over, put his arm around her, and stuck a glass of wine in her hand. He couldn't easily ravish her while she was holding a glass of sticky sherry, he thought. It was all he ever wanted to do when he was alone with Sally, but so far he had managed not to try. He wondered, though, how long respect would hold out over yearning.

Sally took a sip and sniffled. "You know you could work for Peter's company. He's enormously successful—it's disgraceful how much money he's making—and he needs people who speak German."

"Aha," Juergen said. "You aren't hoping for advice. You are hoping for a job for me."

Sally smiled at him, and he almost promised to dig ditches for her.

"I sell automobiles," Peter Blake said. "If I knew what was going to happen in Europe in the next five years, I could probably get rich."

"You are rich," Roger Stiller said. He grinned at Peter. "Comparatively speaking."

It was a family dinner for, as Eden put it, "kin and their attachments." That included Janessa and her doctor husband, Charley Lawrence; Sally and Juergen; India and her artist, with whom the family was still pretending she was not actually living; and Frank, who had come for something to do with the IWW and to hit his half-brother up for a contribution. They had quarreled for a good hour about the union question, but India thought that Peter had given the money to him. Frank looked pleased with himself.

Sally, in not a particularly subtle fashion, had turned the conversation to the unrest in Europe. Europe was constantly in a state of unrest, as far as India could tell, and most of the time the Germans seemed to be poking a stick into it. She liked Juergen, though. The whole family did.

Peter ignored Roger's comment and leaned toward Juergen while Eden's maid cleared the table. The gentlemen would smoke cigars and drink brandy, and the ladies would remain to join in their conversation, having long ago forsaken the custom of excusing themselves to another room. Eden put a decanter of sherry on the table as well and wound up the gramophone. She put "Rings on My Fingers" on it, a cheerful counterpoint to the gloom of politics.

"I'm thinking seriously about winding up my investments in Germany," Peter said.

Juergen looked shocked. "But your mother's family. Your trustees—"

"Will have to lump it. I'm not going to have my factory over there confiscated to make machines of war, and particularly not aeroplane engines."

"Aeroplanes!" Sally looked horrified. "Dropping things out of the sky?"

"If you think mankind isn't going to employ something as useful as the aeroplane to kill himself with, you have too sunny a disposition," Peter said.

"Peter's a pessimist," Frank said, but he didn't look as if he really thought so.

"On the contrary, I imagine he knows whereof he speaks," Roger stated, poking in the pocket of his vest. "My dear." He smiled winningly at India. "I've left my cigarette case in my overcoat."

"I'll get it." India went into the hall where the coat tree was, glad of the chance to miss part of the conversation. Even the gramophone wound down, as if dispirited.

"Why the hell do you wait on that ass?"

She turned to find Frank in the doorway, grimacing with disgust. She balanced the cigarette case in her hand and said defensively, "I don't wait on him."

"What do you call that?" Frank pointed derisively at the case, a gold one, her Christmas present to Roger. "From I.B. to R.S., with love and servitude forever," he said mockingly.

"Oh, stop it, Frank!"

"I won't," Frank said. "You wouldn't fetch and carry for me, and I've known you a good deal longer than three years."

"I don't fetch and carry for anyone!" India protested. "If I choose to do Roger a courtesy, that is my business. He returns the kindness, I might add." She turned away to rejoin the party.

"Name something."

She stopped. "Damn you, Frank, you could at least be civil."

"You're being evasive," he said.

She stepped toward him and looked him in the eye. "You have no right. Not the right to criticize my behavior or even the right to have an opinion about it."

"Then I shall confine myself to criticizing him. He's a lout."

"And you are a dog in the manger!" India snapped.

"No doubt. But that doesn't improve him." His face softened as he looked into her weary, angry one. "I haven't seen you in a long time. I really came to see you. I can catch old Pete anytime. Can I take you to lunch?"

"Roger won't like it," she said automatically. But Roger probably wouldn't notice, she thought, if he was working. The gramophone started again as they walked back into the room. Eden had put on a Scott Joplin rag and was trying to entice Peter onto the floor. Mike and Roger were rolling up the rug.

"Dance with me," Frank said. He took her hand. "We can give your lout his cigarettes."

The last remark was loud enough for Roger to have heard, but he made no comment if he did. He merely touched India on the nose with one finger and took another swallow of brandy instead. "Thank you, my sweet. I'll have a puff while you cavort."

"He'd do better to smoke the cigarette," Frank said as he took India's arm and steered her onto the cleared floor. "Unless of course he just wanted to prove he could make you go get them. Does he always get drunk at dinner?"

"Roger works at a very intense level," she said between her teeth as they began to dance. It was hard to argue in ragtime. "If he needs to unwind in the evening, that is hardly any concern of yours."

"Juergen might want to talk about it." Frank swung India around so that she could see Roger and Sally. Roger had his arm around Sally's waist.

"Let us trot the turkey trot, glorious golden lady," Roger was saying. He had a little trouble with "glorious" and "golden." "Abandon yon Teutonic swain. Pretty American girls ought to stay in America."

"Roger, stop it!" Sally hissed. She shot an uneasy look at India.

"My lovely lady is dancing elsewhere, and I am a man of passions, who likes a little variety." Roger's arm tightened around Sally's waist.

"Well, I'm not it! And India's my best friend." She brought her heel down hard on his instep.

"Shall I detach your Lothario for you?" Frank inquired.

"No!" India said, her cheeks burning. Behavior she could overlook in Greenwich Village left her mortified in Eden's drawing room. And making advances to Sally was worse than chasing his models. She left Frank standing in the middle of the floor and took Roger by the arm. "It's very late, dear, and you have a date to go fishing with Mr. Schultz tomorrow, do you remember?" She grabbed their wraps off the coat tree and edged him toward the door. "We've had a lovely evening, Eden."

"I never thought you were so bourgeois," Roger said minutes later, leaning back in the motor cab that India had hailed. He hadn't helped with that, just stood against a lamp-post whistling while she got her skirts splashed with mud.

"This was my family, Roger!" India snapped. "I don't mind if you want to get soused with friends, but not in front of my family."

"That's the trouble. You get with your family and you turn into a stiff-neck." He snorted. "You used to be fun."

India glowered out the cab window. There was no point in arguing with him in this mood. A certain amount of liquor made him blind to anyone's wishes but his own. He'd probably apologize in the morning, and if he had a sufficient hangover, she could probably get him to apologize to Sally, too. India supposed Sally was used to such overtures; everyone who saw her fell in love with her, or into lust at the very least. It had only been a matter of time before Roger tried it, she supposed.

The cabbie pulled up outside their Tenth Street apartment building, and India paid him.

Roger followed her sulkily up the stairs. "I don't want you to see that Blake fellow anymore," he said as she unlocked their door.

"Frank's an old friend of mine. You don't have the right to choose my friends."

"I've got a right to keep you from making a fool of yourself over him," Roger said. He stuck his chin out aggressively.

"I'm not the one who—" India bit off her sentence, knowing there was no point in going further. Right now Roger had it worked out to his own satisfaction: She had misbehaved, not he.

"Go to bed," she said wearily, and gave him a little push through the door.

III

Roger

Roger was still asleep when India got up in the morning. Ernie Schultz was pounding on the door, and she prodded Roger out of bed before answering it in her wrapper.

"Slugabeds!" Ernie was a big, bluff fellow who painted cheerful comic scenes of tavern life and fished every moment he wasn't painting. "Out! Out!" He shook the bedclothes at Roger, who disappeared blearily into the bathroom. "Had a little too good a time last night, did he?" he said to India with a wink.

"A little." India wasn't going to make any excuses to Ernie. He had known Roger longer than she had. But a day on the river with Ernie would straighten Roger out, and he would probably come back penitent and reasonable, with flowers. He always had before.

India shooed them out the door and dressed herself with relief. She always got more done when she was alone, from making up the bed and turning the room into a parlor again to ordering her own mind, shaking the fluff and dust out. She remembered that Frank wanted to have lunch with her, and decided that she would. Roger wouldn't be back until dusk.

Frank telephoned, he said, to see if she was too hot to touch and, assured that she wasn't, came and took her to Mama Rosalia's. They ate spaghetti and shared a bottle of Chianti.

"I don't know why I do this to myself," India said.

"What in heaven's name are you up to now? The papers are full of the anarchist menace."

"Just the ones that think a decent wage and a six-day week will crumble the foundations of democracy," Frank said.

"What are you *doing* it for?" India demanded. "Pure high-mindedness? You don't belong to the working class."

"I do if that's where I choose to be."

"Well, *why* do you choose to be? Why not go into politics or law and change things from the top, where you might actually accomplish something?"

"Like Uncle Toby?" Frank asked. "Tell me what he accomplished. All his efforts at reform got him voted out of office after one term. And the last thing he tried to do in Washington was keep us out of a stupid war with Spain. You know what success he had with that. He got spat on for being a pacifist. I'll get spat on from down below, thanks, where something will get done. Reform doesn't get legislated; it happens when the downtrodden get mad enough to fight back."

"I suppose I should be glad you found your calling." India thought crossly that she was the one who had told him to figure out what to do with his life, to stop drifting. She should have known that what he chose wouldn't be compatible with hers. She looked at him wistfully, and the same electric glow that Frank always seemed to radiate washed over her. She wouldn't let him come up when he brought her home. She knew what would happen.

They strolled leisurely to her apartment after lunch, and when they got there, India pulled a handful of letters out of the brass box by the front door and held them in front of her like a shield. "I have work to do this afternoon," she said. "I've shilly-shallied long enough."

Frank accepted her reasoning with grace and left.

India went upstairs reading the mail, and by the time she got to the third floor, she had forgotten him entirely because of a seething, swelling rage. She unlocked the door, still reading. The other letters fell out of her hand, and she kicked them angrily across the threshhold. She stared at the page again:

> *. . . similarity to the new piece at First Chicago Bank. We regret the necessity to withdraw the commission. Your work follows by separate post.*

India was waiting for Roger when, fishy and cheerful, he came up the stairs at dusk. He handed her a paper cone of late roses, bought from a pushcart on the way home, and a creel full of fish. "Roses for my rose," he said, propping rod and reel against the brass bed. "Fish for her supper."

India put the roses on a table, carefully, her hands shaking. Her knuckles clenched around the handles of the creel. "Do you really expect me to clean these and cook them for you?" she said through her teeth. "You son of a bitch, *Lane's* turned down my painting. They just happen to have their offices in Chicago!"

"Chicago?" Roger blinked at her.

"Where you sold the painting you *stole* from me!" She flung the creel away from her. It smacked into the wall and rained fish.

"You're hysterical," Roger said. "What are you talking about?"

"You know very well. The girl under the trees. *After the Storm.* You stole my entire composition. The editor of *Lane's* saw it in the bank and sent mine back—he accused *me* of stealing from *you!*"

"Don't you think 'stealing' is a little harsh?" Roger said plaintively. "You know what pressure I was under. After I sold the first piece there, I had half a dozen buyers and nothing to send them. I'm not an illustrator—I can't churn out work indefinitely regardless of whether I feel any spark."

"So you took *my* idea!" India shouted. She snatched up the letter from *Lane's*, balled it up, and flung it at him. "*My* work. You bastard!"

Roger narrowed his eyes. "It was just a magazine illustration. I gave it depth. I made it art."

"Depth?" India screamed. "How dare you? Is that all you owe me? I haven't complained when you've come home too drunk to walk! I've ignored it when you've made advances to my friends! I've made excuses when you sleep with your models! I've even cleaned your damned disgusting fish!" She saw them on the floor and picked one up in each hand. "I cleaned your fish for you!" India threw one at him.

It splatted against his coat and left a slimy, iridescent smudge.

"Stop it! You are hysterical." He started toward her.

"Don't you come near me!" India threw the other fish. It caught him across the face and flopped wetly on the floor. She heaved a third, its silver body arcing end over end.

"Get a grip on yourself," Roger said. He watched her warily, ready to dodge anything else she threw, but his voice was condescending. "You ought to be flattered I saw something in your little painting. Usually they're just fluff, but this one had something."

"Get out!" India screamed. "Get out and don't ever show your face here again." She aimed another fish at him, the last.

Roger snatched up the cap he had laid on the bed and jammed it on his head. "I have no intention of staying in the same apartment with a woman who cannot control herself," he stated.

India began to throw his clothes and his paints out onto the landing. He tried to pick them up as faces popped out of doors up and down the hall.

"You're a thief!" she screamed, heaving canvas after canvas at him. His paint case popped open, and tubes of paint scattered on the floor. He stepped on one in an explosion of vermilion splatters.

"I want to sue him," India said. She drummed her nails —short, thick, paint-stained nails—on the desk, making a sound like teeth clacking together.

"For plagiarism?" Mr. Zimmerman looked interested. He was a short man with a bushy brown mustache. She had picked a lawyer from the Village on the theory that he would be familiar with Village matters and possibly enlightened enough not to look down his nose at a female client. Unable to stand living in the apartment she had shared with Roger— or to pay the rent on it—she had moved to a studio in the old stables along MacDougal Alley, and Mr. Zimmerman's office was only a short distance from it. "I don't believe I've ever had a case involving art before. What is your evidence?"

"The painting that *Lane's* sent back with this letter," India said, smoothing the wrinkled letter on the desk. She regretted having crumpled it, now that it was evidence. "I was working on it long before Roger painted that—that—whatever it was he sold those baboons in Chicago."

"Have you actually seen the painting in Chicago?"

"No, but I am, by God, going to," India said. "I'll photograph it. Can we force them to let us take it to court if we want to?"

"I imagine so," Mr. Zimmerman said. He listened to the racket in the street outside for a while, as if it might tell him something about the explosive young woman sitting opposite him.

The coo of pigeons under the eaves was punctuated by the squawks of chickens being transported below in the street. There was a restaurant on the first floor of Mr. Zimmerman's building. The proprietress was an anarchist from Illinois, Mr. Zimmerman had told India, and her cook was rumored to have once been the lover of Emma Goldman. "What are you hoping to get from your suit?" he asked her.

"To make a fool of Roger Stiller. He made a fool of me. *Lane's* thinks *I'm* the plagiarist. Word gets around. Everyone else will think the same if I don't do something."

"Would it damage your income?"

India thought. "Most likely. But it's my reputation I'm concerned about. And the insult. He as good as said that his work matters and mine doesn't."

"Well, let us stay somewhat concerned about your income," Zimmerman said. "It's your strongest card in court if you want to nick him for serious damages."

"Oh, I do. I most certainly do," India said.

On the way home, a fairly short walk, India thought about the prospect with pleasure. Roger had suddenly come to embody men for her, and everything she didn't like about them. The attitude that a man's work was important and a woman's was not was the same one that kept women from voting. *How could I have lived with him?* Was she that enamored of a pretty face and an insinuating smile? Or just with the idea of a man who would stay put? Well, look what it had got her.

Muttering, India dodged past a pushcart full of kitchen knives and pots. She stalked back to her studio with the intention of taking the next train for Chicago. Her place was still full of crates and boxes, and God knew what was in them, she thought. She had put things in at random, in a fury, and she wondered whether she could find everything she would need for the trip. But she had to go, she decided. She had to see for herself what Roger had done.

It didn't take long for the Village to hear all about India's allegation and decision to sue Roger Stiller. While she was away in Chicago, the community talked it over at length, and by the time she got back with the photograph of the painting, the story had even gotten into one of the newspapers. It was a very small paragraph but enough to cram her mailbox with letters asking her what on earth she thought she was *doing*. Opinion seemed divided as to whether Roger really had stolen her design, and if he had, on whether India ought to sue him over it. After all, they had been living together. "A woman scorned . . ." said some of the male artists, shaking their heads over their beer.

India set about doing exactly what Zimmerman told her to. She polled her friends to learn which of them had seen *After the Storm* on her easel before Roger's first sale to the Chicago bank—and found that a number of those who had, blanched at the thought of swearing to it in court.

"Roger's an old friend, you know. I hoped you two would make up this spat."

"This is not a lover's quarrel," India said through clenched teeth, but her witnesses boiled down to three: Ernie Schultz, Sally, and May Fraley, the model who had posed for Roger's Chicago bank painting and for several others earlier in the year. Depositions, date changes, and finally a countersuit clogged up the process until after the New Year. Roger—or his lawyer—waited as close to each court date as possible to request a postponement to suit the schedule of a vital witness or because of unexpected ill health on someone's part.

"Now he's suing *me*!" India said, snapping her teeth at the papers in her hand. "How could he?"

"You lived with him," Zimmerman said cheerfully.

"That was an aberration. I'm not normally such a damn fool."

India wanted to go back and erase the last three years, rub Roger out with art gum, dilute him with turpentine. The last year she had lived with him, with her thirtieth birthday looming, they had even talked about having a child. India shuddered at the thought. It was a wonder she hadn't had one by accident; she had tempted fate sufficiently. Maybe if all he had cost her was a stolen drawing, she was lucky. Several friends said so. Ernie Schultz suggested that it was an excellent reason to drop her suit.

"Roger's not a bad fellow, you know, just impetuous."

"Never."

Everyone who knew them came to the trial when it was finally under way. Ernie Schultz sat on one side, and Roger Stiller's other cronies sat on the other, shaking their heads sorrowfully. Such a shame, they said. May Fraley brought several other girls with her, three of whom had modeled for Roger. They looked at him uneasily, with sidelong glances.

Roger was dapper, the personable gent. He smiled kindly at India as he took his place and received a stiletto gaze in return.

"Try not to look so much like Lizzie Borden," Zimmerman whispered to her.

Mr. Purcell, Roger's lawyer, had an imposing Vandyke beard and a gimlet eye. He turned it on May Fraley.

"And now, Miss Fraley, please state your, er, occupation for us."

"I told that gentleman before," May said. She looked at Mr. Zimmerman, who had already examined her.

"Well, just tell us again, please."

"I'm an artist's model." May clutched her pocketbook in her lap. She had on a high collar and a big beehive hat, and she seemed to be trying to hide inside it.

"I see." Mr. Purcell inspected her. "And did you pose for Mr. Stiller?"

"I already— Yes, I did."

"In the, er, altogether?"

"I object, Your Honor." Zimmerman stood up. "That is what artist's models usually pose in, and Miss Fraley, like all of us, has a living to earn. We are interested in what she saw, not what she wore."

"Your Honor." Purcell turned toward the judge. "I don't wish to embarrass this young lady in any way, but where we are concerned with the veracity of a witness, what she is or is not inclined to wear may be a reference to her character. So may her other actions, which I am coming to."

India glared at him, outraged, while the judge also inspected May Fraley, who was twisting her hands around her pocketbook. She was a wispy blonde with the air of an appealing waif. Many artists used her, and she looked as if she would rather have been nude in front of all of them than clothed in front of Mr. Purcell.

"Overruled," the judge said. "But counsel will try to keep in mind that Miss Fraley is not on trial here."

"Certainly. Now then, my dear. *Did* you pose, er, nude?"

"Yes, sir." May compressed her lips and looked away from him.

"And did you pose in this fashion for other gentlemen as well?"

"I'm a model," May said. "What do you think I did?"

"That's what we're trying to find out, my dear," Purcell said unctuously, and India put her head in her hands. She wanted to pull her hat down over her face like May's beehive. She knew what was coming.

"And did you ever have any, er, relations with any of these gentlemen, while you were in this unclothed state?"

"Relations?" May said. "That's not your business."

"Objection," Mr. Zimmerman said. "It isn't."

"We'll narrow the inquiry a little," Mr. Purcell said. "Did you ever have relations with Mr. Stiller?"

May shot India a panicked look and an equally terrified one at Roger. "What kind of relations?"

"Carnal ones, Miss Fraley," Purcell said dryly.

"I don't remember." May looked at her toes.

"Come now. Mr. Stiller is a handsome man. Surely he would be memorable. Unless, of course, there were so many others—"

"No!" May said. "You aren't gonna make me out fast! Mr. Stiller made advances once or twice. He—"

"And how far did those advances go?"

"He gave me a watch," May said.

The jury clucked its tongue, collectively.

"Let me try to spare your blushes," Purcell said. "Did you or did you not have carnal relations with Mr. Stiller, before or after the watch? All you have to say is yes or no."

"Yes," May whispered.

"Damn satyr," Zimmerman said under his breath.

"And what happened after that?"

"Nothin'," May said.

"Weren't you perhaps angry? At this cavalier attitude toward your virtue?"

"No," May said.

Purcell raised his eyebrows. "It meant so little to you? Do you routinely have meaningless affairs with men?"

"No!" May said angrily.

"I see," Purcell murmured. "Only with those who give you watches. And now you have testified that Miss Blackstone, to whom you have done a considerable wrong, I should say, despite that couple's unmarried state—" he cast a critical glance at India "—is the true author of this work of art. That you in fact saw it on her easel long before Mr. Stiller began his version."

"Yes, I did, and I know when he started his because I sat for it."

"Yes. Interesting how your loyalties have shifted from Mr. Stiller to Miss Blackstone, presumably at about the time that Mr. Stiller ceased to pay his attentions to you. Thank you. That will be all, dear."

Mr. Zimmerman, having launched his smallest ship first, proceeded to bring out the big guns. Sally took the stand, and one glance at her told Purcell not to try the same tactics. She was impeccably dressed from head to toe in russet silk and fox furs, and she told the court of her friendship with India, her charity work at the Women's Hospital, and her daddy the senator. She had, she assured them, seen the picture in question on India's easel on several occasions.

"Well, of course I did," Sally said, laughing. "I posed for it."

"In the altogether?" Zimmerman asked kindly.

"Certainly not," Sally said. "Miss Blackstone does not require the enticement of undraped women in order to make people look at her pictures."

"Thank you," Mr. Zimmerman said.

Mr. Purcell questioned her memory for dates, and Sally produced her pocket calendar.

Ernie Schultz took the stand looking like a dog being dragged to the vet.

"Well, I do remember it. Quite some time ago. Round about the spring, I expect. I saw Miss Holt sit for it."

"You're quite certain?"

Schultz grinned in spite of himself. "I always remember Miss Holt."

Purcell was jocular and sympathetic to Mr. Schultz's position, thrust into the middle of a quarrel between his friends. And did he have any way of knowing that Mr. Stiller had not already begun his painting? Just because Mr. Schultz hadn't seen it, did that mean it did not exist?

No, Schultz said, looking apologetically at everyone. He scrambled down from the witness stand before Purcell had even finished excusing him.

Zimmerman called India to the stand. Had she ever seen Mr. Stiller's painting before she went to Chicago to photograph it? No, she hadn't. Had she left hers on the easel, or propped against the studio wall in plain view? Yes, for months.

She was dressed for the occasion in a plain blue serge suit and a severe navy hat, but it didn't stop Purcell, on cross-examination, from discussing her unmarried state.

"Were you perhaps not enraged that Mr. Stiller refused to marry you, and decided to achieve at least a financial gain from the situation by selling his designs as your own?"

"Mr. Stiller did not refuse to marry me," India said icily. "I refused to marry Mr. Stiller."

"Come now. You deliberately chose the role of outcast from polite society? What kind of woman are you?"

"Objection!"

Purcell's cross-examination continued to be punctuated by howls of outrage from Zimmerman, nearly all sustained. But an innuendo made was an innuendo heard, even if the jury had been told to disregard it.

"I warned you you were in for this," Zimmerman said to India at lunch. "Purcell isn't going to let go of it."

"It's all he's got," she said. "I can take it."

"Just don't get mad at him," Zimmerman said. "Men don't like an aggressive woman. They like females they can rescue."

"And you wonder why I don't want to get married," India muttered.

"Well, if you'd married him," Zimmerman said philosophically, "you couldn't sue him."

In the afternoon he put Roger on the stand and played out the rope with which they hoped he would hang himself.

"Do you consider yourself a serious artist?"

"Certainly," Roger said.

"And Miss Blackstone's work—how would you describe that?"

"Miss Blackstone is a magazine illustrator." Roger's mouth tightened. "I do not think her work could be described as serious. It is very rare that a woman has the capacity for serious work."

"And yet you were her lover for three years," Zimmerman said flatly.

"Certainly. She is a personable female, or was until she went mad and began imagining that I was stealing from her. I do not require artistic talent in my female companions. Frankly, I find them more attractive without it. Too many dealings in matters best left to men make a woman unfeminine and unreliable."

"And so you did not consider her work particularly important?"

"It paid the bills," India muttered from where she sat. Sally put a hand on her shoulder and shushed her.

"In terms of art?" Roger asked. "No."

"Then if someone had stolen one of her ideas, that would not be particularly important either?"

"I don't know."

"Isn't that what you said to Miss Blackstone when she accused you of doing so?"

"I don't remember. Maybe. No, I didn't say that!"

"Then you said it was important that you had used her design?"

"I didn't use her design!"

"Then how do you account for the similarity?"

"I told you. She copied her design from mine."

"Six months before you painted it?"

"No! After. How do I know when she stole it? She was in my studio all the time."

"Doing what?"

"Cleaning!"

"Kind of her," Zimmerman said, "considering how unimportant you felt her work was, to clean up after yours."

"That was her business, to keep the place clean."

"I see. And what did you contribute to this cozy nest?"

"What any fellow would. Income. I paid the bills."

"All of them? Isn't it true that Miss Blackstone paid a larger share of the bills than you did? That she in fact made more money than you did?"

"I don't know. I don't pay attention to money."

"Too artistic, we presume," Zimmerman said. "I'll leave the jury to wonder why a woman who made more money than you did should need to steal ideas from you."

"The jury doesn't like him," Sally said. "Did you see their faces?"

"Good men and true," Zimmerman said. "They don't hold with artists who let their women support them. Unfortunately, they don't care for ladies who get overly independent, either. A little more shrinking violet when they take this up again wouldn't hurt."

"I'll try," India said between her teeth. The case had been continued until the day after next.

"Stiller's got a list of witnesses to call yet," Zimmerman said. He looked at it and shook his head. "All men. All artists. The gentlemen's club is closing its doors in your face, my dear."

The Village grapevine sent out new shoots by the score overnight. Everyone had an opinion. They debated them over wine and minestrone at Mama Rosalia's, and the ranks were drawn. Could a woman do serious work? Even some of the women felt that the answer might be no. Women were the helpmeets of bohemia. And India admittedly did commercial work. What would happen to their collective integrity if this fellow, a serious artist, were convicted of plagiarizing from a woman illustrator of magazines? Some of the men shook their heads sorrowfully and knew where their duty lay, but the rumor ran round and round the Village, like a mouse in a bucket, that Stiller had indeed stolen the picture.

Sally spent the day out of court going through India's wardrobe and decreeing what she should wear for the second day of the trial. "You don't want to look fast, and you don't want to look like a bluestocking." Sally held up a tan wool dress with a draped bodice and a black satin belt. "This might do, with the right hat."

"He steals my picture and then accuses me of theft, and I have to worry about the right hat!" India paced the apartment talking under her breath, and jumped when the telephone shrilled at her from the wall.

In a moment, though, she turned to Sally and held out the receiver. "It's Juergen."

Sally's hand went to her mouth. If Juergen had tracked her down here, it was important. If it was important, it was bad.

His voice sounded tinny, as if he were down a well, but she could hear the desperation in it. "They're sending me home."

Sally leaned against the wall and closed her eyes. "When?"

"Next week. I have to see you. Tonight."

"I have to be in court tomorrow, early."

"Sally—"

"I'm going home. Meet me there." Sally turned to India. "I don't know what I'm doing. They're sending him back to Germany. I'll get to court tomorrow morning, I promise."

Sally's maid let Juergen in. He was tight-lipped and white around the mouth. The maid took his topcoat and hat with avid interest. "Bring Mr. von Appen a whiskey," Sally said.

"And then go away," Juergen said tiredly, losing his usual good manners.

"Sit down," Sally said. "Juergen, they can't send you home!" She clenched slim fingers together, twisting them.

"They can do anything they want to do."

He looked, Sally thought, as if someone had beaten him.

Her maid brought the whiskey, and he took a sip and set it down. "They were quite explicit. Given the political situation, it is felt that I am perhaps not reliable."

"What political situation?"

"The one which every hothead in Europe seems determined to make. Germany is quarreling with the English again. Or they are quarreling with us. It depends on how you look at it. And Americans are felt to be suspect."

"It's because of me, isn't it?" Sally took his hand and wailed, "Why can't you just *stay* here?"

"We've been through this," Juergen said miserably. "What do you want—more years of dithering over how we can marry and where we shall live? Sally, just come with me. Marry me and come with me. If you're willing to do that, they can't object to you."

"Who couldn't? Your mother?"

Juergen smiled, the best effort he could manage. "No, darling, the Diplomatic Service."

"And your mother?" Sally said stiffly.

"We don't have to live with her."

"She hates the idea of me," Sally said with conviction. "It would be dreadful. Juergen, please stay. My family likes you."

"I cannot. You know I cannot." A moment passed before he moaned and said, "How am I going to live without you?"

"I don't know," Sally said. "How am I going to get along without you? I want to get married, I want to have a normal life like other people. That's all I've ever wanted. I'm tired of living alone, I hate it."

"Then come with me." He closed his arms around her, kissed her, and held her against his chest.

She tried to think through the fright of losing him, but it was making her head spin. The thought of living in Germany appalled her. She had met the other Germans from the consulate, and they had been stiff and condescendingly gallant. But they couldn't all be like that. His mother and sisters would hate her, though, and what if there was a war? Yet how could she live without him?

"I cannot stay," Juergen said quietly. "I serve my country. And particularly if there is a war, I cannot stay. What kind of man would that make me?"

"But you want me to give up mine."

"I am afraid I think that for a woman it is easier. Perhaps it is not. I do know that I don't want to be without you. I don't want to be . . . lacking, all my life, for want of you."

Sally took a deep breath and bit back the howling sobs that bubbled up in her throat. "I won't go with you. Not now, I can't—not sight unseen. But I'll come for a visit in a while, when you've had time to talk with your family."

"When?" Juergen demanded.

She sat up and looked at him. "In a few months. When you can tell me I'll be welcome. And then we'll see." Her mouth was firm, and she had her no-nonsense look.

Juergen tightened his arms around her. "If you came now you would be welcome. My *wife* would be welcome."

"Things I do on the spur of the moment are always wrong," Sally said. "I'll come in six months."

She kissed him again, agonizingly, and made him leave. Then she got into her nightgown and lay awake all night, caught between the twin terrors of going to Germany and losing Juergen.

In the morning Sally slipped into the back row of the spectators' benches, whispering apologies to the bailiff and the people whose feet she stepped over. The trial had already started. Mr. Purcell was chatting jovially with an artist whom she had met at India's one night. He was quite sure he'd seen the painting on Roger's easel, oh, months before the date in question. Roger must have put it away for a while to simmer. Sometimes it took time before the right image came into one's head.

Sally drew in her breath in a fury. She could see other artists, a herd of them, all male, nodding and looking solemn. No question of old Stiller's lifting ideas from his little lady, the witness on the stand said, shaking his head. She did a different kind of work entirely. Not to be offensive, but not much there to steal, you know. But sometimes the ladies got angry if you didn't take them seriously. He expected that was what had happened.

"She's cooked," a voice said in Sally's ear, and Frank Blake sat down beside her.

"What are you doing here?" Sally hissed.

"Just the sweep-up man," Frank said, "come to pick up the pieces. I never liked that bastard."

"You wouldn't have liked anyone," Sally said astutely. She rubbed her eyes.

"You look horrible. What's the matter?"

"Juergen's being sent back to Germany."

"Aw, hell," Frank whispered. "Are you going with him?"

"I'm terrified to," Sally said. "What if it was unbearable, even with Juergen, and I'd already married him?"

Frank flinched. "A terrible life with someone you love. Worse than being alone, do you think?"

"Infinitely," Sally said. "If you love them enough, it would be agony."

"So what are you going to do?"

"Talk to Peter, I think, about what it's really like. Maybe if I went with Peter, and he introduced me to people, it might make it easier. Maybe they wouldn't dislike me so much. I'm the reason they're sending Juergen back, the beasts."

"They may dislike Peter fairly shortly, too," Frank said.

Sally put her hand on his wrist. The last witness was stepping down. It had been a brisk parade of genial gentlemen artists, not unkind about Miss Blackstone but blunt in their assessment of her abilities.

"She used to do better work than he did," Frank said between his teeth. "Before she got interested in making money and playing house."

"Be sure to tell her so," Sally said with unusual irony. "That's bound to cheer her up."

The jury wasn't out for long—almost, it seemed to India, as if, like her work, she didn't matter very much. She had known since this morning that she was going to lose, had known when she'd seen Roger's parade of witnesses. None of them had said anything conclusive, but they had all been men, and so was the jury. She was the intruder.

The jury foreman coughed and studied the notes in his hand. "If it please Your Honor, we find Mr. Stiller not guilty of plagiarism." He glanced at Roger for a moment with a mild distaste, as if, although plainly in the right, there was still something not square about him. The juror coughed again, almost a *harrumph*. "In the matter of the countersuit, we find Miss Blackstone not guilty of the same charge."

The sudden uproar in the courtroom subsided when the judge whacked his gavel on the bench and said, "This court is not yet dismissed." He glared at Roger Stiller and India and their respective lawyers. "Someone has wasted a great deal of my time. However, since the jury has so found, I will leave any further verdict to public opinion. Dismissed!"

"A sound plan," Frank said, loud enough for Roger Stiller to hear. "Public opinion has an excellent nose."

Stiller spun around, his face flushed. Ernie Schultz and one of the morning's witnesses grabbed his arm, but Stiller pulled away, glaring at Ernie and then at Frank.

India pushed her way through the enthralled crowd, with Mr. Zimmerman behind her. "We may not have got any money out of him," Zimmerman said philosophically, "but his name is mud."

"I wanted the money," India said darkly. "His name won't stay mud. They're all such jolly old pals." Then she noticed Frank. It was the first time she had seen him since he took her to lunch the day she got the letter from Chicago. She imagined he must have known about the trial. "Come to see the show?"

"It seemed more tactful not to watch the festivities," Frank said. "I just came for the denouement."

"I didn't know you were in New York," she said.

"Well, to tell the truth I just got here. I was going to be a gent and not show up until the shouting was over, but Mike sent me down to find Sally."

Sally peered at him blurrily.

"I didn't want to just blurt it out between witnesses," Frank said. He took Sally's hand. "Gran's gone. Mike just got a wire from your father. We're summoned home for the funeral."

"It'll give her something to take her mind off Juergen," Frank said to India over dinner. He hoped it would. Sally looked dreadful. She had refused to come out and eat with them. Frank imagined she was going off somewhere to wrangle with Juergen some more.

"Certainly," India said. "Nothing like a death in the family to distract you."

"Gran was ninety-two," Frank said gently. "She had a good long go. Went to Oregon with the first wagon train."

"It's a pity there aren't any now. I'd like to go somewhere."

"I told you he was an oaf. How are you holding up?"

"I'm going back to work," India said with a sigh. "I have bills to pay. Zimmerman's, for instance. Assuming anyone will hire me."

"The world's hard on females." Frank attacked his steak.

He must be flush, India thought. Usually he bought her spaghetti.

"It's the unfairness that makes me so angry." Her fists clenched into balls around her knife and fork. "They knew he stole that picture from me, and they turned him loose anyway, because they thought it didn't matter."

"Lots of people out there the world thinks don't matter," Frank said. "That's why I do what I do. Bill Haywood thinks I'm useful because I can put on airs like a gentleman when I need to, but he doesn't quite trust it either. He'd sooner I came from the wrong side of the tracks."

"If you were female, he wouldn't notice you at all."

"Put your money where your mouth is. Go march for the vote. I'll be in New York for a while, after I get back from Portland. Plans to lay. And some folks to hit up for money, folks that have it. Maybe I'll tap Dad for a contribution while I'm in Portland. There, got a laugh out of you."

India chuckled ruefully.

He would come see her then, Frank decided; give her time to let her anger at Stiller dissipate. It probably wasn't prudent to leap too quickly between the other fellow's sheets when the lady in question wanted to take after the other fellow with a poker.

IV

Cologne

Her grandmother's funeral in Portland was the most depressing event Sally had ever attended, even for a funeral. It rained constantly, and the old house was sodden with it, dampness in the bathrooms, mildew on the ceilings, mud in the hallways from someone's boots. Toby and Alexandra were depressed—Grandmother Eulalia's last illness had been a harrowing one. Frank had a fight with his father because he had actually had the nerve to ask him for a contribution, and the parlor was thick with furious tirades about the Wobblies —as the members of the IWW were now known—and the socialists. And the subject of who was going to run the old place when Toby and Alexandra were too old hung in the air. Everyone looked at Sally; Aunt Cindy, Frank's mother, intimated that her niece was undutiful not to stay home now.

"Mama's only fifty-six," Sally said, more tartly than she meant to. "She hasn't got one foot in the grave."

"Your father is seventy," Aunt Cindy said.

"And a tough old bird," Frank added. He dragged his mother off to discuss Gran's jewelry with Alexandra. Everyone was in black and looked like a nest of weary crows.

Sally retreated upstairs to her old room and stared at the mildew on the walls until her mother came in to inform her that it had been decided she was to have Gran's cameo and pearl eardrops.

Juergen would be gone by the time she got back to New York. She had written to him in Germany already so there would be a letter waiting for him. Some piece of herself seemed to be missing. When her parents asked after him, she couldn't gather the energy to tell them what had happened. They would be relieved, she supposed, and she couldn't bear to tell them she might follow him. It was too soon for that, anyway. She looked in the mirror at her black funeral dress and thought that she looked as if she were decomposing with the damp herself.

Peter Blake caught her in the hallway when she finally emerged. "Frank told me," he said. "Said you didn't want the family to know, but you'd a notion to talk to me about it. Come on."

Sally followed him into a little upstairs parlor that had been Gran's. A fire had been lit to chase the damp, and Gran's knitting was still sitting next to it.

"I miss her," Peter said wistfully. His mother, the German, had died when he was two, and Gran and Aunt Cindy were the only mothers he remembered. He was brown-haired, as his birth mother had been, and her beauty had somehow been transmuted into an engaging plainness in his face. He had a cheerful mouth and ears that stuck out a little.

"What's it really like in Germany?" Sally asked. "To live there?"

"A little stately," Peter said. "Not what you're used to here. I've always enjoyed myself in Grevenburg. Of course, it helps to be my mother's heir—rather like the young squire coming home. I've a cousin who inherited the title, but my mother is remembered fondly."

"You're a connection of the von Appens. Would that help?"

"It would if Juergen wanted to marry me," Peter said. "Unfortunately, *you're* a connection of the mannerless American who married her and snatched me out of Grevenburg."

"Juergen wanted me to go with him."

"Don't you do it," Peter said bluntly.

"I said I'd go for a visit. And we'd see."

"When?"

"In six months. When he's had time to talk to his family."

Peter shook his head. "He can talk to his family until he's blue in the face, but it won't do any good. Even if they could be persuaded to like you, no one else would."

"How do you know? You make them sound dreadful."

"I just came from there. They're no more dreadful than anyone else, I suppose, but there is a great deal of bad feeling against England and, by extension, America just now, and it's going to get worse. I've shut my factories down. Sold the machinery outside of Germany."

"Oh, Peter, you don't really think it will come to war?"

"You stay out of Germany," Peter said. "Don't even go for a visit."

Which was all very well for Peter to say, Sally thought, putting down her money in the Cunard office nearly a year later. Peter wasn't in love with someone in Germany. Peter wasn't in love with anybody, as far as she could tell; Peter appeared to be immune. But you couldn't make yourself *stop* loving someone, Sally had discovered. She hadn't really tried as long as Juergen had been in New York. But after he had left for Germany, she had tried to stop loving him, with determination. It hadn't worked. She could get numb, until she didn't feel it so much, but as soon as she let herself feel anything, she could feel Juergen again, even now. And nearly a year had passed.

It had taken him six months to talk his mother and sisters into agreeing to Sally's visit. Sally didn't know what he had threatened them with, but he had finally written to say that they would be delighted to receive her. But then his mother had taken sick with some debilitating stomach complaint. The doctors weren't sure what it was, Juergen had written, but she couldn't possibly receive company. In a month she should be well. In two months. When she had been sick for five months, Juergen wrote abruptly that she was completely recovered and was looking forward to meeting her prospective daughter-in-law. Juergen would be waiting for her. Cologne was very beautiful in the spring.

Sally sailed for Germany and wrote her parents that she was doing so simultaneously, which resulted in an enormous upheaval of cables and frantic letters that came far too late to stop her. India was hauled before the family court and could say truthfully that Sally had told her nothing, but that she thought Sally had been bitterly unhappy this last year.

Sally, at sea, cast any guilt she was feeling over the stern into the liner's wake, flung it openhanded to the seagulls, who would eat anything. She was twenty-eight, old enough to know what she wanted, and she wanted Juergen. The closer she got, the faster her heart thudded against her ribs when she thought of him. She conjured his face out of the clouds and the roiling sea foam, slept with his picture under her pillow, and told gentlemen who expressed interest in her company at dinner that she was engaged to be married.

She landed in Le Havre and took a train to Cologne, where Juergen met her with a bouquet of roses nearly bigger than she was and a tightness around the mouth that seemed at odds with the expression in his eyes when he looked at her. "Oh, my darling," he said quietly.

Sally flung her arms around him, and everyone stared at them. After a moment Juergen set her away from him and stood drawing her in as if she were oxygen. "Dear God, you are so beautiful." He sent his driver for her trunk and tucked her into a Benz motorcar. "You'll just have time to dress for dinner. Mother and the girls are expecting you." Again, Sally noticed that little tic by his mouth.

The von Appens lived near the Tempelhaus, and Uncle Rudolf, Frau von Appen's brother, kept offices nearby. He and Juergen's father had inherited the winery started by Juergen's grandfather, but since his father's death, Juergen explained, Uncle Rudolf ran the business alone. Juergen had been expected to take over but had developed a talent for foreign languages and diplomacy and found his niche elsewhere.

"I suppose I'll have to do something with the winery when Uncle Rudolf dies," he said, "if the girls haven't married by then. The Rhine vineyard country is very beautiful. I want to show it to you."

Sally peered around her with interest. Cologne was old and stately and elegant. A Gothic cathedral with slim lacy spires towered over the skyline. It had, according to the guidebook she had bought in New York, taken five and a half centuries to build. The city went right down the banks of the Rhine, and the riverine smell of deep water, coal smoke, and fish drifted faintly on the air. Blending with them was the scent of chocolate, tobacco, and eau de Cologne from the manufacturing district. A pleasant mix, Sally decided. It might be easy to like Cologne.

The driver pulled the car up outside an imposing stone house and opened the door for Sally. She half expected him to click his heels—and he did. Juergen led her inside, through a cavernous entrance hall adorned with suits of armor and enormous portraits in gold frames, to meet Mother and the girls.

Frau von Appen was a very straight woman—that was Sally's immediate thought. Her pale champagne dress, very much the color of the family vintage, was nearly pencil-shaped in its severity; her back was utterly upright, as if some invisible governess still placed books on her head; her chin was perfectly centered above her high linen collar. She held out a hand and said in excellent, pleasantly accented English, "How do you do?"

"How do you do?" Sally said. "You are very kind to invite me."

"Allow me to present my daughters."

"The girls" proved to be approximately Sally's age, with their mother's stiff carriage but a great deal of Juergen's good looks. They stepped forward a pace, gave her identical greetings, and stepped back.

"No doubt you will wish to change," Frau von Appen said. "We will see you at dinner."

Dismissed, Sally practiced her German on a maid who spoke no English, bathed in a small tin bathtub filled with a kettle, and put on a dinner dress she had bought in New York to dazzle Juergen. It had a draped front of pale blue crepe de chine sewn over with purple wisteria blossoms, and a skirt slit and knotted at the knee to lift one side elegantly above her ankle. The pompadour out of style now, she had pinned her hair in gentle waves over her ears and knotted it in the back. A purple silk band with a white aigrette held the waves in place.

Juergen appeared satisfactorily dazzled. Mother and the girls inspected the dress and asked Sally as she sat down whether all American girls were fast.

"I beg your pardon?" Sally blinked at them.

"Do they all wear dresses like that—showing their legs?" Crista asked. She peered at Sally as if she were perhaps a new species.

"German girls wouldn't dream of hitching their skirts up like that," Ilse said. They both nodded.

"American girls are possibly a little ahead of us in fashion," Juergen said. "You ought to go to Paris more often, Ilse."

"Where do you come from, Miss Holt?" Mother inquired.

"Why, Portland, Oregon, originally," Sally said. "But these days from New York."

"I don't know where Portland, Oregon is." Frau von Appen appeared to be proud of that. "Why do you live in New York?"

Presumably you know where that is. "I like the city," Sally said, smiling as graciously as possible. "There are wonderful libraries, and the symphony, and the opera, and the art galleries."

"In Germany we have far better cultural achievements," Frau von Appen announced.

"How nice," Sally said.

Juergen flushed and shot a look at his mother.

"I understand that you work. In a hospital," Crista said.

"I'm a volunteer," Sally said, well aware that to have been paid for it would set her down several rungs on the social ladder. "My sister is a physician there," she added for effect.

"Your *sister*?" Ilse raised her eyebrows.

"She founded the hospital, as a matter of fact." Sally decided she might as well begin being straightforward, as she meant to continue that way. "It is a hospital for the women of the tenements and does a great deal of good."

Mother clucked her tongue. "Why would a lady wish to waste her time that way?"

"They have dreadful slums in New York," Ilse said. "Quite as bad as in London. Perhaps it's necessary."

"Dr. Lawrence is very well known in New York," Juergen said. He glanced at Sally, and a flicker of amusement passed between them. That Dr. Lawrence was well known for advocating contraception was probably something that should *not* be mentioned. It was controversial enough in New York.

"I have heard that New Yorkers are all unhealthy," Crista said.

"It is the air," Mother informed her. "Not like the clean air we get from the Rhine. Americans all have lung disease."

* * *

"And Germans *do* have *some* manners," Juergen said the next day, torn between fury and embarrassment and laughter. "Mother's just outraged that I haven't fallen in love with anyone over here."

"I'm sure she's tried," Sally said. They were motoring through Cologne toward the vineyard country, dismissed with a parting shot from Mother about the loose appearance of going out alone without so much as a driver. Sally wondered what Mother's efforts to interest Juergen elsewhere had encompassed. "And there hasn't been anyone in the last year?"

"Not a soul," Juergen said cheerfully, turning south. The family vineyards lay beyond Bonn, in gently rolling hills green with vines. They had a picnic hamper of Strasbourg pâté, dark bread, and a bottle of the family's Riesling. Well into the countryside, they passed a farmer with an oxcart and a small girl trying to catch a chicken. The sun was warm, and when Juergen stopped the car at midday outside a long empty shed full of barrels, Sally could hear bees.

They had talked of this and that for most of the drive, but now Juergen turned serious. "This is where we crush the grapes, the first stage. We've had a good spring—the ice saints brought fair weather—so it will be a good harvest. You see, this is another reason I can't leave. Someone will have to mind the business after Uncle Rudolf. It's all that Mother and the girls have to live on."

"They hated me on sight," Sally said.

"They hated you before you got here. It isn't personal, darling. Once they know you, they'll come around. Mother came around to your visit."

"You threatened her with something."

Juergen laughed. "I threatened to go back to America."

"My God, Juergen." Sally stared at him. "I believe you did. Did you mean it?"

Juergen smiled and slipped an arm around her waist. "We don't have to live with her. She has the girls under her thumb. She can do without me."

"I wouldn't dream of living with her," Sally said flatly. "Do you think Ilse and Crista might like me, after a while?"

"Who could help but like you?" Juergen said, which wasn't an answer.

He took her hand, and they walked through the vineyards. The vines were old, hoary gray trunks, pruned and staked, their new shoots leafy pale. They reminded Sally of green ringlets on an old gnome's head. "What are the ice saints?" she asked.

"Mamertus, Pancratius, and Servatius. They are extremely obscure in the Christian calendar everywhere except along the Rhine. Their saints' days are May eleventh, twelfth, and thirteenth. If they're in a good mood with mankind, they bring three days of warm weather, and the harvest in October will be fine. If they're in a temper, they bring a frost."

"Does that spoil the vines?"

"Only the new ones," he explained. "But there are always new ones. Vines give out, and the oldest have to be replaced each year. And Uncle Rudolf is always trying new varieties."

"Will I meet Uncle Rudolf?"

Juergen hesitated. "I expect so," he said finally, a little too casual in his tone.

And what is wrong with Uncle Rudolf? Sally wondered. Perhaps he, too, hated Americans. And was there an Aunt Someone? And all the little Someones, who also would hate Americans? But the vineyards were near Bonn, and Sally had the notion that perhaps she and Juergen could live there. The sight of his face, carefree now and unbearably dear, was enough to make her think she was willing to try it. There had been no talk of war the night before, and war seemed infinitely far away from this sun-drenched vineyard and the slow roll of the Rhine beyond.

She met Uncle Rudolf at the end of the week, after five days of sightseeing expeditions that kept them blessedly out of Frau von Appen's house. Despite Mother's disapproval, they stayed in country inns more picturesque than comfortable and saw the Drachenfels, Cat Castle and Mouse Castle, the Rhine Gorge above Bingen, and the ruins of Ehrenfels looming in Wagnerian drama over the river. Juergen pointed out the Lorelei Rock, onto which a sweet-voiced sprite was said to have lured hapless boatmen to their doom. Sally drank in the misty gorges and terraced vineyards, the castles, many still occupied, towering on their cliffs, and fell in love. She could live here, she thought while riding beside Juergen between a pear and an apple orchard. A green woodpecker flashed across the road in front of them, and somewhere down the mountain she could hear a church bell calling folk more pious than they to services.

They spent their nights in separate rooms, content now to wait, certain of their future, although nothing had actually been said. On Tuesday they returned home to Cologne.

"Uncle Rudolf will be here for dinner," Mother informed Juergen before they were quite in the door. "Please do not make an uncomfortableness by discussing your plans with him." She addressed him in English, and Sally was unsure whether it was out of deference to her or to make quite certain that she knew what Frau von Appen was saying.

Uncle Rudolf proved to have no attachments, much to Sally's relief. Mother and the girls were quite enough. *It's my punishment for having led a charmed life, I suppose*, she decided, and she set about being charming.

Uncle Rudolf was small and round, with a very Prussian mustache, which seemed at odds with his face. He beamed at her rosily from behind a monocle. "Ah! A very pretty one, Juergen. I am jealous."

I can deal with him, thought Sally, the accomplished flirt. He was just like all the nice old uncles, the judges and generals of her father's generation, who pinched her cheek and told her what they would do if only they were ten years younger. It wasn't until she felt Uncle Rudolf's hand slide over her knee at dinner that she began to think she had miscalculated.

She moved it quite firmly away, but it came back and squeezed a little. Sally looked at Juergen for help and saw that his cheeks were flaming. He knew what was happening. Uncle Rudolf squeezed again, and Sally dropped her fork in her lap, poking the fat fingers quite sharply as she picked it up again. The hand withdrew.

Uncle Rudolf turned to other matters, but he gave Sally a sly wink. "It is good for Juergen that you are an American and not an Englishwoman, eh? The English will see what Lord Haldane has cost them when we invade their country."

"Invade England?" Sally goggled at him. The failure of the neutrality pact—England had declined to remain neutral if Germany started a war—had been a constant topic of conversation over the past few days, but this was the first time she had heard anyone mention invasion. *Invade England?*

"Certainly," Uncle Rudolf said. "England comes to the end of the time when she can treat Germany without respect. The emperor has made it clear that our time in the sun has come."

Juergen bit his lip. "We trust that that will not mean war, Uncle."

"War?" Uncle Rudolf spluttered. He set his wineglass down rather too hard, splattering the contents on the tablecloth. Sally noted that his contempt for all other nations did not prevent him from drinking French burgundy; the Rhine Valley lacked the sun for the great red wines. "Of course there must be war. The mongrel peasants of small nations can no longer be permitted to take what is Germany's due."

"The neutrality pact may still be achieved," Juergen said. "The chancellor and Prince Lichnovsky, the new ambassador, are hopeful."

"Bah!" Uncle Rudolf said.

When dinner was over, Frau von Appen decreed that Ilse should play the piano, and everyone settled in the best drawing room to listen to her. The drawing room was decorated in deep red, with heavy gold-fringed curtains and a massive carved highboy, on which stood a collection of Dresden china shepherdesses simpering at china shepherds.

"And how long do you visit with us?" Uncle Rudolf whispered, plumping himself undaunted onto the sofa next to Sally.

"I'm not sure," she answered, wishing she still had the fork. His hand rested on the sofa between them, and she watched it suspiciously.

"Not too long, eh? It's nice Juergen has a friend. You can tell the Americans we are not so bad as their newspapers make out, eh?"

"Shh! Ilse is playing," Sally whispered.

Ilse played Beethoven with authority, and Uncle Rudolf drummed his fingers on the sofa in time to the piano. Sally edged away. When Ilse coughed and asked for a glass of water, Sally leaped up with as much alacrity as possible to fetch it for her.

Frau von Appen looked at her oddly and said, "We have servants to do that."

"That is all right. No need to trouble them." Uncle Rudolf huffed to his feet. "Fraulein Sally and I will fetch it."

Juergen had stood, possibly with some idea of nipping that in the bud, when there was a thunderous knock at the door. A maid materialized to open it, and everyone waited. When the maid came back to fetch Juergen and his mother, Sally found herself in the pantry with Uncle Rudolf after all.

She filled a glass at the scullery tap and looked around her for a toasting fork. Uncle Rudolf beamed and pinched her cheek. "American girls are so delightful. So informal and easy to know, eh?" He edged closer, backing her against the sink.

"Not that easy," Sally said firmly. "Juergen will be very angry with you if you don't behave."

"Juergen knows I can't resist a pretty girl."

"You'll have to, or I'll make a scene." She stamped suddenly on his instep, and when he hopped back, she whisked around him through the door. "American girls are very forthright, too."

She heard Uncle Rudolf hobbling after her as she presented the glass of water to Ilse. Sally was determined not to look at him; it would probably only encourage him. Uncle Rudolf was probably capable of interpreting having his foot crushed as flirtation. She flushed, hoping that Ilse and Crista weren't aware of that disgusting little scene, and then realized that a gelid silence had overtaken the room. Angry voices came from behind the double doors that closed the drawing room from the entrance hall. Crista and Ilse, and now Uncle Rudolf, stiffened, listening.

They were speaking German, and Sally could catch only a few words through the anger and the muffling doors. She heard Juergen's voice, tight, under stiff control, but acid in its fury. The male voice that argued with him was demanding, and there was something insinuating in its tone. Another spatter of words flew like furious hornets, with Frau von Appen speaking also, her tone icy and contemptuous. There were footsteps, and then the front door closed with an angry bang.

When Juergen slid the double doors open, Sally could see that his face was flaming. He looked nearly angry enough to be violent.

"We must have a family talk. Immediately," Frau von

Appen said tightly to Uncle Rudolf. She glanced at Sally. "I am sure that Fräulein Holt will excuse us."

There was no way to decline, and Sally had no wish to overhear family crises anyway. She said, "Certainly," and took her leave. Juergen was staring furiously at the wall. She wasn't even sure he had seen her go.

In her room Sally undressed and climbed into the big four-poster bed, carved of some dark wood and overstuffed with a feather mattress. After a moment she heard two more sets of footsteps patter up the stairs. It appeared that Ilse and Crista had been dismissed, too. Soon the house was silent, and after a few minutes of anxious thoughts, she fell into a fitful sleep.

Sally dressed in the morning hoping that whatever storm had arrived last night had blown over. She was pulling on a silk kimono when a peremptory tap rattled her door. "Come in," she called in German, thinking that it was the maid. It was Juergen.

Sally wrapped the kimono around her corset cover and knickers in a hurry. "Whoops. You're up early, darling. Thank heavens you're not Uncle Rudolf."

"I have to talk to you." Juergen's jaw twitched.

"Certainly. Sit down." He looked dreadful, white where he had been flushed last night. She patted the bench in front of the dressing table, perched on the edge of the bed, and again said, "Sit."

Juergen closed the door and sat, putting his head in his hands for a minute. Finally he lifted it. "I was very lonely without you," he said abruptly.

Sally nodded, perplexed.

"I told you I hadn't fallen in love with anyone else."

"Oh, no," Sally whispered.

"I didn't," he said. "I don't think I will ever be able to love anyone but you, no matter what happens. But I made love to someone else." His mouth twisted, and he added bitterly, "I slept with someone else."

Sally flinched.

"Not with a prostitute," Juergen said. "With a 'respectable' girl, because I am a damned fool."

"That was her father last night," she said with certainty.

"And Gerda," Juergen said.

Gerda. Sally examined the name, like picking at a scab.

"She is—with child. She says it is mine." Juergen held himself very carefully, very still, as if pieces of himself might break off.

Sally took a deep breath and waited for the room to stop spinning around her in sickening swoops. "Is it?" she asked him.

"No! I saw her. She is showing already. I was with her only two months ago. Before that I was in Berlin for six months. You know that. I wrote you letters."

"What does her father want, then? Money?"

"He wants me to marry her," Juergen said bitterly. "I am a catch. They are shopkeepers."

"Oh, Juergen, how could you?" Sally's eyes started to fill with tears, and she wiped them away.

"I told you," he said miserably. "I am a damned fool. She—she made it very easy. I think maybe she already knew she was pregnant. Perhaps I am a better catch than the man responsible."

"Can't you prove you were in Berlin?" Sally's mind went first to the practicalities. She would think about how she felt when she could bear to.

"Very likely. After there has been a great scandal and everyone knows and we are all made wretched, including Gerda. But maybe not. Not to the satisfaction of public opinion."

"How important is public opinion?" Sally whispered.

"In my business, it is very important. And public opinion is coming to dinner tomorrow night." His mouth twisted. "I insisted that Mother invite our friends to meet you. To meet my future wife. I cannot disinvite them now."

Sally felt sick. "And everyone will know?"

"Everyone knows now. When I threw them out last night, they went straight to tell the world and a lawyer, I think."

Later, when Sally came downstairs, wondering how much of the usual enormous German breakfast she would be able to eat, it became clear that Ilse and Crista knew, despite their banishment from the drawing room the night before. They looked sideways at her and snickered.

Juergen was still white-faced, but he had managed to still the twitch by his mouth. He looked blank, Sally thought, as if the only way to blot out his anger and his misery was to blot everything else out. She felt desperately sorry for him.

"I hope you will enjoy our party tomorrow evening, Fräulein Holt," Crista said with relish, buttering her toast. "All of Juergen's old friends will be there."

"Not quite *all*," Ilse murmured.

"All that Fräulein Holt wants to meet. I'm sure they will be eager to meet *her*, too. We must make sure they do not mistake her for someone else."

"Be *quiet*!" Juergen snapped, and they blinked at him innocently.

"That is enough," Frau von Appen said. "This is indecent talk for girls." But she gave Sally a slow, sly look of satisfaction.

Sally got through the party by pretending that her German was not very good and she did not understand what anyone was saying. She danced with Juergen and the other gentlemen who asked her, including Uncle Rudolf, with a bright, fixed smile on her face, even when she overheard one of Juergen's diplomatic colleagues say to a tall young man in military uniform, "Well, she's beautiful enough, and apparently perfectly stupid. Maybe she doesn't know."

"Then Juergen should marry her!" the military man laughed. "She's the perfect wife!"

"He'll have to put a leash on his mother first."

Juergen gave no sign of hearing any of the innuendos and amused remarks that ended in guffaws behind cupped hands, but no one thought he was stupid. The mothers looked at him with frosty disapproval, and their daughters, with heightened interest, like rabbits, Sally thought irritably. He looked proper and as impervious as one of the Dresden china shepherds, but when everyone had left, he flung himself down in a red velvet armchair and poured himself a shot of whiskey three fingers deep.

"You will make yourself sick," his mother said.

"Just drunk," Juergen said.

Sally fiddled dispiritedly with the silk cording that had come off the hem of her ball dress when Uncle Rudolf had stepped on it.

"I hope you weren't too bored, Fräulein," Mother said,

"listening to all of Juergen's old friends chatter about things that don't concern you."

"I had a lovely time, thank you," Sally said, and slunk up to bed.

At breakfast the next morning, Juergen was sober and showed no sign of a hangover. "We are going out," he said, before his mother or sisters could open their mouths. "Ask Cook for a picnic basket. We want a drive in the country."

Mother made an exasperated noise. "Drive in the country? You have been driving in the country for over a week! Are you not needed at your work?"

"I took a leave for Sally's visit, remember? And I imagine my superiors would prefer that I not make an appearance just now, anyway, until I have settled my difficulties." He stood up. "I thought we might take a walk first," he said evenly to Sally. "While we wait for the hamper. Then you will know the worst."

She wasn't certain what he meant, but she went with him, certain it would be preferable to eating sausage with Mother and the girls. His meaning became clear in a few blocks.

"I thought if you could brave it out now, it wouldn't be so bad later," Juergen said.

"Last night wasn't bad enough?" Sally flushed.

"It will get worse," he said grimly. He offered her his arm, and after she took it, they made their progress past the tobacconist's on the corner, from whose open door a masculine voice shouted indeterminate threats. A woman burst into loud sobs.

"Gerda's father," Juergen said between his teeth. "When he finds out it isn't mine, he's likely to beat her to death."

Sally didn't feel particularly sympathetic toward Gerda. She caught a glimpse of a round face, red with tears, and a coronet of brown braids before Gerda flung her apron over her face and fled into a back room. *Oh, Juergen, how could you?* was the thought that declined to go away.

They walked on doggedly in silence until finally he said, "To hell with the hamper," and they got on a tram and rode it to the zoological gardens. They stared at the monkeys in their cages, and the monkeys stared back with depressed faces.

"They're too human," Sally said with a shudder.

"My darling." Juergen turned her around so that she looked at him instead of the monkeys. "You can't let this spoil it."

"Spoil it?" Sally said, flabbergasted. "Everything is different. It's horrible. Your family snickers at me, and your friends wonder if I am too stupid to know, or just too prideless to complain."

"If I apologized on my knees, would it make a difference?"

"I don't know. They are all standing around licking their chops at the thought of your having to marry this woman and humiliate me."

"There is no question of my marrying this woman," Juergen said flatly. "It is not my child. I have told you it isn't. And my lawyer now has witnesses that I was in Berlin. They weren't hard to find—I went to the office every day. And Gerda was seen with a student from the university."

"I don't want to look at animals in cages," Sally said abruptly.

They took the tram back into town, riding in silence. She knew that Juergen wanted desperately to talk to her and didn't know how, and she took a sort of sadistic pleasure in keeping her silence.

They got off the tram and walked again, her first expedition into the heart of the city. The cathedral spires rose above the skyline, attended by the spires of lesser churches. The cobblestoned streets were narrow, caught between steep slate roofs that were pointed like card houses and adorned with carved gables and attic window boxes full of flowers. Most were brick, but some of the oldest were stone, their facades blooming with stone flowers, fruit, and vines. Around the whole ran the Ringstrasse, an elegant boulevard newly constructed where the old city walls had once stood. They took a motor cab along its broad circle, and Juergen said, "I will build us a house out here, out of the old city."

"In Cologne," Sally commented. Her voice was flat, not a question. So they wouldn't be able to live in Bonn, near the vineyards. They would be in Cologne, near Mother.

"A villa," Juergen said, as they passed a row of elegant ones. "Everything the way you wanted it."

"And what about the war?"

"There won't be a war," he said. "Not with America."

Did that mean there would be one with England? Peter Blake said almost surely, and so did Sally's brother Tim, who corresponded with a reporter in Berlin.

She felt numb, drained, as though she were a glass and someone had drunk what was in her. Juergen put his arm around her in the shadow of the cab, and she leaned on his shoulder, trying to pretend they were in New York, trying to separate the war from Gerda and from the fact that his family hated her.

When they returned home in the late afternoon, after lunch at a café, Frau von Appen launched into a tirade about the picnic hamper, their waste of good food, and their lack of consideration. Juergen's lawyer was waiting for him in the library, she added.

She looked at Sally, taking in the hat with the red silk geranium drooping over one eyebrow and the pencil-slim skirt that showed her ankles. "You should go home, Fräulein," she said acidly. "Juergen does not wish to say it, but it is an unpleasant time for a visit."

"Be quiet, damn you!" Juergen shouted at his mother. While Frau von Appen goggled at him, he spun on his heel and stalked into the library.

Sally fled up the stairs.

She left the next day, white-faced and resolutely holding back tears while Juergen pleaded miserably with her all the way to the station.

"I will manage my mother, I promise."

"It isn't just your mother! Juergen, I simply can't do it. If I marry you here, I'll be trapped here with your mother and sisters, and with all your friends who disapprove of me, and everyone who knows about Gerda laughing at me. And if there's a war, I won't be able to get out."

"Gerda is past history. My lawyers have found the father."

"It doesn't matter anymore," Sally said wearily. "It's too much. If you'll come to the States, I'll marry you. But not here."

"Oh, dear God." Juergen took her hands and bent his face to them. Sally could feel hot tears on her knuckles. She bent her head down and laid it along his hair, desolate, holding him until the car got to the station.

It didn't take long, once she was home in New York, for Sally to know that she couldn't have stayed in Germany. She found a pile of letters from her brother Tim, who was frantic and frothing. The Balkans were going up in smoke, he wrote, and ultimately it would boil down to England versus Germany, and fairly soon. It was his bet that America would become involved, since the Germans were making noises about the Panama Canal.

Americans still considered England a kind of racial homeland, or at least the Americans who mattered—the ones with money—did. Everyone of British stock was incensed with Germany, and German immigrants learned not to offer any comment about Germany's side of things. Assuming it had one, Tim said, and that pretty well summed up the American attitude. *Don't* go back to Germany, he added for emphasis.

Frank Blake was in New York, at least for the time being, and while he wasn't living with India, he was with her most of the time, as far as Sally could tell. They scooped her up and took her under their collective wing, which meant that she went to a number of unusual parties in the Village and listened to socialists and anarchists debate each other over who could save the world. India's artist friends and Frank's union men were less interested in a possible war, which seemed very far away to them. More immediate was the Lawrence, Massachusetts, textile strike, in which the IWW had managed a wage increase that would affect something like three hundred thousand workers. India and a number of socialist women had formed a committee to look after the strikers' children. Frank had inveigled her into that, but really, India said, one could not believe the conditions the mill workers lived under. And when the mothers tried to put one batch of children on a train, the strike police drove them off with clubs and took the children themselves.

Frank and India listened sympathetically to Sally's account of her stay in Cologne, and Frank muttered and cursed Juergen until Sally said desolately that it wasn't Juergen's fault. She should have known she couldn't stay in Cologne when she met his mother. Gerda was just the finishing touch.

By the next year, even in circles preoccupied with matters closer to home, most people were taking more interest in the flash fires erupting in Europe.

"Bonfires," Frank said one night at a party at the elegant Fifth Avenue digs of the newest of the rich bohemians, a Mrs. Mabel Dodge. "Germany keeps throwing sticks on them."

"Not everyone in Germany wants a war," Sally said quietly. "There are many, mostly in the diplomatic offices, who still think it may not have to happen."

"Oh, it will happen!" someone said. "Prussian pride has its dander up. I can spot a German a mile away these days."

"I have a friend," Sally said. "A friend in Germany, who knows—"

"Well, I wouldn't mention it if I were you," a thin woman clear across the room said angrily.

Mabel Dodge fixed them all with a smile of immense power. "Now we shan't fight over friends' friends," she said firmly. "That isn't our topic for tonight. Remember that we are discussing Revolt of the Masses."

All the same, Sally learned not to mention Juergen, not at Mabel Dodge's salons and not at the hospital or the Literary Evenings or the Thursday Night Musicale, either. When he wrote that his lawyer had won his case without ever taking it to court, and that Gerda's father had sent her away to the country and threatened to shoot the university student on sight, Sally folded the letter and put it in the box with the rest.

V

Ben

After Sally came back from Germany, it seemed to India that everybody—herself included—was constantly fighting over things no one cared about ten years ago. It infuriated her to the point of inner explosion that women couldn't vote. Roger Stiller and his humiliation of her gave her emotional heartburn, and what she had seen during the Lawrence textile strike angered her to the point that she distrusted the entire justice system.

"We'll make a rebel of you yet," Frank said cheerfully.

"I don't want to be a rebel," India retorted. "I just want things to be fair."

Frank and Bill Haywood, with whom she and Frank were dining, doubled up with laughter.

The IWW was fighting the other labor unions over the purpose of organized labor. More radical than most, the IWW wanted one union, all the workers of the world, organized to bring about social revolution. Daniel DeLeon and the other old socialists called them agitators and bums, but the IWW Wobblies weren't interested in war in Europe, which was refreshing. As far as they were concerned, war was just an opportunity for the haves to divide up the spoils and further suppress the have-nots.

Haywood frequented Mable Dodge's salons, where he took a shine to India, particularly after she painted some posters for the Wobblies' efforts to recruit migrant workers and didn't charge him for them. She was making money

again now and had divorced herself, figuratively speaking,
not only from Roger Stiller and his cronies but from beating
her head against the wall of male disregard for female artists.
The magazine-reading public didn't care about the sex of the
illustrator. They adored India's creation, the "Blackstone
Girl," and her agent had begun to sell her work in England.
The struggles for recognition and status among classicists
and social realists, cubists and abstractionists, fauvists and
expressionists, ceased to interest her particularly. She let the
Armory Show of 1913, which was supposed to carry forth the
banner of modern art, go by with a sniff and a curt nod to a
few old friends who had work exhibited.

Her Wobbly posters caught the eye of a reporter or two
who recognized the signature, and the editor of the *Gentlewoman's Handbook*, now the *Ladies' Book*, suggested to her
ever so gently over tea at the Knickerbocker Hotel that doing
that sort of work might not be in her best interests.

"I told him that where I sold my own work was my
business," India said irritably to Mabel Dodge, whose ex-
pressive dark eyes flashed with amusement. "As long as he
thinks I'm making money from it, the old devil will reluctantly refrain from arguing with me. God forbid I should give
the Wobblies anything for free, though."

"He's afraid you'll slip devious messages into your pictures," Mabel said. "Convince all his lady readers to leave
their husbands and become revolutionaries."

Mabel made an odd revolutionary herself, India
thought, in her white-walled apartment furnished with a
white marble fireplace, a polar bear rug, and uncounted
gilded mirrors. But Mabel was no lightweight when it came
to being a rebel. Sinclair Lewis and Lincoln Steffens frequented her salons, and so did Carl van Vechten and Walter
Lippmann and the poets Edward Arlington Robinson and
Amy Lowell, who smoked cigars. There was always a topic
for the night, among them Sex Antagonism, Union Organization, Revolution, Women's Rights, and Psychoanalysis, which
Mabel was among the first to try. It didn't help her difficulty,
and another doctor took her tonsils out instead.

India had become something of a celebrity herself, but
it wasn't in the most pleasant fashion. She was the woman
who had sued Roger Stiller, who was beginning to become a
big name. The rumors that Stiller had stolen the picture still

circulated, and consequently a few of Roger's closest friends felt obliged to be vicious to India. She made the rest uncomfortable merely by her presence.

"I feel like Hester Prynne," she told Frank. "Only I have a big scarlet *T* for Troublemaker emblazoned on my bosom."

"Then get out of town for the summer," he advised. "Take a vacation."

"Turn tail? I will not."

"I wasn't suggesting a week at the seaside," Frank said. "Come and do something useful. I always used to promise I'd take you on the road one day."

"That was when you were bumming on freight trains."

"We'll let you ride on the plush." He smiled. "We're going to California to give the ranchers hell. It's time the pickers got a fair shake, and the IWW is the union to do it. But no one knows what to do with the babies and the mothers. Those women are pretty near beat to death, and their kids are dying of disease like flies; they're out in the field when they're four years old. If there's a strike, we'll have the same problem we had at Lawrence."

India thought about it. There wasn't any good reason to stay in New York for the summer. She could paint anywhere; maybe she could sell some paintings of the pickers' children and stir up public opinion at the same time. Maybe it would even brush the taste of Roger Stiller out of her teeth.

In a week she found herself on a Northern Pacific train heading for Sacramento. She paid for a private compartment for the sake of comfort and half expected Frank to share it, but he grinned and hopped back down on the platform. "I've got my ticket," he said, flashing her a red pasteboard IWW card.

When the train stopped in Chicago, he was there, a little disheveled, with a pair of cronies, who looked at India and were struck dumb by an actual woman in a tan linen traveling suit and a Panama hat. He had been riding in a boxcar, she discovered, and the IWW card had indeed functioned as a sort of ticket. The Wobblies claimed the boxcars as their own, nonunion men not permitted, and the brakemen, often members themselves, looked the other way. Even the railroad police could often be intimidated by a boxcar full of men who would fight together instead of running separately. India could see the hobo jungles from her window as the train slid through the outskirts of cities. She thought about what Frank had told her: There were more workingmen than bums in them now—men who couldn't get a job, who followed the harvest or the cotton-picking or any rumor of work just to get enough to eat; men with families, who sent money home or brought their wives and children with them because they had no place that was home.

Maybe the Blackstone Girl would take up a career of do-goodism, India thought. She could work in Sally's hospital, teach migrant children, and march for the vote. Would all the girls in Evanston and St. Louis and Milwaukee who wanted to be like her follow suit? It would be interesting to find out.

But when India and Frank got to California, she found there was no time to open her paint case. Frank took her into the fields, and if she had been shocked by Lawrence, she was appalled by what she saw here. She had always thought of farming as a bucolic occupation, hearty families with eleven children working their own land. Her own parents raised cattle and worked their spread with hands who lived there year-round. What was called a ranch here, she discovered, was neither a livestock spread nor the family farm of her imagining. It was an open-air factory, a hellhole, and the workers weren't even permitted to stay all year. When the crop was picked, the ranchers ran the pickers off the land. They were undesirable elements.

And nothing in her summer at Lawrence—trying to teach the ABCs and elementary sanitation in a place where the workers were refused the basic necessities for that— prepared India for the Durst Ranch. She had been called a tramp and a whore, an agitator and an interfering bitch by the bosses at other sites, but here she was a nonperson, one of the lost, a being whose continued existence simply did not matter.

Too many of the California ranchers had grown angry at the Wobblies, and Frank decreed that they should go to the Durst Ranch, the largest employer of agricultural labor in the state, as anonymous workers. They joined a flood of men and women answering E. C. Durst's advertisement for hops pickers, with the promise of ample work and high wages. "You'll see," said Frank. By the end of July there were two thousand eight hundred men, women, and children on Durst's ranch, and no truth to the advertisement.

Over two thousand of them camped on a bare hillside—some in tents Durst rented to them for two dollars and seventy-five cents a week—and shared eight small, overflowing toilets. Flies were everywhere, the temperature rose to nearly a hundred and five, and Durst refused to provide any water nearer than wells a mile away. Even Wheatland stores couldn't deliver groceries because Durst had a half-interest in a grocery of his own.

For all this, India discovered, nursing blistered hands and nausea, the pay rate fluctuated daily. Durst had advertised for far more pickers than he needed, and as long as hands were plentiful, pay continued to drop. No matter what the rate, ten percent was withheld daily to be distributed at the end of the harvest to the "loyal" ones who stayed the whole season. But Durst, not the pickers, decided who stayed. *We are not people,* India thought, eating biscuits and gravy from a tin pan under the dubious shelter of a patched tent. *We are a commodity, like the hops we pick. We don't matter.* And she could leave anytime she got sick of it. What of the others?

On the second day, Frank and Blackie Ford, a veteran Wobbly, drew up a list of demands for Durst, and the pickers endorsed it. Everyone knew they couldn't spend the season like this.

The demands were minimal: uniform minimum wages, free water in the fields, decent camp conditions. When presented with the list, Durst shrugged his shoulders.

"Get ready," Frank said. "Something's going to happen."

"What?" India asked uneasily.

"I don't know, but I think Durst's crazy. This goes beyond the usual grasping business practices. People are dying. We're asking for a mass meeting tomorrow, but we're in a jam—Blackie says he's counted twenty-five different languages or dialects in this crew, and between us we only speak about three of them. Maybe that's what it is with Durst; he just doesn't think they're people."

The dusty air, hot as an oven, was perfectly still, but it didn't need a breeze to carry the stench of the overflowing toilets and what little food there was rotting in the heat. A baby was crying in the tent behind them, a thin wail that sounded like some animal's dying cry. In the tent on the other side, a roofless three-walled enclosure of canvas, another of the IWW men was teaching a mixed group of Chinese, Japanese, Italians, and Poles to sing songs from the IWW book.

> *"The long-haired preachers come out every night,*
> *Try to tell you what's wrong and what's right.*
> *But when asked about something to eat,*
> *They will answer in voices so sweet:*
> *You will eat by and by, in that glorious land*
>   *above the sky, way up high,*
> *Work and pray, live on hay,*
> *You'll get pie in the sky when you die!"*

India chuckled. The Wobblies had little use for evangelists, except for the brand that ran soup kitchens. As far as they could tell, the rest were hand in glove with the bosses to promise "pie in the sky" instead of a decent wage now.

A straggling chorus of voices soared up to the dark sky in air that was still stifling hot, like being in an oven. The child's wailing ceased—into sleep, India hoped.

"Tomorrow," Frank said. "After the picking."

Neither he nor India went into the hops fields the next day. For every day they worked, there was someone who needed it who didn't. Frank spent the day conferring with Blackie Ford and with Herman Suhr, a genial bulldozer of a man who was accounted to be slow in his mind. Herman might be slow, but when he grasped an idea he had it forever. Fair treatment for workers was Herman's idea, and he spoke it simply and convincingly over and over. No violence, Frank and Ford and Suhr said; don't give anyone an excuse to retaliate. Call for a general strike, and if all the pickers stay solid, Durst will have to meet demands or watch his hops rot.

India got a shovel and dug out trenches around the overflowing toilets and threw the dirt inside on their contents. Clean trenches were better than this. Her back felt as if someone had stepped on it, and her hands were blistered from palm to fingertips. She was dirty and flea-bitten, and she laughed in acid amusement at Frank's idea of a vacation. When he crawled into their tent that night, she couldn't even

smell him, she smelled so bad herself, and when he reached
for her, hands like sandpaper invading her bedroll, she let
him and worried only mildly about getting pregnant. She
hadn't brought any of the things she had learned to use to the
camp, and would have thought twice about putting them
inside herself in all this dirt if she had. But surely no life
would have the nerve to get its start in hell.

The next afternoon the pickers gathered under the
scorching sun, desperate for anyone who could show them
some way out. Durst had gone beyond even the normal brutality of the migrant camps. Some pickers, the ones who
could, who hadn't spent their last nickel to get here, had
already left. A band of high school boys and girls from San
Francisco and Oakland and Sacramento, hoping to earn some
money and spend a healthful summer in the countryside, had
been the first to go, gagging and horrified. The ones who
were left were the desperate.

Blackie Ford began to talk of a general strike. He held a
sick baby up and shouted, "It's for the life of the kids we're
doing this!"

India reached out and took Frank's hand. This was
change. This was history in the making. It terrified her, and
it was exhilarating at the same time. The migrants began to
sing, two thousand voices with what sounded like as many
accents. India wondered how much of Blackie Ford's speech
they had even understood, or how much of the song, but
they sang with enthusiasm. The IWW had learned early that
song was powerful.

Frank pulled his red songbook from his pocket and let
her follow along. The cover said *Songs to Fan the Flames of
Discontent*, she noted with a grin.

"Subtle," she murmured.

"Most of these are by a fellow named Hill," Frank said.
"A Swede. He's got a knack for it."

Two thousand voices reviled the nonunion worker for
accepting the myth of American success. A panicked Durst,
convinced that the migrants were going to riot, had reacted
by calling the law. The district attorney, the Yuba County
sheriff and his deputies, and a special posse roared through
the hops fields in time to hear the derisive last verse:

*"Poor Block he died one evening, I'm very glad
        to state:
He climbed the golden ladder up to the pearly gate.
He said, 'Oh, Mr. Peter, one word I'd like to tell,
I'd like to meet the Astorbilts and John D. Rockefell.'
Old Pete said, 'Is that so?
You'll meet them down below.'*

*Oh, Mr. Block, you were born by mistake,
You take the cake,
You make me ache.
Tie a rock on your block and then jump
        in the lake,
Kindly do that for liberty's sake!"*

Durst screeched his car to a halt with a furious boot on the brake pedal. The sheriff's special posse piled out of it. "Get 'em off my land!" Durst shouted.

India started to stand up. Frank pulled her back down. "Wait. Don't do anything until I tell you."

The deputies converged on the speaker's platform. Blackie Ford held up his arms and shouted, "Take it easy, folks!" With furious despair the crowd watched the deputies surround him. A few shouted catcalls and worse things. A deputy, eyeing their numbers with unease, fired his shotgun in the air.

"Oh, the devil! The damn fools!" Frank said, grabbing India now and pulling her to her feet. All around them the crowd of migrants erupted in a furious flow like lava from a volcano. They converged on the deputies who had hold of Ford, and the deputies, in a panic, fired back indiscriminately. "I'm getting you out of here!" Frank shouted at India as they ran through the mob, heads down.

The air was full of roiling dust and the sound of gunfire and the angry howling that a mob makes when it has lost all control. The lawmen were armed but badly outnumbered and undisciplined. India saw a member of the posse laying about him with a baseball bat, and another firing blindly into the crowd without even aiming. A terrified child ran past her feet and disappeared into the melee before she could pick it up. They stumbled over a man who knelt on the ground vomiting, blood running from his mouth. A deputy's club struck India on the back of her head, and she fell forward into a blackness across which spun whipping spirals of yellow light. Frank lifted her and dragged her, and after a moment the blackness passed and she could see again, everything brighter than before and wavy at the edges.

The hops pickers and the lawmen battled each other in desperate fury until exhaustion slowed them. Then slowly they receded, both sides limping away, leaving the wounded and the beaten, the rats and the flies, and four dead men: the district attorney, whose name no one had cared about until now and everyone would know afterward; a sheriff's deputy; and two pickers, a Puerto Rican and an English boy. The hops pickers fled like victims of an explosion or an earthquake, bewildered, defeated, unsure of how it had happened.

Frank and India stumbled along with them and hid under a bridge over a stream while Frank looked at the knot on India's head and peered suspiciously at her pupils.

"I'm all right," she said. Blood was matted in her hair.

At night they slunk back, with a handful of other hops pickers, to try to salvage their meager possessions, wondering what was going to happen now.

They found out when they straggled into Wheatland and saw people being arrested. Frank got them a room at a cheap hotel in a hurry, and they made themselves respectable enough not to catch the eye of the law.

The Yuba County officials had to blame somebody, and they couldn't blame themselves, so they charged the IWW with the deaths of District Attorney E. T. Manwell and the deputy. (Nobody cared about the dead pickers.) While ranchers everywhere screamed about the Wobbly menace, local deputies and Burns Agency detectives set out up and down California with John Doe warrants charging anybody they fancied with inciting a riot and first-degree murder. The press joined the clamor and printed the usual parodies of the IWW initials: I Won't Work, I Want Whiskey, International Wonder Workers, Irresponsible Wholesale Wreckers.

Wobblies and migrant workers were locked up in every small town in California, out of reach of any defense council. For weeks no one knew where Blackie Ford was. Finally Yuba County indicted Ford and, to India's disgust, Herman Suhr for the murders of E. T. Manwell and the deputy, despite the fact that neither had been seen near either victim and that both had been heard repeatedly counseling the pickers against violence. The IWW sent Austin Lewis to take charge of the defense, and he got the trial moved to Marysville in a change of venue. Marysville was somewhat less hysterical in its assessment of the IWW than Wheatland, but not much. Frank followed them, giving Lewis what assistance he could, since he had seen the riot, and India followed Frank, taking time now to paint the migrants, their children, and—until the local sheriff threatened her with arrest—the Burns detectives and their prey.

They took rooms in a boardinghouse in Marysville, respectably refraining from sharing the same one. The landlady looked at them suspiciously and made it clear that she didn't stand for that sort of thing. India had no desire to be a small-town scandal, although Frank said regretfully that it would have been cheaper. She could have gone home, India knew, but she didn't. She was in the thick of it now; going home seemed like turning tail.

From the arrests in August until the trial in January, the newspapers connected the IWW with every suspected case of crop destruction, sabotage, and even any murders that were, as Frank put it, "hanging around loose." A young reporter for the Associated Press named Ben Richardson moved into the boardinghouse and said to Frank, shaking his head over a game of poker one night, what the hell did he expect when Wobbly agitators went around frothing about class warfare on every street corner?

"Gives the middle class the pip," Ben said. "They think they're going to be murdered in their beds."

"Some of the fellows get carried away," Frank conceded. "I've tried to keep a lid on them. But, damn it, it *is* class warfare."

Richardson grinned. He was young, probably about twenty-three or twenty-four, with a shock of brown curls and a choirboy mouth that seemed at odds with the gleam in his eye. Frank had seen him climb up the outside of a three-story jail, while citizens threw rocks at him, to talk to the prisoners inside. Now Richardson was considering the possibilities of a poker hand. He looked sideways at India. "Have you folks figured out which class you're gonna belong to, when the war starts?" he inquired.

"I'm an artist," she answered. "That puts me in a class by itself."

"I'll say," Richardson said admiringly. "A hell of a poker player, too."

"She cheats," Frank said.

"You think anybody who can beat you cheats," India retorted. She put fifty cents on the table to match Ben Richardson's. "Call."

Frank folded. He picked up the deck.

"One," Ben said. Frank dealt it.

India smiled serenely. "Pat," she said.

Richardson looked at her with interest. "Bet you two dollars anyway," he suggested.

Frank watched Ben with growing unease while India put her two dollars down and turned up four queens. Ben winced and folded his cards. "Filled it, too," he said mournfully. *"La belle dame sans merci."*

"I dealt her the damn queens," Frank said irritably.

Ben Richardson put his chin in his hands, not bothering to shuffle and deal. "Pure witchcraft," he said, gazing at India. "I doubt you had anything to do with it."

More newspapermen appeared, including one from Tim Holt's San Francisco *Clarion*, which, like the Associated Press, was more balanced in its coverage than most but still had no love for the IWW. The Wobblies were too rackety, too populated with bums and bindlestiffs and possibly dangerous immigrants importing Marxism. Ben Richardson said that India was the first lady Wobbly he'd met, and she said she wasn't one at all—she was an artist. Show me, he said, so she did—the watercolors she had done of the camps and the bums asleep under the water tower.

"Do you think anybody will buy those?" he asked.

She shook her head ruefully.

"Someday," he said. "I'll eat my hat if you aren't famous someday."

India chuckled. He was awfully cute, and so obviously smitten with her.

She found it easy to be with Ben in the days that followed. He gave her a bunch of chrysanthemums he stole from the City Hall flower beds and took her clear to Sacramento to the moving pictures. He wasn't critiquing her art when he swore she was prettier than the Blackstone Girl. The Blackstone Girl hadn't a patch on India, Ben said.

"That's my friend Sally," India said. "You haven't met her. They all fall in love with Sally."

"Nope," Ben said. "Not me. I've got me a girl. Well, I'd like to anyway." He looked at her wistfully.

Frank watched this exchange and rolled his eyes. He hooked his hat off the parlor hat rack, jammed it over his eyes, and stalked out.

Ben looked thoughtful, and when India had gone upstairs to wrestle with an unsatisfactory sketch, he fetched his own hat and went after Frank.

He found him, as he had rather expected he would, in the Feather River Tavern down the street. Frank was hunched on a barstool nursing a beer under a giant stuffed bass that represented the tavern's sole decorative motif.

Ben slid onto the stool next to Frank. "Beer," he said to the bartender. The bartender drew a glass and slid it down the bar, leaving a trail of foam. "Nice place," Ben commented, eyeing the bass.

"Bucolic," Frank agreed. "Do you fish?"

"Not very successfully. I catch the occasional boot or the fish that's too dumb to be suspicious. This is supposed to be good country for it."

"Nah, they're all up on the walls." Frank grinned.

"Hmmm." Ben studied his beer. "You've, uh, known Miss Blackstone a long time, I guess."

"This is rather an abrupt change from fish, isn't it?" Frank said.

"The fish were a ploy," Ben said.

"To break the ice? Ease into the subject of women?"

"It's a riddle," Ben said. "How is a woman like a fish?"

"Cold-blooded," Frank said.

"Actually, I don't know the answer," Ben said. "I just made up the question. Miss Blackstone doesn't strike me as cold-blooded."

"Is that why you're still calling her Miss Blackstone?"

"One doesn't wish to presume." Ben lifted his glass and drank off about half of it. "You never answered my question."

"Which one was that?" Frank drained his beer and held his glass out for another. Ben thought he might have had several already.

"How long have you known Miss Blackstone? India."

"How cold is a fish?" Frank took a swallow from his refilled glass and wiped the foam from his mouth with the back of his hand. "Hell, man, I don't know."

"You don't know how long you've known her?"

"I don't know the answer to what you're really trying to ask."

Ben studied the stuffed fish on the walls. There were two more bass and a salmon and a constellation of iridescent trout. They arched away from their plaques, forever frozen in air. "I don't quite know how to put it."

"I generally find that if you put it in the baldest terms possible, there's the least room for misinterpretation," Frank said.

Ben drained the other half of his beer. "Well, then, are you going to marry Miss Blackstone?"

"No."

Ben sighed, unsatisfied with that. "Are you in love with her?"

"Probably," Frank said gloomily.

Ben thought that over. "With all due respect, old man, aren't you asking rather a lot of her?"

"I'm not asking anything of her," Frank said. "I haven't any right to. If you'll buy me another beer, I'll tell you the story of my life."

Ben sighed and motioned to the bartender. "You're getting maudlin, Blake, and I don't want to know your life story. I want to know if you'll punch me in the teeth if I court Miss Blackstone."

"I won't punch you in the teeth," Frank said. "But if you'll take the gypsy's warning, I'll give it to you: Don't do it."

"Bit of a dog in the manger, aren't you?"

"Probably."

"Probably," Ben said. "You got anything here you can say with certainty?"

Frank peered at the foam that slid down the side of his glass as if there might be hieroglyphics in it, some code with instructions for him. "I can say I've got a job to do here. I can say it's probably my life's work. It took me a long time to find it. I'm not sure India's found what she wants. I'm not sure where our paths converge."

"But they intersect," Ben said.

"Yeah." Frank shook his head. "Sometimes they run along a little way together. Best times I've had in my life."

"But not good enough to get married and settle down?"

"India's got more sense." Frank turned his head and looked Ben in the eye. "India doesn't want to get married either. It ties a woman down worse than a man."

"Not if the man doesn't tie her," Ben said.

"Horseshit." Frank's eyes narrowed. "You'd offer a woman that kind of marriage? Complete independence?"

"I would if I wanted her bad enough," Ben said soberly.

"Ah, Christ," Frank said. "Go away. Go do whatever you want to. You don't need my permission."

Ben nodded. He left some money on the bar for their beers.

Frank watched him go, and then he put his head in his hands, running them through his hair, fingers hard over his skull as if some new lump or protrusion might suddenly be there, a phrenologist's key to his psyche. If Ben Richardson offered India that sort of marriage, what might she do? Frank stared at himself in the mirror behind the bar. A battered face stared back, hair sticking up wildly. He slicked it down with one hand. *What do you want, Blake?* The mirror image didn't have anything to say. *There was a time when you were pretty upset about taking advantage of her. What happened to those highfalutin principles?*

This time the mirror had an answer: *She doesn't want to get married either.*

That doesn't absolve you from asking, pal.

Oh yeah? The mirror image pointed a finger at him. Frank wondered if anyone else could see it. *What if she said yes? And then where would we both be?*

The fish above the mirror seemed to be in agreement, mouth open in anticipated consternation.

Frank didn't want to converse with himself anymore, especially since he thought he was either drunk or crazy. He turned away from the fish and pushed his way out through the saloon's double doors onto the sidewalk. The sky was a hard, bright, robin's-egg blue of the sort that California might produce at any time of year. Only a faint thread of cloud was snagged on it, high up. The sun hurt his eyes. Frank bypassed the boardinghouse and went to confer with

the IWW lawyer, Austin Lewis, about the defense's evidence
for the trial. At least there he was sure of his ground.

Ben filed his daily story on the AP wire and went looking for India. He found her in the landlady's garden, cleaning
out fall flower beds.

She smiled at him and pitched a snail past him into the
road. "It's that sketch of Durst and the deputies, just before
the riot," she explained when he asked her why she was out
here. "I did it from memory, and I can't make it right, so I
thought I'd do something useful instead of swearing at it.
The deputies all keep coming out looking like pigs. It must
be my subconscious."

"Very likely." Ben got down on his knees beside her and
pulled grass from the border. "How neatly psychoanalysis
explains everything. That in itself should make one suspicious. It's entirely possible that the deputies did look like
pigs. One wears one's character on one's face."

"A horrible thought indeed," she said. "I might look like
anything in a few years."

"I feel certain that your character is steadily improving,"
Ben said. "You can only grow more beautiful."

"So you think I should just let the deputies be pigs?"

"You may have hit on a new expression in social realism." Ben found another snail and flicked it toward the road.
It was dusk, and the shadows of the eucalyptus trees whispered above the roofline. The snail shell clattered against the
stones by the garden gate. Footsteps stopped, and there was
a muttered curse.

"You'll hit someone with those if you don't watch where
you're throwing them," India said.

"It's only Blake. Let's throw more."

India laughed, delighted by his playfulness. She rocked
back on her heels and said, "It's too dark to work. I can't tell
weeds from flowers."

"It's a nice evening," he said.

The sky was still turquoise but darker, as if ink had been
poured over it, India thought, and the moon hung in a thin
sickle above the dark eucalyptus. Ben edged a little closer to
her.

She looked at him. His eyes reflected a gleam of light
from somewhere, the parlor window maybe. Frank had gone

past them into the house, muttering, and there was no one else in the garden. Ben slid an arm around her. It seemed easy to lean into his arm, rest her head against his. They watched the moon rock in the sky above them. It looked like a cradle, India thought, or the outline of a big-bellied woman, pregnant with who knew what. The air turned cold as the last of the sunlight went out of the sky. Ben's warmth was like a cloak around her, his wistful smile close to her ear so that she could feel the warmth of his breath.

If she turned her head, he would kiss her. It would be awfully easy to let that happen.

But he was ten years younger than she was, and Frank was watching their courtship with a jaundiced eye. And what had Frank ever gotten her but a lump on the head? The hell with Frank. She turned her head and let Ben kiss her out there in the garden under the landlady's dusty eucalyptus trees, and after that it didn't seem much trouble to let him in her bed, too.

Ben wore an ecstatic expression for most of the next day, and Frank grabbed India by the arm in the upstairs hallway.

"What the hell do you think you're doing?"

"Whatever I'm doing is my business," she said.

"Boy, you sure know how to pick 'em," Frank said disgustedly.

"And just what do you mean by that? Ben is one of the nicest men I know. You like him yourself."

"I think he has rocks in his head, hanging around with the Black Widow. Are you in love with him?"

India was silent.

"He's in love with you," Frank said. "Don't you think that's a little unfair?"

"I think it's not your business," India said between her teeth. "You have no right to any claim on me."

"That's right, I don't," Frank said grimly. "I just didn't think you were such a louse."

India's eyes opened wide. "I'm a louse?" she said quietly. "I'm a louse because I'm interested in a man who might *be* there once in a while? Whose idea of a good time isn't getting his head knocked open in a riot?"

"You had one of those," Frank said. "Old Roger was

always around, except he turned out to be a little more intimate with your artwork than you wanted him to be."

"And what precisely has that got to do with Ben Richardson?"

"If you pick 'em on the grounds that they'll stick around, you may be surprised. And Richardson is going to take off whenever the AP sends him somewhere else."

"I wasn't planning to spend my life in Marysville either. I don't see what you're getting at, Frank."

Frank looked depressed. "I don't know what I'm getting at either. Can't we go somewhere and talk about this?"

"I don't see anything to talk about," she answered stiffly.

"Well, not talking about it somewhere else would be a lot more private than not talking about it here. Old Lady Muncie comes by to shake out the sheets or clean the grate every time she gets a sniff of something interesting. You can holler that there's no hot water till you're blue in the face, but whisper in someone's ear and she'll pop up like a toadstool." There were banging sounds from down below to indicate that the landlady was up and raking out the stove. "Don't think she won't know what you've been up to if you aren't careful. I'm going to laugh like hell when you get evicted for moral turpitude."

"I told you we didn't have anything to talk about," India said. But she turned her head warily toward the stairs as the banging ceased.

"Ah, hell, India, just give me a few minutes. I can't stand the way I feel right now."

She looked at him curiously. This was the closest she had seen Frank come to an admission of jealousy. He had hated Roger, and so it had been easy to attribute his possessiveness to a selfless urge to save her from herself and a bad match. No one could help liking Ben, which must make that harder. There was something in Frank's eyes she hadn't seen before, a hunted look and a kind of furious misery. She relented. "Come out by the chicken house," she said. "Mrs. Muncie's already been to get the eggs."

The hens were bobbing and clucking under the eucalyptus, looking for the last of the corn the landlady had shaken from her apron an hour ago. The air smelled of dry straw and chicken droppings. Frank leaned against the wall of the chicken house while Mrs. Muncie's rooster flapped its wings at him.

"Richardson sounded me out about you yesterday," he said finally. "Asked me what my intentions were."

"Oh, lovely," India said. "Did either of you ask what *I* wanted?"

"No," Frank said miserably. "I think I'm afraid to. I don't know what the hell I have to give you."

"I don't either!" India snapped.

He looked as if she had hit him, and her throat tightened. Everything she felt for Frank was still there, was always going to be there, but what use was it?

"I love you," she said quietly. It was the first time that either of them had spoken the word, at least to each other. "But I need something more. Someone who's *there* at least part of the time, someone who doesn't forget my existence periodically."

"I know you do." Frank dug the toe of his boot in the ground, stirring up a fine dust. "It's not even unreasonable. I don't know what the hell's wrong with me that I can't give you that."

India buried her hands in her paint apron, wrapping it around and around them. "I don't either," she said. "Maybe it's not you. Maybe it's me. Maybe I'm asking too much, trying to stay clear of marriage and tie you down at the same time."

"Richardson'll try to marry you," Frank said.

"I am reasonably sure that Ben does *not* want to marry me. I'm ten years older than he is. So you can relax about that."

"I got the distinct impression that he might," Frank said. "But I told you that for your benefit. I might relax more if you did get married. At least it would shut the door on—"

"On you and me?" India asked him. "I—Frank, I don't know. It would be a lot easier with Ben if I didn't know you."

"Yep," Frank said.

"And don't tell me there aren't other women," India said indignantly, finding a new irritant. "Because I don't believe it."

"I haven't told you that," Frank said. "Although there seem to be fewer now that I'm not a spring chicken. Pardon me, girls." He bowed ironically to the clucking hens, and India's lip twitched.

"Spring rooster," she said. "Sprung rooster. Poor Frank. I don't think I believe you."

"I didn't say I'd become a monk," he said defensively.

"I may not want to get married and have four babies in a pram," India said, "but I want some stability. I'm no spring chicken either. I tried once with Roger, and it blew up in my face. I tried with you, and it's always been like having the north wind for a lover, or something equally erratic. Ben may be a reporter, and yes, I know they're all crazy—I probably don't want a man who's not a little crazy—but compared to you he's a monument to stability."

"Compared to me? Is that what you do? Compare them to me?"

India drew in her breath to say no. Frank's eyes pinned her down. "Maybe," she said.

"Poor Ben, then."

"You think a lot of yourself."

"I think you aren't going to shake me out of your skin just because you want to. I'm not universally that memorable. Plenty of other women have been able to forget me successfully. But not you."

"What makes you so sure?"

"Because I can't jettison you either. I've tried."

"Why did you try?"

"It seemed the kindest thing for both of us."

"Wonderful," India said. "Like euthanasia."

"I don't know what's wrong with me either," Frank said. "I have a long history of people not knowing what's wrong with me, starting with my parents," he added bitterly. "All I can figure out is that I have some unique urge to torture myself. I want you, and I want to stay on the road, and I won't give up one for the other. You have every right to more than that, as you pointed out."

Then why do I feel guilty about it? India thought. *Damn you.* "You make me feel worse when you're reasonable," she commented.

"A secret weapon," Frank said with a half smile. He stood a little away from the chicken house and held out his hands. She came toward him before she thought what she was doing.

The hens flurried around their feet, pecking at her boot-laces as if they might be food. India put her hands in Frank's and looked searchingly at him. What she had thought was there was there, all right.

"I love you, damn it," he said. "I'm sorry."

"I know you do." India let out her breath in a long sigh and leaned her head against his chest. "I have to try this," she said into the red flannel of his shirtfront. "I have to see what happens."

"You go ahead and try, honey," Frank said. "I won't put a spoke in your wheels."

"Truly?" India lifted her head again.

"Truly. I'd be an awful son of a bitch if I did." He touched her hair, running his palm over it. "The learned phrenologist says you're a faithful woman and only ought to have one fellow at a time."

India stepped back a little bit. Ben was a sweet boy, with an intriguing streak of the devil, and fine company. Maybe it would work. It hadn't worked with Frank, despite the charged air between them every time she saw him. *Alternating current*, she thought, *push-pull*, and then decided that she didn't know enough about electricity to explain that analogy. There would be something idiotic about it, and Frank would laugh at her. And anyway, being with him was more like sticking her finger in a light socket.

"I won't make a stupid speech about continuing to be friends," India said. "Of course we will. We always have been. But I have to see."

"You bet." Frank sounded falsely hearty to both of them. The rooster decided it had finally had enough of their intrusion and stepped between them, flapped its feathers again, and crowed. Frank laughed at it. "Come on in to breakfast before Chanticleer here busts himself."

They turned back up the chicken yard to the back porch and saw Ben leaning on the porch railing, smoking a cigarette. *Oh, no*, India thought, but Ben didn't say anything. He flicked the cigarette into the flower bed and went into the house ahead of them. He poured India her coffee at the breakfast table with a careful face and gave no indication to Frank of remembering their conversation of the day before or of having seen anything in the chicken yard.

As soon as Mrs. Muncie was out of the way, Frank vanished to Austin Lewis's offices, and India made herself particularly affectionate toward Ben. His face lit up, and he kissed her happily as if he knew something had been settled. He seemed to have no illusions, or moral revulsion, over whatever had been between her and Frank but said cheerfully that he was glad he'd beat the fellow out, and she didn't want a Wobbly, really she didn't—they weren't reliable.

They stayed in Marysville until the trial, and a week before the date, Frank got word that the authorities in Salt Lake City had arrested Joe Hill, the man whose songs the IWW sang so joyfully. He was accused of murder, of shooting a grocer and his son in the course of a robbery. Rumors flew. Hill had been framed. Hill had been with a married woman that night and refused to compromise her honor by claiming an alibi. Hill had been treated by a Salt Lake City doctor for a gunshot wound that night.

Frank got ready to go to Utah and see what could be done about defense lawyers. Ben's ears pricked up, and he bought a train ticket, too, whether because of the newsworthiness of the situation or because India was going, she wasn't sure. On January 24, 1914, Blackie Ford and Herman Suhr were sentenced to life in the Folsom State Penitentiary.

The IWW started a pardon campaign on the grounds that both had been railroaded, and Ben shook his head. "Won't do you any good. Not unless you can rein in the more outspoken members."

"This isn't a monarchy," Frank said. "We've all got our heads busted open for free speech. We can't turn around and say it doesn't apply here, not this time, just this once."

All the same, the pardon campaign was run in what India was beginning to recognize as typical IWW style—cooler heads on one hand securing the support of respectable Californians and petitioning to Governor Hiram Johnson's sense of justice and fair play; F. H. Esmond in *Solidarity*, on the other hand, demanding capitulation and threatening sabotage and a general strike: "Unless Ford and Suhr are freed outright by the Appellate Court, the cat and his kittens are coming to enjoy a merry picnic in the hops fields of California."

Johnson refused the pardon, but he set up a commission to regulate conditions in the migrant camps, with the secondary goal of draining off the IWW's influence. The commission suggested to ranchers that they could best combat the IWW by improving conditions and warned migrants sternly that violence would do them no good. None of which worked. It was not lost on the migrants that while they had been peaceful no one had cared about them; only after they had rioted did the state grow solicitous.

In Utah, they found the sentiment of press and public much the same as it had been in California. It began to look as if Joe Hill was being tried for being a Wobbly. The Salt Lake press constantly referred to Hill's connection to the IWW and the IWW's connection to sabotage and anarchy. Ergo, he must be a violent anarchist . . . and guilty as hell.

It took a while for the IWW to plow through all the rumors and find legal help. Hill didn't help. He repeated his story that he had been with a woman and kept on refusing to name her. Half the IWW thought he was gallant, and the other half thought he was a damn fool.

In June a jury found him guilty, and in July a judge sentenced him to death.

Why do we even try? India thought. *All the decks are stacked.*

After Hill's sentencing the law in Salt Lake City was out in force. Frank set up a soapbox in the park anyway and began an impassioned speech, calling for protests to the verdict, appeals for clemency to the governor. Furious, despairing Wobblies crowded around him, and the police called for reinforcements. India, following Ben as he wriggled through the crowd, saw them coming and clutched Ben's arm.

Ben shook her off. "Get out of here, sweetheart. This isn't going to be a picnic."

India didn't move. She stood watching, outraged, as the police converged. Ben's notebook and press card seemed to be some shield, but the cops were grabbing spectators at random, clubbing them, stuffing them into police vans. She saw Ben, press card stuck in his hat, duck past one and push his way, arguing, past a second. Frank was thrashing in the grip of two officers. Next to her, a boy who looked about fourteen tripped over a policeman's outstretched boot. He fell with a crack of chin and teeth on the brick walk.

"He didn't do anything!" India grabbed at the cop's hands. "Let him alone!"

The cop kicked the boy in the ribs and grabbed India

instead. He twisted her arm behind her back. The boy rolled away, spitting blood.

"Agitator," the cop said. "We don't allow that in Salt Lake City."

India flailed her free arm, clawing and biting at him, but he was big and burly, and his hobnailed boots stamped a path through the crowd like a determined elephant. She gave up and let him drag her, spitting with fury.

He shoved her into the police wagon with a horde of bloody Wobblies. As the door slammed in her face, she saw Frank being stuffed into another wagon. There was no sign of Ben. The driver started the van, and she lurched against a ragged shoulder. A grizzled face with a newly missing tooth smiled at her. "Keep yer chin up, girlie."

At the police station a matron in a blue serge suit looked at India with apparent disgust. "In here." She motioned India into a cell already occupied by four other women. One was nursing a bruised jaw and looked as if she had just been picked up in the park. A second was drunk, singing quietly to herself. The other two wore a bedraggled finery of feathers and laddered stockings and sniffed at India with the disapproval one form of outcast often shows for another. There was no toilet or beds, and India assumed that meant they wouldn't be there long, just until the cops sorted out who they were and released those with whom they had no business.

She sat down to wait on the cement floor, beside the woman with the bruised jaw. When something damp began to seep through her skirt, she got up again in revulsion, but sat down once more, finally, when her legs wouldn't hold her any longer. She was wrong about a brief stay. No one came to see about them until the next morning, although the whores shouted and pounded on the bars with their shoes, and the drunken woman had a convulsion. While the others watched with dull-eyed disinterest, India tried to keep her from swallowing her tongue and shook the cell bars, screaming, "Someone is sick in here!" No one came. The drunk woman settled finally into a thick snoring, and India slept fitfully beside her.

In the morning when the matron appeared with a ringful of keys, she motioned India out.

"This woman is ill," India said.

"Nah," the matron said. "She has fits." She pointed India down the hallway and through double doors at the end. "Someone's here for you." The matron pursed her lips. "Men oughta know better."

"May I—is there a bathroom?" India said, gritting her teeth.

"Nah," the matron said.

Ben was at the front desk, signing something. India halted ten feet away from him, embarrassed, and the matron pushed her forward. Ben put his hand to her forehead, as if she might have a fever. "We'll get you home, sweetheart," he said, ignoring the stench that came from her clothes. "Isn't there a place where the poor woman can freshen up?" he demanded of the sergeant behind the desk.

"Take her," the sergeant said, and this time the matron did, muttering.

When they got to the boardinghouse where they had rooms, she found that Frank was out on bail, too, and they had a date with the judge the next day. Swift justice was Salt Lake City's motto.

"What the hell were you doing there?" Frank demanded. He had a black eye.

"Innocent bystander," Ben said, "and we shall so prove."

The judge declined to believe that. When India brought her sketchbook as proof of her bona fides, he lectured her on wasting her God-given gift on riffraff.

"The Blackstone Girl is a suitable model for any young lady in this country, or so I have thought. My own daughters admire her greatly. When you associate with saboteurs and layabouts, you cheapen yourself and you cheapen her. I am deeply troubled by this, and I am going to fine you one hundred dollars so that you will think about the example you are setting for the innocent young women of this country."

Frank got a five-hundred-dollar fine and was ordered out of Salt Lake City.

"Cheer up," Ben said. "If you hadn't been such a nice girl, you'd have got the same."

"He sounded as if that stupid girl is more important than I am," India fumed while they bought tickets in the railway station under the watchful eye of a Salt Lake City cop.

"She is," Ben said. "She's more beautiful than life and twice as sweet, like the sugar bride on a wedding cake. And she is always well behaved."

India sulked while the train rattled across Nevada back to Sacramento, and when they got there, she discovered that the fine and the night in jail had gotten into the papers. If Ben hadn't done it, someone else would have, and it was, after all, his job. He'd made that clear to her, but it felt awkward, like being caught naked. Influential people all over the world were protesting Hill's sentence, and several women's magazines ran editorials praising India for taking a stand. Her father wrote to her, a letter that began by huffing irritably and ended as a full-blown tirade. Her mother added a placatory postscript that if only India would keep out of the *papers,* Father wouldn't be so upset.

"Ah, my love, it's the price of being a pioneer," Ben said.

He was sprawled across her bed in an unbuttoned white cotton undershirt and drawers, fanning himself in Sacramento's stifling July heat with a copy of the local paper.

"I'm not a pioneer," India said. "I'm an artist."

But these days no one seemed to know what they were. Everyone was watching the horrors going on in Europe, and the world landscape and even the people around her seemed to change like metamorphosing insects before her eyes. On June 28, 1914, two days after Joe Hill's trial, the archduke Francis Ferdinand, heir to the Austrian throne, had been shot in Sarajevo with his wife. Now, a month later, Austria-Hungary was at war with Serbia, and in only a handful of days Germany had declared war on Russia and France and invaded Belgium, and England was in it, too.

Ben poured water from a pitcher by the bedside onto his chest and let it trickle down his ribs. "Hotter than an oven. I hate Sacramento." He rolled over and looked up at her. "The office says it's time to move on, love."

"Move on? To where?"

"Your Wobblies don't look so important with a war on. But I'm thinking of chucking the whole thing and joining up instead."

"*We* aren't at war!" India protested.

"No, but poor old England is. And if you ask me, the

Germans need smacking. A lot of Americans are going over.
They need men to train as flyers."

"In *aeroplanes*?"

"It's been talked of," Ben said. "There's a notion you
can mount guns on them. And you can certainly drop things
out of them."

"You're going to learn how to fly an aeroplane—across
the *English Channel*?" India looked at him in flat disbelief.

"I wish you'd marry me before I go."

That stopped her flat. "Marry you?"

Ben grinned. "Who knows what you'll be up to while
I'm gone if I don't get a grip on you." He got up off the bed
and put his arms around her. "Unless you're afraid I'll come
back in pieces. I'd understand that."

"It's not that," India said. "But you can't just go and get
married in the middle of a war when you don't know what
you're doing."

"I know just what I'm doing."

"Would you have asked me if you hadn't been leaving?"

"Well, maybe not this soon. But I damn well know what
I want when I want it," Ben said.

India closed her eyes. The war seemed to have gotten a
grip on this room. She could feel its dark vibrations through
the floor, aeroplane engines and the muffled thud of distant
explosion, coming nearer. "Not like this," India said. "I can't.
Not in the middle of this."

Ben didn't press her, but she knew he'd be there with a
ring if she changed her mind, up until the day she saw him
off on a train for New York. He wasn't the only American
heading for England. The papers were full of news of American volunteers, although sentiment was strong for America
itself to remain neutral.

The IWW was against any involvement in the war—as
far as they were concerned, it amounted to the bosses sending the workers off for cannon fodder and dividing up the
spoils. Frank had a less jaundiced viewpoint but nevertheless
showed no signs of going to England. Part of the reason for
his disinclination to go might have been his absolute aversion
to the army, his father's career, but when he said he had
work to do here, he spoke the truth. The IWW was still
trying to get a pardon for Hill. Letters and telegrams came
from all over the world, from union members in Stockholm

and Berlin, from the Swedish ambassador and even from
President Wilson. Sympathetic non-IWW Americans paid for
lawyers, appeals, and pardon hearings. None of it did any
good. On November 19, 1914, Hill was executed by a firing
squad. The night before, he wired to Bill Haywood, "Don't
waste any time in mourning. *Organize*."

Frank said grimly, through two-thirds of a bottle of
whiskey, that Hill's execution didn't mean there wasn't anything more to be done here. But India couldn't stand to sit
still any longer. She got a letter from Ben, who said that so
far he had only managed to get himself into the British Army
but that with lies and perseverance he was determined to
wriggle into whatever it was they were doing with aeroplanes
—it was all very hush-hush. A miserable letter from Sally
came, saying Juergen had joined the German Army, but he
could still correspond with her, as long as America was neutral. Sally said she kept trying to turn that into a comfort and
couldn't. India's mother wrote again, to say Father had
calmed down a little, but they didn't really think she was
doing anything bad, but that was how it looked, especially
now with all these troubles abroad. Her cousins in England
were all in the army, Mother said, and her girl cousins were
training to be nurses.

India went back to New York with no real purpose, except that with Ben gone and Frank in the dark mood he was
in and drinking too much, she couldn't find any joy in being
where she was. In January, German zeppelins began to drop
bombs on the English coast. All the hospitals there were full
of maimed civilians. Sally was white-lipped and silent, and
the night India returned to New York she slept on India's
sofa, under the dust sheet that had covered it for a year, and
cried all night. India looked out the window and thought
about what it would be like to have death raining down out
of the sky, and to have the Germans thirty miles away across
the English Channel. How did Sally stand it? It was bad
enough to be worried about Ben, but at least India could talk
to people about him.

Tim Holt came out to New York from San Francisco and
tried to get Sally to go home to Portland with him, but she
wouldn't budge. She had a row with Tim, and then Mike and
Eden, and then Janessa and Charley got into it. Everybody
had a plan for Sally, except Sally. Finally they all went away

again, and Sally continued working for Janessa in the women's hospital, practically burying herself in it now. India did a painting of her as a British volunteer nurse, and it sold very well in colored prints; her agent sold it in England as a recruiting poster.

Another letter came from India's mother: Her father was going over to England to see if the War Office could use him, and was irate that America wasn't in the war. One of her cousins had been killed at Ypres, a blond boy she remembered dancing with at someone's debut in London. All those cousins began to come back to her, lined up like paper dolls in evening clothes in the big elaborate sleeves and belled skirts of 1898. That had been the year of the war in Cuba, and India had been eighteen. They bowed, swaying in her dream, and danced out of sight. All her family was over there, except for those that were in Rajputana, and she supposed they were fighting, too.

She wrote to Frank that it didn't seem to matter what she thought about it all, what she *felt* seemed to have a louder voice, and if there was something that Ben could do, there must be something that she could do. The hospitals were full, and the English were turning all the big houses into more hospitals. Copper Hill, a house outside London where she had once gone for a party on a long-ago visit, was a hospital now. She would go there. If they couldn't use her, they could turn her over to someone who could.

She sent a cable and bought a ticket, looking uneasily at the sky outside the ticket office, as if here, too, things might begin to fall from it.

PART TWO

1915–1918

VI

London

The letters from Juergen stopped coming. Sally wrote to him in Cologne, and at the military address he had given her, but he never answered. Her letters never came back, either.

"It may not be such a good idea to go on writing," her brother Mike said. He and Eden had asked Sally over for dinner, and she had just joined them in the parlor after clearing the table. "You may get him into trouble with his own people."

"Oh, no." Sally looked terrified. "I hadn't thought of that."

"Darling, can't you forget about him?" Eden asked. She was surrounded by balls of wool, which she was furiously knitting into socks to send to the British soldiers. Most people didn't want America to get into the war, but there was the feeling that her citizens ought to help out the allies in all other respects. "Can't you find a nice boy over here and try to be happy?"

"No," Sally said. "I'm just hanging on by my fingernails, waiting for the war to end."

"It's going to be a long haul," Mike said. "Or that's what Tim says."

"Tim doesn't know everything!"

"I think he probably knows this."

"Then why don't we get in the war and get it over with?"

"Let me see if I understand this," Mike said gently.

"You want to beat Germany as soon as possible so that you can go drag Juergen out of the wreckage."

"I suppose so," Sally said. "Oh, I can't stand it. I feel like a penned wolf over here, reading the news in the morning paper and getting everything secondhand and not doing anything about it. India's over there. She's *doing* something. I'm going to go, too."

Mike sat back in his chair with a frustrated sigh. "What you're thinking is that England is closer to Germany than America is, and you might find something out. You have bats in your belfry."

"I don't care," Sally said stubbornly. "I can't bear it. Mike, you and Eden knew you belonged to each other when you were twelve years old. And everybody in the family made trouble when you got married because you were so young, but you *knew*." She got up and paced, knocking over Eden's knitting basket. "Can't you see how *I* feel?"

"Possibly," Mike said with the ghost of a grin. "Well, you have more training than most of those poor women who've been dragged into nursing. You ought to be useful."

India's cousin Babs professed herself glad to have any help she could get at Copper Hill when India presented her with a cable from Sally. Babs was Lady Barbara Pickering, the daughter of a duke who was the nephew of India's maternal grandfather. Leo, Babs's husband, was an army man, now engaged in trying to turn Britain's civilian population into a new army while the old army held on desperately in France. His family were respectable gentry, but financially he had his army pay and not much else. The money for Copper Hill's upkeep came from Babs.

The house was enormous, a monstrosity built during the Restoration on the site of a ruined abbey, and Babs ran it as a hospital with the same proficiency with which she had ruled it as a household. Her children were at school, and when they came home for the holidays, she tucked them up in the servants' quarters. "Their rooms are all full of wounded now." Babs was brisk, red-haired, and terrifyingly efficient. Even India's father declined to cross her and so raised no argument over India's traveling to London. He was at the War Office, and India saw as little of him as possible, on the theory that they would only have a row if she did.

"Well, it does overset a man to have his daughter get famous, I expect," Babs said. "I know dozens more people who are dying to meet you. They'll be thrilled to find they can meet the artist *and* her subject."

India had discovered, to her mingled amusement and horror, that the Blackstone Girl was even more popular in England than in the States. Babs had given a party for her when she had arrived, a scraped-together, wartime party, with punch and biscuits and a hoarded bottle of champagne in the music room, with the ambulatory patients among the guests.

"You gave us all a whole new look," confided a slim young woman who managed to be elegant even in a Voluntary Aid Detachment uniform. "A sort of an attitude. And that little wave over the eyebrow. Half the hairstyles in London are your doing. It's funny, I thought you'd look more like your drawings yourself."

India glanced vaguely at her dress and stammered, "Well, no. I don't use myself for a model."

"It's such a shame. I was hoping you could tell me how to do that wave. My hairdresser simply can't get the knack of it."

It's just Sally's cowlick, India thought. *Is this my contribution to the world, a new look in female fashion? One that I can't even wear successfully myself?*

The Blackstone Girl seemed utterly unimportant to her in the face of the things she was learning to do with the Voluntary Aid Detachment—or VAD—in London: treat amputations, for example, and men with lungs burned by poison gas. She had a stronger stomach than anyone but Babs, and had learned to deal with gangrene without gagging and to back up the trained nurses in the surgery. At night sometimes she dreamed she was back in the migrant camp on the Durst ranch. There didn't seem to be much difference.

She had no idea where Ben had gone. She had looked for him, even asked her father at the War Office, pretending to be asking for a friend, but Edward Blackstone said he had no information. And the wounded continued to stream in. They had been patched up in the field and then sent on to England, some of them raving and half out of their heads. There was horrible news from everywhere, thousands killed fighting the Turks at Gallipoli. They were calling it a World

War now, and there was talk of submarines and air raids on London. Zeppelins were already dropping bombs on the coast, and no one thought it would be long before they got as far as London. At night there were hardly any lights in the streets, except for the searchlights crisscrossing the sky. And there were no men, other than the wounded.

When India came off her shift, she would go up to her room, a tiny one that used to belong to the children's nanny, share a shot of whiskey with Babs and the other women, put her aching feet up, and smoke one of Babs's cigarettes, wondering what her father would think of *that*.

Everything was going to be different after the war, Babs said. "Women have done too much. We won't go back. When you've changed a tire and unplugged the drains because all ablebodied men are in the army, it does make you wonder what else you can do. I swear I'll go to jail with Mrs. Pankhurst if we don't make progress getting the vote."

"I just want the men back," another nurse sighed. She curled herself on India's bedcovers and rubbed her feet. "I'm sick to death of being brave and modern, if you want to know the truth. I want Harry back in one piece and a cottage somewhere to raise babies in."

"Oh, we all want that," Babs said, and India wondered if she didn't, too, and if not, why. What was wrong with her?

"I want Peter and Clare to have a normal life, God knows," Babs went on. "With time to play cricket, and go to dances. And ride." She sighed. "God knows when we'll have horses again." All the Copper Hill horses had gone to the cavalry.

There was a rumpus of shouting and a clanging bell from downstairs, and they flew off the bed and out of the chairs, stuffing swollen feet into shoes. India clattered down the stairs, adjusting her cap. Babs's seemed to stay on in any high wind, its veil falling in perfect folds. "What on earth?" she demanded at the foot of the stairs.

"It's Lieutenant Sellow," one of the patients said. He was out of bed, trying to steady the lieutenant. Three of the junior probationers clustered around, one with the emergency bell still in her hand. The senior nursing sister was shooing them away while the lieutenant stood staring at her, his eyes blank. His pajama top was buttoned up one button off, and under it they could see a thick red blotch forming.

"What is this man doing out of bed?" Babs demanded.

"Well, he wouldn't stay in," the other patient said.

"Guns," Lieutenant Sellow said. He turned to the window. Everyone froze in horror, but the only guns were in the lieutenant's head.

Babs took his hand. "Let's get you back in bed," she said softly. She looked over her shoulder. "Sister Merton, do you think we ought to send for Sir Henry?"

"If you can find him. The doctors are all spread thin," the sister said. She lifted the lieutenant's pajama top and looked. "But you had better try."

Between them, Babs and India and Sister Merton got Lieutenant Sellow into his bed, where he lay staring blankly at the ceiling while his reopened wound pooled blood. The sister rebandaged it. Every few minutes he would try to sit up, and India would gently push him back down again. The third time she took his hand, which was clawing at his bandages, and held it. "Reload," he said, as if he were trying to find ammunition in his bandages.

"Likely to be how he tore it open," Sister Merton said. "He'd best be watched."

"I'll sit with him," India said. He wouldn't let go of her hand anyway. They got the bandage tight again, and Babs went off to see that everyone else was settled down. One of the night nurses offered to take over for India, but he still wouldn't let go.

Sir Henry Haverford came at three A.M. , looking nearly as done in as the lieutenant, and clicked his tongue in despair. "That's the third time he's opened it up. As far as I can tell, he *wants* to die of it. Poor blighter, I can't say as I blame him. I've just come from a batch of civilians brought in from Folkestone. The zeppelins are busy tonight. The world's gone to hell. They're after the shipyards, of course, but you can't tell what you're dropping your cargo on from the air, and I don't believe the Germans care."

The lieutenant opened his eyes at that. "Guns," he said distinctly. He closed them again, and his hand went limp.

Sir Henry felt for a pulse, but India knew from the stillness of Lieutenant Sellow's fingers that it was gone.

India spent the rest of the night looking out her tiny window at the searchlights sweeping like speeded-up clock's hands across the sky, and waiting for whatever it was that the lieutenant had kept hearing.

In the morning while she was making beds, someone tapped her on the shoulder, and she dropped the blanket with a faint shriek.

"Nervy, aren't you?" Ben said. It really was him, in a Royal Flying Corps uniform and with an even cockier grin than he usually had. "I wanted to surprise you," he said sheepishly. "I didn't think you'd throw your apron over your head like a terrified housemaid."

"Where did you spring from?" India asked him, sheer delight at seeing him bubbling up inside her.

"I'll tell you in a bit. See if they'll turn you loose. I don't have but twenty-four hours."

They went and found Babs, and she said, "Certainly, go on. Don't be ridiculous, no one is indispensable. Come back tomorrow and we won't even ask where you've been." In half an hour India found herself in street clothes, driving down the stately drive in an army car with Ben.

Copper Hill sat about a mile from the village of Maystone, which was outside London. Not far outside, but far enough to seem like country.

"Where are we going?" she finally thought to ask him.

"Just as far as the Green Man. That's the local pub in Maystone, in case you don't frequent it. I took a room upstairs. For myself and my wife," Ben said as he drove. "Some days in advance. Every soldier on leave wants a room. Probably for the same purpose."

India didn't say anything, just let him drive her along the narrow lane. Once they stopped for a flock of sheep. She watched the green countryside go by, marveling at the depth of its leafy peace. She wouldn't have known there was a war on except for all the old men doing calisthenics on the village common, practicing to defend their sheep from Germans.

"Your name is Shotwell," Ben said as he pulled the car up in the yard of the Green Man. "Should you be asked."

"What?" India said.

"*My* name is Shotwell for the duration," Ben said with a chuckle. "It seems the English don't want Americans in their air corps, at least not Americans who've never seen the inside of an aeroplane and who have to be trained. They'd rather train one of their own who'll stick around after the war. And there's fierce competition to get in."

"What did you do?" India demanded.

"Found a sympathetic pal who scared up a British birth record for me. The poor soul's name was Reginald Shotwell, but I wasn't about to turn it down on those grounds."

"Reginald?" India said. "Do I have to call you *Reginald*?"

"Not in bed," Ben said happily. He got out and opened her door for her.

"What happened to Reginald?"

"He went to the dogs in India, but fortunately he wasn't in the army, so there weren't any reliable records of his demise."

"But what about his family?"

"They should be grateful to me," Ben said unrepentantly. "I'm redeeming his reputation. To tell you the truth, I don't suppose they know a thing about it. My pal just happened to know where he might find what I needed. I honestly don't think anyone's going to raise a fuss. I think my commander knows. I fed him some taradiddle about being raised in the States to account for my accent, but I really don't think he's interested as long as I can fly the plane. And I am hot stuff at that."

"Are you?" India supposed she shouldn't be surprised. The whole escapade seemed infuriatingly like Ben. She wondered how much he wanted to defend England and how much he just wanted to fly aeroplanes.

He gave her his arm, and they went into the Green Man, where they were given a seat at a mullioned window. Outside they could see the pub's sign swinging slowly in a light wind: a green face made of leaves and tendrils.

"The original forest god," Ben said. "Local custom keeps the darnedest things alive."

They ordered the plowman's lunch of beer, thick bread, and cheese and sat munching it happily. "Reginald!" India giggled. "No wonder I couldn't find you."

"Did you try?" Ben's eyes were eager.

India smiled at him. "Yes, I tried. I even braved my father, who's made use of his British birth to come over and work at the War Office. I told him you were the hometown swain of a fellow trainee. If I'd told him *I* wanted you, he'd probably have had you shot on sight."

"All the more reason to be called Shotwell."

"But not," Ben said later, upstairs in the room under the eaves, undressing her with eager, loving hands, "in private. Oh, God, India, baby, sweet darling, I think about you all the time." He kissed her neck and talked into her hair. "I think about you when I'm flying. The first time I went up, I was scared witless. I kept saying, 'India, India, India,' like some kind of spell. I felt as if I could float on your name."

"I did look for you," she said. It seemed important that he have that acknowledgment. "How did you know *I* was here?"

He pulled her down on the bed, shedding his shirt. "Oh, God, you are so beautiful. I heard from a friend of a friend who knows Lady Barbara. 'The noted illustrator India Blackstone.' He said he'd heard you were an 'original.'"

India chuckled. "They're all disappointed I don't look like the Blackstone Girl. I feel like Dr. Frankenstein, but my monster is coming over this month to work at the hospital, so maybe they'll be happy with her."

"What's she sailing on?" Ben stopped kissing her for a moment to hear the answer.

"A Cunard liner," India said. "Why?"

"The Germans are threatening to sink Allied ships in waters anywhere near the British Isles."

"But this is a liner!"

"They didn't make a distinction."

"Submarines?" India said in horror.

"I think so."

"Ohhhh." She buried her face in his shoulder.

Ben kissed her again. "It would take a lot to catch a Cunard liner. And there'll be too many Americans on board. The Germans don't want to push America that far. We might figure things out and get into the war," he added disgustedly.

India didn't ask him why he had brought it up in the first place. She pulled him to her, and they made love, quickly at first, like pots boiling over, and then again slowly, watching the long twilight turn purple through the tiny window.

"When do you have to leave?" she said into his ear.

"In the morning. I told you that." He yawned. "I'm sleepy, blast it. I wanted to stay up all night."

She pulled his head onto her shoulder. "Sleep on me. It's nearly as good." She hugged him tighter. In the midst of war, it had ceased to matter whether she loved him or not. She needed him.

In the morning, Ben drove her to Copper Hill and left her on the doorstep with a kiss that was of enormous interest to the junior nurses leaning out the window.

Babs chuckled when India came through the front door. "What an attractive young man." She was in the front hall with Sister Merton, checking off supplies on a clipboard.

India blushed and was further discomfited by the discovery of an equally attractive gentleman in a Lancer's uniform, upon whom she had never laid eyes before, standing in the cavernous hall behind Babs.

"This is Robin," Babs said. "My youngest brother. He was in Egypt, I think, when you were here last."

"How do you do?" India waited for Captain Lord Robert Cochrane to inspect her olive skin and register disapproval, but he didn't. The English army was relentlessly fussy about any entanglements between its members in the colonies and women of native blood, and the whole of the British populace wasn't much better. The Cochrane family had felt that India's maternal grandfather's liaison with her grandmother, an Indian woman, had been unwise at best and immoral at worst, and only those of India's generation were the least bit accepting of it. Several old majors had already told her that she was a charming woman, most unusual. "Edward Blackstone's girl, eh? Rich as Croesus, old Edward," they would say. But she knew they didn't want her to marry their sons.

However, Robin Cochrane, who had some of the same brisk charm as his sister, merely held out his hand and said with apparent sincerity that he was delighted. He was dark-haired but otherwise looked very much like Babs, with a determined chin and a cheerful expression. "Are you here for the duration?" he asked.

"As long as we can keep her," Babs said. "Her fellow's just gone back to France."

Robin looked at India. "What regiment is he in?"

"He's in the Flying Corps. I'm afraid he's pretending to be British."

"If he can fly, we're glad to have him." Robin smiled. "Aerial reconnaissance is the best tool we have."

"I think he's more interested in shooting Germans," India commented. "They've begun mounting Lewis guns on the aeroplanes to try to shoot them out of the air."

"Good heavens!" Babs said.

India chuckled. "Ben says that the pilots were going up with pistols and rifles before that and dueling with the German pilots. Machine guns are more efficient."

"Can they bring down a zeppelin?" Babs asked practically.

"I think so, if you shoot enough holes in it. Ben says they're learning to fly in formation, so aeroplanes with guns can escort the ones making bombing runs and drive off the German gunners."

"Zeppelins!" Babs looked at Robin plaintively. "I sound like a terrified old fussbudget, but I could cope with the world better when the cavalry were our most fearsome weapon."

"We aren't quite antique yet," Robin said. "The French cavalry actually charged German planes on the ground on the Aisne and took out a number of them."

"Ben says the Germans are threatening to sink British ships, even liners, with submarines." India sighed. "I'm worried about Sally."

"Is that your friend? Babs told me she was coming over. What's she sailing on?"

"A Cunard liner. The *Lusitania*."

"I don't think they could catch the *Lusitania*," Robin assured her.

The day before the *Lusitania* would make her run across the Irish Sea for Liverpool, the captain ordered the lifeboats swung out and uncovered, but no one felt any sense of foreboding. After all, the *Lusitania* was a liner, and there were so many Americans on board. Surely Germany would have more sense than to attack it. However, they drew the shades in the main lounge that night, kept all the doors closed, and forbade smoking on deck after dark.

The lounge was stuffy, and Sally yawned her way

through the concert and went to her cabin early. She had fallen into the habit of sleeping when she grew restless, to try to make the time go faster. She felt like an outsider, a pariah with a German lover; she couldn't even carry on a normal conversation.

In the morning they could see Ireland, and everyone breathed a sigh of relief. The fog had lifted, and the sea looked welcoming, somehow not as deep as it had felt when no land was in sight. Sally was in her cabin packing her clothes—though it was far too early, and the steward would have done it for her—when the ship gave a bump somewhere down below. It shuddered, and then there was another shock, an explosion this time. Sally flung herself to the porthole and looked out to see the sea receding precipitously as the ship tilted to starboard. She heard running feet and screams in the corridor.

Oh, my God, we're hit! The knowledge buffeted her, driving all sense out until she made herself stop and think. *Life belt. Get my life belt. Passport. Handbag.* The ship was heeling farther. She grabbed her things and ran, abandoning everything else. She fled up the stairs, trailing the handbag and trying to put on the life belt as she went. The stairs were tipped at an angle and jammed with panicked crewmen and passengers. Climbing them was like trying to walk on the walls.

Sally found that she couldn't breathe from sheer fright. *It was a U-boat,* she thought. *But Juergen isn't in the navy.* Why that mattered, she couldn't decide.

She came out of the stairwell gasping and staggering on the inclined deck. She could still see Ireland off the port, the high side of the ship, but now it looked farther away than it had, separated by miles of fearful water. Everyone instinctively turned in that direction, but the lifeboats hung too far in against the ship on that side and couldn't be lowered. Passengers milled frantically around her, wailing for lost husbands and children. Sally turned toward the starboard side, which was tilting fast into the water, and tightened the tapes on her life belt. The ship must be filling up below. *What will I do?* she thought as the *Lusitania*'s nose settled in the water. The lifeboats were full.

Swim. Surely the ship had been seen from shore, from the lighthouse on Kinsale Head. And there were fishing boats in sight—farther, though, than they had seemed in the morning when the ship was upright. Water began to lap at her ankles. *It will make a horrible suction when it goes down,* she thought. *I have to get away from it.*

"Mama!" Sally looked down to find a child clutching her knees, a girl in a white pinafore, her face red and screwed up with terror.

"I'm not Mama," she said. "Where is your mama?"

"Mama!" The child's wail was despairing, bereft. She held harder to Sally's knees, wrapping her arms around them. Sally looked frantically around her for the mother, but she was nowhere to be seen. Under them the ship lurched, and then the child was waist deep in water. Helplessly, Sally untied the tapes of her life belt.

"Hold still." She fought the child's grip on her until she could get the life belt on. The tapes were too long, so she knotted them around the girl's waist, the cold water making her fingers stiff. The ship began to settle under their feet. Sally picked the girl up, swung her back and forth as though it were a game, and flung her out over the water, as far away from the ship as she could throw.

Sally's handbag floated away, and she watched it with a laugh that was near hysteria. Silly, futile thing; the ocean wasn't going to ask for her passport. She couldn't bribe it not to drown her, either. She kicked her shoes off in the knee-deep water, then her dress, pulling it over her head. She didn't swim very well, and it would be easier in her shimmy.

The water closed over her, awful and cold and salt-laden, like being pickled in brine. Sally clawed her way upward, fighting against the pull of the ship, bumping into debris and other people, her lungs burning by the time she got her head above water. The passengers who had made it to the surface bobbed among a flotsam of loose planks, chairs, tables, oars from the portside lifeboats. Sally grabbed a floating section of wooden railing and clung desperately to it. She didn't see the child she had given her life belt to and knew she would never find her in that chaos.

Near her a woman in the water was praying out loud, Hail Marys said through chattering teeth, and another woman was shrieking, "Cecily!" Was that the child? Sally bowed her head over her piece of railing, spitting up water. Had she thrown the girl far enough out from the ship? Had the child drowned in panic anyway? And why had she given up her life belt? There hadn't been anything else to do.

The ship was gone, leaving only a long, slow swell on the water and the debris, human and otherwise, that floated on it. Already Sally's arms ached. Would Juergen know she had been on this ship? Was he even alive? The thought that he might have been killed jolted her into an anguished howl of pain. On its heels followed a silent prayer: *He didn't want a war. He tried to keep it from happening. It isn't fair to kill him.*

The sun on the water was making her feel woozy but somehow distanced from her situation. She was no longer so terrified. It must be the cold, she thought, and wondered how long she could hang on to her railing before she passed out and let go. She wriggled herself farther up it until she was half on. Any farther and it sank under her weight, leaving her face in the water.

Where were the boats? she wondered, and then tried to figure out how much time had passed. How long did it take to die in icy water? Why had the ship sunk so fast? It couldn't have been more than twenty minutes from the time it was hit. That had been before she was so cold, before the water began to make her mind numb. She had heard two explosions. Had there been munitions on board? There weren't supposed to be munitions on a liner. Maybe if she drowned, Juergen would forget about her and marry a nice German girl. She didn't *want* him to have a nice German girl.

"Aye, she's alive! Got a death grip on that rail. Come on, lass, let go of it and we'll have you aboard."

The voice came out of nowhere, out of the cold water for all Sally knew. There was a hand on her wrist, and fingers trying to pry hers loose from the railing. She opened her eyes, and a face under a fisherman's cap spoke to her in a thick Irish brogue.

"Turn loose, lass. I'm not here to save the railing."

Another pair of hands was around her waist. Sally did what the voices were telling her to and was pulled from the water and into the boat. A shivering steward, his white uniform stained with oil from the water and his forehead crusted with dried blood, was already aboard.

"Dusk comin' on," one of the rescuers said. "Look

sharp." The sea was still littered with bobbing shapes, most of it debris now, but it was hard to tell. Were there still bodies floating among the rubbish?

"These two are nearly done for," the other man said. "Get 'em aboard, and we'll have another look round."

The little boat bumped against the fishing trawler from which it had been lowered. It was plain that Sally couldn't climb the ladder, so they stuck a life ring over her head, hooked her arms over it, then sat her in a sort of sling and told her to hang on. She gripped the ropes with the same viselike hold she had had on the railing as she felt herself being pulled up and then onto the trawler's deck. A fisherman helped her stand up and take the life ring off. He put a blanket around her and took her inside, where there were more half-drowned people and some bodies as well. Someone gave her a cup of scalding tea. It was warm where she was, and she was so tired. She swallowed the tea, and her eyes closed as she put the cup down. She curled in a ball in her blanket, her wet yellow hair making a puddle under her head.

Over the whimpering of the injured and the sobs of those who had lost husbands, wives, and children, she could hear the fishing trawler's crew steadily cursing the Germans for being uncivilized pigs, for being murdering Huns. *Would they have saved me if they'd known about Juergen?* Sally wondered as she drifted into exhausted sleep.

The boats worked against the failing light, gathering in bodies alive and drowned. Those who had got away in lifeboats were towed to Kinsale Harbour by a Greek steamer that had been nearby. The British fleet and fishing vessels from the coast picked survivors from the water and took them to Queenstown, thirty miles away. Sally saw nothing but chaos there. Families were separated. There weren't enough beds in the hotels to accommodate the survivors. Temporary morgues had been set up for the unidentified bodies, and weeping survivors were looking in them for their lost. The Cunard office on the quayside had posted a list of known survivors, but it was short; some of those picked up were in no condition to say who they were.

Sally said her name firmly to anyone who would listen. India knew she was on the *Lusitania*; surely she would come looking for her, or send someone. A volunteer took her to a pub, where other volunteers were sorting out some of the less badly hurt. The barmaid gave her a comb and a dress to wear.

"You'll feel better with clothes on, that's for sure. 'Tis bad enough to nearly drown without having all these great louts looking at you in your shimmy."

"I don't have any money to give you for it," Sally said. "But someone is coming to fetch me. I think. They'll have—"

"Never you mind," the barmaid said. "Drink your tea. There's not much food left, but I can find you a sausage and a nice egg." She bustled off, leaving Sally curled in a huge chair by the coal fire, her hair fanned out and drying on her shoulders.

After a while it occurred to her that she could send a message to India through the Cunard office, and she walked down to the quay and did so. She stood to one side while she waited for an answer, watching the survivors who clustered frantically around the office. She hoped she would see the child who had worn her life belt, but the chances were probably small. That didn't mean the girl was drowned, Sally told herself. No one could find anyone tonight, and she didn't even know the girl's name.

The shrill voices rose around her like frightened birds. Hundreds had been brought in dead, and who knew how many more had gone down with the ship and never surfaced. The morgues were full of drowned children, one woman said, sobbing. Another woman sat wailing on the floor in a corner of the office. She clutched a two-year-old boy to her and howled *"Artie! Artie!"* over and over, her face red and slick with streaming tears. The little boy seemed to be in shock.

"Tch." Another woman looked at her sympathetically. "Her husband. He got her and the boy into a lifeboat and wouldn't come with them. Put another woman in instead. She's been crying for him all night. I saw him in the morgue." She jerked her thumb at the distraught young man in charge of the Cunard office. " *They* can't bring him back. Murdering stinking Germans!"

Sally closed her eyes and leaned against the wall, waiting until the message from Copper Hill came. It was from Babs. *Already left*, it said. *Stay put. Hold on.* Sally told the hunted-looking man in the Cunard office where she would be and went back to the pub to stay put by the warmth of the coal fire.

By the time India came, Sally was asleep again, curled in the same chair but full of sausage and egg. It was late afternoon of the next day, and she had spent most of her time in that chair (there were no more beds to be had) trying to soak up enough of the coal fire's heat to feel warm again. Her skin was warm, but inside there was a frozen core that would not thaw.

She looked up to find India bending over her, her dark brows knitted together with concern. Over her shoulder Sally noticed a pleasant-looking Lancers captain with a valise in his hand. "Have you been sleeping in that chair like that?" India demanded. "You'll get pneumonia or something. You sound terrible."

"I haven't said anything yet." Sally was groggy, and her chest hurt.

"Your breathing," India said. "Let me listen to you."

"I'm all right." Sally tried to push her away, but she was beginning to wonder if she was. Her lungs felt—tight. She took a deep experimental breath, and India frowned as she listened.

"A month's VAD training and they all get that way," the captain said over her shoulder. "You might as well let her."

Sally blinked at him across India's hat.

"I'm Robin Cochrane," he said. "I'm sort of a cousin. I'm Babs's brother. I was on leave at Copper Hill when we got the word, so Babs sent me along with Miss Blackstone here to see if I could help."

"How extraordinarily kind of you," Sally said, "to give up your leave." She looked at India curiously, but he didn't seem to belong to India.

"I only came home yesterday," he said, confirming this. He looked at Sally appraisingly. "Fortuitous, I call it."

She took a careful breath—it was beginning to hurt to breathe—and gave him the smile that always bowled men over, whether she wanted it to or not.

"I think we ought to get you back to Copper Hill, where you can be seen to right away," India said, straightening up. "The doctors here are run off their feet, and I don't think there is any medicine left in Queenstown by now. Have you cabled your family?"

"Oh, my Lord, *no!*" Sally sat up fast, and India grabbed her.

"Slow down."

"I'll do it," Robin said. "Give me the addresses. We brought you some clothes." He handed her paper and pen and put the valise beside her.

"I don't know what I was thinking of. I must be out of my mind," Sally muttered as she wrote. "Your cousin will be inundated with telegrams by now, and everyone will be frantic. I am an *idiot*, I was so tired, I just—"

"You're done in," Robin said gently. He took the addresses and departed.

India helped Sally to her feet. Both her arms were sore from hanging on to the railing, and something was definitely wrong with her lungs, but with help she put on one of India's dresses, too big and too long, and combed her hair and pinned it up again. She had to rest when they had finished.

With the same efficiency that he had shown on the trip out, Robin got them all on a train for Dublin and then across to Holyhead. He dealt with customs inspectors and intelligence police concerned about Sally's lack of a passport, while India, who had acquired the deepest possible suspicion of authority, and Sally, who was feeling worse by the moment, watched him admiringly. When they got on the train for London, Robin propped Sally up with pillows and commanded her to lean on his shoulder. He sent for tea and put a little whiskey in it from a flask in his pocket, and for a while she felt warm inside.

"You're so kind to use up your leave this way," she mumbled.

"Not at all. I was just going to spend it with Babs." Robin gave India a look that said she was not to mention that he had been on his way north to spend it with friends in Scotland.

VII

Robin

Babs installed Sally Holt in another of the tiny servants' rooms on the top floor of Copper Hill and got Sir Henry Haverford up to see her. Sir Henry diagnosed bronchitis but said that Miss Holt appeared to be made of tough stuff, and if she would just stay in bed for a few weeks, she would pull through nicely.

"I understand you've already had hospital training," he said. "As soon as you are well, everyone will be fighting to get their hands on you."

"They'll send her to France," Babs said gloomily. "We train them, and then they get shipped out to somewhere else."

"They may want to retrain me," Sally said with a chuckle, which she broke off because it hurt. "My work was entirely in a volunteer capacity, and at a women's hospital."

"None of us had had any experience with wounds, to speak of," Sister Merton said briskly, tucking in Sally's blankets around her. "If you're trained at all, you are ahead of most of the VADs we get here. Present company excepted," she added, but it appeared to be for form's sake.

"We're learning," Babs said meekly.

"Indeed you are, Lady Barbara. But you're right. They'll take this one away from us."

"How much training do you have to have to go to France?" India asked. Sally thought she sounded restless.

"More than you have had, Miss Blackstone," Sister said.

"I will give you credit, however. I've never asked you to do anything yet that you didn't care to."

"A miracle in itself," Babs muttered, and Sir Henry and Sister Merton looked at her with a certain amount of sympathy. "Many of my friends and acquaintances want to 'do their part' in a manner that does not require them to dust or mop floors or empty bedpans."

"France," Sally said thoughtfully. It had never occurred to her to go to France, but maybe that would be a good thing. Surely the work there was even harder, and she wouldn't have time to think. And in the back of her head, unadmitted, was the secondary knowledge that it was closer to Juergen. What difference that would make, she couldn't have explained.

"Not France yet," Robin said. "First we have to get you well." He sat down beside her bed and looked at the others in the room as if he expected them to leave.

Babs raised an eyebrow. "We have rounds to make. Since you've appointed yourself nurse, Robin, I'll leave you to fetch anything Sally needs." She bent her head toward India as they went down the stairs. "Things come on fast in a war, don't they?"

"I think Sally is a little non compos mentis at the moment," India hedged.

"Robin isn't. I hope she's not engaged to be married or something."

"No." India saw no point in elaborating. And Robin was a dear—darling, competent, and dashing, with a store of funny stories, mostly told on himself. He had entertained India with them on the trip to Queenstown, to keep her back from the edge of panic. He was relaxed where Juergen was stiff, adaptable where Juergen was incapable of adapting. *Maybe*, India thought to herself, *just maybe . . .*

Robin spent most of his remaining three days of leave in Sally's room, fluffing her pillows, making her lemonade and hot tea, and then, as the supreme proof of his devotion, learning to make coffee like an American, because Babs's cook simply would not. This achievement was seized on with cries of joy not only from Sally but from India, who pleaded with him to teach the cook, because the cook had no intention of listening to India and wouldn't even let her in the kitchen.

"It's fearful stuff," he said, watching indulgently while Sally swallowed hers. "You Yanks all must have tin tummies."

"We got put off tea during the Revolution." Sally grinned. "Found something better. So there."

"I found something better, too," Robin said. When she flushed but didn't respond, he added, "I wish I could have shown you London, but I'll get another leave eventually, and we'll do it."

"They may send me to France," Sally murmured.

"Not if you don't want to go. You aren't in the army, you know. And in any case, so much the better. France just happens to be where they're sending me. If I write to you, will you send on your address?"

"Of course."

He took her hand and kissed her knuckles. "I won't take advantage of a woman who's still an invalid, but you'll hear from me," he said happily. "Believe it or not, I never fell in love with anybody before, so I'm not certain how it's done, but I promise you I'm going to be hard to get rid of."

He departed, and Sally could hear him whistling on the stairs and then the general commotion of his leave-taking. He was sweet, she thought. It wouldn't hurt to write to him. And he probably fell in love all the time . . . Anyone that good-looking would have packs of women pursuing him.

Robin's first letter came a week later. He must have written it the minute he landed, India said, mildly annoyed because she hadn't received one from Ben yet.

"I think he wrote it on the boat," Babs said. "It takes forever to get mail."

Sally opened it and read it. It was full of chat, only mildly ardent, as befitted a man who had only just begun a courtship: nothing embarrassing or that required a specific answer. It was entirely satisfactory, and Sally got out her note paper and started a long reply. There wasn't much else to do while she recuperated except to listen to India's and Babs's tales of the wards and for gunshots in the distance.

The guns were the only way they could tell if bombs were coming. The zeppelins were almost silent and had to be right overhead for them to hear their humming. The zeppelins were very sinister, Sally thought. She saw one once, working its way in from the coast, floating like a fat cigar pinned by the searchlights that turned it silver. Then she had heard the pom-poms start up, but nothing seemed to hit it.

At the end of May, when Sally was recovered and beginning to do light work in the ward, the zeppelins got through to London. Everyone had said it would happen before long, but no one was prepared for the terror of fire and rubble and smashed buildings. India and Sally were watching from a darkened window, thinking that Copper Hill was surely far enough away to be safe, when there was a huge *thump* and a burst of flame from the yard. They heard shrieks and breaking glass from below, and then the stable roof went up in flames.

India and Babs flew down the stairs with Sally behind them, tying the sash of her wrapper; she had just come off duty and undressed. The patients, those who were ambulatory, were hanging out the windows and shouting at the sky.

"Bastard!"

"Must have had one left and couldn't bear to waste it."

"Or he was going in, got too excited."

"Come on, you fellows that can walk! Get the hoses on that roof!"

They heard a distant siren wailing. "Lord," Babs said, "that could have come down through this roof."

"It's a good thing Jerry hasn't any aim," a major with a patch over one eye said. He joined a half-dozen other pajama-clad men in the yard, and they turned the garden hoses on the stable roof. Bells were sounding the alarm in the distance, and the zeppelin was floating away like a bloated oval. "Come on, shoot!" the major yelled at the gun batteries. "Or get an aeroplane up there!"

India took four of the VADs down to the scullery, and they brought up the buckets that had been put there, ready for the raid no one had really expected. Beyond the stable was a pond, home to a flock of ducks who were nowhere to be seen, and the women started a bucket brigade from it to the flames. India heaved five-gallon buckets along it, glad of the muscles she had acquired in the last few months. Sally was not permitted to carry buckets and was chased inside by Sister to see to the wards, where all the wounded men were calling for nurses, wanting to be told what was going on.

"Just a little fire in the stable roof," Sally said comfortingly, tucking a boy who didn't look old enough to have been allowed in the army back into his bed. "There now, I hear the engines coming. No need to be nervous."

"It's the fire. I was burned once, you know." The boy held out gauze-bandaged hands. "Now I've got such a horror of it. I know pilots who carry a pistol up with them, in case the aeroplane catches fire."

"The stable was made of wood. This house is stone. It would take a lot to catch it on fire," Sally said. *It would take a bomb that landed just a hundred feet to the left of that one.*

India was outside and could feel the heat from the burning stable on her face. Hot ash was falling in her hair, and she could see the faces next to her glowing like coals in the red glare. The men of the local engine company had come and were pumping water from the pond, but they weren't going to be able to save the building. It would just be a mercy if they could keep it from spreading to the hay barn. *That* would make a bonfire.

Sister Merton came down the line, peering at each of the men from the ward. "You'll do," she said. "And you. You, certainly not! Get back to bed before you undo all Sir Henry's work!" They were the best of the lot, the nearly convalescent, hobbling on crutches, with arms in slings. The rest could only lie in bed and listen to Sally assure them that the house was stone.

The wards were lit with the ghastly glow of the fire for most of the night, and the hay barn did go up, after the stables. At least there were no horses or hay in them to burn, Babs said grimly. But the firefighters had kept the flames from the house.

At four in the morning, India went up to her room, ash-covered and grimy, her arms aching from the bucket brigade. She considered herself in the mirror. Her cap and veil were gone, and she found that she liked herself better this way. At least she had been fighting something, even if it was only the fire. She took out Frank's last letter and Ben's, and read them again.

Rhodes-Moorhouse got a VC for the bombing run that killed him at Courtai, Ben wrote, *and yesterday the French dropped 87 bombs on the prison*

*gas works at Ludwigshafen, more power to them.
No other news except that I have a beautiful new
Bristol Scout to fly, and I've had a machine gun
mounted on it, with which I nearly gave a Boche
pilot heart failure. I didn't have the luck to hit him,
but it's quite exciting, diving at 120 mph and firing a
machine gun.*

Frank wrote,

*I now have a collection of California cities to
which I have been politely requested (sometimes
with a club to the head) not to return. We have
finally organized an Agricultural Workers' Organization, with Walter Nef to head it and a start to be
made during the Kansas harvest. Do you want to
hear Joe Hill's will? To wit:*

> *My will is easy to decide,
> For there is nothing to divide.
> My kin don't need to fuss and moan—
> "Moss does not cling to rolling stone."
> My body? Ah, if I could choose,
> I would to ashes it reduce,
> And let the merry breezes blow
> My dust to where some flowers grow.
> Perhaps some fading flower then
> Would come to life and bloom again.
> This is my last and final will,
> Good luck to all of you.*

*Are you still ministering as Ministering Angel
over there? I thought how useful it would be to have
a resident nurse the last time I got in a tussle, but I
suppose your efforts are all for the Cause.*

*Do you hear from young Richardson? Is he
airborne yet?*

India folded both letters back into their envelopes, unbuttoned her soot-stained uniform, and threw it in the laun-
dry to be washed. In the morning she told Babs what she was
going to do, and Babs's eyebrows shot up into her hair.

"You don't know what you're getting into," Babs said
bluntly.

"Yes, I do," India said. "I've done things you wouldn't
dream of, I'm afraid."

She told the Red Cross that, too, and after they had
tested her, giving her a car to drive on a hair-raising trip
through back lanes and timing her, they had to admit that
she probably had.

"We do have a few female ambulance drivers," the offi-
cial who received her driving report conceded. "But I can't
say that I approve of them."

"I don't want you to approve of me," India said
brusquely. "I want you to give me a job. I've had some VAD
training as well as being able to drive. That ought to make
me useful."

Her examiner looked at the folder in his hand. He had
gray hair in a short military cut and heavy fingers that fiddled
with the edges of her folder. "Why aren't you satisfied with
nursing?" he demanded.

"I want to fight them," India said. "Not pick up the
pieces. Men always leave the pieces for the women, but I'm
not a ministering angel. I haven't the patience. I'd fly an
aeroplane if they would let me."

"Heaven forfend," the Red Cross man said wryly. "Content yourself with an ambulance, Miss Blackstone."

It took two weeks to get the necessary inoculations and
papers and transport orders, and Sally watched wistfully as
India went shopping in London and came back with divided
skirts, which she said were easier to drive in.

"Stop moping," India said. "You look like a spaniel.
They'll let you go to France."

Sally gave a tremendous sigh. "I don't know why I want
to. As it is, I'm terrified all the time here. But I've had too
much time to think. I can't stand it if I have to think anymore."

"Oh, lamb." India put her arm around her. "Is it still
Juergen?"

"I don't even know if he's alive," Sally said and burst
into tears. "And nobody *cares*. Nobody *wants* to know. He's a
German!"

India patted her again ineffectually and tightened the
strap on her valise, trying to make herself stay sympathetic

toward Sally and not to equate Juergen with the pilots of the zeppelins that were bombarding London or the captain of the U-boat that had sunk the *Lusitania* and killed over a thousand people. It wasn't easy.

Babs drove India to the station, still shaking her head in disapproval, but India felt light as she stepped onto the train and lighter still boarding the Channel steamer, packed with civilians and soldiers. It was like shedding a nun's habit to shed the VAD uniform, which to India looked far too much like a habit; the custom of addressing nurses as sister added to the effect. There was something about nursing that she found claustrophobic and littered with rules on behavior. The VADs lived under the matron's scrutiny and were hedged about with must-nots designed to preserve their chastity and reputation. Watching men die seemed to India a far greater horror, and likely to have a more lasting effect, than going dancing in clubs forbidden to good girls. It was the dying rather than the rules—which her age gave her authority to ignore anyway, she believed—that had slowly made her feel as if she were wearing an extra-tight corset, trapped and a little queasy. How quickly the wounded could be transported from the front to the hospital mostly determined whether they lived or died later, she had found. But it was at the front, in those critical hours, that she could at least do a little fighting back at the Germans who had maimed them.

There were two other drivers going over to France, both men. They gave her an interested look but made no unsuitable comment, particularly when, after their arrival at Boulogne, they had to drive the new ambulances being unloaded to their base camp in the dark. The base camp was a Belgian farmhouse taken over as an evacuation hospital, and it was shelled regularly. That was why they went in at night, Victor Gerard and George House, the other two drivers, explained. Harder for Jerry to see.

"We transport the wounded at night, too." They waited for her to flinch.

"Sensible," India said brusquely. She looked them both in the eye. "I'm older than you are. Don't teach your grandmother to suck eggs."

They laughed and bought her a beer in a French tavern and taught her to sing "Mademoiselle from Armentières."

Victor, from Liverpool, had something wrong with one foot that wouldn't hold up on a march. George was American and rich. He'd personally paid for the ambulance he brought over, and he groused continually that President Wilson was writing *notes* to Germany over the *Lusitania* instead of declaring war.

After the first hour on the road, they followed nose to tail like circus elephants, headlights turned off and taillamps lit. A big searchlight swept the sky beyond a ridge of trees, and India and George tucked their ambulances as close together as they could, trying not to lose sight of Victor, who supposedly knew the way. They arrived at about ten-thirty at night, mud-spattered and missing a headlamp, which George had run into a signpost with no sign affixed to it. India was shown to her quarters, which she was to share with another woman.

Maida McDowell was in her twenties and had blond hair bobbed off at the base of her ears. "Welcome to the Grand Hotel. I see the valets took good care of you," she said, pointing India to a cot opposite her own.

The rest of the furniture consisted of a packing-case dressing table, with a packing-case seat, and a long wooden pole to hang clothes on. The evacuation hospital occupied the farmhouse proper. From what India could see in the darkness, their own quarters had formerly housed the chickens that now wandered disconsolately in the road, roosting in hedges.

She fell on her cot exhausted with barely a civil word to Maida, who she discovered in the morning was to be her driving partner. She also discovered that she did not get to keep the beautiful new blue ambulance she had driven from Boulogne. It was destined elsewhere. Maida's vehicle was elderly, with dented fenders and an inscription painted in gilt on its side that read:

PRESENTED BY THE TOUNGOO AMBULANCE GIFT FUND
ZEYAWADDY
TOUNGOO DISTRICT BURMA AMBULANCE

"She has more go than she looks," Maida said, "if we only had decent petrol to put in her. The stuff we're getting now you have to strain through a chamois first."

The first day was quiet: no sound of shelling. A rumor went around that the Germans were cooking something up, and there were bound to be casualties by night. That notion fizzled, though, so Maida took India through the little village a mile beyond the base camp, to see what was left of it. There was not much, but the taverns still standing did a good business from the troops constantly traveling back and forth along the road. Next Maida took her up to the evacuation hospital to introduce her around. She seemed to know them all, even the *blessés*—the wounded—who had been brought in by other drivers. The matron was taking advantage of the lull to have the floors scrubbed down, the endless rivers of mud and blood washed away. The smell of disinfectant lingered in the air. At the evacuation hospital only the most dreadfully wounded were operated on. All others were re-dressed and sent on to base hospitals, or on to England. India thought of Babs's old stone house outside of London and felt, for reasons she could not articulate, unaccountably free.

The next day there were casualties. They could hear heavy firing not far away, and Maida, cocking an ear, told India which guns were the Germans' and which were the Allies'. They all sounded alike to India. The windows rattled, and the whole shed vibrated so much that its tin roof hummed. It wasn't long before she and Maida were called out, along with George and Victor.

"They'll start coming out almost right away," Maida said. She was driving, and India rode beside her. "First the *petits blessés*, the ones who can walk. Then the worst hurt will be laid out on stretchers at the dressing station for us to pick up. This ambulance will hold three *assis*, the ones who can sit, and four *couchés*. Those are the stretcher cases. We'll make the run back in the dark. Jerry has a horrible habit of dropping bombs, the filthy beast."

India hung on to her seat as the ambulance bounced over the rutted road.

"You should see it when it rains," Maida said. "Lord, what a muck."

There were troops moving along the road, as well, and civilian refugees from the town up ahead where the fighting was. Half the buildings along the road had been bombed or shelled to ruins. Over everything was the boom of the guns

and the screech of shells. India had to force herself not to
duck when she heard one—they were landing in the front
lines up ahead, at least in theory.

It was nearly dark when they got to the dressing station,
the twilit sky illuminated every now and then by star shells
or the flash of guns. The wounded were packed on stretchers
in rows against the side of a shed that afforded them only
minimal protection.

"If there's no stretcher bearer, you load them yourself,"
Maida said to India. "The faster we get them to hospital, the
better chance they've got, especially head cases and hemorrhage. There isn't much they can do for head wounds out
here but put a dressing on to keep the dirt out."

They loaded four stretcher cases, trying to decide who
was the most desperate among the bleeding, moaning men.
Mixed in among them were a few German wounded, who
were brutally left for last. "I know it looks callous," Maida
muttered, "but if someone has to wait, it won't be our boys."

The assis were helped in after the stretchers, and they
began the trek back to the hospital. If no more casualties
came from the front the next day, Maida said, they might
take the ones who could be moved on to Boulogne.

Halfway there one of the blessés, a man with a thigh
wound, began to bleed badly, splattering blood over the inside of the ambulance. Maida stopped, and India put one of
the assis in front with Maida and crawled in the back to see
what she could do while the ambulance jolted on, through
pitch darkness now, the sky flaring behind them with star
shells. India found that a tourniquet had slipped and got it
tight again, but the man's face was ashen under the dirt, and
he wasn't but half conscious. He was a big man, a Scot in a
torn kilt, and whatever he was murmuring was in a brogue so
thick she couldn't understand it. The ambulance thumped
along the road, wheels dropping into potholes, while she
kept her hand on the blood-soaked dressing to hold the tourniquet on.

When they reached the hospital, they unloaded the
couchés, including the Scot, turned them over to the hospital
orderlies, told the assis to follow the orderlies, and turned
around for another run. "You drive this time," Maida said.

India climbed behind the wheel. The ambulance was
clumsier than the new one she had driven from Boulogne,

and the rutted road felt like railroad tracks. She gave it as much gas as she dared in the darkness—headlamps only made you a target—and tried to remember all the turns she had seen Maida take.

The landscape of war had altered some. The British had moved forward a bit, driving the Germans back, and the new wounded were in an *abri*, a dugout shelter not a hundred yards from the trenches and barbed wire of the front. India homed the ambulance in on the faint flicker of candlelight that came from the back side of the abri, and they flung themselves into it as shells came down around them. All the blessés here were stretcher cases except for one man with half his arm shot off who miraculously could still stand and walk. The pain had made his eyes glassy. On the stretchers were a chest wound, two mangled legs, and a man with a bloody mess where his eyes had been. They were just gone.

The drive back had the surreal quality of a dream in which all the lights go out and the dreamer is left in a landscape suddenly unfamiliar, confronting monsters. Shells dropped around them, shrieking as they came down, lighting the road with sudden fire and burning out into dreadful blackness again. What moon there was, was covered in cloud, and India drove with her head out the window, feeling her way.

Maida looked behind her. "One more run, I think. We'll have to get them all out by morning. I think the shelling's dropping off."

Already weary beyond exhaustion, India didn't answer. Maida poured a cup of cold tea from the picnic flask she kept in the ambulance and handed it to her. India drank it while she drove, the tin cup rattling against her teeth.

They made a third run and limped back to the hospital at four in the morning. India fell on her cot and went to sleep without undressing. At daylight she woke from habit, and Maida told her to go back to sleep. "No more now. We'll take these out to Boulogne tonight." India closed her eyes and fell back into unconsciousness. That night after Maida woke her, they drove to Boulogne.

"You'll get used to it," Maida said. "You get to be nocturnal, like owls. Get up in the dark and go where they send you, keep an eye on the sky for Jerry."

But they didn't need to look for Jerry. They could hear

him, the angry buzz of the aeroplane engines and the whine and shriek of shells. India stared into the unmarked darkness, trying to pull landmarks from it. *This is where I'm going to live during the war,* she thought. *Out here in this dark.* The war seemed to have taken everyone and tumbled them into the dark. The only color was red, for blood, and even blood looked black at night. The idea of worldwide war was too much to comprehend, all the hundreds of thousands dead, a whole generation of young men if this kept up. She could only manage if she narrowed it down to this ambulance, *these* few men.

Over the next months, she found that she could keep her sanity by confining her world to the inside of the ambulance. A fast-moving turtle, she thought. They didn't always go between the base camp and the front, or the base camp and the rear hospitals. They were just as likely to be sent to Etaples for supplies—paraffin, antityphoid serum, and once a pair of guinea pigs—or to transport the medical teams. Occasionally there were single casualties, the maimed victims of mines or unexploded shells, and the nearest ambulance would answer the call. In between there were days of no motion at the base camp, when India and George taught Victor and Maida to play poker. Maida and George, India suspected, were falling into one of those wartime passions that any damned fool but the fools involved could have told them would come to no good.

And then the guns and the aeroplanes would start again, fire would fall from the sky, and India would crawl inside her turtle shell for another drive through the flames.

After India sailed, Sally did her best to get sent to the hospital in Etaples and was outraged when she was judged too delicate to go.

"I'm in perfect health!" she raged.

The matron in charge of VAD placement thought otherwise. "You have a rasp in your throat still. You have been nearly drowned. If you want work, I will give you work, but not in Boulogne. You may go to Deerfield, where there is a hospital for serious surgical cases and too small a staff. That way if you collapse, you may be sent back here with a minimum of trouble." She nodded her head briskly as if that was that.

It appeared that it was. Sally packed her bags, thanked Babs profusely for her care, and took the assignment at Deerfield. It wouldn't do to go on staying with Babs, with Robin writing her ever more affectionate and suggestive letters and Babs watching her like a cat at a mousehole and extolling Robin's virtues as they charted temperatures in the ward. Babs clearly adored Robin and would be hurt if Sally didn't.

Deerfield was a sprawling country house near Coventry that had been turned into a hospital for touch-and-go cases— men who might live if they had sufficient attention and round-the-clock nursing. The owner, a young baronet just come into his inheritance, had been killed in France, and the family, an uncle and two old aunts, had decided to give the house up to the medical service for the duration of the war. The new heir, if he lived, was a distant cousin in the Flying Corps.

Sally's ward had been the music room, and a dust-sheeted piano and a harp still sat at one end. There were twenty beds, and she shared her shift with a sister. A smaller room just off the ward had been turned into an operating theater, which was in use a great deal of the time. Nearly a quarter of the men here were dying, Sally discovered, and dying slowly. Changing dressings meant stopping hemorrhage, draining and reinserting rubber tubes, pushing intestines back through gaping wounds. Progress was measured in minute increments. A patient who was no worse than the day before was to be rejoiced over.

Sally's patients were all officers, some of them younger than she was. There were dying privates in other wings, a ward full of head cases, and in one small separate wing a few badly wounded German officers, prisoners transferred from France. On her first morning the matron gave her a tour, showed her where the dining hall was, gave her permission to brew coffee on a gas ring in the scullery, and turned her over to a formidable sister to be shown the ropes in the ward.

If Sally wanted no time to think, she got it, and with some aggravation she wondered how Étaples could possibly be worse. Her feet ached constantly; all the nurses went to work every day with them bandaged. She never got enough sleep. As the months wore on other things grew scarce, too— butter and sugar. It seemed petty moaning over no sugar for her coffee, but when her father mailed her a pound from the States, she was ecstatic and tied it up in little bundles for Christmas presents to give to the other nurses on her ward.

Deerfield got draftier as winter came on. The sisters and VADs went on shift bundled in sweaters over their uniforms and wearing woolen stockings.

Robin wrote to her from France, and she wrote back, describing as cheerfully as she could her day on the ward; the sense of loss, the *ache*, when someone died, even if she hadn't known him; her efforts to tune the piano so that it would be playable, to give them something to listen to. One of the other wards had a Victrola, and someone had donated some records, but most of them were things like "Lead, Kindly Light," and the men were always asking for popular songs. They didn't seem to care if the piano was out of tune. She told him she had taken some of her hoarded sugar to the German prisoners because naturally the best of everything was kept for their own men, and she felt so sorry for the others.

Robin wrote back, *You have the kindest heart of any woman I have known. If I'm ever captured, I would hope to find a nurse like you behind the German lines. I may be home for Christmas. Save me some of your sugar, and if possible a kiss.*

Robin came home for Christmas but not on leave. Babs telephoned Deerfield to tell Sally that he had been wounded.

"They've taken off his right leg," Babs said tightly into the telephone. "He's being very good about it. He wants to see you. Can you come to us for Christmas?"

Sally went up to London the next day, and Babs took her to the hospital where Robin was. He looked ashen around the mouth, and there was a horrible empty space under the sheet where his leg should have been, but he gripped Sally's hand with startling strength. "Now I'll get well," he said. "No more hunting for me, I suppose—they've taken the knee, too—but horses will be a luxury after the war, anyway."

Sally sat beside him and felt tears sliding down her face. "What will you do now?"

"I suppose I will have to find a desk job," Robin said. "No more cavalry for me, either. Would you fancy me as a banker?"

Sally managed a smile. "You wouldn't be bored?"

"That would depend entirely on my other circumstances." He started to say something else, and his mouth tightened suddenly as a spasm of pain flickered across his face. "It comes and it goes," he managed after a moment.

At that, the sister in charge shooed Babs and Sally out but told them they could come back in the evening, and perhaps in another few days he might be transferred to Copper Hill to recuperate. "It's having family about that does them good," she said.

"Having *you* about will do him good," Babs said in the car going back to Copper Hill. "He's not out of the woods yet, despite what he says. I asked the sister. His leg is badly infected. They may have to take more off." Her gloved hands clenched on the steering wheel. "Oh, God, it is so beastly. What has *happened* to the world?"

Sally spent her holiday leave at Copper Hill, helping to trim Christmas trees in the wards and going twice a day up to London to see Robin. He willingly did everything the nurses told him to as long as Sally held his hand, even when it came to changing the dressing on his leg. It was amputated just above the knee, and he was fiercely determined to keep that much, to make an artificial limb easier to fit.

"I'm not going to spend my life in a bloody bath chair," he said through gritted teeth.

"Certainly not," the nursing sister said briskly, while Robin's fingers clenched around Sally's. "Not if you behave, Captain."

They wouldn't let him go, though, not before Christmas, so Sally brought him some chocolate, and the hoarded sugar, and the kiss as well, before she took the train to Deerfield.

"I'll write to you," Robin said, while the print of his mouth was still warm on hers. "And maybe they'll cut me loose from here." His eyes gleamed despite the pain, and he kissed her again while she was still bent close to him. "I have a plan."

How could he be so cheerful, Sally wondered, with one leg gone, a man who had been in the cavalry? She suspected that she might be the reason. And coming from a man as kind and sweet, not to mention as beautiful, as Robin, that was something to be cherished.

She wrote to him from Deerfield, and to Babs as well, a little less stiffly now, as befitted someone who might become a sister-in-law. She still didn't know what she would do if Robin asked her, but two weeks after her return to Deerfield, she found him there, propped up in her ward and grinning from ear to ear.

"I told you I had a plan," he said, laughing.

He looked better, heavier, and the infection was nearly cleared up. They still wouldn't let him out of the hospital, so he had called in all the favors he was owed by anyone useful and arranged to have himself sent to Deerfield.

Sally discovered that he could probably have had a bed in Windsor Castle had he wanted it. He was due to get the Victoria Cross, according to hospital scuttlebutt. When she tried to pin him down, he just said cheerfully that it had happened on Vimy Ridge, that he had pulled another fellow out from under his dead horse and had gotten him away—facts she already knew. He had been in the hospital since November, trying to hang on to his leg, and hadn't agreed to let them amputate until weeks later. Hadn't let anyone tell Babs until it was inevitable.

"I rather wanted to show up to see you on both feet," he said sheepishly. "Do you mind it dreadfully?"

"I don't mind it except for you!" Sally said. "Robin, how can you even think it would make a difference to me otherwise?"

"I know a fellow, lost his arm. His fiancée couldn't face it. Couldn't look at the stump. Said it made her sick."

"Well, he's better off without *her*! If she didn't show her true colors over an amputated arm, she'd have shown them later." Sally was indignant, and he looked so sad lying there that she didn't stop to wonder if the conversation was going where she hadn't meant it to.

"I don't know how much money the family will have after this war," Robin said. "Everything is changing. But I suppose it will help to be a war hero, even if it's embarrassing. There are fellows who will give me a job afterward on the strength of it."

"And so they should," Sally said. "I'm beginning to hear the pieces you haven't been telling. Lots of the other girls have fellows who were at Vimy Ridge. You can't hide your light under a bushel."

"Huh-uh." Robin shook his head. "The heroes are here, women who've never had to work before, doing scut work like scullery maids. I'll be pleased about *my* light, such as it is, only if you are."

"I am proud of it." Impulsively, Sally picked his hand up from the sheet and kissed it. He held on when she started to let go and with his other hand fumbled in the little box beside the bed. He unearthed a snap-front leather jewelry case from beneath the day's newspaper and his journal.

He took out a sapphire ring and balanced it in the palm of his hand. "I had Babs send this on here. It was my grandmother's." When Sally didn't protest, he slipped it on her hand. "It fits!" he said in astonished delight. "I thought I'd have to have it sized."

Sally looked at the sapphire blinking benignly on her finger. A safe harbor, she thought, a way around the rocks. She was off duty, and the night staff were making their silent rounds, murmuring to each other now and then. The lights were almost all off. Sally leaned forward in her chair and laid her head on Robin's chest, careful not to jostle him. She could feel his heart thumping steadily under his nightshirt. She laid her hand on it to feel its steady thud echoed in the ring. *I have something to do with my life now,* she thought, half amazed that she wanted to.

And over the next few months it was sweet relief to be able to talk: to talk about Robin, about their plans, about what her father said when she wrote that she was marrying an Englishman. The wedding would have to wait until after the war, until her parents could safely travel over. There was no hurry now; Robin wasn't going anywhere, except to the Midlands to train officers for the cavalry. She could talk and plan, trade pictures of wedding dresses with the other VADs, nearly all of whom were engaged or thinking about it. She could speak her beloved's name aloud without fear of censure.

In the spring Robin was sent to Copper Hill to recuperate, and Sally got a few days' leave and joined him there. Babs's husband, Leo Pickering, came home on leave, and there was a family party. The Cochranes and the Pickerings were almost like the Blakes and the Holts, Sally thought. They were devoted to each other, pried incessantly into each other's business, and offered each other good-natured opin-

ions on all subjects. Copper Hill felt like another version of
the Madrona, and Sally said wryly to Robin that it was comfy
for now, but when they were married, could they please live
in London?

"Of course," Robin said. "I knew what I was doing
when I picked a city girl."

The king himself pinned the Victoria Cross on Robin's
chest, and the whole family went to London to see the cere-
mony. Robin's father, the Duke of Terrill, and his older
brother, Tommy, who was nearly as blind as a bat and consequently confined to civil defense work, came up for it and
treated Sally as if she had always been in the family. New
blood was an excellent thing, said the duke, and Tommy
peered at her and said she was prettier than Robin deserved.

In the summer Robin returned to his regiment—at his
own insistence and after pulling another handful of strings—
and Sally went back to Deerfield. She wrote long, reassuring
letters to everyone in her family, who wasted no time writing
back, demanding photographs, and trying to work out how
this marriage would make them all related to the Black-
stones. They professed lighthearted horror that she had
bobbed her hair. And through all the gay, chatty correspondence, she could read, if she were candid, an underlying
current of relief on everyone's part that it wasn't Juergen.

By the fall of 1916 the world seemed to have settled into
the war. Thousands were dying, but nothing much was being
accomplished. In America, Wilson won the presidency again
on the slogan "He Kept Us Out of War," but the country was
leaning more and more toward getting into it after all, outraged by submarine attacks and Germany's callous attitude.
Britain and France had also been ruthless in the name of
necessity, but they always managed to convey that it was
with deepest regret. Germany gave the impression of enjoying it. After the *Lusitania* went down, a commemorative
medal was struck in Berlin, showing the sinking liner on one
side and a queue of passengers at the Cunard ticket office on
the other, buying tickets from a death's head.

In Britain, Lloyd George became prime minister, and
everyone at Deerfield said that now something would happen. Sally quit drawing wedding dresses in the margins of

her diary; who knew when she would get married, and the fashions were changing too fast.

Deerfield was still full of slowly dying officers, and Sally was elated when she got a letter from India to divert her attention. India wrote from Belgium that both sides were using gas now, but since she couldn't see to drive at night in a gas mask, she had ripped hers off and driven through a kilometer of gas without it. She had been lucky not to hit a patch. She had seen Ben once. Maida had been transferred, they were always short of drivers, and India was driving alone now. There had been heavy casualties on the Somme, German as well as French and British. The cavalry had ridden into action through waving wheat, lances glittering, and been mown down by German machine-gun fire. Then the fall rains came, and the front was churned into mud. No-man's-land looked like the moon, India said, pocked with shell craters, cut on either side with trenches and barbed wire, littered with dead bodies in the rain. Cars bogged down; even the artillery mules bogged down, floundering up to their bellies in mud. Nothing seemed to happen. Endless munitions were produced in the factories to kill endless men, and nothing changed, and nobody won. The day before she had picked up a German boy who had lain in no-man's-land for two days and who couldn't do anything but stare at her and ask her for an orange, of all things, until he died.

Sally folded the letter and went to see if the German lieutenant in the Deerfield ward was still alive. He was only twenty and gradually bleeding to death from the subclavian artery. No one could do anything about it, and he was afraid. The nurses at Deerfield were growing progressively less sympathetic as the war dragged on, and less inclined to sit with him. Sally had begun to speak what German she knew to him when she was off duty. It seemed to make him a little less frightened. Most of the other German officers knew her by now, and sometimes she would read the newspaper to the ones who didn't read English. The nurses on duty were glad to have her—it let them off the hook if they didn't feel like comforting Huns, as one of them said.

This evening there was a screen around the boy's bed, and Sally sighed with weary resignation. Everyone in the ward knew it was coming, but she felt a sense of loss all the same, and wondered whether there was some girl in Germany wondering why her world had fallen apart.

"He just went," a sister said when Sally stepped around the screen. "I think it was peaceful. Poor soul, *he* was past doing us any harm." The lieutenant's face looked like a wax carving. Sally pulled the sheet up as the sister said, "I'll send the orderlies for him. We're run off our feet tonight. The Red Cross in Etaples, in its wisdom, has chosen to send us four more half-dead Germans to deal with, and we're full up already. I'll have to put one in this bed. I don't see why they can't keep them in France!" She bustled off, and Sally saw that more cots had been jammed into the end of the ward, and the VADs taking temperatures could barely get between them.

Sally went down the middle aisle to see if there was some way she could help—as if, she thought, irritated with herself, she could make it up to the poor dead lieutenant that way. But she stopped stock-still, her stomach turning over like a falling stone, when she saw the man in the last bed but one.

It was Juergen. His whole torso was heavily bandaged; she could see the bulky dressings through the thin broadcloth pajamas. He was thin, his face nearly skeletal, and he watched the VAD who was coming down his row with blank eyes.

Sally put her hand to her mouth and thought she was going to faint. She had pleaded to be sent to France on the thin, demented hope, admitted to no one, that she would somehow find Juergen there. But to find him here in England, when she had learned not to think of him every night . . .

He turned his head and looked straight at her, as if her thoughts had somehow spilled over him. His eyes widened, and the look of longing that leapt across his face made her heart sink.

She went to his bed. "I didn't know you were here," she said to him in German. The VAD could hear everything.

"I couldn't write," Juergen said. "But you knew that."

Sally nodded.

"Why are *you* here?" He looked puzzled.

"To help." Sally looked straight at him. "I was on the *Lusitania.*"

Juergen closed his eyes in misery. "I am glad I did not know that," he whispered.

"They gave the schoolchildren a holiday in Berlin," Sally said.

Juergen nodded.

"How were you wounded?"

"Machine-gun bullets," Juergen said. "On the Somme. Damage to the lungs. They sent me here. I am lucky to be an officer. The privates get less care."

"Are you in much pain?" Stupid question, only a fool would ask that, but she had to ask him something, had to talk somehow; it was like talking to something through the bars of a cage. Whose cage, she wasn't sure.

"I am supposed to live," Juergen said. "I have been told so."

"And your family?" *Kindly, polite, Lady Bountiful asking after the wounded,* she thought fleetingly.

"The girls are nurses," Juergen said. "Like you."

Sally stood by his bed. There was nowhere to sit. One of the VADs on duty looked at her curiously. "India is in France. Driving an ambulance."

"She would be good at it," Juergen said. "She is fearless. You have to be."

Sally's face crumpled. Tears slid down her cheeks. "Was it—horrible? They would have made you wait, wouldn't they, until the French and British wounded were taken in?"

"War is horrible," Juergen said bleakly. "This one has taken everything I had." He looked at her in such misery that Sally felt sick with it, sick with the grasp of things that wouldn't let go. She twisted one hand in the other to keep herself from reaching out for him, and Juergen's eyes followed the movement. He saw the ring, for the first time, she thought. "Is there . . . a man?" he asked. He sounded to Sally as if his mouth were full of broken glass.

"Robin Cochrane," Sally said. The tears wouldn't stop. "He's a cousin of India's. He lost a leg at Vimy Ridge. I'm going to marry him."

Juergen turned his head away from her and closed his eyes.

VIII

The Front

It wasn't long before the news was all over the hospital. All the sisters and VADs in the German ward spoke at least a little German, and rumors uncoiled at the ends of the grapevine. Matron was sympathetic; a few of the VADs who had known Robin before the war were spiteful. Sally found she could not function knowing that Juergen was there, on the other side of the house; yet going to see him was like walking on knives. She went stoically through her duties, not speaking to anyone who didn't speak to her first. Some of the girls cut her at the dinner table, and Matron let her cry on her ample shoulder. But the worst came when someone wrote an anonymous letter to Robin.

Robin called Babs. He was worried, and he couldn't get leave. Babs came to see her instead. Matron took them both into her office, and Sally burst into tears, this time on Babs's shoulder.

"I didn't know he was going to be here!" she wailed. "I never told Robin about him. We weren't ever engaged. He was just someone I fell in love with years ago, and it didn't work out."

"I should think not," Babs said. "Well, you can't stay here with him, that's certain. That's asking far too much of you."

"There is no place to send Captain von Appen," Matron said firmly. "Not until his wound is healed. Then he will be sent to a prisoner-of-war camp."

"You'd better come back to Copper Hill, then," Babs said.

"I can't just cut and run," Sally said. "They need me." *Juergen!*

"I think that would be best," Matron said. "I am sorry you have had to cope with this, and I know that some of the girls have not been kind. But I am afraid I cannot foresee that getting any better, and I do not have time to cope with a discipline problem."

Sally nodded. It was easy this way. They would make all the decisions for her. "I have to tell him that I am leaving."

"No," Matron said firmly. "I think it would be better if you did not."

So Sally went back to Copper Hill, and Babs managed to find enough for her to do so that she had no idle time for thinking. But this time it was even harder not to think, though she didn't tell Babs that. Babs was convinced that she had rescued her future sister-in-law from an embarrassing and awkward situation. A few rumors trailed Sally to Copper Hill, but Babs made it clear she wouldn't stand for that, and Robin's friends backed off.

The first night she was there, Sally had sat down and written a long letter to Robin, explaining all about Juergen and apologizing for not having told him. He had written back immediately, relieved that she was at Copper Hill. He was jealous, he said, but manfully attempting not to be, and after all, he should pity the poor fellow since Sally was going to marry someone else—himself.

At Christmas, Robin came home on twenty-four-hour leave, enfolded Sally in his arms, and promised her that everything was all right. In March he was sent to work in the War Office in London and came home exultant that he could see her almost every day. And he told her that Captain von Appen had been sent to a POW camp in France.

"I thought you would want to know, so I've been checking on him. It appears that he will live; I should feel a lout if he didn't. But he's safely out of England now, and you needn't be terrified he's going to pop out at you from behind any more corners."

Juergen! "I'm sorry, Robin," Sally whispered.

"It will be all right," he said. "And America is going to

come into the war any minute now—they should have known Wilson wouldn't stand for submarine attacks on neutral shipping. Then we'll get somewhere."

President Wilson had broken off relations with Germany in February over the threat to neutral shipping, and the Germans proceeded to sink American ships. The German secretary of state, who had apparently lost his mind, offered Mexico German help in taking back New Mexico, presumably to keep the Americans busy elsewhere. A clerk in the German legation in Mexico City was bribed, and the text appeared in American papers. On April 6, 1917, the United States declared war.

With that a curtain came down, obscuring any last faint hope. *Now we are enemies, Juergen. My country is going to fight yours.*

The United States had a great navy but virtually no army. Men had to be conscripted and trained, just as they had twenty years ago when the country went to war with Spain.

The Allies were in need of the Americans' help. The Russians had overthrown the czar and were fighting among themselves over what to do next. Under the French General Nivelle, the Allies attacked the German front again and again and gained only six hundred yards and slaughtered troops in the hundreds of thousands. The French Army began to mutiny. Pétain took over, began putting the pieces back together, and said, "We must wait for the Americans and the tanks."

Meanwhile, British shipping was losing ground. Only one in four that left port came home again. Lloyd George rammed the idea of convoys down the British admirals' throats, and the British began to sink submarines. Finally tanks came, in sufficient numbers to smash a four-mile hole in the German lines at Cambrai, but the infantry couldn't keep up with them, and the cavalry were easily blown to pieces by the German machine guns. Then the Americans began to arrive.

Mike wrote to Sally that Frank Blake, of all people, had joined the army.

Sally read the newspapers every morning, dutifully cheering for the Allied victories, and tried to envision married life with Robin. The vision wouldn't come. Her mind

stayed blank. When she tried to picture him across the
breakfast table from her, no one seemed to be there.

Meanwhile, he *was* there nearly every morning, asking
solicitously how she was doing and whether she was getting
enough rest. He still said that the women were the heroes.
On the days when he didn't spend the night at the War
Office, they chatted over tea, and all that Sally could feel was
that she had somehow been caught in one of her brother's
moving pictures. She was playing out a role that was only
make-believe, had no substance behind it. When the action
ended, she would look around and see that the scene ended,
too, in painted flats that went no farther than the camera's
eye. Behind them there would be nothing at all.

I loved him last year, she thought desperately. She
stared at the sapphire ring on her finger until she was cross-
eyed, trying to convince herself that it was real. She still
loved Robin—she knew that because she didn't want to hurt
him—but how could she marry him if every morning across
the breakfast table she would hope to see Juergen?

And how, she wrote desperately to India, who always
seemed to know how to do what she wanted, *do you jilt a
war hero with only one leg?*

You just do it, India wrote back brusquely. *Don't be
caught up in patriotic fervor.*

But that wasn't much help. India wasn't living with his
sister.

Everyone in America was caught up in patriotic fervor.
Having waited so long to get into the war, they were now
one-hundred-percent, red-blooded patriots, even the ones
who had disapproved. They had to be or risk having their
windows smashed. Woodrow Wilson had predicted as much,
and he seemed to know his people. Spy hysteria was ram-
pant. Everyone saw Germans under the bed. Government
posters urged citizens to report anyone "who spreads pessi-
mistic stories, divulges—or seeks—confidential military information, cries for peace, or belittles our efforts to win the
war." Names of such suspects were to be sent to the Department of Justice.

Rumors flew. Joseph Tumulty, the President's secretary,
was said to have been imprisoned as a German spy and shot.
Tumulty had to publicly proclaim his innocence and the fact

that he was still alive. Horses being shipped to France were said to have been infected with bacteria, and Mexican bandits were poised on the borders to invade Texas. A *New York Times* headline claimed "Red Cross Bandages Poisoned by Spies." Reaction ranged from the simply silly—school systems banned the teaching of German, sauerkraut became liberty cabbage, and dachshunds became liberty dogs—to the horrible—citizens with German names lost their jobs, some were tarred and feathered, and a young man with a German name was hanged in Illinois.

IWW members, including Big Bill Haywood, were arrested for attempting to cripple the national war effort by organizing workers and for speaking against the government. General Henry Blake braced himself for the public disgrace of having his son tried for treason. To everyone's surprise, Frank Blake, who was thirty-nine, eschewed his union's antiwar sentiments when he joined the army.

Frank wrote to India:

> *Father wrote me quite a stiff letter congratulating me on finally "becoming a man." Mother says I'm too old (a notion which occurred to me the second morning in cantonment) and that I could do a useful job here. Brother Peter is making aeroplane engines, as he predicted, for our side. Haywood says I've been co-opted by the government. I don't know quite why I did it except that it seems to be time to bring this bloody mess to an end, and it's becoming obvious that it won't be done without America. As it is, a whole generation of European men has been wiped out, and a whole generation of women will spend their lives alone as a result. I don't know what that will mean in the long run. In the meantime, I have become Father Superior to a platoon of farm boys, stock clerks, and youthful bank tellers, none of whom are more than twenty-five. All are eager to go and kill the Kaiser. From my jaundiced viewpoint, I wonder, of course, how many will come home again. In the meantime we learn rifle sighting and aiming, gas warfare, personal hygiene and care of the feet, military discipline, and how to darn socks, something I was*

already proficient at. We are supposed to be in
France in sixteen weeks.

There was no telling what the idea of war would do to
people, India thought, the idea of all that death. It provoked
people to fight and mate, as soon and as often as possible.
She thought about Sally and wrote her another letter, longer
this time, when she should have been catching the only sleep
she was going to get for a week, trying to explain that notion:
that things she thought she might want to do because there
was a war on might be things she would regret when the war
was over. Also, war made people do things because *other*
people thought they ought to. Sally wrote back to ask wistfully if that meant that she wasn't entitled to any sort of life at
all, if she couldn't trust her own instincts *or* anyone else's?

India decided that the subject had become hopelessly
garbled, and since she didn't trust her own instincts, either,
she felt completely inadequate to give further advice—she
had bobbed her own hair and was wearing trousers filched
from George. And in a fit of madness, on their last meeting,
she had told Ben Richardson she would marry him.

Ben always came without warning. Sometimes he would
spend his whole leave tracking her down from one post to
another and return to his squadron without seeing her at all.
But fates conspired, as he put it, in the spring of 1918 to land
them both in the same place at the same time, and India
slipped him into her quarters in the dark, grateful now for
Maida's absence. As the only female driver at the base post,
India had a luxuriously solitary lodging, with scavenged oil-
cloth on her packing-crate dressing table and a candle in a
china holder to supply light. The electricity in the drivers'
quarters had been out for weeks.

"We can all see in the dark by now anyway," India said.
She stood Ben in front of the candle and looked at him,
scrutinizing his face. He had transferred into the American
Air Service when the United States first got into the war, and
had spent some time at home training pilots. When they sent
him back to Europe, he was the grand old man of his squadron from the start, with twenty-seven kills to his credit from
his Flying Corps days. Now he was up to thirty-seven, and it
showed in his face, India thought, the responsibility for all
those deaths and maybe the knowledge that his own might

be no more than one slow reflex away. He didn't talk about that but instead seemed almost manic. He danced her around the candlelit shack and kissed her as if he were starving.

Only later, propped up on one elbow, squeezed beside India on her rickety cot—they had tipped it over once and landed on the floor in a tangle of howls and blankets—did he tell her that he had been to the funeral of Manfred von Richthofen, the Red Baron.

"A Canadian got him, the day before I came over," Ben said. "He didn't even know whom he'd shot down till they telephoned. Richthofen's plane went down near the trenches, and some Australians pulled him out. They gave him a funeral procession and an honor guard, and we all went over for it. They buried him at Betangles, and British headquarters sent a wreath. It was the oddest thing. Like a game almost. 'Our worthy foe.' They fired three volleys, and the bugler played 'The Last Post.'"

India thought about Sally's description of anti-German sentiments in her letters. The nurses at Deerfield wouldn't have felt that way about Richthofen, not when they had patched up the fliers he had shot down.

"What happened to Blake?" Ben said suddenly. "They were arresting Wobblies right and left when I was over there."

India chuckled. "He joined the army. I'm still not sure why."

"Have you seen him?"

"No," she said absently. She was still mulling over a military funeral for a German enemy who had shot down eighty of their own planes. "No, he hasn't shipped out yet."

Ben put his arms around her, her apparent lack of interest in Frank Blake seeming to please him. "I always thought you were too good for that guy. He isn't going to change his spots, you know."

"No," India admitted.

"Whereas, on the other hand, *I* am an excellent choice and will write a best-selling memoir of my flying days as soon as the war is over, and be able to support you in the style to which I know perfectly well you were at one point accustomed." He kissed her ear.

"Ben, what are you getting at?"

"I am getting at, since you seem to be over whatever was between you and Blake, who has a screw loose if you ask me, now would be an excellent time to get married."

India opened her eyes wide. "I didn't not marry you because of Frank."

"So you think," Ben said. "So you can marry me not because of him, too."

"I'm older than you are."

"I can count," Ben said. "You're very well preserved. And I myself am getting older daily." He tightened his grip on her. "India, honey, don't you think it's time you had a normal life like other people? I won't stop your painting. I'm proud of you. I won't even stop your gallivanting off to do good for the migrant worker, as long as it's not with Blake. Why shouldn't we get married?"

"I don't know," India said, though she was thinking, *There must be a reason.* But in bed with Ben by candlelight, safe for a few hours from the horrors outside, she didn't know what it was. Ben's body was urgent, nearly as urgent as his cajoling voice, and it was easy to give in to it, easy to take pleasure where she found it, easy to stave off war with the notion of a "normal life" afterward.

"Then we will," Ben said. "I'll scare up a padre on my next leave. Do you want a wedding dress?"

India started to laugh. "No! No, not unless you do."

"Wouldn't be caught dead in one. And I like you in trousers." Ben stroked her flanks.

"I thought maybe you'd be horrified by them," India said. "But they're so much easier to get about in. The blessés don't even realize I'm female half the time."

"Poor blessés," Ben said. He ran his hands over her breasts and nuzzled her bobbed hair. "I like you like this. Don't grow it out again."

It was a good sign if he felt that way, she thought; a fine sign.

So she was going to marry Ben. When he had gone back to his squadron, promising to show up in a month or so with a padre, she wondered if she had lost her mind. Some mornings the knowledge that she was going to marry Ben seemed to give a solid core to her existence: She knew what she would be doing after the war. On other mornings she felt herself flailing, as if she had flown into something's web and couldn't get out again. It was all very well to give Sally advice. What could she say to Ben when he came back? She didn't even have Juergen for an excuse. She must be going to marry him. She felt slightly dazed by that.

Frank wrote that he was shipping out at last, but his second letter from the front reached her before the first. He was a sergeant now, in charge of a machine gun. The Germans had mounted an offensive that had pushed the Allied lines back nearly to Paris, and huge numbers of reinforcements and supplies were flowing in.

India's unit was sent to Esquennoy just behind Montdidier, toward which the German attack was being directed. Driving in, she saw tanks for the first time and nearly went off the road staring at them. Here were turtle shells indeed, steel boxes with treads on them and mounted guns. They could batter down anything, from the looks of them.

The ambulances were housed in the empty end of a closed factory, the drivers quartered in tents pitched on the pockmarked grounds of a nearby park. That night the Germans bombed Breteuil and an aviation field a quarter-mile away, and India lay awake listening to the shell fragments from the antiaircraft barrage fall like rain in the nearby woods. The next day she and the other drivers sat on the stone wall of the park, waiting to be called out, and watched shells drop into Breteuil.

The aeroplanes were up again, bombing as soon as the shelling stopped. A formation that someone said was American fliers went up after them.

It was like watching hornets, India thought, horrified and exhilarated at the same time. They chased each other through the clear air. The German planes were painted in gaudily splendid colors, red and green and yellow and silver. The Flying Circus, the British called them, half sneering and half admiring. The sound of machine guns came harshly over the whine of the engines, and India put her hand to her mouth. A burst of fire came from an American aeroplane, and a green German Albatross turned nose down. Flames flared past the fusilage as it dropped. India saw a boiling cloud of flame as it hit the distant ground.

Two other German fliers converged on the American pilot, and they all wheeled in the sky, black now against the sun. There were cheers from the other observers on the park wall as the Germans took flight, the Americans on their tails. They could still hear the guns, but the aeroplanes were specks in the sky now.

The next day the drivers were called out. After her experience of the day before, India now watched the sky for aeroplanes with the caution of a mouse when owls are out. Shelling had been going on all day, and the ambulances crept in low gear past troop convoys, infantry, and terrified refugees fleeing the German advance. Her knuckles tightened on the wheel until she had to force herself to loosen them. All around them the bursts of antiaircraft fire kept up, punctuated by the dull boom of shells hitting and the screech as they went overhead. But she made it without incident to where the wounded were waiting.

On the way back she passed Victor Gerard on a motorcycle. He stopped and shouted to her that he had been sent to deliver orders to the regimental surgeons to pull back.

"It's bad!" he shouted.

The German advance went on for days. Three ambulance drivers were wounded and one killed, his car blown to bits. Through it all India stumbled blindly, slinking down dark roads with her load of blessés, hiding under trees when German aeroplanes were overhead. The pilots peppered the road with machine-gun fire every time an incautious driver turned his lights on. The Germans had a new kind of flare as well that lit up the whole countryside and exposed bombing targets. The night sky looked as if someone were turning electric lights on and off very fast. All India's nightmares about things that fell from the sky were a waking reality now, illuminated by a harsh red light.

It wasn't until two weeks later that she learned that Ben had fallen from the sky, too.

Victor Gerard told her, just before she would have seen it in the newspapers. Ben's plane had been hit and had gone down slowly, in a long glide that suddenly flipped nose over tail and crashed. A French farmhand had pulled him out of the wreckage and held him while he died. Victor gave her the Paris paper. All the fliers were heroes, larger than life. When a noted one died, it was news. India stared at the paragraph, full of French enthusiasm for Ben's exploits. Her stomach knotted up into a tight ball.

The next day the captain gave her three days' leave. She

stared at the slip of paper, with no notion of what to do with
it.

"Go to Paris," Victor said. "Get the hell out of here. You
haven't taken leave since I can remember. Go *away*, will
you? Take some time to mourn the poor man."

Numbly, India changed into the divided skirt she hadn't
worn in months and a clean uniform blouse. When was the
last time she had been to Paris? When she was seventeen,
with her mother and father. She had wanted to stay and
study art. Father had been appalled. What did it matter now?
she thought.

But when she got there, it was as if time had tilted,
sending all its contents colliding with each other. The pris-
tine Paris she remembered was battered now, shelled by a
gun mounted seventy-one miles away that everyone called
Big Bertha. She went, for no other reason than that she had
been there once, to a café where she had had tea with her
parents, but this time she saw shells come down on top of it
and a waitress die. Horrified—by what she had just wit-
nessed as well as the gradually solidifying reality that Ben
was dead—she stumbled through the streets, full of terrified
civilians and American troops.

She had no idea how long she had been walking when,
like an incongruous new episode in a shifting dream, she ran
into Frank. Literally ran into him, caroming into his chest as
everyone ran for the cellars.

She jerked her head up, staring at him as if he were an
apparition, and she didn't resist when he pulled her down
cement stairs into a wine merchant's cellar.

"Get in here. Tuck your arms over your head."

He looked as unlike himself as she could imagine, his
pale hair hidden under the broad-brimmed hat. His uniform
had sergeant's stripes on its khaki sleeves. India stayed
crouched beside him, and they were joined by the wine merchant—a morose-looking septuagenarian with a fluttering
gray mustache—two schoolboys, and a French *poilu* in put-
tees and horizon-blue uniform. When the bombardment
ceased, they all came blinking out into the sun.

Frank put an arm around India to steady her. "I've been
looking for you. Have you . . . heard about Richardson?"

"That's why they gave me leave," India said tightly.

"I didn't know," Frank said. "We're east of here, near

Verdun. When I heard he'd gone down, I pulled all sorts of scams to find out where you were and then came chasing you into Paris with a supply convoy."

"I was going to marry him." India looked at Frank, and she could feel her eyes well up with tears.

"Oh, God," he said. "Here. Come and we'll find a place to eat."

He took her to a restaurant with sidewalk tables, which had been stubbornly reoccupied as soon as the bombardment ceased, and led her inside so she wouldn't have to look at the sky. A waitress with a voluminous apron led them to a corner table and made a fuss over them.

"Now that you Americans have come, the pigs of Germans will be sorry!" She put a basket of hot bread on the table and beamed at them, assuming that they were a courting couple. "*My* fiancé, he is with Pétain."

"We'll have whatever is the house specialty," Frank said hastily.

It proved to be *boeuf bourguignon,* and they gobbled it, starved after months on front-line rations. India ate steadily, stolidly, not talking, and drank three glasses of the red wine that Frank ordered with it. He watched her silently.

Suddenly she jerked her head up, the realization that this was *Frank* sitting across from her hitting her for the first time. "Where have you been? Are you all right? Frank, *why* did you join up? You're too old for the draft." She grabbed his arm, fingers clenched on his sleeve.

"Not anymore," Frank said. "There's talk of upping the age to forty-five."

"My brother, Winslow, is working in a munitions plant," India said. "You could have done that."

"If I am going to blow someone up, I would prefer to do it personally, so that I am very clear on what I have done. And what's eating you, anyway—I thought you were steamed up to come out here and fight the Germans. I had the distinct impression you thought *I* ought to, too."

"That was—"

"Before Richardson got killed," Frank said. "Will you loosen your grip on my arm?"

India stared at her hand. She unclenched it and put it in her lap. "I should have congratulated you on making sergeant," she said, grasping for normal conversation. "With your background, I should have thought you'd have been an officer, though."

"My schooling and innate good breeding, not to mention my father's name, made that suggestion come up rather regularly," he said. "I turned down officer's training until they gave up."

"Why?" India swallowed the last of the wine in her glass and poured more from the bottle on the table.

"My covey of baby gunners, I suppose. Eighteen-year-old farm boys ready to go kill a Hun. They hadn't the foggiest idea of what they were getting themselves into. I couldn't see bailing out on them."

"Did it make any difference?" India muttered. "Did your being there keep them sane?"

"Maybe," Frank said. "I don't know. We're all scared to death all the time. But like I said, if I'm going to kill someone, I want my hands on the gun. I don't want the option of telling God it didn't count because it was at long distance."

"Ben said something like that," India said, tears choking her. "He said he'd rather shoot it out with another pilot or strafe a column than drop bombs. He said he'd make an exception for the gasworks, though. People working there were evil."

"We use gas ourselves." Frank sighed deeply. "It's just the latest horror."

India put her head down on her crossed arms on the table, the wineglass tilting dangerously.

"You've had dinner," Frank mumbled. "Maybe I ought to just let you drink dessert and put you to bed." He paid the tab, bought another bottle of wine, and tucked it under his arm. India stood up, less drunk than he had thought she was, but her face was twisted in pain.

"I have a room," she said. "In a *pension*. I caught a ride here with another driver. He dropped me off this morning, so I got a place first thing. I was very organized this morning."

"Well, you're a mess now," Frank said. "Do you remember how to get there?"

"You call a taxi. I'll give him the address." She stood like a cigar-store Indian and stared blankly at the crowd in the streets while Frank hailed one.

They climbed into a disreputable vehicle with tires that

looked about to disintegrate, and India stared at the upholstery while they jounced through Paris—rather too circu-
itously, Frank whispered, but he wasn't certain. The driver
made much of the "gallant Americans," so perhaps the roads
he said were bombed out really were, and it wasn't all a
matter of how large a fare he could stick to the gallant Americans.

Frank took her up to her room in the pension, which
had a chipped iron bedstead, painted white, and a thin hand-
pieced quilt over a rocklike mattress. A handful of bedraggled garden flowers in a water glass gave it an air of rakish
gaiety.

"When I was seventeen, this was the kind of room all
the art students lived in," India said. "My father was horrified, because it looked like heaven to me and I desperately
wanted to be one of them." She sat in the slat-backed rocker
beside the bed and pushed it with her foot.

"You're done up." Frank sat on the bed and picked up
her foot, unlacing her boot. "Here, give me the other. Why
were you going to marry Richardson?"

"He wanted me to," she said sadly.

"Plenty of people have wanted you to do things. You
aren't generally that malleable."

"It seemed like—" India spread her hands helplessly.
"Like a way to keep from going mad. A way to hold on to the
future."

"A future that might have been hell, if you'd both lived
to enjoy it. Did you think of that?"

India nodded, and tears streamed down her face, suddenly, silently. "After I said I would. But how could I tell
him that?"

"The poor chump was in love with you. I told you that
in California, remember?"

"Of course he was in love with me—why do you think
he wanted to marry me? Give me some more wine."

Frank produced a pocketknife with a corkscrew. "You'll
have to drink out of the bottle. It would be too depressing to
let those flowers die."

"I didn't love him, Frank!" India wailed. "Not like that.
I didn't love him. It's not fair!"

Frank popped the cork. "What's not fair? To you?"

"To Ben." India took the bottle and tipped it up, taking a

long swallow. "It's not fair not to have loved him." She sniffled and wiped her hand across her nose.

"It wouldn't have been fair if you'd married him," Frank said grimly.

"Do you think he knows?"

Frank looked dubious. "I think you're getting in over your head here."

She burst into tears again. She climbed out of the rocking chair and lay down on the bed beside Frank, burying her face in the pillow. "I feel awful! I feel rotten! Using Ben to pretend everything was going to be jolly after the war. Why didn't I cut him loose and let him find some nice girl? Now it's too late!"

"You've lost your marbles."

India sat up and looked at him, her face hot and slicked with tears.

"If you'd cut him loose, he wouldn't have had time to find a nice girl," Frank said gently. "And he'd still be dead."

"I can't bear it that he's dead!"

He handed her the bottle again, and she drank more. He drank some himself, a hefty swallow. "Of course you can't, honey. You aren't heartless. You cared about him or you wouldn't even have *thought* about marrying him. Is it that important to you, getting married?"

India scrubbed at her eyes with her fist, but the tears wouldn't stop. They just flowed, as if whatever valve should turn that faucet off was gone. "I never thought it was. But he wanted to, and he wanted me to go on painting, and I thought—"

Frank touched her cheek. "You thought you'd be like other people, huh, honey? Well, maybe you could have."

"I'll never know," India howled. She buried her face in her hands. "I'll never know, and I didn't love him, and it was wicked to do that when I didn't love Ben!" She sobbed harder, great choking, strangling sobs.

"You made him happy," Frank said.

"He got killed! They shot his plane down!"

"Because you didn't love him? Love is powerful, but I doubt that it's a shield against antiaircraft fire."

"Because I'm stupid!" India wailed. "Everything's gone to hell, and I must have done something to cause it!"

"You aren't stupid, but you sure are drunk," Frank said

gently with a tentative smile. "Honey, I'm sorry. It's rotten about Ben, but you didn't kill him by not loving him. You might have made him miserable later, you know. Is it that important to you to get married? If you want it that bad, I suppose *I* could marry you."

Was this Frank talking? Was this how she had agreed to marry Ben, on a high charge of emotion?

"If love's what's important, I can give you that," he went on. "I'd be a rotten husband, but I'd love you."

"No," India sobbed, her shoulders shaking with knotted-up misery. "Half the time after I'd said I would, I was desperate, trying to think of a way out of it, trying to figure out how not to. And then he got killed. I have to write to Sally." She looked around as if trying to find a pen and paper. "I have to tell her not to do it. She can't marry Robin if she doesn't want him—she may make something happen to him!" India's dark eyes were frantic now, and she clutched Frank's hand as if he were Sally, or as if he could give her the message.

Frank detached his hand and clasped India's with it instead. He pulled her against him. "You are not responsible," he said fiercely into her ear. "You did not shoot that plane down."

India collapsed against his chest, still sobbing, the sound thin and sad.

"You didn't do it," he said again. She was knotted into a ball against him, and he pulled at her knees, trying to straighten her out. "Lie down, damn it. You need to sleep."

He managed to lie down himself, and she stretched out with a sudden sigh, still plastered against his chest. "Sleep," he said into her hair. "Sleep while you can."

IX

Armistice

In the summer the German offensive waned, battered by the same forces that had always frustrated the Allied advances. Land once taken could not be held; enemy lines once broken could not be held open. But this time when the Allies advanced, the Americans were behind them, and the Germans began to fall back. British tanks overran the Hindenburg line. There began to be talk of an armistice. Neither side believed the war could be won outright. Germany started to negotiate.

In the trenches there was very little difference to be noticed. The war to end war, to make the world safe for democracy, continued to blow human lives to hell. As the Allies advanced, the stretcher carriers and ambulance drivers went with them. India found herself driving her vehicle through a no-man's-land as desolate as a plague city must have seemed when the Black Death ate its way across the countryside. For fifteen miles the terrain was blasted with shell holes, water-filled gun emplacements, blackened tree stumps, and demolished concrete blockhouses. Dead and decaying horses lined the single road that snaked through the nightmare. Slogging along it was a convoy of mud-covered men and wagons and artillery. Wagons mired at every step, and India felt her car's tires sinking in the muck. Rain drizzled around them, not enough to put out the hellish glow of a burning munitions dump to the east.

Just before dawn the *saucisses*, the sausage-shaped ob-

servation balloons, went up, and the Belgian and British batteries began to lay down a barrage to clear the way for the
troops who were to attack at dawn. The blue-gray horizon
burned like the Fourth of July in hell, with red, white, and
green star shells that screamed through the air with their
passing. As the convoy bogged deeper in the mud, India's
unit huddled for protection from stray shells in an abri,
where they found the nalf-buried leg of a German soldier.
George House flung it away with a bellow of disgust, and it
lay sinking again into the mud outside.

India huddled inside the abri and closed her eyes. They
had had no sleep yesterday, and the supposed rest days before that had been occupied with working on their cars, trying to keep them running on makeshift parts and bad
gasoline.

She was actually sleeping when the shout came that the
shelling had passed them by and the convoy was moving
again.

But as the convoy straggled on, three German planes—
which had begun to fly in daylight now, desperate to strike at
the advancing Allied lines—approached to bomb and strafe
the road. India flung herself from the ambulance and dove
under it, listening as the British planes went up to meet
them. Their battle filled the sky with a roar of engines, joined
moments later by the spatter of a line of machine-gun bullets
along the road.

India pulled herself under farther. Was this how it had
been for Ben? But Ben would have been in the air, fighting
back, not pinned under a car. Again the urge to *fight* them, to
kill them herself, washed over her.

When the aeroplanes had gone—out of ammunition or
driven off, she was not sure—she crawled out and took the
wheel again. The countryside was littered with human
corpses and abandoned German artillery, stuck in the mud.
India gritted her teeth and tried not to wince when shells
screamed overhead. They were landing well away from the
convoy, the Germans shooting back at the British and Belgian artillery. A saucisse went down, collapsing like a bag.

At last the convoy crossed the dreadful empty land and
came again to roads through woods and deserted towns,
where some semblance of houses still stood. As a wagon a
hundred yards ahead of her rolled through a crossroads, it

separated into pieces with a sickening *whump,* and a cloud of dust and flame rose into the air. India could feel the shock wave tremble through her car and slew it sideways in the road. The convoy milled in confusion, and someone shouted curses at the engineers who had missed the mine. The line of cars and wagons veered around it, while the stretcher bearers picked up the injured and put them into an ambulance that had been called from the line. Nearby in the infantry column, four men were dead as well as the wagon driver, and six more wounded by the *éclat* from the mine.

India pulled her ambulance around the hole, which was deep enough to bury a two-story house. She tensed, waiting to feel the dismembering fury of another mine. Nothing exploded. The convoy drove out of the village onto a slightly better road, and India tightened her shaking hands on the steering wheel. Frank had gone back to his gun crew near Verdun. Was he in this advance? she wondered. Was he even still alive? Would she know if he wasn't? The morning after she had sobbed in her drunken misery over Ben, she had wakened to find herself still dressed, cradled in Frank's arms on the bed. The buttons on his uniform tunic had left an imprint on her cheek. She touched it now as if it might still be there.

India's post and billet were in a bakery that somehow, miraculously, was still functioning. She went to sleep with the smell of fresh bread in her head, and half a loaf of it in her stomach, and woke at two A.M. with orders to evacuate three couchés and an assis with a shattered arm. The road was still a sea of mire and shell holes, and the wounded moaned and shrieked every time the ambulance dropped a wheel into one. Columns of men still passed her in the night, and at nearly every mile India had to ask them to help her heave the ambulance out of a hole. The assis, an English Tommy with a Cockney accent, climbed out each time to lighten the load, but they usually had to take the couchés out, too. She wasn't sure Tommy was right in the head, but they carried on a conversation of sorts as they drove through the night. He called her luv and she called him Tommy, and he told her about his "missus" and little girl in London.

"She's got red hair like her old man," Tommy said. "Like a regular flame. You can't see it under the mud and the tin hat, but when I was in civvies I used to fair light up the sky. You got any little uns?"

"No," India said. "No chick nor child. Would I be out here?"

"Dunno what you Yanks might do, women or men. You're all a little crazy, aren't ya. Lord, I hate these tin hats, like bein' in a bleedin' can, they are."

"They keep your brains dry," she said. Tommy was wavering on the edge of coherence. How long could a body stay sane with half an arm blown off?

A shell screamed overhead, and India looked around wildly. A burst of flame and rubble shot up like a geyser to their left.

"Jerry doesn't want us using his leavings," Tommy said.

The shells fell around an abandoned pillbox that the British had taken over. The Germans had deliberately built them with thinner walls to the rear so that if captured, they would not be as impregnable to German fire as to the enemy's. But this one was holding.

"It'll take a direct hit to smash that," Tommy said as they lumbered by. India gave the ambulance as much gas as she dared, the gearbox protesting her attempts to shove the wheels through the clinging mud. They could stop and take shelter in the pillbox, she thought, but that was the target.

The shells rained down around them, screaming as they fell. A couché in the back cried out as one went overhead. Then the landscape was lit up in a red blaze of light.

"'Strewth!" Tommy said.

The ground erupted in front of them, shooting rock and flame into the air. India felt its heat and the slam of the explosion, blowing her body back against the seat of the car. The wheel wrenched itself from her hands, and something thudded into her legs. She heard the couché scream again.

She woke in a fever dream of pain and terror. A face in a driver's uniform and tin hat swam in front of her and vanished again. She was moving upward, lifted. The sky was on fire, the flames burning holes in the night until nothing was left but blackness. She could still hear the couché screaming.

The next time she woke she screamed herself, her voice rising as the car jolted into a pothole and her right leg exploded with pain. She fell backwards into darkness, clung to it, tried to fold it around her, but with each jolt was wrenched back into consciousness. The roar in her head blotted out the thunder of the guns. Only the voice of the wounded man in the back of her ambulance could get through the sound.

She woke again, still this time, with a face peering at her from under a Red Cross cap and veil. A hand reached out and smoothed a cold cloth across her forehead. "She's awake, Sister," a voice said.

Sister looked down at her. Slowly, India brought her into focus. Somewhere she could still hear the scream. "My blessés—" she tried to say. It came out a barely intelligible slur.

"You're at Étaples," the sister said. "They sent you on here to us. Do you remember the evacuation hospital?"

"No." India tried, but she couldn't remember that part. "My blessés," she said again.

"I don't know," Sister said. "They pulled you out of a smashed ambulance. One man came in with you, a Brit with a mangled arm." The sister was Australian, with a ruddy face and a no-nonsense look about her. "You worry about yourself for now. You did all you could for those poor men. Your ambulance took nearly a direct hit."

"My leg hurts," India said. It was the first thing to penetrate her consciousness, that pain. Appalling pain.

"I'll get you something for the pain," Sister said. "But the leg's in a bad way. You're going to need more surgery. Do you think you can stand up to that?"

India gritted her teeth. "I can stand up to what I have to." She looked at the sister with sudden panic. "They're not going to take my leg off!"

"You'll have to talk to Doctor about that," the sister said soothingly. "Let Miss Evans get your temperature, and then we want you to rest." The VAD appeared again with a thermometer.

"I want to see the doctor!" India looked around her wildly. "And why are those screens up?" She knew what screens around a bed meant.

"To give you some privacy," Sister said. "We don't have room here for a ward just for women."

"Oh."

The VAD read her temperature and inscribed it on a chart. Sister gave her a white pill and a glass of water. No amount of pleading produced the doctor, and when the white pill took effect, India slipped into the darkness again. It carried her like a stretcher. No more potholes. Blessed stillness.

When she woke, the doctor was there, a little man, balding and precise, with an Oxford accent—the antithesis of Tommy's. India opened her eyes and said, "You aren't going to take my leg off."

"You've lost a great deal of blood," the doctor said. "The leg is infected. It may poison your whole system. The dressings will have to be changed three times a day, and it will hurt like the devil. Even if we do save it, you will have a bad limp." He didn't have time to mince words.

"Try," India said. Her eyes squeezed shut and tears ran out. "Please."

The doctor sighed, as if he must hear the same argument daily from fools who would rather die than lose a limb. "Let's have the dressing off, Sister, and we'll look."

It hurt, hurt horribly like flame or red-hot pincers. India bit down hard on a corner of the sheet while the VAD held her hand. When they were done, she was shaking, empty as a glass that had been upended.

"You may hold your own," the doctor said. "We'll see. Sister, that leg is to be re-dressed at each shift." India closed her eyes, her stomach heaving at the thought, but she didn't say anything.

For a week she wavered between consciousness and blackness, rousing with the pain of the dressings being changed and sinking afterward into Sister's white pills. Tommy came to see her once, his pajama sleeve pinned up over an amputated arm. None of the other blessés had made it, he said.

He clucked his tongue. "You let the surgeon take that leg off, luv. There'll be lots of us after this war. You won't be alone."

India shook her head.

Tommy shook his, too. "They're sendin' me to England tomorrow. An arm's a small price to pay for goin' home."

Home. A letter came from India's mother, frantic with worry and grief. India's brother, Winslow, had been killed in an explosion in his munitions plant. Everyone suspected

German saboteurs. Winslow, who had never gone to war, dead of the war anyway, from German saboteurs or just American mistakes. He'd been such a good boy, her mother wrote. He'd kept a journal, and now she read it every night along with her Bible. . . .

India thought about him while she slipped between consciousness and dream, like walking between two rooms. A lot of people were there: Ben, Winslow, Roger Stiller . . . Tommy and Frank, and the couché who kept screaming. He was still in one of those rooms, but India never quite saw him. He was a wraith at the edge of her vision. Where was she going? *Please, don't let me pace between these two rooms forever.*

Sometimes she thought of letting them take her leg just to get out. What did God do about amputated legs if you rose in your body at the Resurrection? And what of Winslow, torn in pieces, all his separate selves thrown to the air? She supposed God had a plan. The padre who came and tried to pray with her sometimes assured her that He did. But she was too tired to pray, and it wasn't the Resurrection that was on her mind. "I don't care what you do with me when I die," she said fretfully. "I want both legs now." She saw the war as an animal, eating parts of people.

The doctor never said anything encouraging during the agony of changing the dressings. After the second week it seemed to India that it hurt marginally less, if pain could be measured against itself. After the third week, the doctor said, finally, "I hope you knew what you were asking for, Miss Blackstone. It appears that you are going to keep your leg. But it will pain you the rest of your life."

"So will a lot of things." India closed her eyes and saw a plane lifting into the sky, coming down in flames, and her brother hurled upward unprotected, arcing like a thrown toy among the star shells.

Consciousness prevailed, slowly closing the other room. India had time to think. Too much time, she thought at first. Then it began to seem like a canvas given her to order the contents of that inner room before it was locked away forever. It might fester, she thought, if she did not. So she tried to think what might come next, how it might be pulled from the jumble, the rat's nest that the past had made. And to wonder how many other rooms her life might have, into which she had not yet ventured. She had once suggested laughingly to Sally that there might be themes, compartments to keep her separate selves safe from each other. What would happen if they met?

At first all that would come to her was what she did *not* want again: death, loss, to be taken in by men, to damage them in return. Then something more specific took shape: She did not want any more of the Blackstone Girl. That image belonged to the years before the war, to coming-out parties and long taffeta petticoats, to corsets and hair that hung past her waist, to a time when men were protection and a good woman didn't need the vote. The Blackstone Girl was gone, blown up by shells, cracked from her egg by machine guns, left bobbed-haired and bewildered, metamorphosed into something that wouldn't suit such an airy style.

What *did* she want? India asked herself. Something more definite, more serious, some vision of art to risk her livelihood for . . . to see if she could paint to suit herself. No more fashion dolls. And for Frank to come out whole, she thought, not blown into terror, scattered on the wind like her brother.

She wanted that.

There would be an armistice—everyone knew it—but still it made no difference in the trenches. Turkey and Austria-Hungary got out of the war, and the Ottoman Empire and the Hapsburg Empire vanished. The Germans and the Allies went on shooting at each other as if they were automated, mechanical death set in motion that no one could stop until the bell rang.

At Copper Hill, Sally got a telegram from Oregon. Her father had had a heart attack and was barely holding on. *Don't come*, her mother wired. *It's too dangerous*. Another telegram followed to say that he had died. Again her mother wired: *Don't come*.

Robin was summoned home from the War Office the next day, and she bounded into his arms, sobbing. He held her tightly and said, "I'm so sorry. So sorry I couldn't have known him."

"*Daddy!*" Sally wept into his coat. She went to bed that night with a shot of whiskey in milk and lay awake staring at the roses in the wallpaper, prewar roses twining sinuously on vinelike stems, roses from when the world had been sane. No one could blame the Germans for Toby's death, but it seemed a part and parcel of the war to her: loss, endless loss.

What was left now? Mother was at the Madrona, where there would be lots of mopping-up to do after the war, but she had a foreman for that. Sally was supposed to be going to London to live with Robin after the war. She would find endless work to be done there. But was that all she had to look forward to, cleaning up other people's messes? Didn't she have a right to make her own, get knee-deep in the mud of them just for the joy of living? There wouldn't be any joy with Robin, just comfort and stability and love of a sort. She had convinced herself to ask Toby what she should do, but now he was gone. *Daddy!* She howled the name the way she had howled for Juergen.

Robin and Babs were solicitous, endlessly. They made plans for Robin to take Sally home as soon as the armistice was signed, and then to bring her mother to London for the wedding. A year's mourning was considered proper, but after the years of war even Sally's mother wrote that she mustn't postpone the wedding; Toby wouldn't have wanted that. *You must go on and be happy now, my darling,* Alexandra wrote. *Your father and I had our love. You must have yours.*

On Armistice Day, Sally told Robin she couldn't marry him. She told him in the middle of all the bells ringing and the champagne and the kissing in the street, because suddenly she knew, and it didn't seem right to let him celebrate and then tell him.

Robin closed his eyes for a moment. "Is it that German fellow, von Appen?"

"I don't even know where he is," Sally said. She didn't say it wasn't.

"He'll be repatriated." Robin's voice was tight, under control. "If that matters to you."

"I'm sorry, Robin." Sally looked at his stoic face, immobile, like a plane of granite. "It would be horrid, for both of us. Marriage isn't a mistake you can undo. I have to undo it now, before it's too late. You have to find someone who'll make you happy."

"That was you." It was the closest he came to pleading.

"I wouldn't have." No one could hear them in all the noise. The convalescents on the next ward were singing

"God Save the King" and "Yankee Doodle" and "Waltzing Matilda" at the tops of their voices, and the nurses were shrieking and crying. Babs had gone to the cellar to root out the last few bottles of hoarded wine, and the VADs were scouting up enough glasses to go around.

"What will you do now?" Robin asked grimly.

"I don't know," she said. "I can't fathom what to do now. I think I have to go home."

"You might stay long enough to be certain of what you're doing," Robin said. "We don't have to tell Babs yet."

"Oh, I have to tell Babs!" Sally was horrified.

"It will make me look like a damn fool."

"It will make me look like the fool," Sally said sadly. "No woman in her right mind would pass you up. I know that."

So she told Babs, because how could she go on staying there if she didn't? Babs was somewhat less stoic than Robin and snapped, "You've lost your mind!" but after that, she was pleasant and encouraged Sally to stay until she was certain, until she knew what she really wanted to do. After all, Robin still wanted her, and to Babs's way of thinking, if Robin wanted her, then he should have her.

Plenty of Babs's friends were not nearly so charitable. The talk of Juergen surfaced again. Sally caught Babs looking through the stack of letters that Sally put out for the post. It didn't take more than a few days for her to know that she had to leave. She had to go home to her mother anyway. That made it a little easier. But the engagement had been announced, and to everyone who asked her when she was coming back, and was Robin going with her, there was the awkward, stilted explanation that they had decided not to get married after all. Robin said noncommittally that he wanted to give Sally time to think. Everyone who looked at his face translated that easily as "she jilted him." In the gossip that circulated so easily through their set, three women accused her of being a German sympathizer and cut her to her face. Robin was white with anger.

Sally packed her clothes, all the things she had bought in London three and a half years ago to replace her drowned trunks, and fled on the first ship to sail after the Armistice, a guilty conscience baying behind her.

                    *   *   *

Frank had survived. He found India at Étaples and told her he was being demobilized. There would be an army of occupation, but that was for the professionals. He looked tight about the mouth and said they had given him an award but that it didn't make up for the loss of two of his crew.

India sat up. "Hand me my wrapper. They're letting me walk some. You can help me."

He handed her the bathrobe—made for a man and donated by some Red Cross committee in the States—and steadied her while she put it on. They walked out of the ward and into the hall, India gritting her teeth. She leaned heavily on his arm.

"How much does it hurt?" Frank asked her.

"A lot. Not as much as it did. I have to walk on it. If I don't, I'll lose it, I know I will. They tried to take it off already."

"I'm glad you didn't let them. I needed someone I knew to survive whole," Frank said.

"Me, too." India tightened her grip on his arm, not so much for balance as for the reassurance that he was still there, solid under her hand. "We used to find dead Germans in machine-gun nests," she said. "Just pieces of them! Oh, God. I always thought of you and then tried to wipe the thought out in case it was a jinx. In case it was catching, you know."

"I know," he said softly.

"I brought you something," Frank said when he came the next day, just before he shipped out. It was a silver-headed cane, old by the look of it and lovingly polished.

"Where did you get it?"

"In a shop. I don't know whose it was. I imagine it has a story, but in these days I don't want to know it. It's new to you. I thought it might be more dashing than the hospital ones, when you're ready for it."

India ran her hand along the chased silver head, adjusting the picture she had of herself to become someone who would need a cane. How much more clearly Frank saw her sometimes than she could see herself.

She looked at him, looked through into the hidden mental room that he had left, where his dead crewmen were, and realized that that acuity of vision worked both ways.

Frank wasn't whole, either, and she didn't know what kind of cane it would take to make him so. She hobbled to him, putting her weight on his gift, and kissed him, leaning her other hand against the dismal khaki of his shirt. She felt his arm tighten around her, and the cheek he pressed against hers was damp with tears.

PART THREE

1919–1929

X

David

Sally Holt, Frank Blake, and India Blackstone went home to the States to find that plague had visited there, too. The influenza epidemic of 1918 had killed between four and five hundred thousand people, more than had died in the war. And strange shifts were taking place in the social landscape of the nation. Its way of life was about to be blown to smithereens by some very big guns. Liquor was about to become illegal, and criminal sources of supply were already happily presenting themselves to customers who felt they had, by God, earned a drink these last few years. Congress had passed another amendment to the Constitution, giving women the right to vote. It was making its way through the ratification process among the states, but it was clear that the women who had fought the war had earned that. They had scrimped, saved, done without, nursed, collected peach pits for gas masks, and done their sons' and husbands' jobs in their absence. They had earned a say in whether their country went to war again.

"This was the war to end war," Sally said to Frank. They had brought India to a show at a Fifth Avenue gallery, because she was supposed to exercise her leg and was inclined to forget that when it hurt. "I couldn't bear another one. Neither could any woman I know."

"Have you found where Juergen was sent yet?" he asked softly. India noticed that he didn't bother expressing his private opinion that as a species humans hadn't learned enough to prevent wars and probably weren't going to.

Sally shook her head, one tight motion with more hopelessness than India had seen from her before. "Let's look at the pictures," she said.

India and Sally had taken their old apartments, sublet during the war, and had them turned out with bleach and carbolic in the mop water. Frank was staying with Mike and Eden, but he was leaving the next day for Chicago to work on appeals for the IWW members still in jail. The war hadn't changed any of Frank's convictions, India thought. He could fight the Germans and then come home and fight his own government.

Sally seemed to relax and enjoy the show after Frank stopped asking her about Juergen. Frank regarded the abstracts with a raised eyebrow. India had to admit that she was glad they had dragged her from her apartment, since there were many interesting people from the art world here that she wanted to meet. Among them was a dark, thin, aquiline woman named Georgia O'Keeffe, who had had a one-woman show at Alfred Stieglitz's gallery and was said to be his lover. She was younger than India, but something in her face mirrored the passionate intensity India felt at her easel.

Or it mirrored the way she *used* to feel, India thought, that summer in New Mexico with Mike and Eden and Frank, before she had come to New York. The summer she was nineteen and had painted from morning to night and had fallen in love with Frank.

"You paint," the aquiline woman said to her after their introduction. "Alfred's told me about you. You're the one who gave Roger Stiller hell."

"For all the good it did me," India said. "I let myself get sidetracked anyway," she added suddenly, but the bitterness she had expected the words to carry somehow didn't stick to them.

"Oh, you can get back on track," Georgia O'Keeffe said airily, as if she had never found it a problem.

And how many years' difference between us is there? India thought, but all the same something knotted inside her seemed to loosen itself, to uncoil. "I've been in France," she said. "I drove an ambulance."

"Well, *that* ought to give you something useful to work

with," O'Keeffe commented. Then she drifted off, screwing up her eyes to stare at the exhibit. India looked after her thoughtfully.

When Frank and Sally took her home, she pushed them out the door, refusing so much as to feed them. She took off the "respectable" dress she had just purchased and tied an apron over an old one. While she had been in France, India had discovered, the Blackstone Girl had been selling prints almost on her own. There was money. It wouldn't last forever—print sales were dropping sharply because the postwar girl wanted a new model—but India thought it might keep her for a year. It was time enough to see if anyone would buy her heart's blood and not her potboilers, to see if she could still make anyone want to.

She thought about what O'Keeffe had said, and it made her think of the people and events she had ordered in that inner room while she was convalescing, stacking them neatly, telling them to wait. She began to take them out now, to consider them in paint. She sat on a stool, to spare her leg, and experimented with pillows.

Two days later Frank let himself in and said, "There's a milk bottle on your stoop turning into cheese. Sally thinks you're dead. You're not answering the telephone."

"I didn't hear it," India said vaguely. She focused on Frank and gave him a sudden grin.

When Frank saw what was on her canvas, he whistled. The couché she had heard so clearly the night she was injured rested among the star shells, supine on the night sky. Below him the aircraft buzzed like dragonflies, bright emblems on their wings. It was exhilarating and beautiful, Frank said, and it made his skin crawl. She turned back to her canvas, and she wasn't even sure when he let himself out.

But the money didn't last, not the way she had thought it would. It was too easy to go out to eat and not take the time to cook. It was too easy to buy paint—the oils she hadn't worked with in so long, a beautiful array of colors, the best ones hellishly expensive. "What do you spend your money on?" Sally would demand, looking around the apartment and inspecting India's clothes. India would point to her paint and canvas.

She had to sell something, but when she took her canvases to the galleries, no one was willing to exhibit them. It took a month or two to think of Roger Stiller.

"The Oriole Gallery as good as told me it's because of Roger," she said between clenched teeth to Mabel Dodge. Mabel was still holding court, although restlessly. Everyone seemed restless now that the war was over.

"He's told them no one from his school will show there if they show me," India told Mabel. "*School!* The Stiller *School!* Roger Stiller an artistic buffoon! What a thing to come home to."

"It sounds as if you need either a lawyer or a very discreet assassin," a masculine voice said with a chuckle. "I'd be happy to provide you with the name of either. Frankly, I think Stiller's work is rot."

"You don't know anything about art, Jerry," Mabel said, and India turned to find a dark-haired man in a tuxedo smiling at her over a whiskey glass—not illegal yet, but everyone India knew was drinking like a fish because it soon would be. He had sleek black hair and heavy bones that gave him the look of being even taller than he was. His eyes were green, a color that India had always found interesting. He was far and away the handsomest man she had ever seen.

"This is Jerry Rhodes," Mabel said. "He makes money hand over fist on Wall Street stealing from widows and orphans."

"Only from the well-off ones," Jerry Rhodes said. "You're Miss Blackstone. I know because someone pointed you out to me. I am a great admirer of the Blackstone Girl."

"Mabel's right," India said with a grin. "You don't know anything about art. I have driven a stake through the Blackstone Girl's heart like Mr. Stoker's hero and am trying to move on."

"I think that's a great pity," Jerry said. "But I'd like to see what you've moved on to all the same."

So India showed him, and somehow, in the weeks that followed, she found herself spending more and more of her time with Jerry Rhodes. Certainly it was a luxury to be taken out by a man who fed her steak and didn't expect her to pay for half the dinner. He said, apparently truthfully, that he found the silver-headed cane distinguished. She took some more of her hoarded money and bought a new dress, gold cloth and black velvet with a draped skirt, and gold kid slippers to go with it. As Sally pointed out, she didn't have anything to wear to the kind of places Jerry was taking her. To her surprise, India rather enjoyed that dress. She felt elegant in it. *I'm nearly forty,* she thought, staring into the mirror before she put it on. *Well, nearly thirty-nine.* Her birthday would come in a few weeks, and *then* she would be nearly forty. Nothing sagged yet, but the sight of her narrow waist under the silk shimmy made her think abruptly of the babies in their carriages that she passed in the park every Sunday. Babies had never occurred to her before; now they seemed to comprise half the population of New York. She had never particularly wanted one until recently, when they had started to invade her dreams and occasionally creep into her paintings.

Jerry seemed to like her work. He introduced her everywhere as "Miss Blackstone, the artist." The remark about the assassin had been a joke, but he did take her to his lawyer and instructed him to threaten Roger Stiller with a lawsuit. (India privately suspected that Jerry could have arranged the assassin, too, had he wanted to.) Not long after the lawyer came into it, a gallery took three of her new paintings and sold one. The critics were supercilious about "a former illustrator of popular fiction," but the collector who bought the painting had a reputation for backing winners.

Sally threw her a party to celebrate the sale and India's thirty-ninth birthday. Frank was still in town, although it seemed to Sally that she rarely saw him since India had begun to go about with Jerry Rhodes. Sally was never sure what went on with Frank and India, but she invited Frank to the party, and he came, carrying a gaudily painted green and scarlet wooden dog, about a foot high, that he said was a footstool. It appeared to be snarling, but the painted white teeth and beady eyes looked very cheerful. It was Guatemalan, Frank said.

India propped her aching leg on it and chuckled at the effect.

"You can use him to frighten door-to-door salesmen," Frank said. He was his usual talkative, irreverent self, but it struck Sally that he seemed to be behaving oddly. *Well, none of us came out of the war the same as we went in,* she thought.

India certainly hadn't. Sally watched as she unwrapped primrose paper from Jerry's offering. Even the way she sat let you know that her leg hurt. India didn't mention it often, but Sally knew it hurt all the time. On either side of India's mouth were two lines that hadn't been there before. She had gray hairs, too, just a few strands or so, but they showed in her black hair.

"I'm afraid I wasn't as imaginative as Mr. Blake," Jerry murmured as India took the lid off a little blue box.

India sucked in her breath as she lifted the cotton inside the box. Under it was a white gold pin set with a sapphire: a delicate, fluid filigree like an exotic flower. "Oh, Jerry!" The words came out with the exhaled breath, a rush of surprise and delight.

He was watching her carefully, Sally noticed, and he seemed satisfied. "I wasn't sure what you might like," he said. "I won't be insulted if it doesn't suit you and you want to choose something different."

"Never!" India said. She pinned the brooch to her new black and gold dress and peered down, trying to admire the effect.

"Look in the mirror," Jerry laughed. "You're making yourself cross-eyed."

Frank raised an eyebrow at the sapphire, which was plainly enormously expensive, but he didn't say anything, and Sally took that as a good sign. Frank had opinions on what he called the conspicuous display of wealth in the form of shiny stones. When he chose to withhold such thoughts, it was generally for tact's sake. A display of tact just now argued that he had no plans to get in the way of whatever might be going on with Jerry Rhodes.

India picked up Sally's present from the table beside her. At her feet was a discarded heap of pink and yellow papers and gaudy ribbons, frothing like sea foam around Frank's Guatemalan dog. "You'll spoil me, sweetie," she said. "You're supposed to do this next year when I can truly claim to be decrepit. Thirty-nine is such a silly age. No one believes you, anyway."

"Especially when you've been thirty-nine for three or four years," Jerry chuckled. "I had an aunt who stayed thirty-nine for five years. I think it may have been a record."

"Even if you *are* thirty-nine, no one believes you," India

said. "They sort of *smile*. Maybe I'll just be thirty-eight again this year, and forty next year." She stuck a fingernail under the knotted ribbon.

"Chronological limbo," Mike Holt said. "Adrift in time."

"What Mother used to call a woman of a certain age," Sally said. "I always wondered why they said that when they meant a highly *un*certain age."

"While men, on the other hand, are held to improve with age," Frank said. "Most unfair."

"Oh, I don't know," India said sweetly. "Then they have to live up to it."

"True." Jerry sighed elaborately. "Dear lady, we are no less vain than your sex. We are simply forbidden to mention it. We must take pride in accomplishment instead, while we view the departure of our hair with equanimity."

"But do you?" India demanded.

"It hasn't departed yet, thank goodness," Jerry said. But Sally saw him sneak a furtive look in the sideboard mirror. "I will consult my psyche and report to you when it does."

"I think the 'thank goodness' is his answer," Sally said. "No one wants to get older. Especially when—" She broke off, her face clouded, and busied herself at the sideboard with a bottle of champagne, keeping her back to them.

"Here, let me do that." Frank took the bottle from her and put a napkin around the cork. "When we have to count up all the things we meant to have done in life and haven't," he said smoothly.

"Heavens, yes," Eden said. "There's learning to crochet. And going to Italy . . ."

"There's getting married," Sally said grimly. "You might as well let the brick fall. I dropped it myself. I had the misfortune to fall in love with a man from Germany," she said to Jerry. "It rather spoiled my plans for life."

"A woman as beautiful as you could find a husband at any time of life," Jerry said gallantly. "Should you feel the need. I am speaking hypothetically, of course. I never married either, but not for nearly so good a reason as yours. Inertia, I suppose. And then the war." Jerry had sailed all his life; he had earned a commission in the navy, but no adventure had befallen him there, or so he claimed. He glanced down at India and said in an affectionate voice, "Possibly it's time I rectified that."

India paused, startled, her fingers tangled in the gold ribbon on Sally's present. It seemed to have snarled about them deliberately, holding her to the echo of his words. *She hasn't known him but three months*, Sally thought as she handed India the scissors.

The echo didn't quite fall away from the gathering with the ribbon. It seemed to buzz in the room as India opened the flat box from Sally and found a tortoiseshell dresser set and two dozen monogrammed handkerchiefs, lace-edged. India laughed delightedly, as if to set aside any unease. "They won't see the inside of the studio, I promise," she said to Sally. She held up a handkerchief. "Not a breath of paint shall cross their lips. Faces. Whatever."

"She uses them for paint rags," Sally explained. "She tucks them up her sleeve and then forgets what they are and wipes brushes with them."

"Not with these. I promise."

Sally sneaked a look at Frank. He was standing at the sideboard, blank-faced, apparently cheerful, but distant. What was it he had once said to India? If India actually got married, it would settle matters between them. Marriage was permanent. Sally's eyes teared for a moment. She was supposed to have married Juergen. . . .

Frank carried the champagne bottle and three glasses by their stems, and Sally snapped herself out of her reverie to bring the rest on a tray.

Frank poured one full and handed it to India. "To life," he said solemnly. "Wherever the road takes you." He poured the rest of the glasses and handed them round, napkin over one arm, the perfect waiter.

Jerry raised his and said, "To the Blackstone Girl, in all her incarnations, present and future."

India smiled up at him. "She seems to be changing rapidly," she murmured.

Frank was silent a moment. Then he said, "To metamorphosis, then," and drank off his glass.

The next morning, before India was even awake, Frank came to her door and said he'd received a telegram and had union business to take care of. He kissed her forehead. "Enjoy your life," he said. "Just don't stop painting."

And what on earth did he mean by that? India wondered sleepily, watching him trot down the stairs. She yawned and pulled her wrapper around her. How like him to appear at seven in the morning, she thought foggily. She closed the door and went back to bed.

The next day when she tried to find out where he had gone, she discovered that Mike and Eden didn't know.

"He flew the coop," Mike said. "Old Frank doesn't change much. I would have thought *you* had the forwarding address." Generally when the family was looking for Frank, it was India they asked.

"No," she said.

"Silly ass. No words of farewell." He looked at her thoughtfully. "Maybe he saw the writing on the wall."

"He said not to stop painting."

"Brilliant," Mike said. "He might as well have said don't stop breathing, I imagine."

Not necessarily, India thought. She couldn't go on painting and live on one sale a year. The money from the Blackstone Girl was running out. Frank knew it, too. She tried to decide if he had been telling her anything else, giving her some unspoken blessing, but she truly had no idea, not this time.

A few days later, Jerry Rhodes produced a diamond ring in a velvet box and asked her to marry him.

The question of money never entered the discussion, but it was a piece of certain knowledge in the back of India's mind when she thought about him. She studied his handsome profile, felt the little ripple of excitement that went down her backbone when he kissed her, and thought that perhaps it was a sign—a composite sign, composed of her work, her last shot at motherhood, and the marriage she hadn't made with Ben. Jerry said quite frankly that he thought it was time he married. He was forty, and his position required a wife. The wife wouldn't have to do any work, he assured her—just paint in the daytime and be a social ornament in the evening.

A trophy, India thought, like the tiger head on his study wall. But was that so bad? He was stable, he was her own age, old enough not to kick over the traces of domesticity, young enough still to be an ardent lover. He loved her. She loved him certainly as much as she had loved Ben. She would have time and money to paint—and maybe children. She had decided to remake her life, had she not?

So she married Jerry the next month, and her friends all approved. So did her father, who had returned to his ranch from London and now came to New York with her mother. He had long financial discussions with Jerry about the stock market and postwar investment.

"Glad you're going to take this girl of mine and get her back in the circles she belongs in." Edward Blackstone clapped Jerry on the back and gave him a cigar.

He proudly walked India down the aisle of Trinity Church, and she married Jerry Rhodes in front of three hundred people, some of whom she had never met. She wore a Paris gown of trailing white crepe de chine, a band of pearls around her forehead to hold her veil, and white kid slippers with pearl buckles. Sally was her maid of honor, ethereal in a cloud of sky-blue silk, and two of Jerry's cousins from Philadelphia were bridesmaids. India, looking at herself in the mirror just before she went out to take her father's arm, thought she looked entirely different, as if someone had stuck a new head on her body.

As she came down the aisle, leaning on her father's arm instead of her cane, she could see Frank in the third pew, his expression interested but noncommittal. India forced herself not to slew her head around to look at him as she paced past. Where had he sprung from? She had sent letters to every place she could think of that he might be but had gotten no answer. Uncle Henry, Aunt Cindy, and Frank's sister Midge were sitting next to him. He had on proper evening clothes.

She turned to Jerry and took a deep breath. He looked happy, pleased with things. She handed her bouquet to Sally, and Sally squeezed her fingers in encouragement. Funny, India thought—she had always thought of marriage as a trap, a box that they would put her in to stop her painting. It had never occurred to her that it might offer freedom.

Jerry smiled at her and squeezed her hand, too. India beamed suddenly, a smile that was enough to set any man back on his feet. Jerry Rhodes had done very well for himself, despite the limp.

India abandoned the various forms of birth control, the mechanics of which were passed from woman to woman but could not be publicly discussed, and found herself pregnant in two months. It was a wonder it hadn't happened before, she thought with horror. Because it had not, she had assumed that she might be too old. But she was very satisfactorily pregnant—sick in the mornings, afflicted with swollen ankles and lethargy, and able to outeat her husband. Jerry took her to the best woman's specialist in New York, who said that a first pregnancy at her age was no laughing matter. He gave her instructions for rest and diet and climbing stairs. She got sicker. With a grave expression he ordered her to bed. India's mother came to stay with her and drove India mad until Jerry, somehow, without causing a scene, managed to make her go home.

Jerry sat at the foot of the bed and rubbed India's feet. "I feel like a cad. Poor kitten, you look so miserable."

"It only lasts nine months," she said. "I'm just not used to having to be still. And I'm afraid my leg will stiffen up," she added fretfully. "I'm such an old crock. You shouldn't have married me."

Jerry kissed the end of her nose. "You are exactly a year younger than I am. I do not think of myself as an old crock."

When he left her, she knew he went and consulted with the doctor again, and she wondered how much he wasn't telling her. But there was no point in worrying; it might just make it worse. And Jerry was so good to her. He would rub her feet and bring her buttered toast and books and lilies and anything else he thought she might like, anything that might take her mind off being too sick to paint, and maybe to carry a baby.

But she didn't lose the baby. She got progressively bigger despite the nausea and began to knit things, a gesture toward expected maternal behavior.

Frank came to see her once and eyed her belly with what seemed almost like apprehension. "You don't look like yourself," he said. He left as soon as Jerry came home. Frank and Jerry found very little to talk about.

As India ran a hand over her stomach, the baby's foot batted against it. It felt unutterably strange to have someone else living inside her. Her bad leg was propped on a pillow, under billows of white silk nightgown. She leaned past the baby and pulled the nightgown back.

The twisted scar was still an angry red, pulling the flesh

of her calf inward in a deep depression, as if a scoop had been taken out of her flesh. But the scar seemed more real to her than the baby, a part of herself despite its ugliness. It showed, too, now that skirts were so short. Hemlines had crept nearly halfway up the calf, which in certain quarters was regarded as the death knell of civilization, but young women went on hemming up their skirts. India loved the freedom of the new clothes. She had her skirts hemmed up, too, despite well-meaning suggestions from the Philadelphia cousins that she should wear them long to hide her deformity. By the time the Philadelphia cousins went home, there was no love lost between them, and Jerry was affectionately calling her "Adder." Jerry didn't mind what the scar looked like, bless him. She might be a trophy, but she wasn't a pinned butterfly. She thought again of the tiger head with a reasonable satisfaction.

The baby came in the middle of summer in 1920, when New York was sweltering hot. An electric fan moved the air around but hardly managed to cool anything. The baby was two weeks late, and after trying to keep her from miscarrying all these months, the doctor was now worried because she hadn't gone into labor. When the pains came, he was there in twenty minutes, his uncombed hair sticking up from his forehead like an elderly cockatoo's crest. India was as white as her sheets with the pain, and Jerry was frantic. The doctor's nurse pushed Jerry through the door, out into the hall.

"Don't do this again," the doctor muttered to India between clenched teeth.

She shuddered as another pain went through her, too weak even to scream.

"Hang on," the doctor said, and then, "Oh, Mother of God."

There was another wrenching pain and then the hot, wet feel of her own blood everywhere. The doctor worked frantically while India swam in and out of consciousness and heard a faint cry that she at first took for the couché of her nightmares and her paintings. When she opened her eyes again, it was a jolt to see that she was in her green and silver bedroom on Fifth Avenue where she had stenciled lilies along the walls, and not at Etaples among the dying Tommies. The doctor's face swam above her, wavy as a fish.

"You have a boy," he said gently.

"Is it all right?"

"The baby is all right. You have lost a lot of blood and have to be very still for a while. If you'll promise me that, I'll have Nurse bring him to you."

India nodded, and they put the baby in her arms. She and Jerry had already picked David for a name if it was a boy, but she found it hard to start thinking of this tiny creature by it. His face was beet red, and he had a shock of black hair that came to a peak over his nose.

"That will fall out," the nurse said comfortably, rubbing the hair, "and then he'll be a handsome young man."

They let Jerry in, and he sat beside the bed and held her hand. *Am I dying?* India wondered suddenly. Their faces all looked like it.

But she didn't die, just as she hadn't lost the baby. Both had been close calls. She knew she couldn't give birth again, and with that realization came an overwhelming love for little David. It came on her suddenly, almost like someone turning a light on, as soon as her milk came in, as if the milk were a flowing river washing up at her feet all the maternal sentiment she had tried and failed to muster while she was pregnant. She studied his ears and toothless mouth, his starfish hands and minute finger- and toenails. Here was creation, certainly.

When she could get out of bed, when they were sure she wasn't going to die, she began to paint him, and to plan a studio of high shelves and easels bolted to the floor, where she could have paints and baby around her at once. There was a nursemaid, but Jerry said approvingly that the woman was severely overpaid and underworked.

Sally had watched with bemusement the transformation in her friend. It seemed strange that India should be the happy wife and mother, the role Sally had always imagined for herself. Sally hadn't *wanted* to be a free spirit. Even now her mother, fretting over what would happen to the Madrona and proudly displaying photographs of Mike and Eden's fat-cheeked babies, asked Sally if there wasn't anyone she would like to see while she was in Portland on her yearly visit. Several old beaux were still unmarried, or even widowed.

Sally peered up at the old red-and-white house with its turrets and gingerbread, as if the men her mother spoke of might be up there at the windows, noses pressed against the glass. Ghosts in her attic. She shook her head.

Reluctantly, her mother produced a letter from her purse, fumbling for it in the dusty sunlight. She looked too old, Sally thought. Her feet were encased in sensible black shoes with laces.

"If you're looking for your glasses," Sally said gently, "they're on your nose."

"I am not," Alexandra said. "I'm not that far gone. Here. This came this morning just as I was going into town to meet you." She handed Sally a thin blue overseas mail envelope with a wealth of stamps on it.

Sally blanched. The thin paper shimmered in the sun.

"I imagine he knew I would forward it," Alexandra said briskly.

"He doesn't know I went back to the old apartment," Sally said. "I wrote to him in Cologne, but they had moved."

"Did you have to write to him?" Alexandra asked.

A flock of starlings swarmed noisily above the trees. Sally held on to the envelope as if it might leap from her hand and fly with them. She slit it open with her fingernail.

Meine Liebe Sally,

It is beyond me to guess whether you will want to know where I am. I can only hope so. I can only hope also that your parents will forward this, as I have forgotten the name of the man you have married, and have not the heart to try to find out. But I thought that you would want to know that I survived my wound and the war. I think of you well and happy in London, and it makes life bearable. You need not write to me if it will make trouble. I only wanted you not to worry about me. I will tell you something funny. I am to be sent to San Francisco by the new government, as soon as our consulate is reopened there. I am bringing Mother and the girls. There is nothing left for them here. But you will be in London. That is irony.

With best regards to all your family,
Juergen

Sally put the letter in her own purse. She picked up her hatbox—everything else had been whisked inside by her mother's driver. "Can I have my old room again?"

"Are you going to write to him?" Alexandra demanded. When she got no response, she cried, "Oh, Sally, not the German again! Tell him to let you *go*!"

"Do you have strawberries in those beds by the kitchen door this year?" Sally asked. "I want to go out barefoot and fill an old straw hat with them, the way we used to."

Sally wrote to Juergen that night, sitting in her old room at the schoolgirl's desk with just a candle lit, so her mother wouldn't see light under the door and look in on her. There were plenty of candles. The old house was sketchily wired and prone to power failures.

Sally laid the pen down halfway through her letter and stared at the closed door, chin cupped in her hand. The candlelight made a circle, like a fairy ring, enclosing her in a world she had not been a part of since childhood. It felt strange to be here and writing to Juergen. Juergen belonged to New York, to her life there. Here on the Madrona he was the alien and interloper that her mother envisioned him to be. The Madrona was American and exuded both the pride and the smug complacency of houses that have sheltered generations of the same family. Sally had tried to explain the Madrona to Juergen once, but it had been hard. He had never lived in a country where there was a frontier.

I wish I'd known Grandpa, she thought. *I wonder what he would have thought of me.* Grandpa was Whip Holt, Toby's father, the first husband of Sally's grandmother, Eulalia. Among the Holt children, he was the stuff of legend. By all accounts Whip Holt had been a loner until he had married a southern belle who'd come west in the wagon train he was leading. It had been the first train into the Oregon country, in 1840, when the United States was trying to settle the territory with its citizens to bolster its claim to the land. The English and the Russians had wanted it, too. There were still Russian place names around.

Whip and Eulalia had built the first house here, but Alexandra and Toby had enlarged it. Civilized it, Sally thought: plastered over and concealed the old log walls, added bathrooms and nurseries for a growing number of children. It was odd to think that Whip's house was still there, embedded in this one. Maybe it was also embedded in herself. Whip Holt had never behaved as he was expected to, so Grandmother Eulalia had said. Maybe it was growing up in his house that had made Sally just a tad rebellious.

She gave a snort of laughter at herself and picked up her pen again. Whip Holt's rebellion had been diluted by the generations until it was barely visible. What had she ever done except not get married? Now she was turning into a highly conventional old maid, as conventional an old maid as she would have been a wife. *I'm not like India,* she thought. *All I ever wanted was to do what everyone expected me to—marry some nice boy and have nice babies.*

Now Juergen was coming to San Francisco. It was hard to say what that might mean. He thought she was married to Robin. Sally's heart lurched, thinking what it would have been like if she *was* married to Robin, what it would have been like to get Juergen's letter. What would she have said to him? What would she have said to Robin? Would she have found an excuse to go to San Francisco, or would she have stayed in London and been a good girl, the way she had always been? It was hard to say. Sally felt that there were two of her, like the house within the house. The one that was writing to Juergen was the one buried at the heart.

She finished her letter, sealed it, and put stamps on it, smoothing the envelope with her fingers. She would put it out for the postman herself, so Mother wouldn't have to see it. Alexandra was old and battered by the loss of Toby, and there wasn't any point in adding to her unhappiness.

Alexandra didn't ask again about Juergen, and in gratitude Sally extended her visit. They put flowers on her father's grave and went through the boxes of his things still left in the attic. They sat on the veranda, drank tea, and talked about him. Alexandra, Sally thought, had need to say his name to keep him with her.

Sally began to drift, the sharp edge of her longing to be back in New York failing with the knowledge that Juergen would be in San Francisco, failing with her mother's need of her. She would stay six months this time, she thought. Why not?

But at the end of it she went to San Francisco—to see her brother Tim, she said. Yet her mother knew the real reason and said flatly as she packed, "It's the German, isn't it?" Alexandra's mouth tightened. "You nearly died on the *Lusitania*. I wonder why you can't remember all those drowned babies."

The first thing Sally thought when she saw Juergen was that he had gotten old; somehow, while she wasn't looking, the war had made him old. But then she saw that it was just lines, that he was still there under them, and what leaped in his face when he saw her brought youth back to the surface with it, so that the old and the young faces flickered, alternating, across each other. It took days of staring at him for them to merge and some picture of Juergen to settle in her head.

He had taken a house for Mother and the girls on Telegraph Hill, a peach-colored three-story affair built after the fire and adorned with masses of old-fashioned white gingerbread, about which Mother complained constantly. It was "foolish."

After one dinner with the family, Sally and Juergen dined elsewhere, and on their second day together, they took a picnic hamper down to the beach below the Cliff House and watched the seals barking on the rocks.

"I love seals," Sally said. "They're so comical. It's very hard to look at a seal and be depressed."

Juergen looked at her and smiled. "They're vicious. They fight like dogs with each other over territory."

Sally chuckled. She had kicked off her shoes and removed her stockings, and now she sat with her toes in the warm sand. "Like people," she said, and gave him a sidelong look. Juergen's mouth twisted, and she wished she hadn't said it. "I'm sorry. I wasn't trying to—"

"I know you weren't. You don't know what it is like now, at home. France and England are determined to punish us, and America is going along with it. There is nothing."

"But you are here," Sally said. "I don't mean to sound brutal, but you are here. And you have your mother and the girls with you."

"I was right," Juergen said. "They loathe it here."

"They would loathe it anywhere outside of Germany!"

Sally snapped. "Juergen, they don't own you. And in any case, here they are. They might as well get used to it."

"Could you get used to Germany?" Juergen asked her. "I remember."

"I'm not in Germany. They're in San Francisco." She felt argumentative and unsympathetic. Frau von Appen and the girls had cost him enough.

"Oh." Juergen stared at the seals. "We are only here a year," he said finally.

"What?" Sally grabbed his hand, made him look at her. "I thought it was indefinite. A long-term post. You didn't say—"

Juergen's lined face stared out at the ocean again, as if he couldn't look at her and talk at the same time. "I thought you were married in London. I wanted to rub your face in it, that you hadn't waited for me."

"Oh." Sally examined his hand in hers.

"When I found out that you hadn't married, I—I thought about staying. Marrying you if you would have me, and staying here."

"But you won't." Sally's voice was flat, but she didn't let go of his hand.

Juergen's fingers suddenly clenched hers as if he were pounded by the rolling surf and she could pull him toward her. "I would marry you. I would marry you this afternoon, or anytime that you would do it. It is only that I can't stay here. I was a pig to think that I might. My country is in ruins; my sisters will probably never marry. I have to be there to try to put the pieces together however the new government thinks will work. It is like sticking potsherds one on another, trying to make something. I have a duty."

Duty. It was an ugly word, plain as mud. *We didn't start the war*, Sally wanted to scream at him. But Juergen hadn't, either. It had just caught him up. How could she ask him to be disloyal to his own country when she felt so strongly about hers?

"If you are beaten," Juergen said, "it does not give you the freedom to be dishonorable."

"Then why can't you *stay* here? Why won't they let you stay? You're an asset to the consulate, you're a born diplomat. You can put pieces together *by* staying here."

"I am suspect," Juergen said. "I am not allowed to stay."

"Because of me? Still?" Sally's eyes snapped.

"Always. I *am* good. That is why I am sent here. But I am suspect and not allowed to stay."

"And you want me to marry you and follow you back to a place where you are suspect just because of me?"

"I want to marry you," Juergen said. "I want more than anything to marry you, but I *must* go back, even if I cannot have what I want."

"Does what *I* want matter?"

Juegen turned to look at her now, held her eyes, wouldn't let them go. "To me, yes. But not to my duty."

"Oh, damn you! Damn your duty. I'm thirty-eight years old. India just had a baby and it almost killed her, but at least she's got one. I may never have one. I may never even sleep with a man unless I sleep with you now whether I'm married to you or not. I've been such a good girl, Juergen. I followed all the rules. Look what it got me. My mother keeps reintroducing me to old beaux who are so old now their first wives have *died*! What have you done to my *life*?"

"What have you done to mine?" he said quietly. He laid his hands on her shoulders, pulled her toward him until her face rested against his cheek. He pulled her straw hat off and stroked her hair. "*Liebchen*. I would make it different if I could. Every morning I wake up and I wish I had died, because when you are dead I think maybe then your reward is that no one has a claim on you. Then I could be with you, just a very quiet ghost with you every day."

"You're a romantic," Sally said acidly. "I'm not. I want love now, in this life, before I'm too old. I could do without babies, I suppose, but not without love."

"Then we sha'n't, if that is what you—don't you think I have wanted nothing else since I saw you? But are you sure—"

Sally sat back from him, so that he could see her face and the determined flare in her eyes. "For once," she told him, "I am going to have what I want."

She took him back to the hotel room she had rented at the St. Francis over her brother's protests and let him in. The room was high, with a view of the hills and the sky hanging like a blue curtain above them. No fog today, just a stiff breeze that whipped the girls' short skirts about their calves on the street below and blew a banker's bowler hat down the pavement.

Sally was not ignorant. She was thirty-eight, and the days when an unmarried woman knew nothing about sexual intimacy were long gone. She had in fact come fairly close with several of her beaux, and extremely close with Robin, but no one but Juergen had ever made her want to give in to the urge that India, for instance, seemed to treat so lightly. For Sally it meant something, some power that the man would then have over her. Perhaps she trusted no one but Juergen.

The whole experience was worth it even before she saw how much he wanted her, saw the look on his face, how his mouth trembled and his fingers trembled as he unbuttoned the row of tiny fastenings down her dress. His hands felt hot, and he started to whisper in her ear in German, things half understood. A seagull perched on their windowsill outside the glass and looked at them curiously.

This isn't the person I was supposed to be, Sally thought as Juergen's naked body slid along hers on the satin bedspread. This was what was supposed to have happened on her wedding night. *I'm too old to begin being wicked now,* she thought wistfully. But despite that, she wanted him dreadfully, felt terrified and exultant just to look at him. Juergen wrapped his arms around her, pinning her to the bed, so that now all she could see was the side of his face and the piece of the room behind his shoulder, a chest of drawers with a three-paneled mirror above it, endlessly reflecting the seagull. Its bright eyes looked knowingly into hers, and it lifted white wings in a blur and flipped into the blue sky.

Later Sally lay in the circle of Juergen's arm and thought, *I've done it now. Now I'm a fallen woman. Mother would be horrified, even at my age. I can't tell my friends. Except for India. The rest of my friends aren't like India. Mike and Tim would want to shoot him.*

"Will you stay?" Juergen whispered. "Will you stay in San Francisco for what time we have?"

So you can convince me to marry you, Sally thought, *now that we've gone this far?* This would make Juergen feel compelled to marry her, she knew; he no doubt hoped, and assumed, that it would compel her, too. *I won't marry you because I've slept with you,* she thought. *I couldn't bear Germany.*

She pulled him to her fiercely. "I'll stay as long as you're here. I'll take what I can get."

XI

Jerry

It was amazing how much *time* a baby took, India thought. David seemed to eat whenever he wasn't asleep. Then when his first ravenous appetite slowed, he slept through the night and began to eat cereals and mashed fruit, with which he mostly wanted to play. India watched, fascinated, as he smeared fruit on his tray or paddled his fingers in cereal, admiring the smacking sound it made. His widow's peak had filled out as promised, and now he had a thick head of wavy dark hair, which India brushed into ringlets around her finger. She had painted him sleeping and waking, curled around a teddy bear and splashing in his bath. She hardly ever showed those canvases to anyone—they were maternal, sappy, far too cute, and they gave her immense joy. Other work went to the galleries, which were beginning to take notice, but the David pieces stayed home. Jerry hung one in his office, and the father of another new baby immediately wanted to commission India to paint his own child. India refused, and the picture in Jerry's office came down, replaced with one of her war pictures.

"My secretary thinks the baby was nicer," Jerry said, mixing her a cocktail in the long slow summer evening while David played with his toes on the rug.

"I just got rid of the Blackstone Girl. I'm not going to do babies. Those pictures of David are for me." She inspected her glass. "Jerry, where is this from?"

"Just off the boat," Jerry said cheerfully.

"You always say that," India said. "It's just occurred to me that I don't ever know what I'm drinking. Not really. And you tasted that stuff that Frank brought the last time he was here."

"Your friend Blake is fairly low on discrimination."

"I know you don't like him," she commented. "The two of you stared at each other like a pair of owls, each one thinking the other was going to try to take his mouse."

"I think he's a blowhard. He thinks I personally go out and browbeat the workingman every day for amusement. We don't have much in common."

India sipped her drink. "Certainly not your bootleggers, thank God. But truly, Jerry, where does this come from? I'd like to know."

"Off a boat," he said. "Truly. But then it gets cut somewhere and rebottled if you're not careful. Howes got a bottle of supposed Benedictine the other day, with seals and all. Then he took a good look at them—someone had resealed it with hot wax and a quarter. It said 'In God We Trust.'"

India hooted with laughter. David pulled himself up on her skirt and batted at her glass. "No, poppet, you're too young. Maybe by the time you're old enough to drink the government will have regained its senses."

"One trusts so," Jerry said. "They've done an excellent job at creating another endeavor for the criminal classes. You cannot legislate mankind's urge to enjoy himself."

"That's what Frank says." India looked at him. "Possibly you have more in common than you think."

"We both like to drink." Jerry emptied his glass and stood up. "It stops there. However, I never demanded the right to pick your friends." He bent over and kissed her on the forehead. "Enjoy your drink while I play with Junior."

It was very relaxing to be David's mother, to bask in newfound maternal instincts and respectability. The trouble was, that feeling of floating calm, of being willing to drift lightly through her days, began to wear off. It could never have been permanent, not for India. And when she came out of it and wanted to work, it became obvious that Jerry didn't notice the change in her. More and more often he was away, meeting with investors and increasingly with the movers and shakers who ran the city. While she had been drifting, enraptured with David, India hadn't really noticed how much he was gone. Now, oddly, while she herself was preoccupied with work, she noticed that Jerry was, too. Or with something. Sometimes when she telephoned his office, he wasn't there. It crossed her mind once or twice that he was having an affair, but he seemed just as amorous toward her as ever. Whatever was preoccupying him wasn't a woman, she thought.

All the same he looked tightly strung. Not tense, but rather exhilarated. His eyes were bright and his attitude sometimes slightly manic. When she asked questions, he slid away from them. But one evening he appeared at dinner with a box from Tiffany's and set it on her plate.

"Open it," he commanded her. He looked excited and boyish.

India opened the box. Inside were a necklace and a bracelet of rubies set in heavy gold spirals. She goggled at them. Jerry fairly often brought her presents, but this was worth nearly as much as their house.

"My God," she said, and decided that was inadequate. "Jerry, it's splendid, it's amazing. But so much money—" *And I'd be afraid to wear it.*

"I happened to come into some money," Jerry said. "Made a good deal. I want people to see what my wife is worth to me." He grinned at her.

"There must be other ways to demonstrate it," India murmured. But the necklace was beautiful, and she knew it would suit her. Jerry always knew what suited her. And this probably meant he wasn't having an affair—unless he felt guilty. It was an awfully expensive guilt offering. She studied him, puzzled. "You're up to something," she said finally.

"I am not." He laughed, mock indignant. "And kindly don't go around saying things like that, either. It takes a lot of time and attention to take care of business these days, and I don't like neglecting you. This is just to prove it."

"Well, it certainly does." India put the necklace on and looked in the mirror that hung over the sideboard. It was beautiful, and she wanted it dreadfully. *And I refuse to feel silly about that,* she thought. *Or guilty, either. I shall wear it out and enjoy it. At least I know he's not having an affair.*

"For goodness' sake take good care of it tonight," Jerry

told her. "It's not insured yet. I'll call Lofton in the morning and have it added to our policy."

"I'll sleep with it," she said.

With Jerry gone so often, India found it easy to spend as much time as she wanted to in the studio, although they were socializing more and more on the evenings that he *was* home. These parties were important, Jerry said, so India went willingly and never admitted to being bored. She had plenty to do. She had David and painting. If at times she felt as if she was being held back on a ruby leash, she ignored it. Still, it was like someone having opened a stuck window when Frank came by on one of his periodic trips through New York.

David had just turned two, and Frank brought with him a rocking horse equipped with a genuine cavalry saddle. Jerry was working late at the office, "making more money," India said lightly. David was introduced to Frank and the rocking horse. He patted the latter and accorded the former all the suspicion natural to a two-year-old. Then he and the horse were whisked off to bed by his sensible English nanny.

Frank looked around India's living room, newly redecorated with black and silver and splashes of vermilion glazed pottery. "The lady of the manor," he commented. "Don't you get restless sometimes, what with that pea under all your mattresses?"

India snorted with laughter before she could stop herself. "Sometimes. I'm painting more, now that David's old enough not to need me every waking moment. I used to think I could paint and baby-sit at the same time, the more fool I."

"You look good," Frank said. "That part of it suits you. You ought to do a self-portrait with him—'Dark Madonna.'"

"I've been doing horses again. I go over to Central Park and paint them. Do you want to see?"

"I always want to see." Frank followed her upstairs to the studio that Jerry had built for her. The limp was still there, he saw, and she used the cane he had given her going up the carpeted stairs. The studio had a skylight, and Jerry had the dormer windows opened up and extended to give a clear north light all day. The horse canvases littered the studio. In a half-finished one they came up out of the ground, their haunches extensions of the hills, their heavy hooves pulling loose from mountains. There were no riders on their backs; no one could have ridden these horses.

"I like the way horses move," India said, biting her thumb and studying the canvas. "I always have. I've started riding again. I thought I couldn't at first, but the muscles in my calf seem to be stretching."

"Does it hurt all the time still?" Frank asked her.

"Mostly," she replied. He wouldn't give her sympathy, she knew; there wasn't any point in it. He just wanted to know how she was doing. His hand touched her shoulder briefly, squeezed it.

"Do you take commissions?" he asked.

"For the Wobblies?" A spark lit in India's eye, the urge to get off the leash a bit igniting her interest.

"We don't have any money."

"You spend it all on lawyers. I'm surprised you haven't had to go to Russia, too." Bill Haywood was there now, waiting for the revolution to come to America.

Frank shook his head. "I don't trust the Communists. But for Haywood it was that or spend his life in jail, and he's old and sick. Maybe the Wobblies are old, too. I don't know how much we're accomplishing now, but I don't quite trust these new unions, either. I guess I'll dance with the one that brought me a while longer."

"What's the commission?" India said.

"The amnesty campaign. We have people in prison still who would be acquitted if they were tried now. Even Senator Borah has said as much, and he hates Wobblies. Public opinion is swinging to our side. I want something to play on that. Your horses made me think of something like that with men—coming up from underground. It was dissent that built America. 'Don't stifle the voices of legal dissent.' Something like that. Get a flag in it somewhere if you can."

"Cynic." India chuckled. "All right. My contribution to the cause."

"Salve your conscience for being one of the haves."

"I don't have a conscience. I'm an artist. I paint things."

Frank snickered. "That's what you tell yourself."

*   *   *

It wasn't until the slogan went on that Jerry, on one of his Sunday morning visits to her studio, realized what she was doing.

"Have you lost your mind?"

India, who was fiercely concentrating, jumped and smeared the brush across the bottom corner. "Damn!" She turned to glare at Jerry. His face startled her. "What on earth is the matter?"

"Blake put you up to this, didn't he?" Jerry's eyes snapped. "I know damn well he doesn't like me, but this is too much."

"It's just a poster. I've done work for them before. You know that."

"You were not married to me at the time."

India felt the blood rushing to her head. "Maybe you should tell me why that makes a difference?"

Jerry took a deep breath. "The IWW are a bunch of traitors and Communists who stand for everything I and the men I associate with find reprehensible. I haven't spoken this bluntly before because of your friendship with Blake, to which you are entitled, but this is too much. I will not have my wife's work on an IWW poster."

India stared at him.

"For God's sake, India, these are the people who blew up half a mile of Wall Street and killed thirty-five people two years ago."

"I know that the government arrested a lot of people they had been longing for an excuse to get at," India said quietly. "They never proved anything. And I can tell you the IWW had nothing to do with it."

"Your faith in them is touching."

"Frank does not lie to me, and he would have known if it was true."

"I have not objected to your friendship with Blake until now," Jerry said stiffly. "Although I have become aware of the terms on which it existed."

India's chin shot out. "You knew about Roger Stiller. I never pretended to be Sleeping Beauty. And furthermore, I have been entirely faithful to you." Goaded, she added, "Have you been the same?"

Jerry's mouth tightened. "I won't be put off the subject. I will not have my wife become an embarrassment to me.

You are to have nothing further to do with the Wobblies or with Blake, at whose door I am well aware the blame lies. And I want you to burn that canvas."

India stared at him, trying to equate this tyrant with the pleasant and untroublesome husband she had assumed she had married. Maybe he had a headache, or a hangover, or the stock market had done something unpleasant.

"Jerry, I don't think we're talking about the same thing. A great many people, even conservative ones, are for amnesty for these people. And in any case—"

"I will not have my wife's name on a *poster!*"

India took a deep breath. "You cannot forbid me to do anything. You don't own me."

Jerry lost his temper. "The hell I don't. I support you. I pay the bills while you paint!"

"And raise your son!"

"That is the usual arrangement between husband and wife. And a perfectly agreeable one to me. But you will not take actions which will offend all of my friends and associates. Do I make myself clear?"

"Would they really be upset with you?" India was bewildered. She hadn't paid much attention to Jerry's business dealings or his business associates. Her head was in a paint palette, as usual.

"I will not have my wife allied with Communists." Jerry's mouth was tight, and there was a little twitch beside it.

"Most of them aren't Communists," India said.

"I don't care if they're baboons!" Jerry exploded. "They *are* baboons—traitors and subversives!" He strode across the studio and snatched the canvas off the easel.

"Put that back!"

He flung it across the room.

"Get out! *Get out!*" India screamed at him. She picked up the canvas. It had knocked an open can of linseed oil off a shelf, and the wet paint was smeared with it. "There! Are you satisfied? What the hell is the matter with you?"

"You remember what I said," Jerry snapped and turned on his heel.

India stared after him, as if a dragon had suddenly erupted from the sink and shot flame at her. They had hardly ever had a quarrel. She knew he didn't like Frank, but that couldn't be all of it. She had gone where he wanted her to, even learned to dress to set off her odd, dark looks and her cane, so that she had actually become fashionable in an exotic way. She hung gracefully on his arm at parties and talked to bankers and legislators. He seemed pleased when someone recognized her name.

Up until now he had been a model husband. He had never even made a pass at Sally, who was still so beautiful that most men did automatically. India sighed. Maybe she hadn't paid enough attention to his business. Should she learn about stocks? Maybe he felt she was making fun of him.

Jerry had gone out by the time she went downstairs, and he didn't come home to dinner. She didn't see him again until breakfast the next morning. She found him at the table, eating a soft-boiled egg, the *Wall Street Journal* propped in front of him. Hesitantly, she put a hand on his shoulder. "I've promised the poster, but I won't sign it. Will that help?"

Jerry looked up at her, swiveling in his chair.

"Do you want to make up?" India asked bluntly.

"I want my instructions adhered to."

"Let's call them wishes," India said. "Then you'll have a better chance."

"You won't sign it? And you won't paint any others?"

"I won't paint any others if it will upset you. It was a favor for a friend, not a piece of art. You don't get to tell me what to paint otherwise."

"Have I ever tried?" Jerry demanded.

"To be honest, no." She held out her hand. "Let's call it a truce."

"Very well."

She sat down at the table, and they ate, rather stiffly. After Jerry left for his office, India picked up the paper and perused it. She had never bothered to read the *Journal* before and found herself bored with it now. It didn't explain Jerry, but the stock quotes were an algebraic mystery to be puzzled over. *Maybe I don't pay enough attention to things*, she thought.

India sent Frank the artwork for the poster and received a letter of thanks in return. Jerry found it lying on her dressing table one evening when they were dressing to go out. To India's outrage he picked it up and read it in front of her.

"That's private!"

"I'm your husband."

"You've never read my mail before!" She got up from her vanity, fists clenched.

Jerry sighed. "I've never had reason to. It never occurred to me that you would get mixed up with the Wobblies again. I thought that was—youthful fervor."

"I'm not mixed up with them," India said. "But I'm not going to change all my political opinions for you. I didn't think you married me for my politics."

"I didn't marry you for *those* politics!"

"I met you at Mabel Dodge's," India said.

Jerry turned to look at her, then said, "I'm in a very vulnerable position. I'm thinking of running for office."

"Well, you can think again," India said, goaded, "because I didn't marry *you* to live in a fishbowl."

"That is not your decision. Are you nearly ready to go? We are supposed to be at the Hanovers' in twenty minutes."

"I will be if you'll let me alone," India said.

Jerry put down Frank's letter and retreated through the door that connected his dressing room with hers. "Arlen's just been appointed to the Trade Commission. Don't talk politics with him."

India glared after him, but Jerry was putting shirt studs in with a nonchalant concentration.

They went with Arlen and Louise Hanover, Wall Street friends of Jerry's, to a speakeasy in Harlem, and no one had any chance to talk politics, much to India's relief. Connie's Inn was among the speaks that catered to the "downtown trade," safe even at night for white customers in evening clothes looking for jazz and food. And a drink.

Americans had all begun to drink like fish the minute someone told them they couldn't, India noted, even the women. Most speakeasies passed themselves off as private clubs and offered admittance cards. They were rarely raided if they paid for sufficient protection. And everyone went. There was no stigma attached—not, India thought sourly, as there was in painting posters for the Wobblies.

Outside Connie's Inn were the smells of poverty: grits and chitlins, yard toilets. It was the music that drew the white customers. There had never been anything like jazz for white Americans to listen to before. The horn man looking for a gig was a constant feature of Harlem, and many of the groups that played the clubs were straight from New Orleans.

Inside Connie's it was dim and smoky, the music winding through the air with tobacco and the faint scent of marijuana smoke. You could buy other things in Harlem, too: cocaine or sexual adventure. White women came with their husbands and stayed safely with them; what their husbands might find when they came alone was another matter.

A group called the Little Ramblers was playing. India saw among the customers three notable gangsters, impeccably attired in tuxedo and the obligatory blonde. She grinned. That made it very unlikely they would be raided.

Despite an evening during which no one said a serious word, Jerry braced her afterward at home for an account of her conversations.

"You were at the table," India said.

"I wasn't monitoring you." He removed his cuff links. "Do I have to?"

"You appear to be trying!" she protested. "We talked about clothes and the trouble Louise's nanny is giving her. I talked about James Joyce with Arlen."

"Good."

India's dark hair stood out from her face, electrified with the force of her brushstrokes. Hairbrush in hand, she studied him. "What precisely are you running for?"

"That's uncertain," Jerry said. "There's been some talk in city circles."

It took India several months to figure out that what Jerry was running for was not an office but simply their current style of life. "Well, of course, dear," Louise Hanover said one day at lunch over chicken salad. "Anyone involved in finance has to be on a good footing with the men at City Hall. And who knows where Jerry will go? But it's just important to be known as someone who's solid on the right issues, don't you understand?"

India understood quite clearly that Louise had asked her to lunch because her husband had requested it: *"Jerry's been having trouble with India. You talk to her, dear."*

"I am attempting to adhere to his wishes," India said, "but he's behaving like a maniac about it. Every time we go anywhere, he catechizes me afterward about who I talked to and what I said. It's becoming ridiculous."

Louise played with her fork and then said brightly, "Well, he's doing very well for you, isn't he?"

Very well. It didn't occur to India that it might be suspiciously well. Keeping the political bosses happy was just a fact of life if you were doing business with them. A wife who painted pictures for the Wobblies was no asset. She modified her views, or at least her expression of them, but it was somehow too late. Jerry didn't trust her.

Two years went by in which they socialized with his friends exclusively, men of power, both the old and the up-and-coming, like the dapper assemblyman Jimmy Walker, rumored soon to replace Red Mike Hylan as mayor now that Hylan was out of favor with Tammany Hall. India liked Walker. He was a cheerful hedonist with a hip flask in his pocket. She didn't suppose he would be a worse mayor than Hylan, though not much better, either. She talked about art with him, and jazz. Jimmy was a connoisseur of nightclubs.

"What the hell were you saying to Jimmy Walker?" Jerry demanded one night the minute they were inside their own door.

"Stop it! You'll wake David!" India stomped up the stairs in a fashion guaranteed to wake him and was perversely satisfied to see him peer around the door of his room. "I told you!" she shouted over her shoulder at Jerry, then disappeared into David's room, slamming the door in Jerry's face.

"Mama?" David was four now, old enough to recognize grown-up dissent.

"It's all right, lamb." India scooped him up and sat down with him in her lap. "We didn't mean to wake you. Daddy's just tired. You can see him in the morning."

David grabbed her dress, twisting his fingers around a silk rosette. "You stay." He butted his face into her chest.

Jerry had left by the time she got up the next morning, but India realized without enthusiasm that they had to go out again that night. Worse, it was a political party in support of Walker's candidacy. *If he does it tonight, I won't go anywhere with him again.*

India fed David his breakfast and discussed the nutritional value of oatmeal with him while he howled for pancakes with jam.

David was calm enough this morning, relatively speaking, but it had taken a long time for him to go to sleep the night before. India thumbed open the mail while she worried about how and why Jerry had changed so, and what their fights were doing to David. Children noticed things. It was no good saying they didn't. Suddenly she was responsible for another person's security. She couldn't just throw fish at Jerry the way she had at Roger Stiller. She didn't even want to. She wanted to go back to their complacent arrangement in which he made money and she was a tiger head he was glad to display, back to the life in which she got to paint and play with David all day.

She opened another envelope. Mabel Dodge was about to embark on further matrimony, India read with a grin. She had met a "wonderful Indian." Her description of his charms leaped off the stationery and practically into India's lap. Mabel had discovered the artists' colony in Taos, New Mexico, several years ago and said it was a breath of fresh air after New York. The breeze had apparently also blown away her latest husband, the artist Maurice Stern, whom she had married after her anguished on-again, off-again affair with Jack Reed, who had subsequently died in Russia. Mabel's life would make a Victorian stage play, India thought, if only it hadn't been so unrepentant. Even in these days audiences liked to have the sinful woman pay for her sins.

India should come to Taos, Mabel wrote. It was a wonderful place to paint. The British novelist D. H. Lawrence was there, writing a novel. He had painted designs on Mabel's bathroom windows.

India read Mabel's exuberant correspondence with a sigh. The way things were now, she would love to go to Taos. It would be a relief to watch someone else's family histrionics instead of her own.

She dressed as carefully as possible that evening, taking pains with her hair and her black-and-silver gown. It came to a deep V between her breasts, and the hem dipped low on one side and high on the other. The dressmaker had altered it so that the low side was on the right, and only the silver cane accounted for India's limp. She pulled her hair back from her face on the other side with a comb of hammered silver knobs.

"You look very elegant," Jerry said when she joined him. He smiled tentatively and touched her shoulder.

India wondered if he was trying to make amends. "Thank you," she said, patting him back because he looked tense.

The party was in the Fifth Avenue brownstone of the head of Jerry's firm. There was a little hush as they entered and then calls of greeting. Someone put a cocktail into India's hand, and the hostess whisked her off to be introduced to a judge who was a patron of the arts. Jerry was already deep in a circle of men. *I'm tired of this,* India thought, but it didn't seem fair to say so or even think it, because she had been happy enough with the arrangement at the beginning. Maybe it was the strain of dealing with Jerry—or with whatever was making him obsessed with controlling her.

She talked about cubism with the judge and wished she had another cocktail—and wondered whether that meant she was drinking too much. When the judge's attention was caught by a fellow male with matters of political importance to discuss, India sidled away and sat gratefully on the end of a nile green brocaded sofa, whose ball-and-claw feet appeared to be about to scuttle away into the next room. Perhaps it would, and she could ride it to the bar and on out into the street. Her leg was hurting tonight.

"If you will be patient," the man on the other end of the sofa said, "I think I can signal the gentleman with the drinks without either of us poor crocks having to get up."

India noted the cane that rested between his knees. "That would be delightful," she said. "I know you, of course, Mr. Roosevelt, but I don't think you know me. I'm India Blackstone Rhodes."

"I thought that you might be," Franklin Roosevelt said. "I'm flattered that you know me. An unsuccessful candidacy for vice president is often enough to obscure anyone."

A waiter in a spotless white jacket appeared with a tray of cocktails, apparently at the slight lift of Roosevelt's finger. "I apologize for not getting up."

"What have you done to yourself?" she said, forgetting that it might not be tactful. The lines of strain around his mouth so closely matched her own when her leg was paining her that she felt some kinship.

"An attack of infantile paralysis, not long after the campaign," he said. "As you can see, it does not confine itself to infants. I walk these days, but not well."

"I'm sorry," India said. "What a snoopy thing to ask."

"Then you may tell me how you hurt yours." He smiled. "There are all sorts of fascinating rumors."

"Oh, Lord, whatever they are, please scotch them. I was driving an ambulance in France, and it was hit. It's been a long time."

"An uncommon woman," Roosevelt said with a smile. "I remember your work from before the war."

India sighed. "I'm trying to ditch the Blackstone Girl and be serious. I'm finding her rather a millstone."

"Difficult to be accused of frivolity when you're trying to be serious," Roosevelt conceded. "I remember the posters you did for the IWW, too. Isn't their latest one yours?"

"Oh, shhhh!" India said. "Jerry's furious about it. I didn't sign it."

"Well, he has a point. The Wobblies' hearts are in the right place, I think. In the main, anyway. But they'll never get anywhere if they can't keep the lunatic fringe from spouting anarchy and sabotage while cooler heads are trying to get something done. It comes of not having any central authority with enough power to control the general membership."

"I'm not sure anyone could," India said reminiscently. "As a group, they don't lean toward central authority."

"No. Which is why other unions will make the next steps in labor organization."

"On the other hand, it does take a lunatic fringe to get anywhere," India said thoughtfully. "When everyone is calm and reasonable, nothing changes. When they do something awful, the government takes notice and starts instituting reform."

Roosevelt chuckled. "You should go into politics."

"God forbid," she replied.

A hand gripped her shoulder, fingers digging in hard enough to pinch bone. "We have to leave now," Jerry said.

India flung her head around to stare at him. "We just got here." Franklin Roosevelt was giving them both a startled, considering look. India thought he was embarrassed.

"We're leaving now." Jerry jerked her up by the shoulder.

India made incoherent speeches of farewell and apology as Jerry shoved her toward the door. Better to leave than to make a scene—and he was clearly working one up.

Once they were on the sidewalk, she pulled away from him. Jerry jerked the car door open. "Get in!"

India got in, and he slammed the door. He came around to the driver's side and yanked it open.

"You don't listen to a word I say, do you?" His mouth was white and compressed. "You stupid bitch, I told you to keep your goddamned opinions to yourself." His hand swung across the space between them, his palm smacking the side of her head.

India's head jolted back from the blow, and she scrabbled at the door handle. The door swung open, and she flung herself out.

"Get back in here!"

"You're drunk," she said, gathering her dignity. She hoped no one was watching them from the windows above. "You go to hell. I'm not driving with you." She set off down the street, too furious to notice whether her leg hurt or not. In a few minutes the car passed her, Jerry looking straight ahead. He didn't slow down.

It took an hour to walk home, and her leg hurt well and truly when she got there. Something horrible was happening to Jerry, but she was still too angry to think straight about it. She pulled the front door open and saw a light still on in the living room. *I'll just pretend I don't see that and go to bed*, she thought, but Jerry came stalking down the hall. He had been drinking more at home, she thought, but it was getting hard to tell. His behavior when he was sober was inexplicable, too.

"We're going to have it out," he said between gritted teeth.

"I'm going to bed," India said.

"You listen to me!" He grabbed her again and raised his fist.

A flash of panic went through India. He was muscular, and she was lame. The light in his eyes was frightening. His fist smacked into her face.

She staggered back and picked up a lamp off the foyer table. It was brass, and heavy. Jerry came at her again, and she swung it into his jaw.

Not waiting to see what she had done to him, she fled up the stairs and locked herself in David's room.

XII

Eleanor

David hadn't wakened when India slid into bed beside him the night before, thanking her stars for the recent replacement of his baby bed with a grown-up one. The next morning she lay stock-still, willing him to stay asleep until she heard Jerry go down the hall and out the front door.

She wondered what Jerry's face looked like this morning and for a fleeting moment hoped she had broken his jaw, although she supposed he would have called the doctor if she had. She had heard him come up the stairs and turn into his own room while she lay rigidly waiting for him to try to break David's door in.

Now as the front door closed, India scrambled out of bed. She had had time to think before she finally went to sleep, and the idea that she and Jerry needed to be away from each other—fast—seemed as solid to her now as it had then. Mabel Dodge's invitation was fortuitous now, a lifeline. That Mabel meant it she had no doubt. Other New York friends had been in and out of Mabel's easygoing Taos establishment. Mabel hardly ever came back to New York anymore, but she liked to import people. You never knew whom you were going to find there—just as long as she didn't find Jerry.

"Mama, where are we going?"

"To New Mexico, darling. To see a friend." India thwacked an unsealed envelope down on the table in the foyer: *Dear Jerry, I am taking David and going to visit Mabel in Taos for a while. You may write me there but don't dare show your face.*

That ought to do it. If he did come after her, Mabel was probably protection enough, and there was always the unknown Indian, Tony.

Taos was three days' journey by train. David spent it with his face pressed to the window glass, India in a complicated inner process in which something tightly coiled inside seemed to unwind, like a snake that has decided not to strike after all. She wondered how much Taos had changed. She had spent a year there in 1899, while Mike Holt was making a movie, one of the first. Now even Taos had a picture palace. That was the year she had fallen in love with Frank and convinced Mike and Sally's horrified doctor sister, Janessa, to tell her how not to have babies.

She wasn't sure Taos had changed at all. They left the train in Santa Fe, David goggling at real Indians, and took a motor bus up through the Rio Grande Canyon to what felt like the roof of the world. The Taos sky was still overwhelmingly, almost frighteningly blue, like crushed turquoise; beneath it the adobes of Taos, plastered with cream and tan and reddish mud, glinted as if they were gold-flecked. It was the chopped straw in the plaster that did it, but from a distance they were magical. Tall blue mountains and the red of the Sangre de Cristo range rose above the plateau. The town plaza with its old well and bandstand were still there, but now there were cars among the wagons and horses. A live chicken was loose in the street, and the white-robed, blanket-wrapped Indians who sat on a sunny corner gave her the same look of mingled interest and amusement that she remembered from all those years ago.

An Indian with his hair in two long rolls like braids met her at the bus station and slung her bags into an expensive-looking Pierce-Arrow that could only have belonged to Mabel. India wondered if this was the much-described Tony but hadn't the nerve to ask.

Mabel's house was an adobe on the edge of the village, to which recent additions had obviously been made. It was far larger than anything of its kind anywhere else in Taos. *Mabel's own pueblo,* India thought.

David had so far been almost silent, eyes wide with too

many changes, but as the car crunched over the gravel and
sand of Mabel's driveway, he erupted.

"I want *Daddy*!" It was a piercing shriek, an anguished
wail of bewilderment. Nothing he was used to looked like
this. There were no tall houses, no paved streets, no proper
grass like in the park. It was dusk, blue shadows were falling
over the landscape, and it was getting dark—no streetlights,
only the yellow glow of Mabel's windows, like cat eyes in the
twilight. There was an Indian in the car with them, and probably Indians in the house. David's tear-streaked face turned
red, and he shrieked again.

"Darling, hush, it's all right." India picked him up as
Mabel emerged from the adobe, wearing a long cotton skirt
and Navajo jewelry around her neck and arms. Her hair was
bobbed in bangs straight across her forehead.

"My dear! Such an exhausting trip. But you're here. You
must meet the Lawrences, and Brett. And now you know
Tony." She beamed at the car's driver. So it *was* Tony. India
held out her hand to him.

India wondered what Tony Lujan thought of it all, but
he shook her hand and didn't say. David was still howling as
they went inside, and he screamed afresh as they followed
Mabel upstairs to a long wide hallway floored with terra-
cotta tile.

"Perhaps he would like his supper upstairs," Mabel said
consideringly.

"I think that's an excellent idea. Maybe just an egg and
some toast." India crooned in David's ear. While they were
alone, she got him into pajamas and led him down the hall to
the bathroom to brush his teeth. The windows were indeed
adorned with squiggly lines in several colors and what
looked like a painting of a chicken. India could see why
Mabel, free spirit that she was, had no curtains on them.
Maybe that had been too much even for Mr. Lawrence.

She met the Lawrences when she had finally got David
to sleep. It was a household of adults; they all stayed as
distant as possible from a screaming four-year-old. Lawrence
was dark, with a beard and a gaunt look, the sort of man,
India thought, who made women want to wrap him up in a
box and take him home to feed him and be his muse. She
suspected Mabel of some such intent and wondered what
Frieda Lawrence felt about that. Frieda was German and

amazingly beautiful still. She had left her first husband and her children for Lawrence. Then there was Dorothy Brett, who seemed to have come with the Lawrences. She was English, an artist, an angular woman in corduroy trousers and a scarf around her head like a cloche hat. There was something in the tension that linked the three women that made India uncomfortable, although Lawrence, at the center of it, didn't seem to mind.

Mabel, wearing what appeared to be a burnoose, gave her a drink and made introductions, while Frieda and Dorothy eyed her appraisingly. After dinner—tamales, with a taste that took India back twenty years—Mabel beckoned her out onto the flat roof of the second story, her burnoose swooping around her in a stiff breeze. "You must talk with Lorenzo more," she said in a passionate whisper. "You will be good for him. He is the man who will give this place a voice. You have been here before. Your soul is in Taos."

I have no intention of being good for him, India thought. *Certainly not.* That was the last thing she needed. But she suspected that Mabel simply couldn't resist the temptation to meddle. The introduction of yet another woman would annoy Frieda and Dorothy so.

"He's a fascinating man," India said carefully. Anyone whose books were regularly banned was bound to be interesting, if only for being a bad boy. India did like what she had read of his work, but she wondered how to make it clear to Mabel that she had no desire to go any further than to be a fan.

In the morning that seemed unnecessary. For some reason Mabel was suddenly on the outs with the Lawrences and announced her intention of taking India to meet other friends. David was sulking and didn't want to go. He up-ended his breakfast dish and smacked his fist into his milk. India apologized, cleaned up, and whisked him out of the house while the other adults looked at her as if she had imported a toad into the dining room.

They put David in the Pierce-Arrow, and Mabel drove. In the clear sunlight, India thought that in one thing at least Mabel had her head screwed on straight—Taos was magical. There was a serenity here that India half remembered, and wonderful colors to paint in the blue and red mountains and the adobe geometrics of the town. She wanted to paint Taos

Pueblo again, where most of the Tiwa Indians still lived.
Tony had come from the Pueblo.

She wondered what had drawn him to Mabel. It
couldn't just have been indoor plumbing. India eyed Mabel
curiously. She was getting plump, not the beauty she had
been, but there was something electric, possibly overpowering about her, and Tony Lujan seemed to stand up to that all
right.

The artists' colony at Taos had grown until it was as
much a tourist attraction as the Indians, and generally more
flamboyant. The artists wore *anything,* Mable said—so liber-
ating. The friend she had decided to descend on was a pho-
tographer whose work India had seen. Eleanor Raspell was
in her seventies, with a knot of thick gray hair and fingers
covered with Navajo rings, which on Eleanor looked as if
they belonged there. Three other women of varying ages, all
artists, lived in the house, sharing space and expenses on a
kind of communal basis, with Eleanor as the grande dame.

India took to Eleanor at once, primarily because David
did. Eleanor looked at his tear-streaked face and got down on
the floor to talk to him. "I don't have any toys, but I have
some magazines with very pretty pictures. Would you like to
see them?"

David nodded, and Eleanor plumped a stack of art magazines down beside him. "And cookies possibly." One of the
younger women bustled into the kitchen and came back with
a plate.

"I've left his father—temporarily anyway," India whispered to Eleanor, wondering with a start what else she might
tell this sweet-faced woman who seemed to invite confidence. No wonder the subjects in her photographs looked so
open, so exposed. "Mabel invited me, and I thought we
should be away from each other for a while. But it's been
hard on David."

"Life can be difficult for a child," Eleanor said, cocking
her head at David. "Adults refuse to be perfect so often."

India chuckled.

"Tell me about work," Eleanor said, and India found
herself doing just that.

Unfortunately, the spell wore off David before the day
was over. India settled in to paint that afternoon in the studio
Mabel had given her, turning David over to the box of toys

they had brought with them. That didn't work—David wasn't used to being on his own. He had a nanny at home. He came into the studio and clung to India's skirts until she put the paints down and cuddled him. The next day, on Mabel's recommendation, she hired a nursemaid in the village, a Mexican girl so unlike his New York nanny that David burst into hysterical screams and ran away from her, slamming doors in her face until he got to India.

After that he was angry at India, too. It was his mother's fault they weren't at home, where things were the way he understood them. When India went into her studio, David got a tube of paint from her box and ran out with it. Scratching her head over a painting on the easel, trying to put the fierceness and serenity of Taos Mountain on her canvas, India didn't notice. In an hour, Tony Lujan brought David to her, almost but not quite by the scruff of the neck.

"There is paint downstairs," he said. David looked oddly triumphant.

India flew down the stairs and saw the adobe wall in the living room daubed red with rose madder.

"David!" She spun around and stared at him.

"I hate you!" he shrieked. "I want Daddy!" He ran past her, swinging his arms, and hurled a pair of china candlesticks to the floor as he passed. They shattered on the tile.

India flew upstairs after him, aghast. She caught him just as he was slamming his own door and pulled him up short.

She knelt on the floor in front of him, holding him by the arms while he fought in her grasp. "What is the matter with you?"

"I hate you!" he howled. "I want to go home!"

"Eleanor's offered to let you have a studio in her house," Mabel said brightly. "Such a fortunate thing, because it's much bigger than this one."

And you're throwing me out with my horrible child, India thought. Had Tony put his foot down? No Indian child would behave the way David had. *Maybe I'm just a horrible mother.*

Eleanor's oddly assorted household didn't seem to think so. They accepted David as simply one more piece of impedimenta belonging to their number. Laura Soames had a dog that peed in the corner of her bedroom every night no matter what she did. Evangeline Flowers had a father who, trying to get her to come back home, had a heart attack in Kansas every other week.

"We all have our drawbacks, dear," Eleanor said, "but we are somewhat less intense than Mabel's ménage. And it did occur to me that if you are here to paint, it might be good for you to be in a household where that's what we all do. Mr. Lawrence does tend to be a little larger than life, and the women there do tend to minister to him, rather than do very much themselves. I thought it might be trying for you."

"Then Mabel didn't bribe you?" India said.

"Not at all. We have a spare studio and bedroom here since Alice left, and it really does take five of us to keep up with the expenses." Eleanor chuckled. "Although I imagine Mabel was happy to get the offer. Mabel only had one child, and he's grown. Heaven knows how she raised him."

"I'm afraid David may be horrid," India said. "But we'll try our best." She looked down at her son, who stood with one thumb in his mouth and the look of a child whose best was likely to be explosive.

"Have you heard from his father?" Eleanor asked in the evening, when David had finally been put to bed—India had stayed until she was sure he was asleep. The three other women, Laura, Evangeline, and Claire Pott, were gathered around the fireplace with a bottle of bootleg whiskey, watching pinecones pop blue and green in the embers.

"He wrote to me at Mabel's, hoping I would come to my senses," India said. Without really meaning to, she had told Eleanor all about it.

"Maybe he will come to his if you give him time to think it over," Eleanor commented. "It is easier to be self-examining if the person you are angry with is not available."

"I feel rotten for David."

"Children are more resilient than you think," Eleanor said. "Of course I've never had any, so I may be talking through my hat. But I am of the opinion that you would damage him more if you subjected him to fighting tooth and nail and to an irrational father."

Those were words of comfort to India—words to wrap around her in the same way that Eleanor's house enfolded her. It was unexpected.

Eleanor's house was an old adobe and not so sparkling as Mabel's; its floors were worn with generations of feet, its beams dark with smoke. The whole top floor had been turned into studios, and the bedrooms downstairs were cramped as a result, the women more interested in work space than living space. India and David shared a bedroom vacated by the departed Alice, who had gone to Paris, Eleanor said.

The population of the house ebbed and flowed. They were at their best as they were now, with five. Claire Pott was thirty, a broad, big-boned blond woman who reminded India of a beautiful cow. She painted luminous landscapes that seemed to float on the canvas. Laura Soames was younger, dark and tiny and thin—she made India think of a roadrunner. She painted flower studies in minature, so intricately detailed that an observer might fall into them, India thought, if he were small enough. Lew, the dachshund with the unfortunate habits, slept in an Indian basket on her studio floor while she worked. Evangeline Flowers was a sculptor in her forties, with a thick mass of red-brown hair, which she tied in a knot to keep it off her neck. Her fingernails were split to the quick from working in stone.

They all took to India with uncritical acceptance, and India fell with startling ease into their routine: up with the first light to make coffee and work, lunch when you felt like rummaging in the kitchen, dinner at dusk with everyone taking turns cooking.

David remained rebellious, and India hired a second nursemaid, this time having the sense to find an Anglo girl who at least looked and spoke like the people he was used to. Her name was Angel and she wasn't very bright, but she liked David and had endless patience. She could read him the same story four times in a row without getting bored, or play tic-tac-toe for an hour until India would have been screaming with the repetition.

"Well, I think she's about four herself," Claire said uncritically.

Evangeline looked at her and commented, "She has wonderful buttocks. I wonder if she'd model for me."

It was a pleasant novelty for India to be in a household where a woman's body parts were considered in the light of art and not under the scrutiny of the latest style or whether they would appeal to some man. The women in Eleanor's household paid no attention to what they themselves looked like, unless they were going to a party. It was like going back in time and finding some earlier self, pre-Jerry. Maybe even pre-Roger.

India had thought that she would miss Jerry, or some man, in bed at the very least, but she didn't. Jerry wrote to her again, but she was absorbed in her work and didn't bother to open the letter for three days. She didn't write to Frank, either, unwilling to discuss her marriage with him or explain why she had gone to Taos—especially since Taos was where she and he had begun whatever it was they had.

Gradually some of the peace of Eleanor's house seeped into David and relaxed the stiffness that would send him into a fury. He made drawings of his own for his father, which India dutifully mailed. As David unwound, some last knot in India untied, too, and she stopped trying to wrestle the Taos landscape onto her canvas. Instead, she began to paint the force that had jolted her life onto this new track—Eleanor's household. She seemed to have found some new depth of vision with which to see it, and a kind of furious joy came over her. The women in Eleanor's house were like the outlines of their own work, bathed in a miraculous light, creation on top of creation.

She produced a fiery portrait of Laura Soames, all sparks and movement, with her flowers exploding in the air around her, a beneficent version of her earlier paintings of the war. Claire was more difficult. India's style was too restless for Claire, but at last she achieved a portrait that seemed to catch some of the light of Claire's luminous landscapes. Evangeline was a muscular figure lifting stones, pulling art from the earth, and Eleanor, a powerful, witchlike form with a camera balanced in either hand.

"Oh, wonderful!" Eleanor laughed. "How like me."

Eleanor had always photographed her housemates, and now with India painting them, they came to study each other as well. It opened another level of seeing to be both painter and model.

India thought again, *I've never paid enough attention to things.* She had let life slide past her, it seemed, while she was thinking about minutiae. Art didn't need a narrow focus but a wide-angle lens. No wonder Eleanor went to the heart of things.

India told her so, and Eleanor said disparagingly, "You're too old to sit at my feet."

"I'm not," India said stubbornly. "I never sat at anyone's feet before. It's probably time. I need to learn what's important."

"Your art is important." Eleanor was making bread in the kitchen, and she talked over her shoulder. "Whatever we do at the moment is important, too. Bread. Potting geraniums. Reading to young David. It's all part of the dance. It's all art. Being a slave to someone else's art is not."

India poked her finger in a puddle of spilled flour. "That's what Roger wanted me to be. But Jerry isn't an artist, and he seems to want the same thing."

"Art is what is important to you to do. Your Jerry feels that way because he has something important that he needs you to be subservient to."

India drew a heart in the flour and cracked a line across it with her finger. "It's so peaceful here without any men."

Eleanor snorted with amusement. "There have been men here from time to time. But never any who stayed. I never could find the right kind. Alas."

"Maybe that's what I mean," India said. "The only one I ever met who was the right kind isn't the staying kind. But just now it seems to me that no men at all is better than the wrong kind."

Eleanor gave her an amused look over her shoulder, forehead dotted with flour. She thumped the bread on the table and kneaded it. "So you say now. You aren't that old yet. I'm not even that old yet."

India chuckled.

"Have you heard from your husband?"

India sighed. "He wants to buy me a gallery. He'll buy me a gallery to run if I come home."

"Is that an apology?"

"I don't know. He thinks it will keep me out of trouble. He's convinced I'm going to embarrass him politically somehow. I can't convince him I don't want to." India added darkly, "And now I *am* starting to want to."

Eleanor dumped the dough in the pans to rise. The house cat, a ginger tom, settled himself on the windowsill

with a fluid leap and a plop. The kitchen smelled like yeast
and the bundles of sage and basil tied to the rafters to dry.
Outside, David was playing with Angel, throwing flat stones
into the stream, trying to skip them.

"If I leave him, he'll try to take David," India said.
"David might want him to. How do I know?"

"You can always come back here," Eleanor said. "This
house is not an either/or sort of place." She untied her apron.
"I'm going to work. Brood while you can, while young David
is distracted."

India stood with her elbows on the kitchen sill, one at
either end of the ginger cat, and looked out into the garden.
Eleanor raised herbs. They bordered the stone path that ran
down to the stream. Around two sides of the house was a flat
stone patio, roofed with a grape arbor. It was hot in summer,
and the scent of ripening grapes sweetened the sage and
chaparral. The sun hung overhead, bright as a bronze gong.
Where did twenty-five years go? How much time had flown
past since she came here to stay with Mike and Eden and
painted the pueblo and the cliff house ruins that Johnny
Rojas had shown her? Johnny had been killed in the war,
Tony Lujan said when India had asked him.

*Are you grown up yet? Have you figured out what you
want?* A bumblebee hummed just outside the window, sus-
pended in his own vibration, a miniature dirigible.

You can come back, a voice said to her. *This will stand
still. You can come back to it.*

At the end of the summer, India and David went home.

Jerry greeted them as if they had been on a prearranged
vacation, a sojourn in the West for relaxation. That was what
he had told everyone, Sally said to India. Frank had been in
town and hadn't believed it, Sally added, but Sally hadn't
thought it her business to enlighten him.

Sally knew the truth, of course, just as India knew what
had happened in San Francisco with Juergen. The von Appens were back in Germany now, much to Frau von Appen's
satisfaction, Sally said with a wry twist to her mouth. "She
didn't like us Americans, and we didn't like her."

David was happy to be home, and for a while getting
the gallery on its feet was time-consuming enough to keep
India and Jerry from spending enough time together to fall

into their old quarrel. India solved the problem of socializing by simply not going with him, when she could avoid it, and by spending evenings in the gallery, overseeing renovations. She christened it the Coyote Gallery, because she intended to show her Taos pictures there—and because it said something about what she felt her relationship to the New York art world to be. Might as well call a spade a spade.

Roger Stiller came with an entourage to the opening of the gallery and wrote a sneering review of the first show. India watched with satisfaction as he overplayed his hand. Roger had grown powerful, it seemed, but power is very annoying to some critics. A few of them brought up the subject of the court case again in print and embarrassed Roger far more than he did India. Young artists, spurned by Roger for not following his style in sufficiently slavish imitation, began to take their work to India. In the four years that followed, the Coyote Gallery got a reputation for being on the edge, for having the newest, most experimental work. Some of Roger's protégés came to her behind his back, but India, allowing herself that much vengefulness, refused to show anything of the "Stiller School." Very satisfactory rumors began to circulate: Stiller was burned out, Stiller was no longer on the edge, Stiller had actually stolen his lover's idea fifteen years ago. And hadn't had another good one since, India said to a critic at an opening, and was quoted in his column.

Jerry seemed pleased. If India was making trouble for Roger Stiller, he could be amused. It kept her too busy to get involved in painting seditious posters to irk the men with whom he did his business. He and India had separate bedrooms now. She had given up pretending she cared whether he slept with other women. She was caught up in her own work, although she was never as satisfied with what she painted in New York as with what she did in Taos. By mutual agreement, she went back to Taos once a year now, leaving David, who was in school, in New York.

Eleanor and her wonderful house were always there. Some of the other denizens changed, but Eleanor and the ginger cat were a constant. The Lawrences went away. Mabel was trying to lure the poet Robinson Jeffers there from Big Sur. The women in Eleanor's house went on working, nobody's muse but their own. It was like breathing pure oxygen after being shut up in a box.

India, who had decided in Taos that she had never paid enough attention to things, had taught herself to see clearly. And she could see, even inside the box, that it wasn't just the serenity of Eleanor's house that made the difference, but the rigid and growing anger that was a part of her marriage to Jerry. Jerry didn't seem to mind. As long as she went to the parties at which he required her attendance and did not express opinions beyond those on art and literature, he was content. That was what he had got married for.

But India had married for freedom—in the way that she had avoided marriage for so long for freedom's sake. If the freedom to paint as she liked had to be traded for Jerry's constant watchfulness, for unending suspicion, it was no bargain. And it was no blessing to her to be able to see that so clearly. There were times when she thought she couldn't see anything else.

Juergen came to New York for a visit—unexpectedly. India watched Sally bloom and then fade again when he went away. Their life seemed to be one of impassioned reunions and wrenching rippings apart. Sally wouldn't go to Germany, and Juergen was trying desperately to turn his country away from the despair and bitterness that had taken root in it since the war. They pulled at each other like people with their fingers stuck in glue. No one expected Sally to marry now. Friends gave up introducing her to eligible men. *Such a shame*, they said.

Frank came to New York in June of 1928 to tell India that Big Bill Haywood had died in the Soviet Union, still waiting for the revolution to come to America.

"I'll miss knowing he's around," India said. She stared thoughtfully at her hands, as if she could read something more to say in their deepening lines.

Jerry stepped briskly into the living room just then, twirling his hat on one finger. "What's the matter? Someone died?" He spotted Frank and said without enthusiasm, "Oh, how are you, Blake?"

"Bill Haywood died," India said.

"Fine thing, too," Jerry said, and he cupped his hands

and called, "Pete! Bring me a drink!" A servant appeared with a bottle on a tray.

"You could at least be decent," India snapped. "I knew him."

"If you're in mourning, I'll leave." Jerry took his drink and went out.

"Sympathetic," Frank commented.

"He hates the IWW. You know that. But I'm sorry to hear about Bill. Are you in New York for very long?"

"For a while, if you'll let me stay. I came to see you. It's been a while."

A smile crept over India's mouth. "Please stay. It would be so much fun. Stay with us."

"How would Jerry take to that?"

"Badly, probably," she said. "I may as well be candid. But do it anyway. I miss you."

"All right." Frank grinned. "You can show me this hot-shot gallery. I understand you are a force and a power these days."

"Marginally." But India smiled, because it was true. Her paintings were selling—when she could bring herself to paint in this house—somewhat better than they ever had. And her gallery was making waves. These days everyone played the stock market, made impossible money on pieces of paper, then bought art like furniture to show they were in the know.

"You look funny," Frank told her.

"I beg your pardon?" India laughed. "You haven't got any more tact than you used to."

"I mean odd. You look like you've grown up some way. Like you know what you're doing. But you don't look as if you like it much."

"That's the price we pay for knowing what it is we're doing," India said lightly. She studied Frank in turn, because he was making her uncomfortable. He was older, that was for certain. There were deep lines scored in his face. He had aged faster than she'd thought he would. His sandy blond hair was thinning, and he looked battle-scarred.

"Do you regret anything you've done?" she asked him abruptly.

"Plenty of things," Frank said. He looked a little startled. "If you don't have anything to regret, you haven't done much."

"Good," India said thoughtfully. The look in her eye gave the word a good-deal of weight.

XIII

Down and Out

Frank Blake was well aware that Jerry Rhodes was not pleased to have him as a houseguest. Jerry was always distant to Frank and often borderline rude. He never let pass the opportunity to make some disparaging remark about the IWW, which Frank understood was irrevocably linked to himself in Jerry's mind. But Frank also knew that he had become a scapegoat for all the afflictions troubling Jerry and India's marriage, so he let Jerry's disapproval run off his back.

For reasons best known to himself, Jerry insisted on accompanying Frank and India to the gallery—to point out to Frank that *he* had bought it for her, Frank assumed. India gave Frank a tour of it with an edgy anger.

"About a third of what's hanging now has been bought," she said. "I think that's something of a record. I'm getting ready to take it down."

"How do you know when to take it down?" Frank asked.

"A few months and it's old hat. You don't want to bore people. I want to hang a Taos show next, but I have a canvas of my own I'm trying to finish for it, and it won't come. I was going to try to work tomorrow morning if you don't mind fending for yourself."

"Tomorrow is Saturday. I'll be home," Jerry mentioned. He thought a minute. "I was going to invite some friends for lunch."

India didn't say anything.

"*I* can fend for myself," Frank said. "I expect Jerry can, too. You've got enough servants to let King George fend for himself."

India eyed Frank affectionately, and Jerry caught her at it. His eyes blazed as he said, "I expect you to be present at a luncheon in your own house."

"You shouldn't," India said tightly. "I might embarrass you."

Jerry stalked out, leaving them to find their own way home.

"He hasn't invited anyone," India said. "He won't, either. Not with you in the house."

"A pariah as usual," Frank said. "And I took such pains."

He had dressed carefully to be seen at her gallery—a gray suit and a dark felt hat. If his hands hadn't looked like a hod carrier's, he could have passed for one of Jerry's friends.

India let out a tight breath. "It wouldn't matter," she said cryptically.

Frank watched them at dinner that night with an increasing sense of unease. David, who was eight now, was home from school in a blue uniform blazer with brass buttons. He sat swinging his feet against the table leg, peering covertly from parent to parent as if he were used to the tension that hummed between them like a storm and had learned to dodge it when it built up a sufficient charge. David looked like his father, with overtones of India when he smiled. He didn't smile very often, and he watched Frank suspiciously when he wasn't watching his parents.

The next morning, as predicted, Jerry made no more noise about guests, and India went up to her studio to paint. Frank settled himself with the newspaper and another cup of good coffee and chuckled at his own appreciation for the palaces of the rich. It just seemed a pity to him that people like Jerry always had to go with them, but until now India had seemed to have no difficulty with that. But whatever was going on now between her and her husband had to do with money, Frank was almost sure. Only money made men like Jerry go crazy.

It was a shame India had married this one, Frank thought irritably, but that had been the point. She had wanted the kid. *And you wouldn't give her that, would you?* She hadn't wanted marriage to begin with, but later on Frank had seen the changes come. Maybe he should have done it, should have married her. *If you don't have things you regret, you haven't done much.* The spark was still there, the deep sexual spark that underlay their friendship and always had. But he was old enough now not to be led by his appetites.

Jerry knew the attraction was there, no denying that. Sexual energy gave off a faintly luminous glow that could be seen by those with a proprietary interest. Frank had seen it with India and Ben. Jerry saw it now, and so did young David, although he wasn't old enough to know what it was.

David came into the breakfast room while Frank was brooding into his coffee. He appraised the guest and said, "When are you going home?"

Frank put his coffee cup down. "I don't know just yet."

David thought about that. "Mother's very busy," he said, and left.

India was past caring what Jerry thought of Frank—or of her, for that matter. No attempt to mend the marriage had worked—not buying the gallery, not the new way of seeing things, not the new way of painting. If anything, things were worse. India saw too much, and too clearly. She could hardly paint now. It was like menopause, like something drying up inside her, until she was frantic. Menopause, when it came, wasn't going to trouble her, she thought, but art was supposed to last a lifetime.

She was trying to be busy, but being busy wouldn't make the images come, wouldn't lift them out of the paint. She was working from sketches she'd done in Taos, a study of Claire and Laura sitting side by side on the leather couch in front of the fireplace, stretched out with a whiskey bottle on the low table in front of them, a half-full tumbler beside it. Laura leaned almost on Claire's shoulder, their faces sleepy with the heat. The effect India wanted was almost there, but it wouldn't come all the way because her mind was jagged with thoughts of Jerry, her back braced for interruption. And when it came, she felt almost as if she had summoned it by her expectation.

Jerry pushed the door open and said, "Oh, are you working?"

"Of course I'm working." India tried to keep her focus on the canvas, keep him out.

"I can't find my pearl studs," he said.

"Well, do you need them?"

"I don't know where they've gone. They're valuable."

She turned around. "Jerry, I don't know where your damned studs are! I don't go through your drawers."

"Well, I thought you might be interested." He sounded aggrieved. "You gave them to me."

Between her teeth India said, "I'm trying to work. Do you want me to stop and *look* for them?"

"I didn't mean to interrupt you. Since it's so important."

India exploded. "You interrupt me every time! You *look* for things to interrupt me with! I don't know what's the *matter* with you!"

"I suppose I thought *I* mattered," Jerry said. "I'll go find them myself."

"Damn you!" India shouted after him. She threw her palette against the wall. "Now I can't concentrate!"

At lunch Frank watched India as she sat in stony silence. Jerry seemed reasonably cheerful, now that he had accomplished his aim. Frank had been able to hear practically all of it, but he had refrained from comment.

He knew it might be better if he left, but he felt disinclined to do so. Jerry was a man who had fostered his wife's career at the beginning. Why was he trying to sabotage it now? He wanted her to run the gallery, Frank thought. He didn't want her to paint.

Now why the hell didn't he? Some deep-seated suspicion of artists as unreliable? After all, Jerry had married the creator of the Blackstone Girl, not the painter that India was turning into. *I know what you don't, pal,* Frank thought. *She was there all along.*

"I'd like to see the Taos show," Frank said casually.

"It will be a while before it's hung," Jerry said.

Frank refrained from suggesting that he stay around until it was. His mouth twitched. He looked at India, and she smiled half behind her hand because what he was thinking was so plain on his face. Jerry's mouth tightened.

"The work is all in storage at the gallery," India said. "I'll give you a private showing, the way I do for big poohbah customers with money."

"Horrors. What a mercenary soul you've become," Frank said.

"It's the atmosphere." India's anger had broken up like floating ice, and now she was using it to needle Jerry. "Money is like humidity in the air. When the level rises, everyone reverts to their worst selves."

Frank chuckled, and they leaned their heads toward each other, a quick, oddly intimate gesture.

David pushed his chair back angrily. It smacked against the sideboard behind him, and India snapped her head around toward him, startled.

"You promised to take me riding, but all you ever do is paint!" he said to his mother. Then he narrowed his eyes at Frank. "You should go home. My mother can't work when you're here," he added with eight-year-old unconcern for the contradiction of his statements. He looked far too much like Jerry just then.

"Maybe you ought to try letting her alone," Frank snapped. "You both seem to be pretty happy as long as you can keep her from having any life of her own!"

David's face crumpled into tears, and he flew out of the room.

"You don't talk to my son in that fashion!" Jerry stood, looming above Frank's chair, his hands clenched furiously on the back of it.

"Maybe you ought to pay attention to the lessons you're teaching him," Frank said. He looked up at Jerry but made no effort to stand.

Jerry jerked the chair back with Frank in it. "Damn you, don't you come here with your Communist ideas. You and your goddamn friends—you're all too lazy to work, think the world owes you a living!" His face was furious, muscles clenched. His mouth worked, and he spat out the words.

India stared at him. "Stop it." She pulled at his arm.

Jerry ignored her. He didn't know she was there, Frank thought. He was too angry to see her, much less to listen. "Think the world owes you a living!" Jerry repeated. He couldn't seem to shake that obsession. "None of you willing to work! Come here and abuse my son, teaching him lies! Keep your filthy hands off him and off my wife!" He yanked at the chair again, and Frank stood up, so that Jerry and the chair flew backward into the swinging door to the kitchen. It gave under their weight, and Jerry staggered for a moment before he flung the chair away from him. It splintered against the wall, gouging holes in the wainscoting.

"Stop it!" India screamed. "This is too much!"

Neither one of them paid any attention to her. Jerry was still shouting accusations of Communism, sabotage, theft, anything he could think of, ranting on about the Wobblies. "Know what you people are like!" he shouted. "Immoral, most of you perverted! Keep away from my wife!"

Frank watched him with a kind of sardonic amusement along with a well-controlled fury. "I could sue you for slander," he said finally, when Jerry paused for breath. "How would you like that?"

"Get out of my house!"

India got between them. "You have lost your mind," she said, staring at Jerry as if he had suddenly turned into a hippopotamus or some other unfathomable roaring creature, no longer human as she understood it. "Frank is my guest. He's *your* guest."

"No one abuses my son!"

"David had that coming," India said levelly. "You're the one who's encouraged him to resent Frank. You're responsible for his attitude."

"The child sees his mother turning into some kind of Communist under the influence of 'Old Pal' here. What do you expect?"

"I expect you to have some sense!" India snapped.

"Actually," Frank said, with a sidelong look at India to be sure she was going to be able to hold her own if he left, "I have to see a man about a dog. I'd probably better be going. I'll be at Mike's," he said. "If you need me."

Jerry shot him a triumphant look and snarled, "We don't need you."

India refused to speak to Jerry for the rest of the weekend, and tried desperately to speak to David, who folded his lips in firm imitation of his father and shook his head.

"David, you were appallingly rude to Mr. Blake. You have no reason to be angry with him."

"We don't like him," David said. "Dad and I don't like him. He made me cry."

"For your information, Dad was rude to him, too," India snapped. She tried again. "Dad doesn't like him because he is an old friend of mine, and Dad is mad at me a lot right now."

"Why?" David demanded, puzzled.

"I don't know." India wondered what that answer would tell David. He had a lot invested in his picture of his father, and it wouldn't help to criticize Jerry. "Just try to be polite to Mr. Blake, whether you like him or not," she said. "You don't have to like him. He's *my* friend."

"Dad says you don't need any friends besides him and me," David volunteered. "Why do you want somebody besides us?"

"David, I don't exist in a bottle, just for the benefit of you and Dad."

"You're my mother," he said. "Dad says you're supposed to spend your time with us."

"Dad isn't being very reasonable," India said gently. "*He* doesn't spend all his time with us."

"He's a man. Men go to the office," David said importantly.

India sighed. "David, I would appreciate it if you would quit quoting your father to me on the subject of what I am and am not supposed to do. He's angry with me, and he's being unreasonable. It's not fair of him to tell you things like that."

David's lip quivered. "I don't see why you and Dad can't get along. All the other fellows' parents get along. I *hate* it when you say things about each other."

"I hate it too, honey," India said. "Can't you come here and sit beside me for a minute?" She took him to the sofa and patted the cushions beside her, holding on to his wrist until he sat down, stiffly, feet on the floor, bottom on the edge of the sofa—as if he wanted to be ready to leave as soon as she let him.

"David, look at me."

He turned his head minutely in her direction.

"David." India put her hand under his chin and turned his face toward her. "This isn't about Mr. Blake. It's about you being unhappy because of Dad and me, isn't it?"

"You and Dad wouldn't be unhappy if it wasn't for Mr. Blake coming around."

"And who told you that? Dad?"

David didn't answer.

"Well, I'll tell you, honey," India said, "it doesn't do to go blaming all your troubles on someone else. Dad and I don't get along when Mr. Blake isn't here, either."

"Dad says you would. Dad says Mr. Blake used to be your . . ."

"What?" India demanded grimly.

"That you used to be his girl. Before Dad. Now you don't love Dad."

"I do love Dad," India said, wondering if she did. *Damn Jerry.* "Mr. Blake is just an old friend."

"Then why do you *fight*?" David's question was a wail of unhappiness. His lip trembled again, and his eyes spilled over with tears.

"I try not to," India said.

"Dad doesn't. He picks fights with you all the time. He says it's because you don't care about him, and he feels bad. Can't you make him feel better?"

"No, I don't think I can," India said. "Dad has to be in charge of how he feels."

"I hate it when he talks about you," David said suddenly. He sniffled and scrubbed his hand across his nose.

"Then don't listen, darling."

"I can't help it! I can't help listening to you, either! Who am I *going* to listen to, if I don't listen to you and Dad? And when I *do* listen, all you do is say bad things about each other!"

"I have *not* said bad things about your father," India said.

"Yes, you have! I won't choose between you. You can't make me choose."

"Darling, no one's trying to make you choose between us."

"Yes, you are. And you're not going to make me!" David's face screwed up, and he burst into sobs. India pulled him into her lap and held him, rocking back and forth, crooning to him. "I want it to be like it *used* to be!" David sobbed over and over. "Why can't you be like you used to be?"

In the weeks that followed, life for India deteriorated. After another shouting match one evening, Jerry put a padlock on the gallery and told India she couldn't have it back until she decided to behave herself. India countered by getting a pair of bolt cutters and going to see a lawyer.

"We have kept Mr. Rhodes from interfering in the business of your gallery since the lease is in your name," the lawyer, Maurice Abbott, said. "Mrs. Rhodes, you must be very sure you can't live with that before you take any further steps that you will regret." Mr. Abbott was gray-haired, solemn, and tall, rather like a serious stork.

"I don't have any options," India answered. "I want a divorce."

"What about your child?"

"David is living in an untenable situation as it is. He hates to come home from school—he never knows what horrible abuse is going to be flying through the air."

"Have you considered that if you go ahead with this, you may lose him? Mr. Rhodes may get custody."

"That is what I am retaining you for, Mr. Abbott," India said with asperity. "I cannot continue to live with Jerry, nor will I subject David to his aberrations."

Mr. Abbott sighed. "I am not without sympathy, Mrs. Rhodes. Mr. Rhodes's behavior during the business of the gallery was bizarre, to say the least. But on the face of it, he appears only to want what most men feel they have a right to —control of his wife."

"Those were not the terms on which we married, and he is not going to change the rules now!" India said.

"Wouldn't it serve your purposes just as well to live apart? We could sue for separate maintenance and, I believe, be successful. You would have to be very careful about forming any other, er, liaisons. That could jeapordize your standing."

"Oh, perfect." India glared balefully around Mr. Abbott's sleekly paneled, well-appointed office. "I can force Jerry to support me for the rest of my life, and I won't have to live with him, as long as I behave like a nun."

"I'm afraid that's the sum of it," Mr. Abbott said.

"But Jerry can do anything he has a mind to? Chorus girls? Fan dancers?"

"I'm afraid so."

India leaned forward in her chair and put her hand on the attorney's desk. "Mr. Abbott, I want a divorce in order to be able to lead a bearable life again. What you are proposing does not qualify."

"Mrs. Rhodes, forgive me, but I know your date of birth. You are nearly fifty. Surely by this age—"

"Would you care to try this prescription yourself, Mr. Abbott? I do not have one foot in the grave. It is quite possible that I might wish to remarry." *Not on your life*, India was thinking.

Abbott sighed. "Very well. You are aware that the only grounds for divorce in the state of New York is adultery. Can you prove that your husband has been unfaithful?"

"He sleeps with his secretary," India said.

Mr. Abbott steepled his fingers together. "Can you prove that?"

India frowned, disgusted. "Not unless I have him followed by a detective."

"Then you had better do so."

"No. I don't want to divorce him because he sleeps with his secretary. I want to divorce him because he is abusive."

"Abuse is not grounds in New York."

"Isn't there anything besides adultery?" She felt panicked, trapped. What if she couldn't get out of this?

"A marriage may be declared null by the court for a number of reasons—fraud of some kind."

"What kind?"

"If either of the parties was under the age of consent, or mentally incapable, or was forced. If there is incurable insanity existing for five years. If there is a physical impairment to the married state."

"What's that?"

"Impotence," Mr. Abbott said.

India chuckled. "Well, we can't try to prove that and adultery as well."

"Mrs. Rhodes, this is a serious matter."

"I am extremely serious, but I thoroughly dislike the idea of having Jerry followed to try to catch him doing something he might not even be doing if *I'd* sleep with him."

"*Don't* say that!" Mr. Abbott said. "If your husband can prove *you* refused to have relations with him *before* he had relations with his secretary—"

"And that's another thing. I haven't got anything against the woman. She probably thinks Jerry will leave me for her

—she's younger. I wish he would, but he won't. He doesn't want a tootsie. He wants a tiger head."

Mr. Abbott looked bewildered for a moment, but then he looked at India, and a certain amount of comprehension seemed to dawn on him. "If he wants to stay married to you, Mrs. Rhodes, it will make it very difficult."

"I want to do it anyway."

Mr. Abbott sighed. "As your attorney, I have to advise you not to. You will pay a very high cost. If you insist on divorce, you would frankly do better to go to Nevada. The residency requirement there is only three months, and the Nevada courts accept extreme cruelty as grounds for divorce."

"Would I be certain of getting it?"

"Does he beat you?"

"The only time he tried, I hit him with a lamp."

"That's unfortunate," Mr. Abbott said dryly. "In that case, no, you would not be certain of getting it."

"Then I'll go through with it here."

Abbott looked grave. "I want you to be absolutely sure of what you are getting into. If you prosecute your husband for adultery, he will be entitled to bring to court allegations against your own conduct both before and after the marriage. It is common knowledge that you lived with a man before your marriage. That will not look good to the judge."

India's lips compressed, and she made a little movement with her hands as if pushing something away.

"It will not be pleasant or pretty. You will be pilloried in public opinion. Your husband will very likely fight the case, since the guilty party in a divorce for adultery may not remarry in this state for three years without the court's permission and on proof of good conduct."

"What if *I* give Jerry grounds for divorce? Do you think he would do it?"

"I have no way of telling. He might if he were angry enough, but you would almost certainly lose custody of your child."

"I won't risk that," India said. "This is barbaric. Why did I get married in the first place?"

"The state has a vested interest in preserving the sanctity of the marriage union."

"I know too many people who are miserably married,"

she said, forlorn. "There's no sanctity in that. I want out. You get me out."

She left feeling that she had somehow been sentenced to jail while she wasn't looking. She would never be free the rest of her life if she didn't do this. *Maybe* Jerry would be willing to get rid of her.

That was a false hope. After David left for school one morning, India confronted Jerry over breakfast and told him where she had been. "You don't want me, Jerry. I'm a constant embarrassment. Let loose of me, and you can see David all you want to. And you won't have to put up with me. If I embarrass you, you can tell your friends that's why you divorced me."

"They will assume that I couldn't control you," Jerry said evenly, not looking her in the eye. He buttered his toast. "If I can't control my wife, I may not appear to be of much use to them."

"Jerry, please. Mr. Abbott says that when couples have agreed, then the charge of adultery is a kind of formality. The husband makes sure he's caught with someone and doesn't deny it in court. No one thinks the worse of him—you probably couldn't find a *judge* who's faithful to his wife."

"Charming," he said. "Except that I don't want a divorce. I want you to behave yourself."

"Why? You know you've been—" India bit her lip and stopped. If Jerry wasn't aware that she knew he had been seeing his secretary, she didn't want to warn him. This was getting more repellent by the minute, she thought; she let the conversation die.

The private detective recommended by Mr. Abbott was repellent, too. Many detectives wouldn't handle divorce work; it was degrading and offended their morals—which appeared to allow everything else. "But I'm always willing to help out a lady," Mr. Blick said, "for a price, of course. Goin' to take him for a good chunk?" He winked at India.

"I just want a divorce," India said.

"Well, Bill Blick is the man to get it for you." And indeed within a short time he produced photographs that Mr. Abbott said would probably do. Mr. Abbott served the papers and obtained an order for Jerry to move out of the house. Jerry went to his club, and the next day the news was all around Wall Street and all through the art world and the Village.

Sally heard it at the hospital, where she was president of the Volunteer Auxiliary.

"Several dear ladies made it a point to tell me," she told India over lunch. "I made it a point to tell *them* that my friends generally kept me informed of their activities, and it was unnecessary for them to circulate the story further. It won't do any good, I'm afraid."

India made a face over her crab salad. "You should see the detective Mr. Abbott made me hire. I wanted to wash my hands after I talked to him. And the pictures he took—like illustrations for a bad novel. Jerry looking furtive, slipping through a hotel door with that poor girl. And even one inside the room. He must have shot it through the window, skulking around on the balcony. They were in bed. It's rather odd to see your husband photographed half naked with someone else."

"Oh, India." Sally looked revolted. "How horrible."

"Well, thank goodness for it. I wouldn't get the divorce otherwise." India felt weary, as if she hadn't been sleeping enough. "You're lucky you didn't marry. It's barbaric. It's like being a slave."

A waitress hovered over them with a coffeepot, and Sally held her cup out. "Sometimes I feel so sad," she said. "Do you? All the plans we made when we were young, all those expectations . . . Nothing really turned out the way we wanted it to, did it?"

"Not noticeably," India said. She studied Sally's face. "I'm sorry about Juergen. I get so wrapped up in my own troubles that I forget I'm not the only woman in the world who's been hard done by. Isn't there any chance?"

Sally shrugged. "We write. Mother hates him. She met him in San Francisco. Tim insisted I bring him around when Mother was visiting. Tim and Elizabeth were perfectly nice, and Mother is never rude, but none of them could get past his being German. *His* mother hates *me*. It's nice all the way around."

India noticed Sally's eyes welling up, though Sally was trying to look away. "They'd like him if they spent any time with him," India said. "Juergen's a man with an unfortunate amount of conscience, I suppose. It makes it impossible for me not to respect him, at the same time that I want to smack him for how he's treated you."

Sally looked broodingly into her coffee cup. "How about how I've treated him? Demanding that he put me ahead of his country."

"Men expect that of women every day," India said brusquely.

"That's different. We don't have the same responsibilities."

India shook her head. In some ways she and Sally were never going to see eye to eye. She suspected that if Sally had married Jerry, she'd stick with him. But then Sally wouldn't have married Jerry without loving him completely. Cynical India was the one who was willing to marry someone she loved just enough to suit her convenience.

"Have you thought what you're going to wear to the trial?" Sally asked, startling her.

"Wear?"

"It's important." Sally seemed to be trying not to brood, so India gave her her attention. "You want to look, well, vulnerable, but respectable at the same time. Maybe even a little frumpy."

"That shouldn't be hard," India said.

"I'll take you shopping. An unbecoming hat will do wonders. *All* the hats are unbecoming this year. I can't abide going around looking like a turtle peering out of its shell. We had such pretty hats when we were young, didn't we?"

"It was a different world," India said.

"Well!" Sally said briskly. She lifted a finger to the waitress for the check. "In *this* world you still have to impress the judge, and I'm not such an old fogey yet that I'm ready to look like Mother Hubbard. How long do you have before David gets home from school?"

"He gets home at three. Mary will be there, but he needs me, not just the cook."

"Of course." Sally looked at her watch. "We have two hours. We'll find you a frumpy hat, and maybe I'll buy a pair of those cute shoes with the rosettes on the toes that everyone's wearing."

They left money on the table and went out into the crisp fall air. A cidery smell from the apple sellers' carts mixed with the scent of wood and coal smoke. India's driver was waiting for them, and she told him to take them to Saks Fifth Avenue.

For the next hour they tried on hats, the sillier the better. A particularly ridiculous one that looked like a jockey's cap with a shortened bill sent them into paroxysms of laughter. An impeccable saleswoman eyed them frostily, but she knew Miss Holt and Mrs. Rhodes, and they had enough money to laugh at her hats if they wanted to.

"Pour le sport," Sally said, tipping the jockey cap at a rakish angle.

India pulled a short, pleated bucket of gray and crimson over her ears. "Ugh."

"No, not that one," Sally said. "Here." She handed India a navy silk toque with a black taffeta flower. "This is perfect. Wear it with that navy suit that looks so nice on you, and no one will say boo to you."

"It's a mercy I have you to dress me," India murmured. "Otherwise I might wear any old thing, go to court in my paint apron."

"You've improved no end since I met you," Sally said with a chuckle. "You have a wonderful style. I just can't resist the urge to manage people. It comes of never having children, I suppose."

"Children," India said. "I have to get home. Do you want us to drop you off, or would you like to come and inspect my closet for the proper shoes?"

"I'll come if I won't be in the way. I'm not feeling very solitary today. There's something about fall that always makes me sad."

"Nor am I," India said. "And you're the only one I have the nerve to be honest with just now. David would like to see you, I think. He's fond of you, and he needs company, too."

They bought the navy toque for India and got home with it before David came from school. It seemed heartless somehow to be shopping for hats, so India took the hatbox upstairs to her room.

"Mrs. Rhodes!" Mary met her coming down the stairs. "This come for you."

India had a lump in her stomach as she took the telegram and tore it open. Telegrams were never good news.

"What is it?" Sally whispered.

India looked at her, stricken. "Mother's dead."

"Oh, darling, no!"

"She had a stroke." India stared at the telegram, then looked at Sally. "She wasn't very old."

"Oh, your poor mother. And poor you." Sally put her arms around India.

India looked bewildered. "How could she die? I just had a letter from her last week."

"I don't know. Strokes are sudden. You know she didn't suffer, though." Sally closed her eyes. "That's always supposed to be a consolation, but it seems like a slim one."

India scrubbed her hand across her eyes and dug in her pocket for a handkerchief. "I wasn't prepared for this. She wasn't sick. I feel as if someone should have given me warning."

Sally laid a hand on India's arm, her fingers tightening in sympathy. "I know. Our parents are always there, and then all of a sudden one of them dies. It's like being abandoned. And you wonder how long until you lose the other one. At least that's how I felt when Dad died. But it's going to hit your father hard. You'll have to go home right away."

India crumpled the telegram in her hand. Home. What on earth would it be like to go home now? She felt a sudden unreasonable surge of anger at her mother for dying now, for not being there when India needed her. Her mother would have hated the idea of the divorce, but she would have forgiven her.

"Call me a cab, Mary, would you?" Sally said quietly. "I'm going to change my mind and go." She turned back to India. "You need time with David. I'll come by again later tonight."

India nodded. She looked blankly at Mary. "My mother has died," she said, trying out the sound of it.

"I'm sorry, Mrs. Rhodes. You want me to call Mr. Rhodes for you?"

"No. Not just now. Just send David up to me as soon as he gets home."

Mary picked up the telephone, and India went slowly up the stairs, leaving Sally in the hall. She saw Sally sit down on a chair to wait for her cab. What a miserable end to the day, India thought dully. Between divorce and desertion and death, they had managed to squeeze in an hour laughing at hats.

She turned numbly through the door into her bedroom, took off her gloves, and set her hat on the dresser. The face in the mirror that looked back at her was pinched and spiteful looking. Was that what grief did to her? Would the ache for her mother be this painful for the rest of her life? She thought about her mother, born in India, raised by her English relatives, married young to Edward Blackstone, so much older than she. Ramedha Blackstone had adored her husband, adored her children. Winslow's death and India's defection had hit them both hard. Now India had to go home, when she should have gone home long ago and more often. Now when it was too late to please her mother . . .

And, oh God, the gallery. India groaned. Tonight she was supposed to meet Stevie Lennox, who was helping her hang the Taos show, at the gallery. If she didn't go, there was no telling what he would do with it. She went into the bathroom and splashed cold water on her face. She felt unpleasantly pulled between grief and responsibilities. How upset would David be? He didn't know his grandmother well— India's fault for not going home—but a funeral was not a reassuring event. She debated taking him to the gallery with her tonight and decided against it. Now that the news was out about the suit for divorce, the Coyote Gallery had suddenly become full of people more interested in gawking at India than in buying paintings.

She told David the news, and he seemed to take it well. When Sally came back later, India left him with her and went to make her appointment.

At the gallery, her acquaintances seemed to take her red eyes in stride, attributing them to the appalling scandal of divorce.

"Aren't you making a mistake, dear?" Stevie Lennox leaned chattily against a column that was going to hold one of Evangeline Flowers's pieces in stone. "You've got the critics eating out of your little hand. Why throw it up over a row with your better half?"

"I suppose a divorce will suddenly make my work no good," India said grimly.

"Oh, it might make it take off," Stevie said. "But it might all go boom, too. There are nasty stories going around. Roger Stiller is telling everyone he knew you when."

India sniffed. "That's old news."

"Not the way Roger's telling it."

India stopped staring at the canvases Stevie had brought her and focused on him. "What does that mean?"

"He's saying you weren't quite, well, *womanly*, you know. A little too interested in the other girls. That sort of thing is all very well for odd ducks like me, so long as we're not blatant about it, but the public doesn't like to hear about it in a woman."

India's eyes flared. "I will find that lying son of a—"

"Oh, I wouldn't," Stevie said. "You'll just give credence to it."

"And on what is he basing this fascinating idea?" India inquired grimly.

"Oh, your little female collective in Taos," Stevie said. "All those women all by themselves. My goodness, they must be up to something. Says he noticed the tendency while you were living with him."

"Oh, God." India's eyes brimmed suddenly with tears.

"Mercy!" Stevie said. "I've never seen you do that before. Here, let me get you a hanky." He pulled a voluminous one from his pocket, and India blew her nose with it.

"I'm sorry," India said. "I just don't know how much more I can take. I got a telegram this afternoon. My mother died. I have to take David and go out to Oklahoma. I—"

"Well, what are you doing in here?"

"I don't know," she said. "Trying not to think about Mother, I suppose. I haven't told them about the divorce. Now I'll have to tell Father." She sniffled.

"It's awful. When my mum died, I thought it would tear me open."

"I haven't been to see them nearly enough. I didn't get along with Father. Now she's gone." India closed her eyes, and tears slid out from under them. "I don't know how David's going to do. They never saw him as much as they wanted to."

"You're too old for remorse," Stevie said. "Brace up. Plain vanilla mourning is what you want; no fancy regrets."

"Should I take Jerry with us?" *And why am I asking a twenty-two-year-old who isn't married and very plainly is not going to be?*

"If I were you," Stevie said, "I'd take the kid and go *stay* there a while, till old Roger runs out of breath. But

Jerry? Not if you don't want to reconcile. Remember how the court will view that."

"Oh, damn the court!" India said, despairing. "My life is more controlled by some judge I haven't even seen yet than it was by Jerry. I can't bear this."

"Buck up," Stevie said. "You're only the scandal of the moment. By the time you get back, all the old hens will have their beaks in someone else."

India wanted to think so. If the divorce dragged on long enough, the gossipers might get tired of it. She lulled herself with that thought on the trip to Oklahoma, the train's rattling wheels producing a long slow chant like bees in the distance. Always they seemed to be receding, and always they stayed with her.

David was a small, silent figure huddled beside her in a stiff black suit that made her think of a crow's feathers. She put an arm around him and drew his head down onto her shoulder. "I'm sorry that everything is so dreadful," she said. It seemed a thin comfort, but what else was there to say?

"I don't really remember Grandmother very well," David said. He shifted inside the suit as if it imprisoned him.

"I know, darling. We haven't been back there very often, but she loved you very much. I wish you could have known her better."

David was silent again, watching the land go by outside the window, flat acres of wheat with a car bumping away from them down a dusty road. "What's a divorce?" he said.

"It's when two people get unmarried." India hugged him tighter, her gloved hand firm against the black coat.

"I didn't know you could get unmarried."

"It's hard to do," India said. "But sometimes people just have to."

"I don't think you have to." David sounded sad. "I think you're just being selfish."

India was quiet a moment. Finally she asked him, "Do you think that I should be miserable for the rest of my life so that your father can have what he wants?"

"What about what I want?"

"You don't get to want things that depend on other people's misery," India said. "You just don't."

David buried his face deeper in her shoulder. From that haven he said, "No one cares what I want."

"I care what you want, darling," India said. "I just can't always give it to you. I love you. Does that help any?"

David sniffled. "Some."

Her father met them at the station with a black armband around his sleeve. His face was drawn, his eighty-nine years hanging heavy on him.

"She was twenty years younger," he said. "How could she leave me? How could she go first?" When they got to his car, his driver helped him in and tucked a rug over his knees. Edward Blackstone looked at his daughter. "I was supposed to go first. Where's Jerry?"

"Jerry's not coming, Father." India put an arm around David, who was beside her in the back seat of the Packard.

"He ought to be here. What's so important that he can't come? Wall Street business?" Edward Blackstone would have understood that. Making money was a man's purpose in life.

"No," India said. "I'll talk to you about it later."

"Dad doesn't live with us now," David announced bitterly.

Edward Blackstone's eyebrows beetled together. "What does that mean?"

India closed her eyes as the car bounced over the dirt road across the prairie from Ada to the M Bar B. "Later," she said.

The house and outbuildings at the end of the road were almost a small village, Edward Blackstone's private kingdom. A mile away was the Martin Ranch, which had once been part of the M Bar B, Edward's partners. They had died in the influenza epidemic in 1918, and Edward had bought out their heirs. Now he owned the whole countryside. In his youth he had gone to New York and London often, taken his wife shopping in Paris. Since the war, it had been hard to get him away from his kingdom. *He'll never leave it now,* India thought, *with Mother and Winslow both buried here.*

The funeral was the next day, in the huge front parlor, with people coming from miles around. India sat by the bed in the best guest room, where her mother's body was laid out, and held the cold hand and cried into the wedding-ring quilt that covered her. All the troubles she could have laid in her mother's lap were a weight with no place to go. Ramedha Blackstone, who had never quite fit anywhere, had understood her rebellious daughter far better than Edward did. What had it been like to be married to Father? India thought. Ramedha had loved him, India was certain of that, but he had been so much older. And overpowering? When she was young, India had painted her mother with a Hindu caste mark on her forehead and the tight, high-boned collar of a Western dress around her neck. Ramedha had complained that the painting made her look as if she were strangling. India had wondered how her mother had seen that so easily.

She wiped her eyes with the sodden handkerchief she had stuck up her sleeve and then called David in.

"I thought you might want to say good-bye, darling," she told him.

David hung in the doorway and looked at the bed. "She doesn't look like I remember her," he whispered.

"No," India said sadly. "She's gone. This is just what she left behind. Bodies look strange because there's no one inside."

"I don't want to stay in here."

"You needn't." India stood up. She straightened the quilt and brushed a hand across her mother's gray hair. Then she sent a shaken David out to the barn with the M Bar B's foreman to see the horses, and while he was occupied, she told her father she was getting a divorce.

"There has never been a divorce in our family," Edward Blackstone said. His hands shook on the arms of his chair. They were heavy with blue veins, as if all his blood ran very close to the surface now.

"Jerry has left me no options, Father." India rested her own hands on the head of her cane, balancing it between her knees.

"You have the option of sticking to your wedding vows!" Edward snapped. "Your mother and I had our problems, but we stuck it out!"

India closed her eyes a moment. She opened them and looked at her father, trying to find some understanding in his face. "You can't know what it has been like. He is irrational. Obsessive. It's like living with a jailer. I can't breathe."

"You aren't required to breathe, then. All your life

you've been at odds with what you were supposed to do—disregard everyone's convenience but your own. Well, this time you are not required to breathe; you are required to think of your family and stick it out like a decent woman."

"I can't," India said.

"What about David?" her father demanded. "Branded as the child of a divorced mother!"

"I am not asking for your advice, Father," India said. "I am simply doing you the courtesy of telling you what I am going to do. I felt that I owed that to you."

Edward Blackstone struggled to his feet, leaning on his chair for support. "Then I will tell you what I am going to do. If you persist in this disgusting and indecent course of action, without regard for your family, you can expect no inheritance from me, apart from what your mother left you. No divorced woman is a daughter of mine."

Edward remained sullen and angry throughout dinner and breakfast the following morning. The funeral brought crowds of people whom India only vaguely remembered, black coats dusty from the road. Her mother's coffin was placed on a stand in the parlor and heaped with flowers, and after the service it was lowered into the ground in a grassy plot where she had planted a rose arbor over Winslow's grave. A matching headstone with her father's name but bare of the date stood beside it. "I was supposed to have been the first," Edward said plaintively to the minister, who patted him on the back and talked about the Lord's unknowable ways.

Edward Blackstone's lawyer asked India to stay until the will had been read the next day, but the day after that, she went home on the train with David, still unreconciled with her father. He had coldly promised a check in a month or two from her mother's estate. It wasn't much, but at least it would be a cushion against whatever whirlwind she was stepping into. And there was a little money of her own, bolstered by rising stock prices—she'd done quite well with America's favorite financial pastime. With alimony from Jerry and income from the gallery, she and David could keep the house. David would be disrupted in his life as little as possible.

India put an arm around him. He had on a cowboy hat a

little too big for him, and his face was unsettlingly waiflike under its brim. She hugged her to him, and he took off the hat and buried his face in her chest.

Despite Stevie Lennox's hopeful predictions, no one had forgotten the Rhodes divorce when India came home. There was a message from Mr. Abbott requesting an urgent conference, and a note from the *New York Times* art critic asking whether she was still planning to mount the Taos show.

Abbott wanted to know that, too.

"Of course I am," India said. "I've postponed it too often with everything that has happened. If I don't get it up soon, the artists may withdraw their work."

"By no means should you go ahead with this show," Abbott said. "With the talk that is circulating, you do not want to add fuel to the fire."

India flushed. "Roger Stiller is still at it? I heard about that before I left."

"Your husband has chosen to call Roger Stiller as a witness at the trial."

"Jerry is a *snake*! He knows very well that the rumor is not true!"

"He has chosen to allege that it is, and that you have been sexually promiscuous with men, as well."

India gripped her cane with both hands. Her clenched fingers shook.

Abbott raised an eyebrow. "I warned you. I did tell you that it would be unpleasant."

"What can I do to counter this?"

"Don't mount the show. Not with pictures of those women in Taos. Or with pictures painted by them."

"I have to! These are friends! They're artists who depend on the sale of their work to live. Most of them aren't in Eleanor's house anymore—they've scattered, they have houses of their own, children to support. I can't back out of the show."

"I strongly advise you to do so."

"I can't. I will not kowtow to that toad. Or to Jerry, either. And everyone knows the show is scheduled. If I don't hang it, it will look like I'm afraid to."

Mr. Abbott spread his hands out. "That might be better."

Sally said so, too, when India described her interview with Abbott. India paced up and down Sally's parlor as she spoke, her cane thumping on the floor. Frank was there, too, and he offered the same opinion. He was in town off and on, keeping a cautious eye on the proceedings. He had come to Sally's tonight to see India, because Mr. Abbott had said that on no account was she to have male guests in her house while the trial was pending. Or female guests, either, he had added, at least not to stay overnight.

"How can anyone *believe*—" India glared into the mirror over Sally's mantel. "And what does one look like, anyway? Should I let my hair grow out again?" She pulled at the dark waves, shot with gray. Her brows were straight dark lines. "Pluck my eyebrows?"

Sally laughed, but she shook her head in bewilderment. "I don't know. I got funny looks at the hospital board meeting yesterday. I think they suspect you're carrying on with *me*."

"Oh, Sally, no!" India looked appalled.

"I didn't even know women did that," Sally said.

"Consider it an educational experience," Frank said. He sat in one of Sally's overstuffed armchairs with a pillow behind his neck. His back hurt almost all the time now. "A look at the far reaches of human desire. But, no, India. You shouldn't hang that show right now."

"I have to," she said. "I would even if I hadn't been going to. Damn them *all*!"

The show went up, and no critic could resist alluding to the divorce, to the charges and countercharges. The paintings of Eleanor's household took on a significance that had never occurred to India. One critic called the canvas of Laura and Claire "a disquieting excursion into forbidden worlds." Another said it had a "dreamlike quality surpassing whatever relationship lies between the figures." They saw in Claire's sculpture "an unwomanly brutality." And everyone pored avidly over Eleanor's photographs of the occupants of her house.

India was well enough known as an artist to be mildly famous in New York. As the creator of the Blackstone Girl, she was nationally known. Now she discovered herself nationally notorious. Columnists discussed her, and her private affairs were argued in letters to the editor. Often the issue of the divorce overrode the sexual rumors. The idea that a woman was not obliged to stay in an intolerable marriage simply because a man wanted her there was to many women a heady one. Those who wrote for and to women's magazines argued the issue in print.

Mr. Abbott looked angrier with her as each new letter appeared. He had told her not to hang the show; it had only fueled the fire. Women who gave too much time to their work were suspect. When did she take care of her child?

A trial date was set for December. "Merry Christmas," India said bleakly.

By the end of October she was almost numb. Nothing said about her could surpass anything that had already been said. Jerry telephoned her daily to castigate, threaten, and berate. David was tormented at school and then sent home for fighting by a self-righteous headmaster. India declined to send him back. He could stay home until the holidays, and then she would decide on another school. She hired a private tutor and argued with Jerry on the telephone about paying his fees.

On the twenty-fourth of October, Jerry didn't call her. It was a blessed relief at first, and then she began to wonder what he was up to. When the telephone finally rang, she snatched it up, ready to tell him to go to hell, whatever he wanted.

It wasn't Jerry. It was Richard Levine, her broker. "We have to cover your margin." His voice sounded tight, as if he were maintaining an elaborate calm that went no further than his lips.

"How much do you need? What happened?"

"Nothing serious. Just a slight market dip, I'm certain. I'll keep you informed, of course. But you need to cover ten thousand in margin."

India thought. "I can do that. But, Richard—"

"I'll keep in touch," he said and hung up. When India tried to call him back, his line was busy.

She bit her thumbnail. Why did he need the money at a time like this? Stocks had gone up steadily. There should be no need to cover her margin. She turned on the radio and sat down in front of its morning-glory-shaped horn to hear the financial news.

They were already calling it a collapse. President Hoover was expected to address the nation the next day. India sat staring at the radio's green eye until eight that evening, when Richard Levine called her for more margin money. Jerry never did call.

The next day it looked as if the market might steady, but Richard Levine needed the rest of her margin. India gave it to him, selling every stock she had to get it. When she went to Abbott's office, Abbott was ashen-faced. Tiffany's was full of people trying to sell their jewelry to raise money. Everyone had bought on margin, putting up sometimes no more than a tenth of the price of their stock. Stock values always rose; it was a wonderful way to make money.

India threaded her way through the crowd in the street. No one was interested in her now. A tearful woman coming out of a broker's office wailed, "How could I lose one hundred thousand dollars? I never *had* one hundred thousand dollars!"

President Hoover in his speech that day declared the fundamental economy of the country to be basically sound. By Tuesday the market had hit bottom. Jerry finally called, to tell her not to talk to the press if anyone asked her about him.

"You don't know anything about finance. You leave any statements to me."

"Like the ones you've been making about me?" India snarled. "Abbott says I am to get an accounting of our finances from you, in view of the situation."

"You'll get it when I'm ready to give it to you," he said.

India turned Abbott loose on Jerry's lawyer, and an accounting eventually came. It *looked* all right, Abbott said. Apparently Jerry had been a cautious speculator, at least with his own money.

By late November it seemed to India that New York had undergone some horrible change, like a plague city. Girders of unfinished buildings rusted along Central Park South. Lines of men huddled outside soup kitchens and flophouses. The crash had taken its toll from the rich down to the poor who had been employed by them. John D. Rockefeller announced that he and his son had been *buying* stocks, in an attempt to bolster confidence in the market. "Sure," said Eddie Cantor, who had lost his shirt along with the other paper millionaires of Broadway, "who else has any money left?" The president of Union Cigar watched his stock fall from $113.50 to $4 in a day and jumped to his death from the ledge of a hotel. Banks and corporations began to fail, and in their debris investigators found sloppy bookkeeping, fraudulent loans, and outright theft. In the glory years it hadn't mattered. There had been plenty of money. "It's retribution for greed," Frank said cynically. "Every chicken eventually comes home to roost."

On the first of December, India discovered that there would be no money from her mother's estate. There was nothing left. On the third, a cable announced her father's death. She packed up David again, and all their black clothes, and went home. Edward Blackstone had been partner in a bank that had failed, and his heart had not stood the strain. India saw him into his grave beside her mother.

"He died angry at me," she said bitterly to the minister.

"He was a good man," the minister said, and talked to India about the unknowable ways of God, although in this instance the minister professed to have a clue. "He hoped to the end that you would come to your senses and keep your family together. He spoke of it often. It may be that the Lord took him to give you light to see by." He suggested that they pray together for guidance.

Fleeing from him, India found herself being patted by the foreman's wife, a thin woman with gray-brown hair twisted into a bun. "He was a stubborn old man," she said, sniffling. "I loved him, but don't you let him bully you from beyond the grave."

Her father had changed his will before he died, India discovered, but it didn't make any difference. There was nothing to leave. Already there was a FOR SALE sign outside Edward's private kingdom.

When she got back to New York, Jerry telephoned her again and said he wanted to reconcile. He promised not to interfere in her work. They would let bygones be bygones.

India stared at the telephone suspiciously. "Is that why you've been telling people I'm a lesbian?"

"Now look here. Neither of us can afford this kind of publicity right now. Let's just make up." Jerry's voice sounded odd, as if he were nervous, not his usual urbane self.

"No, thank you, Jerry. I don't think you really want to do that." *And I don't trust you,* she thought.

The divorce trial was scheduled for mid-December. India put up a Christmas tree and red bows in the windows in an attempt to give the house some feeling of celebration for David's sake. Outside, the city looked frowsy. It had lost its magical glitter, the sheen of frivolity and prosperity. People were talking about a depression. A lot of the speakeasies were closed.

The divorce trial provided the populace with entertainment. India went into the courthouse on Mr. Abbott's arm, leaning on her cane. The crowd in the street jostled to get a look at her. "Atta girl!" someone yelled. Someone else spat at her as she went by.

India flinched, thinking of her last court appearance, the suit and countersuit with Roger Stiller. The bastards weren't going to win this time, all those men closing ranks against her. She wouldn't get them on her side, Mr. Abbott had warned her, unless she was willing to play the victim. *Fine,* India thought with gritted teeth. Fine, she could do that.

The evidence of Jerry's infidelity was presented. His secretary was called to testify, a step India hadn't wanted to take but that Abbott had insisted on. The woman left the stand in tears. Roger Stiller was called.

India hadn't seen him up close in years. She was intensely satisfied to see how much he had aged, and at the same time pleased with her own appearance, her navy blue suit, conservative hat, her cane. Roger looked dissipated.

Yes, indeed he had had an affair with Mrs. Rhodes, before the war. "We lived together for a few years. Those were free and easy times."

"You were not married?"

"No!" Roger laughed.

Jerry's lawyer looked grave. "Why did you not wish to marry Miss Blackstone, as she was then?"

"Well, to be frank, I thought there might have been a few before me. And very likely a few around the same time as well. There was an odd kick to her gallop. Well, look at that show at the gallery—I thought I saw a bit of a tendency that way then." He chuckled with elaborate care. "A man likes to think that he's all a woman wants, you know."

On cross-examination he could produce no names other

than Frank Blake. No female names. "But look at those pictures," Roger said, nodding sagely at Mr. Abbott. "I'm an artist myself. I know the clues, believe me."

"I don't," Mr. Abbott snapped. He elicited from Roger a reluctant account of their parting and the lawsuit over the picture. By the time Roger stepped down, it was clear he had a grudge, but India's face was flaming with fury and embarrassment.

Witnesses to good character were called on both sides, and finally India and Jerry themselves. India testified that she wished a divorce because her husband had been unfaithful. She managed tears. Jerry admitted to sleeping with his secretary, accused India of sexual promiscuity during their marriage, and then unaccountably claimed to want her back. But except for Frank Blake, Jerry also could provide no names to back up his accusations. Instead, he provided a great deal of innuendo and said that he had not approved of India's going to Taos—he thought that household an unhealthy one.

Frank, who considered his sexual activities to be no business of the court's, cheerfully lied and said he had never slept with India at all. They were merely childhood friends.

Jerry's attorney reiterated the fact that India had had an affair with Roger Stiller before her marriage. India's attorney pointed out that Jerry had known that.

India sat with her jaw clenched, fiercely staring at the wall.

"I told you what you were in for," Mr. Abbott whispered in her ear as he sat down. "I hope this is worth it to you."

"Is he going to give me the divorce?" India whispered back.

Abbott didn't answer. The judge disappeared. India put her head in her hands. Jerry stared at the clock on the wall, looking as miserable as India. The courtroom was overheated and stuffy with cigar smoke. The reporters in the back were making bets.

Finally the judge reappeared, and everyone stood up. India's throat felt hollow, and her pulse was racing. What if she was tied to Jerry for life? What if there was no way out but killing him? The thought flashed through her mind that she might do it.

The judge settled himself at the bench. After everyone was seated again, he spoke. "With regret, the court grants a decree of divorce to Mrs. Rhodes. It has become obvious to me, after hearing the accusations traded in this courtroom, that this couple is unable to reconcile and never will be able. Legally, Mrs. Rhodes is entitled to a divorce on the grounds of infidelity, and she shall have it, but the court is well aware that that is not the true issue in their difficulties. Accordingly, Mr. Jerome Rhodes, as the guilty party, is enjoined from remarrying for a period of three years without approval of the court, and custody of the minor child is granted to Mrs. Rhodes. But Mr. Rhodes is to have substantial visitation and as complete parental rights as possible, after a schedule to be devised by this court at a later date."

India unclenched her fingers from the arms of her chair. There was more, but she didn't listen to all of it. *Free* . . . She was to have the house, Jerry was to pay alimony and child support for David, Jerry was to have David for Christmas. . . . Her head was reeling with relief, and she felt faint.

Mr. Abbott touched her arm. The judge had finished, and the reporters were converging on them.

David duly spent Christmas with his father, and India thought the house seemed emptier than ever with its decorations. They looked like spiderwebs to her, festooning the empty rooms.

David acted strange when he returned. India thought something must have been odd about the visit, but he was noncommittal.

"Did Dad talk about me?" she asked. She wouldn't put it past him.

"No!" David said shortly.

"David, darling, I'm so sorry this had to happen. I want to be sure you know that none of it is your fault. Sometimes life is just awful, but the troubles between your father and me are *our* fault. Dad's and mine. We both love you."

David sat on the sofa beside her, and India turned the radio on to the A&P Gypsies Orchestra. She cuddled him while they listened to the music.

"Dad gave me a sled for Christmas."

"I know, darling, I saw it."

"It's big. It must have cost a lot," he said proudly.

"I expect it did. Do you want some dinner, or are you full of ice cream?"

"Dinner," David said.

They got up and went into the dining room, where India's cook, whose salary Jerry was obligated to go on paying, had laid the table for two. India pressed the buzzer under the rug with her toe, and Mary came in with platters.

"It's my night off, Mrs. Rhodes," she said, "so I'll just set these out before I catch my bus."

"I expect David and I can fend for ourselves, Mary." India gave David a grin. "You can learn to wash dishes."

India gave a little sigh of relief when Mary left. She felt all right tonight, as if life as a divorced woman was going to be all right. She and David had lived alone together all through the divorce proceedings, but Jerry had somehow still been there, like an amputated limb. Now he was gone, and she and David were a legitimate team.

India watched David slurp his soup. *He's unfolding,* she thought. He had looked before like an origami bird that had been pressed into stiff attention. Now he was loosening his paper feathers. Maybe she'd teach him to cook, too, on Mary's full day off. They could learn together, book in hand.

She didn't hear the front door open, didn't hear the footsteps until she saw Jerry standing in the dining room door. Then it seemed that she could hear them printed on the air, their urgent echo trying to force her attention. She heard the click of the lock, turned with a key she didn't know he still had; the steps on the polished parquet; the softened tread on the Aubusson carpet, repeated over and over, forever, like a needle stuck in a phonograph groove.

He had a gun in his hand.

"Leave the room," she whispered to David. "Now."

David's chair screeched on the floor beyond the edge of the rug. He froze.

"Stay here." Jerry lifted the gun, its blunt barrel pointing at India. "You ruined my life," he said evenly.

"Jerry—" She tried to stop the hammering in her chest. "Put that down, Jerry."

"I won't forgive you for it. You ruined everything. You took away everything I wanted." His eyes were bright, too bright, glittery and chancy looking, and his face was hollow.

India wondered if he had been drinking heavily, or trying other things.

Her hands clenched in her lap, her eyes searching for some weapon. She couldn't just sit here and let him shoot her. But was he really going to? She wouldn't put it past him to threaten her with a gun just to terrify her. The look on his face left her uncertain. Some rational piece of him had gone away somewhere and left the door open. Anything might come through it.

"If you do this, it will just make matters worse." Her voice sounded tight in her throat, struggling to get out. "It won't make your life *better*."

"You always think you know everything," Jerry said. "You don't know anything, or you wouldn't have left me." His hand tightened on the gun, and India heard the safety snap off.

She flung herself out of her chair, grabbing for David, trying to pull them both away. The gunshot splintered the air, and she spun, shrieking, terrified that she was hit. They said you didn't know at first. . . . Or David! She tried to pull him down behind the table, out of sight. David screamed.

But it wasn't David bleeding on the floor; it was Jerry. He had put the pistol in his mouth. The rug beneath his head was soaking up the blood.

India let go of David and knelt, gagging, beside Jerry. How many times had she done just this? Taken a pulse, looked for the angle of the wound, cradled the blessé in her bloody arms?

"Get the operator, get an ambulance," she said between her teeth, but Jerry was gone, dead. She got up and opened the window, the way the nurses at Étaples had always done, to let the soul out. She didn't want Jerry's soul in here. Then she took David into the next room and held him in her arms, staining his new pullover with tears until the ambulance came.

The police came, too, and reporters who had gotten wind of the shooting. Sally and Frank came after India called them. When the police left and the men from the coroner's office had taken Jerry, Frank threw out the reporters. The doctor gave David something to make him sleep.

"Do you want something, too?" Frank said. "I'll get it for you."

"No." India shook her head. "I'm afraid to go to sleep."

"Dear, you really have to." Sally handed her a glass with a shot of whiskey in it. "Try this, then."

"I'm afraid to." India stared into the fire. One of the drying garlands of greenery had come loose from the mantel and trailed along the hearth. Frank tucked it back in a shower of needles.

"You'd better take these down." He straightened up. "What's eating you? Are you afraid he's going to haunt you?"

"I don't know," she said. "He really loved me, and I drove him to this. How could I have done that to him? I don't know what he might want to do to me."

"People generally get more reasonable when they've shuffled off this mortal coil," Frank said. "He's not after you, poor bastard."

"He killed himself because of me." India's eyes filled with tears. "They won't even let me take up the rug yet. I have to look at it. David has to look at it. All because of me."

"I don't think so," Frank said. "I've been hearing things."

"*Nobody* is responsible for someone else killing himself!" Sally said. She gave India a fierce look. "Now drink your whiskey. We're both going to stay here tonight. You're going to need help with David."

In the morning David woke screaming from a drugged nightmare and flung himself at his mother, beating at her with his fists.

"You killed him! You killed him!"

Sally scooped him up and took him away while India looked despairingly after them. She ought to be able to comfort her own child, she thought, but David went into paroxysms of hysteria whenever he saw her.

After she numbly ate breakfast, India went to the nursery to try again to talk with David. Sally was with him. He didn't like Frank, but he had always adored Sally.

"Darling, please let me talk to you."

David shook his head miserably. "I don't want to. Sally says you didn't make Dad do it, so I guess you didn't, but I don't want to talk."

India had to be content with that. At noon the district attorney came to see her.

"You can have your attorney present if you like, Mrs. Rhodes, but I really don't think it's necessary."

"What is this about?" India said suspiciously. "My husband shot himself. That much was obvious to the police."

"Yes. My condolences. This is about Mr. Rhodes's financial affairs."

An attorney was beginning to sound unpleasantly necessary, so India sent for Mr. Abbott. By evening she knew everything there was to know about Jerry's financial status and sat at the kitchen table grimly eating scrambled eggs.

Mary hadn't shown up. She didn't want her name in the paper, India supposed. Frank and Sally had gone home at India's insistence. She wasn't worried about Jerry haunting her now. He had lost that opportunity when he had shot himself in front of her and their son. How like Jerry to try to blame that on her, too.

David, sitting across from her, angrily poked at his eggs, as if he could hurt them. India couldn't blame him.

"I have to talk to you," she said. "We have to think what to do. There isn't going to be any money at all."

"Dad had money." David didn't look up from his eggs.

"No. He didn't. That's why he shot himself. You're too young to know these things, but I don't know what else to do but tell you."

David didn't answer.

"Dad lost his money in the stock market," India said. "Only it wasn't his money. It was other people's money. Anything of his that's left will have to go to pay them back."

David stared at his plate. "Is that why the men were here? Was it their money?"

"No, darling, things don't work like that. Thank God. They were from the district attorney's office. Kind of like the police."

"The police?" David's mouth quivered.

"It's complicated," she said quickly, "and I'm not sure I understand it, but they think that Dad was handling money for criminals, too. Bootleggers and people like that. Hiding it for them. It's called laundering it, because you take dirty money from dirty businesses and make it come out clean."

David cocked an eye at her finally, interested in spite of

his misery. "I read about that in *Daring Dick*. The villain was hiding money from the white slave trade."

"You read about that in *Daring Dick*?" India asked him, momentarily diverted. Maybe she would have to reassess her son's collection of pulp fiction. "Your father was about to be indicted and very possibly sent to prison. He couldn't face it, I don't think."

"Prison?" David's face was pale.

"I'm afraid so."

"Will . . . we go to prison now?"

"No, of course not. We had nothing to do with it."

And then it occurred to her that Jerry had hit the ceiling with good reason when she painted posters for the Wobblies. The FBI was far too interested in the Wobblies, and he wouldn't have cared for their attention. She supposed he wouldn't have seemed very useful to the Mob if he couldn't control his own wife. Poor Jerry. Had he gotten in too deep, deeper than he'd meant to? And then couldn't get out? The hell with poor Jerry, she thought then, viciously. Look what he'd done to his kid. She couldn't send David back to school in New York now. And then, wearily, *It doesn't matter. I can't afford it*.

"We don't have any money, though," she said practically to David. "Just what I can earn."

"There's the gallery."

India sighed. "We can't stay here. I won't put you through that."

David's mouth relaxed, as if he had been gritting his teeth. "I've been afraid of that," he mumbled into his plate.

"Well, you won't have to," India said briskly. Better to be making plans. Better for David. "We'll sell the gallery. That will give us something to go on with."

"What about the house?"

"We'll sell it, too, but we won't get much, I'm afraid. Who could afford to buy a house like this now? But we can't pay the property taxes on it, so it will have to go." The gallery was probably worth more, she thought dispiritedly. It was alive, a going concern. Her own creation. What would she do without it? And how Roger Stiller would laugh when she left.

"Where will we go?" David asked plaintively, and India focused her attention back on her son.

She looked at the telegram that had come before dinner.

HORRIBLE NEW YORK, it said. COME TO TAOS.
LOVE, ELEANOR. Apparently the news had made the wire
services. She handed the telegram to David.

"I hate Taos," he muttered.

"You'll hate it here, too," India said. "With no money. In
an apartment somewhere. With the other boys ragging you at
school." She might as well lay it on thick. It wasn't anything
but the truth.

"I hate it everywhere!" David flung the words at her.
"How could Dad *leave* me? Why did you make him do that?
It's your fault! Why can't things be the way they used to be?"

"David, I didn't—"

"You wanted a divorce! Why can't *you* be the way you
used to be?" He slammed his chair back, his face running
with tears. "I hate it in Taos! I won't go!"

"You don't have any choice," she said to his departing
back. She heard him stumble noisily up the stairs, then slam
the door to his room. Silently, she finished her eggs and
scraped David's into the garbage. How on earth did a person
know the right thing to do? Maybe she was going to bumble
along making horrible mistakes her whole life. "You don't
have a choice," she muttered at the ceiling, in David's general direction. "Neither of us does." She thought about her
gallery, about having rubbed Roger Stiller's nose in her success, and burst into tears.

The tears lasted as long as the dishes. She dried them
up with the last plate and went upstairs to do the one thing
she was certain she was supposed to do: cuddle her angry,
bereft child.

PART FOUR

1930–1941

XIV

Taos

Eleanor Raspell was alone now. The other women had been young, or younger than she, and had moved on to lives of their own. At seventy-five, she was looking down the wrong end of the telescope, she said.

Sitting in front of the adobe fireplace on a summer night, mending one of David's socks, India wondered what wind had blown them here. David was not really here at all, so distanced by resentment was he. For a while India, too, had felt it stifling her, encasing her in gelatin, until she had almost forcibly shoved it out of her way so she could get on with her life.

She had felt odd at first planning to be in Taos not just for a visit but to stay. She hadn't known how deeply she had belonged to New York. But soon it began to seem normal to get up in the morning and work in the garden or to hitch Eleanor's old horse up for a ride into town. There was no money. Eleanor's arthritis was so bad her fingers couldn't work a shutter anymore, and she never had been rich. A little money came in from reprints of old work, and India sold Taos scenes to tourists in the bookstore in the plaza. The Lawrences had gone, Lawrence had died, and Frieda had come back. Dorothy Brett was still here, and Mabel Lujan. They were reputed to be writing books about their lives with Lawrence, all three of them. India renewed a cautious acquaintance—the three spent their time complaining about one another to people but closed ranks when outsiders threatened. David called them the witches.

He was miserably unhappy, but India thought he would have been anywhere. Taos just gave him concrete grievances to settle on: There was no car, only the horse and dilapidated wagon, since Eleanor's old Ford had given out. To a New York City child that was unthinkable. The single picture show ran scratchy, fluttering reels on antique equipment. Only a handful of Anglos lived in Taos, even counting the artists, and most of them didn't have children. The school was populated mainly by Spanish-speaking Mexican boys and Indians from the pueblo. David was scornful of the boys his age because academically he was two years ahead of them, but the real source of his displeasure was that he was different. The teacher liked him, but no one else did.

And there was Frank. Frank came through Taos—happened by, as he always said—two months after they had moved, put on a tool belt, and went over the house and barn, making repairs. After that he hitched Eleanor's horse to a borrowed plow and enlarged the small garden plot. He settled in, booted feet stretched on the hearth in front of the fire, while India did the mending and Eleanor watched with envy, her arthritic fingers folded in her lap. He told stories of his days in the Yukon trying to dig gold, of his experiences in the California oil fields, of the Wobblies and how many cities he'd been in jail in. He talked about riding the boxcars and the rods, a genuine hobo.

To David, Frank's presence was too much, but Eleanor loved him. She loved David, too, and without saying a word forbade them to quarrel in her presence. David sat beside his mother on the worn leather sofa, eyes on the far wall, away from Frank. He was pretending not to listen, India thought, but she could tell he was. *Daring Dick* had very little on Frank Blake in the adventure department.

Frank left, and India planted her vegetable garden. Her leg ached all the time from stooping and kneeling, but the expanded garden would feed them all if she learned to can. New York surfaced in her mind and was slapped away, pushed back into the little room where she used to keep the wounded soldiers and Ben spiraling out of the air in a burning plane. Jerry lived there now, and she shoved New York in with him, trying to find in the garden some escape from the contents of that interior attic. It began to seem to her here in Taos that she could discern other rooms, more spacious, and she stumbled awkwardly toward their light.

Only when the dealer who had bought Coyote Gallery wrote and asked if she had something new to send him—she was still hot in New York—did she break down. In the art world scandal added spice. She could go back now; she would be able to get by in the Village. But David couldn't, and all the money in the world wouldn't change what New York meant to him.

She went into the barn and buried her face in Taffy's broad bay shoulder. *I have to paint,* she thought. *Not pueblo scenes for the tourists. It will all slip away from me again.* But how could she work on other pieces when the pueblo landscapes made enough money to buy shoes and stamps and toothbrushes, and the garden was growing? How long ago had it been when she could paint all day and tell the cook there would be eight for dinner? *An hour a day. I have to have that much.*

In 1931 no one had any money. With Eleanor, India had found a certain companionship in poverty, but David wasn't adjusting to their new spartan way of life. Not surprising, India thought. All across the country people were being broken by the collapse of the economy. It was the worst in the big cities, where breadlines snaked down the block, and on the marginal farms where the sharecroppers couldn't hold on through the drought that seemed to dry up the water as soon as the stock market had dried up the cash. Taos had never been rich, nor had the pueblo, but being one of the many poor there was no consolation for David. He longed for the New York he remembered and could not be persuaded that it would not be that way now, not for him.

"I hate it here! I won't go back to that school!" He stood, red-faced and furious, glaring at India across the potato hills in the garden. The first year's crop had been successful but hadn't fed them through the winter. This summer India had planted more. "This is Hicksville," he said with a year's worth of stored venom. "You said to try it, and I tried it. I tried it for a whole goddamn year!"

"David!"

"I'll swear if I want to," he announced. He looked at his mother with eleven-year-old condescension. "*You* don't care if we're stuck in the middle of nowhere, driving a stupid *horse*! You like it here! You couldn't wait to get away from New York! And from Dad! You stupid *cow*!"

India lunged at him, but he darted off through the garden, stepping on the cucumber vines. *"David!"* She stood shaking with fury, subduing the urge to run after him, limp along in humiliation with her cane and shake him, weeping and demanding an apology. Instead she went to look at the cucumbers and found that he had snapped the biggest vine off at the ground.

The next few days were an armed truce. India disappeared into her studio at dawn for an hour to paint as she liked, then emerged to fix David's breakfast and watch him retreat into his room until he left for school. After that she weeded the garden and painted watercolors of the plaza for the few tourists who still had money to buy them. When she had finished her work, David came home from school, scuffing his shoes in the red dust and dragging his books behind him by their strap, so that they too were broken and coated with dust.

He gave India a baleful glare, half of anger and half of embarrassment over what he had said to her, and went off to do his homework with Eleanor. Eleanor's gray head bent next to David's dark one over a page full of decimal fractions. *I was too old to have children,* India thought. *I don't know what to do with him.* David shot her a look from under dark brows, then quickly turned his eyes back to the paper.

India went into the kitchen to start dinner. The last corn lay on the old tiled countertop, buttery yellow under the pale green husks. She picked off the few corn worms that had evaded her applications of mineral oil to the silk, and cut away their damage, listening to Eleanor and David murmuring in the soft blue twilight. After a while Eleanor got up and turned the lights on, and a few moments later the radio, signifying the end of homework. India looked through the door into the dining room.

"When does *he* get here?" David demanded abruptly. "And don't ask who. You know who I mean."

"He's coming tonight," India said evenly. Frank was due through on another of his periodic stops. Lately he came more often, to fix whatever was falling down that India and Eleanor couldn't manage, but also, India suspected, because he was lonely. She was always achingly glad to see him—that never changed—and without Jerry between them it was easy to just fall back into the old ways. India smiled a little and took a vase from the sideboard to put some flowers in.

"Coming tonight," David said, mimicking her. "Flowers! That's disgusting. How old are you anyway, Mother?"

"I don't have one foot in the grave," she said mildly.

"Well, it's disgusting to watch," David said.

India stopped, vase in hand. "Would you care to explain that?"

"I don't have to explain anything." He went to the radio and made a production of adjusting the dial, trying to get Albuquerque.

"Then possibly you shouldn't make remarks in the first place," Eleanor said calmly.

"*I* know why she wanted to leave Dad," David said darkly. "And she's almost as old as you. It's—" He fished a word out of his vocabulary lesson. "It's ludicrous."

"Go to your room!" India snapped, losing all good intentions.

She and Eleanor looked at each other as he left.

"He'll get over it," Eleanor said.

India sighed. "What? His father's death, or the conviction that anyone over forty is dead from the neck down?"

"Oh, that doesn't come until you are forty yourself." Eleanor chuckled. "And in any case one's parents are not supposed to be interested in that sort of thing. Children reserve the right to focus their parents' attention entirely on their fine selves."

India was quiet for a moment, and then she said dubiously, "Do you think I should tell Frank not to come if it upsets David?"

"Are you out of your mind?" Eleanor pushed herself half out of her chair for emphasis. "You have a child for twenty years. You have yourself for a lifetime. Kowtow to David now by cutting off your friends, and when he's gone, what will you have?"

"Just checking," India said. "That's how I feel, but I've always been considered unnatural."

"So you are," Eleanor said briskly. "By current standards. I always was. Try to stick with it."

India went to cut some flowers for the vase. She whistled a little under her breath. Frank was coming, and she had been painting again, *really* painting. She had already sent two canvases to New York. She put daisies in the vase and smiled. Frank was coming. If only David . . . bother David.

David ignored Frank at dinner and vanished with the abruptness of a slammed door as soon as he had finished the food on his plate. Eleanor went into the kitchen to do the dishes, and India took Frank into the garden.

"Nice," he said, smiling. "Very down home. You should have a sunbonnet."

"I do. I look a fright in it." India inspected him, noting again how old they had gotten. His thinning sandy hair was ruffled by the evening breeze from the creek. The lines etched in his face crisscrossed weathered skin tanned dark by the sun. A farmer's tan. His upper arms, torso, and legs would be pale, she thought. He was still good-looking, but now in a battered way, which spoke of the abuse his body had been subjected to over the years. She wondered what he saw when he looked at her. Gray in the dark hair, thick streaks of it, more every year? Lines around the eyes, veins that stood up on the backs of her hands? The cane had been with her so long she couldn't think of it as a sign of aging, only an extension of her usual self.

He wrapped an arm around her in the shadows of the rustling corn, which creaked and whispered as her arms went around his waist. She buried her face in his chest. His thin cotton shirt smelled of gasoline fumes from the bus he had ridden into town. They stood there until the darkness enveloped them, throwing stars against the sky overhead, blotting out the mountains' silhouette and the edges of the garden. The house was quiet now. Without speaking, they turned in mutual agreement toward the patio doors, under the dark murmur of the grapevines, and silently went up the stairs. India's room had windows that opened onto the flat roof, and she pulled them wide to let the night in, the faint murmur of evening bugs, the warbling of hunting coyotes in the distance.

Frank was a familiar shadow in the darkness, body remembered over the years. Her hands, as calloused now as his, slid roughly over his skin. She had never had a lover who fit her so well, whose body locked to hers so perfectly. She had never told him that, half afraid to. Now she was old, and inclined, naked, to mourn lost youth, the taut body of twenty and thirty, even the grace of forty. When she was sixty, would she want to be fifty?

After an hour of lovemaking they lay companionably, India's head in the crook of his arm, not caring that her breasts were fifty-one years old and sagged sideways off her chest and onto his. She could hear his breathing, deep and regular in her ear, but she didn't think he was asleep.

Finally she stretched and sat up, reaching for her wrapper.

"I want a drink."

Frank roused himself and said, "I'll come, too. It's a good night for talk. We haven't talked."

India smiled. Talk usually meant arguing about whatever came to mind, impassioned, full of wild gestures and emphasis. It was one of the things she liked best to do with Frank. Jerry had hated it when they stayed up all night, planning Utopia or arguing about the future of industrialization. India shivered with silent anticipation. They could talk till dawn if they wanted to.

In the kitchen she poured them each a whiskey in a highball glass, and they slipped up the stairs again.

"I just want to take a look at David," India whispered outside his door. "Make sure he actually got undressed." She hadn't seen him since his departure from the table. When angry, David would suddenly go from fury to sleep as the adrenaline gave out.

He wasn't there. The room was empty, the bed still made. India flung the windows open and stared onto the roof. Its flat, empty surface held only faint starlight.

She switched on the light. "Frank!"

"Oh, hell!" he murmured when he saw the room. It was a shambles, clothes pulled haphazardly from drawers, toy chest upended. "He took off."

"Oh, he wouldn't." India tried to convince herself, staring at the mess.

"What's missing?"

She took inventory. "His jacket. Some clothes." She pawed among the contents of the toy box. "All his money. The blanket off his bed. Oh, no."

"Take it easy. We'll catch up to him."

Eleanor came to the doorway, enfolded in a voluminous nightgown. "What is it?"

"David's gone," India said. She felt nausea roll her stomach over.

"How much money did he have?" Frank asked.

"Not much. Five dollars maybe. Where has he *gone*?" India looked wildly at Frank and Eleanor as if they could answer.

"Where do you think he's *trying* to go?" Frank asked. "Is he the kind of kid to go hide in the chaparral to scare you?"

"He hates this place," India said. "He wouldn't go off and try to live in it."

"If he took his money, he's going someplace," Eleanor said. "Not just hiding."

"Where does he want to go?" Frank said.

"New York," India said. "Oh, *no*—"

"I wouldn't put it past him," Frank muttered. "He asked me a lot of questions about riding freights the last time I saw him. I thought he was just trying to make me prove I'd really done it."

"Well, *that* has to be stopped!" Eleanor said.

"He can't hop a freight till he gets to Santa Fe," Frank said. "Or Raton. He'll have to take a bus first. It'll take me five minutes to get clothes on." He was wearing only trousers and an undershirt.

"I'm going with you," India said.

"Not a good idea."

"But he hates you, Frank. That's why he ran away."

"That won't stop me from bringing him back," he said. "You watch."

"No. I'm coming."

In ten minutes they were hitching Taffy to the wagon, one small bag between them thrown in the back. Eleanor was on the telephone to the Taos police, to the bus station, to authorities in Santa Fe and Raton when they left.

The bus station was closed when India and Frank pulled up, one dim bulb burning inside, behind dusty windows. But the dispatcher was there, roused from bed at home by a sympathetic telephone operator. He remembered selling a Santa Fe ticket to a kid.

"Didn't notice him much. Thought he was one of those

pueblo boys. Had a hat on, and he was good and dirty." The
dispatcher yawned. "You want me to call Santa Fe?"

"They'll grab him off the bus in Santa Fe and hold on to
him," Frank assured India as they climbed into a car they'd
rented from the local garage. There wasn't another bus, and a
car would be faster. Taffy would be fine until the next day.

But when they got to Santa Fe, climbing stiffly out into
the three A.M. darkness, the bus station *didn't* have him. He'd
slipped by them somehow, the Santa Fe station manager
said. Or he'd pulled the cord and gotten off before the station. The driver remembered somebody doing that, but he
hadn't paid attention to whom.

"He's only eleven years old!" India said. "Didn't anyone
wonder where he was going?"

"Lady, these reservation kids are practically grown by
eleven. Lots of loose kids on the road these days anyway. We
ain't baby-sitters."

"Skip it," Frank said. "Come on." He pulled India out of
the station by her arm.

"Where are we going?"

"Jungles," Frank said. "*I* am."

"With me."

"No. I'm not going to have to look out for you *and* the
kid. It may be tricky. You stay in the car." He opened the
door and got into the driver's seat.

The car slid over the railroad tracks and bumped along a
frontage road that paralleled them, past the Santa Fe train
station where in the distance India saw a solitary porter
asleep on a handcart. The few houses here gave meaning to
"the wrong side of the tracks," and the vacant lots between
them were overgrown with sage and creosote bushes and
waving fronds of ocotillo.

Frank pulled up where the road dead-ended at a wash.
"You wait here. Lock the doors."

He was gone into the darkness before India could protest. She sat, silently cursing him and frantically imagining
David's lifeless body sprawled along the tracks, cut in half by
a roaring train that her mind would not cease imagining. *Oh,
David* . . .

Frank came back up out of the wash alone. At least an
hour had gone by; it felt like all night. He slid into the
driver's seat, shaking his head. "The little shit's gone."

"Frank—"

"I'm not feeling sympathetic." He backed the car abruptly, its wheels spinning on the sandy road. "There's no excuse for stupidity. Or for doing this to you." He put the car in forward gear and slammed his foot down on the accelerator.

"What do you mean, he's gone?" India said.

"Kansas City," Frank said. "Two old 'boes claimed he hopped the cannonball mail. I've got no reason not to believe them."

India put her hand to her mouth. "How could he? A moving train?"

"He had help," Frank said grimly.

"What help?"

Frank was pulling the car out onto the highway, going northeast. "What I've been afraid of. Some jocker liked his looks. I ran into some myself when I hit the road, but I was seventeen and mostly too big to mess with."

"I don't know what you're talking about!" India snapped. "*I* never hit the road."

"Jockers will pal with a kid," Frank said, driving. "Show him how it's done, protect him. But there's a price. If David's lucky, it'll take his pal a while to get around to explaining what it is."

"Oh, my God." India put her knuckles in her mouth, biting down on them.

"It won't do him any permanent damage," Frank said callously. "Might make him think twice about such a damn fool move next time."

"You don't like David any more than he likes you!" India shouted at him. "Be quiet. Just be quiet!"

The trip to Kansas City took them well into the next day, and they were going slower than the cannonball mail. But David and the jocker couldn't just step off one freight and onto another like they had tickets, Frank said. And they'd have to eat. And who knew where the jocker wanted to go? "And I do like the kid," Frank added, seeing India's face in the dusty light. She looked anguished, older than last night. "I get peeved when he thinks it's his privilege to abuse you because his old man was a heel."

"How do you expect him to feel?" India said, taking David's part now. "Jerry was his father. And he's dead. How can he possibly not be angry? And it's not David's fault he looks like Jerry," she added astutely.

"Touché." Frank looked at India with growing concern. "You need to eat, too. I'm going to park you in a restaurant over by the stockyards. Ma's home cooking. Not fancy but not dangerous. You wait there."

"He may not come with you," India said.

"He may be glad to see me."

"Shouldn't we call the police?"

"And scatter every bindlestiff in the jungle, David and his pal included? 'Boes don't offer much information to the police." Frank parked the car outside a dilapidated café with a sign that said MAUREEN'S.

"What are you going to do?"

Frank didn't answer. "I'll holler if I need you." He stripped off his overcoat and the heavy gold signet ring he wore. After contemplating the contents of his wallet, he stuck the red IWW card in his pocket, along with a two-dollar bill, and handed the rest to India.

"Won't you need more money?"

"I'll be lucky if I don't get rolled for my boots," Frank said. "I've been living on the plush too long." He set off down the street, and India saw him turn into an alley that led toward the tracks.

I can't eat. I'll throw up, she thought, but she went into Maureen's anyway.

Frank was betting that the Kansas City jungle was where it had always been. Unless the railroad went in with bulldozers, the hoboes lit like pigeons in their accustomed spot, returning after every raid. He skirted past the depot water tower, stopping to read its cryptic messages: Willie Dee had gone to Frisco; there was field work in Omaha; Pete J. should look up Shorty in Des Moines. Frank grinned. It had been a while since he'd scratched his own name on a hoboes' blackboard. The grin faded. Maybe it was his fault the damn fool kid had run off. Sheepishly, Frank was aware that he saw David more as an extension of Jerry than of India; he decided that he'd probably better work on that.

The Kansas City hobo jungle was screened from the tracks and from the stockyards that bordered them by a tangle of scrub trees and brush, tall grass threaded with nearly

invisible trails. The faint smell of woodsmoke overlaid with
tobacco and onions drifted through the thicket. Frank
stopped a minute, thinking over his plans, and went on. He'd
stopped on the way and bought a cheap pint of bootleg
hooch and a stewbone and tied them in his old red ban-
danna. He dusted himself down with dirt before he went on,
sighing at the scratches he put in his new boots.

There were four hoboes around a fire, boiling coffee
grounds in a number-ten can. A battered saucepan sat in the
coals beside it. They looked at Frank but didn't say anything.

He squatted by the fire, hunkering down. "I don't believe I know you boys," he said after a minute's silence.

"Don't know you," one of them said.

"Don't get through here much." Frank considered. He'd
used Fritz—a childhood nickname—as a road name once,
but these days Germans were out of favor. "Frank," he said,
untying his bindle and taking a swig of the pint. He held it
out to the man next to him.

"Obliged," the man said.

"Thought you might be a bull at first," another said. He
looked appraisingly at the newcomer.

Frank chuckled. "It's been a while since I was on the
road, and that's a fact. But I ain't no bull."

The pint went around the fire, but it didn't wipe the
wary suspicion from the men's faces. The youngest was
maybe eighteen, thin and pinched, with bad teeth. The eldest was grizzled, with no teeth to speak of. A battered cap
clung to his skull as if it had grown there. "What exactly
might you be, then?" he inquired.

Frank took another swig and capped the pint. "Lookin'
for my sister's boy. Damn fool kid, about eleven." He cocked
an eye at the mulligan in the saucepan and dropped the stew
bone in it. "Figured I might be on the road a while. Hope I
haven't lost my manners." Mulligan was made of anything—
wild onion, stolen chickens, the leavings of back-door hand-
outs. There was a lot of meat on Frank's bone, and they eyed
it respectfully. They didn't say anything else, though.

Frank uncapped the pint again and passed it to the thin
boy. The hoboes eyed each other uncertainly and the pint
with avidity.

"Dark-haired kid?" the thin boy blurted out. "Come
from Santa Fe?"

"More'n likely," Frank said. "You seen him?"

There was a dubious silence.

"Kid like that showed with Roadhouse this morning," the boy said.

"You gon' get the shit beat outta you," one of the others muttered.

"If this is his uncle, likely he'll be glad to see him," the thin boy snapped. "Which one o' you bastards is gonna tell Roadhouse I told? I'll tell him it was you!"

"Where's Roadhouse?" Frank said quietly.

They looked at each other. Finally the grizzled man shrugged and jerked his thumb over his shoulder at the thicket beyond the clearing, away from the direction Frank had come. A thin plume of smoke identified a cooking fire. "He don't socialize much," he commented.

Frank stood up.

"Handy with a knife, too," the grizzled man added.

Frank nodded. "Obliged." He put the bottle, still a third full, down by the fire.

The path through the thicket on the other side was less defined, as if it had been trampled out only recently, mostly a matter of bent blades in the tall grass that was going to seed among the thorn trees. Frank went cautiously, eyes on the smoke, but the man was waiting for him before he got to the fire.

"What you want?"

Frank took stock of him. Roadhouse looked forty maybe, a big dark-haired man with a belly that hung over his belt buckle. He wore an undershirt and greasy khaki pants that might once have been army issue.

"Passing through," Frank said. He started to step around the man.

"Pass on over yonder," Roadhouse said. "I ain't fond o' company."

"I heard you had company." Frank looked at him appraisingly.

"Get on away," Roadhouse growled.

"I'm looking for my nephew." Frank smiled. "Dark-haired kid, about eleven. Decided to run off when he got mad at his ma. Only trouble is, his dad's a senator. This gets in the papers there's gonna be cops all over, and it's gonna get mean."

"I ain't seen no kid," Roadhouse said, but his eyes were wary.

"Then you won't mind if I give him a holler. Might be hiding out where you can't see him."

"You get outta here," Roadhouse snarled. His hand went to his belt.

"David!" Frank bellowed the name as he jumped Roadhouse. He got his hand around the man's wrist while his knife was still in its scabbard. They rocked back and forth, wrestling, free hands clawing at each other. "David!" Frank shouted again, and out of the corner of his eye he saw the boy's face, dirt-streaked and wide-eyed.

"Stop fighting me now and I won't cut your liver out," Frank gasped. Roadhouse writhed in his grasp and pulled his knife hand free. The blade came with it, the edge slicing into Frank's palm as it went.

"You better run," Roadhouse grunted. "You, boy, you get on back to the fire."

David stood, frozen, watching them. Frank backed away from Roadhouse, circling, looking for a way to get past the knife. He had a knife of his own, in his boot. When he got enough distance between them, he went for it. Roadhouse saw it, and his expression changed some. "You ain't related to no senator," he growled. "And you ain't no punk's uncle."

"He's coming home with me," Frank said.

"He don't wanna. That's how come I picked him up in Santa Fe. He was lookin' for someone to pal with. Ain't that right, kid?" His voice was scornful, and he didn't bother to look at David, who was behind him to his left. Roadhouse was defending his property. Until he was through with that, David would stay where he'd put him, just like a coffeepot or a bedroll would.

"You tell him what pallin' with you was gonna mean?" Frank asked.

"You get on outta here!" Roadhouse lunged at him, and Frank sidestepped, moving in close as Roadhouse lunged by. "I'm gonna cut you bad, old man!"

Frank grinned wolfishly at him. He was maybe ten years older than Roadhouse, but he'd been in as many brawls, and what's more he hadn't been living on scraps and garbage and bad coffee. On the other hand, Frank's left hand was dripping blood, and it hurt like hell, the pain a distraction. David was behind Roadhouse, and Frank jerked his eyes away from him and back to Roadhouse when he saw the boy begin to move. He concentrated on keeping Roadhouse looking his way.

"You kill me, you'll have cops down on you like hornets," he observed. "I tell you, they're looking for this kid already. I just want to save his old man some publicity he doesn't need."

Roadhouse spat. "You ain't got no proof o' that."

"Proof'll come when some mob drags you outta the county jail and strings you up. This isn't some lost kid that nobody wants."

"He was thumbin' rides at the bus depot." Roadhouse guffawed and moved in closer, knife ready.

Frank saw David in a blur behind Roadhouse and lunged as the rock in David's hands came down on the man's head. Frank's knife went fast across the bum's wrist, sending out a spurt of blood. The blade fell as Roadhouse clapped his other hand across it, trying to stop the flow.

"Run!" Frank shoved David ahead of him, and they thrashed through the tall grass, past the startled men around their fire, bumbling through the scrub trees to the tracks. Frank boosted David up the embankment above the tracks, and they lit out into the dusky twilight, running away from the water tower.

David stopped, gasping, bent over, hands on his knees, and Frank grabbed him by the collar. "Keep moving," he said.

David looked at him, his face tear-streaked, and stumbled on. He was crying by the time they got to the car, which was still parked outside Maureen's. India saw them through the window and came flying out.

"Oh, God! Baby!" She pulled David to her. "Are you all right?"

David gave Frank a baleful glance. "I'm fine." He scrubbed his face with the back of his hand, leaving dirty wet streaks down both. "*I* didn't ask you to come get me!" he blurted.

Frank spun around. "You want me to take you back there?"

"I don't care what you do! I was all right. I hate Taos!" He burst into tears again.

"How'd you like Roadhouse?" Frank asked him.

David buried his face in his hands.

"Stop it!" India said.

"No, you stop it." Frank pulled the car door open and pointed at the back seat. "Get in." He gave David a push. David scrambled away from him into the car. "You get in, too," he said to India. When they were both inside, glaring at him, he turned sideways in the driver's seat and said, "Kid, you are going to hear some home truths whether your mama likes them or not."

"This isn't the time—" India said.

"*I'm not through!*" Frank's voice filled the car, shocking David into a goggling silence and India into an outraged one. Frank didn't bother looking at her. He faced David across the back of the driver's seat. "Who in the hell do you think you are that you get to run your mother's life? Are you under the impression that she was put on earth for the sole purpose of wiping your butt every time it needs it? After she moved away from New York—where, incidentally, she was *happy*—so *you* wouldn't be made fun of by the other little assholes in school! After she goes out and digs in a goddamned vegetable garden every day to keep you fed! So you run away and scare her and worry her and maybe get yourself killed and make her miserable the rest of her life, just because you don't like the company she keeps? Because you don't like *me* in the house?"

David stared at him, openmouthed.

"And then when I come along and pull you out of that jocker's little nest in the brush before he gets your pants down, you tell me I didn't have to bother! For selfish, manipulative, spoiled brats, you take the cake, kid!"

David tried to put his hands over his ears, buffeted by the sound of Frank's voice, which had begun as a yell and hadn't dropped in volume.

India grabbed Frank's arm. "I'll defend myself, thank you!"

Frank took a deep breath. He dropped his voice to a level of tight calm and peered at David over the seat. "I don't hate you, kid. Yes, you've got reasons not to like me. But you don't get to tell your mother *she* can't like me."

David stared at him again, lip out.

Frank scratched his head. He looked drained. "Jesus,

this is why I never had kids. Listen, David. You've been through a bad time, and I guess you'd rather it wasn't me that had to come after you." He took another breath, trying to turn himself into a reasonable man and not a raging maniac. "But the fact is, the stories I told you gave you the idea, and that made it my responsibility, whether I liked it or not, or whether you do. This wasn't something either your mother or you could deal with. I've been a lot of bad places. I'm better at dealing with bad men than your mother is." He looked away, trying to give David some privacy. "And, uh, if there are things you want to talk about, about what happened back there, and, uh, you want to talk to me about them, that's fine. I've been there. I know what it's like. I wouldn't blame you, or make fun of you."

David was silent, but Frank interpreted that as thoughtfulness. He looked at India. She didn't seem to have anything to say at the moment either. He started the ignition and slid the car out onto the street.

By the time they got to Taos, India and David were both asleep, dark heads lolled against the upholstery. Frank climbed out stiffly, eyes gritty, neck aching, and turned to stare at them through the windows. They looked unsettlingly alike to him now, as if sleep smoothed out the sharp edges in David, the anger that was Jerry. Frank wondered if, having refused to father children, he was fated to be stuck with this one.

XV

Madrona

Sally Holt rode the train into Portland with the feeling of having stepped by mistake onto one of those children's rides that circle amusement parks, quarter-scale cars endlessly looping the same track, stopping at the same siding. She felt too big for the Pullman compartment, as if all her life had been compressed into it; and she had been here before, in what felt like the same black dress.

Tom, her mother's foreman, was waiting for her with the ranch truck when she got off. He gave her a hug and threw her bags into the back, hefting her trunk in after them. "You come to stay?"

"Of course not," Sally answered, thinking, *Then why did I bring everything?* "I don't know."

"I'm sorry about Miz Alex," Tom said. "It was—bang, in a minute, like that. I was with her. She just went over in the saddle."

"She was too old to be working the horses," Sally said. Tom snorted. "You try to stop her."

Sally sighed and shook off the feelings of guilt that were plaguing her. Did it do any good to be with someone who was dying? Those who survived were more in need of company.

"What state are we in?" she asked Tom.

"Tim's here," he said. "Mike and Janessa are coming. I guess there'll be a family council, figure out what to do next. The place is still running, but it's been hand to mouth lately."

"You'll stay?"

"I will if you don't sell," Tom said grimly. He had been born on the Madrona, the old foreman's son. For a minute Sally had thought he was his father. She was still half inclined to think that the battered black felt hat he wore *had* been his father's.

"Sell?" The word knotted up like a ball of wire in her stomach.

"None of you brats want to live here." Tom grinned. He was younger than all of them.

But *sell*?

Sally thought about it while the minister read the service for burial in the church that her mother had always attended. Alexandra would be buried on the Madrona, of course, next to Toby, but the church was full of Portland people, faces Sally remembered from childhood. She stood sniffling and fumbling with her hymnbook while they sang "Rock of Ages." How long had it been since she had been to church here, listened to these voices, smelled the scent of tobacco and peppermint and gardenia cologne?

She looked at her brothers and sister, their profiles stairstepped down the pew beside her. Only Mike was a full brother—Toby had been widowed twice before Alexandra—but they had all let Alexandra mother them, even Janessa, who hadn't been much younger. Janessa was seventy now, with grandchildren of her own. Time seemed to Sally to be whipping by like the speeding countryside that blew past a train window. Mike had gray in his mustache, and Tim was almost all gray now and a grandfather himself. Frank and his sister, Midge, sat in the next pew, heads bowed. They would be gone again the next day, though. It was the Holts who would have to decide what to do about Holt land.

"I am the Resurrection and the Light," the minister said.

The casket sat at the center of the nave, in front of the altar, heaped with flowers. The scent was too heavy close to the casket, as if a woman had overdone her perfume.

"Whosoever believeth in me—"

Familiar words, heard too often by now. What had Sally said to India when India's mother had died? That they were at the age for death, for having death begin to affect them, to

take people they loved, to take parents. The war had taken
people, brutally and erratically, but her parents had remained a constant. Now they were both dead, and she realized she was old. *What have I done with my life? And who'll
come to my funeral?* she thought irritably. Sally was the
youngest of them, the baby. *Nieces and nephews who barely
know me?*

They stood again, and frantic hunting through the
hymnbooks separated the churchgoers from the habitual hea-
then. The organist began to play, and they sang, faltering
over the half-remembered lines of "Shall We Gather at the
River."

The beautiful river, Sally thought. That was the Willamette River, flowing past the land she had explored in youth,
past the country of her birth. Was Mother there now, wading
in its shallows? Sally imagined her, in old-fashioned floor-
length skirts held high above the water, ankles silvered with
it.

> *"The beautiful, the beautiful river . . .*
> *That flows by the throne of God.*

"I don't want to sell land that Mom and Dad are buried
on," Tim said. He and the other family members were gathered around the kitchen table at the Madrona after the funeral, after the mourners and guests had gone, patting them,
telling them what upstanding citizens their folks had been,
how if they needed anything just to *call.* But what they
needed was to figure out what they wanted. "How long have
we been on this place?" Tim demanded, as if longevity on
the land pointed to an automatic answer.

"Damn near a hundred years," Mike said. "But are we
on it? Do any of us live here?"

"Does that matter?" Janessa said. She was the oldest but
the most firmly entrenched away from the Madrona. Tim was
in San Francisco, and Mike was in Los Angeles now, making
movies there because the weather was good. The rest, the
wives and husbands, the children, the grandchildren of Toby
and Alexandra Holt, stood back, away, not bound by the
fierce, unexpected tie that held the other four to the land.

"What about Aunt Cindy's children?" someone said, and
the rest shook their heads.

"Frank has a wandering foot," Sally said.

"Or a screw loose," Tim said.

"Midge has her own life."

Everyone had her own life, Sally thought. Except her. She had teas and committees and volunteer hours at the hospital, and a dwindling income that had depended far too heavily on her father's investments in the stock market and her mother's high-stepping show horses, which no one could afford to buy now. "Might as well hook 'em to a plow," Tom had said.

"I want it," she heard herself saying.

"Sally-belle?" Tim snorted, putting on the thick southern drawl that Alexandra had never lost. "You're gonna leave New York and live down on the farm?"

"Shut up," Sally said. "Do any of you want to do it? If you don't want to sell it, someone has to live on it. You can't leave it all on Tom. Land won't flourish if the owner doesn't live on it."

"And how do you know that, Miss New York?" Mike inquired.

"I know it," Sally said stubbornly. She found herself digging in her heels. Before, when Mother was still alive, she had resisted what she knew was the family sentiment that she ought to marry some nice local boy and settle on the Madrona. Now that she wanted to, minus the local boy, they didn't believe her. "Do any of you want to do it?"

"No," Janessa said flatly.

"Then let me have it." Sally's eyes filled suddenly with tears. "What else have I got?" She stood up, pushing her chair back awkwardly from the table.

"Sally, honey—" Tim started after her.

Mike grabbed his arm. "Leave her alone. She had a letter from that damn German again today."

Eventually they all went home. Sally saw them off with relief, shedding their solicitousness and unspoken sympathy a layer at a time until, as the last carload left, she felt finally unencumbered. If only she could have managed to shed Juergen, too, with the departure of those who knew about him.

I used to be a country girl, she thought suddenly. Memory pulled her backward, into the Madrona's heart. She was four, riding into town in the buckboard with Tom's grandfather. *I used to love it then. Maybe I've grown too old to be Sally-belle any longer. We need to keep the Madrona.* It sounded fine at the moment. There was purpose in it, anyway.

But that night she dreamed about Juergen, and her mood rocketed back toward desolation. She woke in the morning feeling like a self-immolated offering, a sacrifice fed to the land. What was she going to *do* all day here?

"Exercise them damn horses," Tom said. "There ain't enough of us. And figure out which ones to sell off. They're eating their heads off."

You couldn't bear to part with any of them, could you, Mother? They poked their noses at her over the gates of their box stalls, big soft lips looking for carrots. The show horses had been Alexandra's darlings, her pets. Sally sighed. "Sell them all," she said over her shoulder to Tom. "I don't know how to train them. If we're going to make this land pay, we're going to have to plant, put some of that pasture under the plow."

"Farm?"

"We already farm oats and alfalfa," Sally said. "Onions and celery can't be that different. If those cowboys of yours want work, they're going to have to learn to do it. Only rich people get rich raising horses these days."

"What about the working stock?" Tom looked horrified, as if she'd ordered him to raise fish.

"Do we still have a contract with the army?"

"We do," Tom stated. "It ain't for but half what they used to buy, though."

"It'll be less every year. They can't compete with tanks. We'll keep the working stock, what you need to run the ranch, and as many remount stock as the cavalry will take a year. That's it."

Before she changed her mind, she turned away from her mother's big darlings, whickering in their stalls, and went down to the lower barns, where she took a heavy-mouthed dun she remembered riding before out of the paddock. She felt like riding something she'd have to fight with.

When she brought him back at dusk, she was as limp as water. She left the ranch hands to their dinner and went upstairs to her mother's old room, hers now, and turned the

overhead light on. She had been all over the Madrona on the
dun's back and could feel its plait etched into her skin like a
tattoo. She found writing paper and her mother's gold-
nibbed fountain pen and sat down to write.

Dear Juergen,
    *I have found a place to hide from you. Mother
died. She was seventy-six, but I feel outraged and
bereft anyway. So I have come home to the Madrona to be the farm girl I always swore I would
not be. I thought I was going to hate it, even this
morning, even last week while I was telling Tim that
I wanted it. Now I don't know. I rode down the
valley, and it seemed to repair things. Knit up holes.
Maybe I will put my hands in the dirt and grow
cabbages, as India is doing in New Mexico. How are
your mother and the girls? I ask, I suppose, in the
hope that they will one day see fit to turn you loose
before we are old. I suppose we are old now. . . .*

Dear Sally, (wrote India)
    *How funny to think of you on a farm, too. Not
that we have what anyone but Eleanor could call a
farm. Truck garden, maybe. There's a little spillover
beyond what we eat ourselves, and we take it to
town to sell. But that's what Eleanor calls it. "Are
you going to the farm?" she will ask when I go out
to weed in the morning. Even David does his bit
with a hoe and a fearful scowl. He seems somewhat
more malleable of late, but it may be only wishful
thinking. He has made a few friends at school, the
few Anglo children here, and a particularly brilliant
boy from the pueblo. Word of his escapade got
around, I think, and has given him some standing.
Maybe it will be enough for him. Frank came last
month, and they didn't actually fight with each
other this time. Frank took Eleanor's rifle and
taught him to shoot—said any country boy ought to
know how. He may have to start shooting us our
supper, although we aren't reduced to eating prairie
dog quite yet.*
    I bought some chickens, for their eggs and to

*eat bugs in the garden. I go out in the morning to
feed them with an apronful of corn and my sunbonnet on. I look like Mother Hubbard. Do you miss
New York? Sometimes I can't think about it without
crying, and sometimes the air here seems so clear
that I think I can see—something. God knows what.
Shall we trade canning recipes and advice on the
best time to plant beans?*

Dear Sally, (Juergen wrote)
 *I hate to think of you growing cabbages when
you love the city so much. Do you go to Portland, or
do you hide on your farm? I will take the right to be
interested, even if you do not accord it to me. Ilse
died last spring, but you couldn't have known that
when you wrote. It is not that they will not turn me
loose; Germany will not turn me loose, we live in
such dire times. I wish you would come here and
see it. See me. Then you might understand. You
might even stay. I tease myself with that notion at
night, that one day you may be willing to stay, that I
may be worth it to you.*

What could be worse in Germany, Sally wondered, than
what she could see on any trip to town, sometimes just by
looking out her back door? They came every day, ragged
weary men, looking for work she didn't have to offer, for the
handout at the back door that was all she could manage.
Thin, despairing women trailed in their wake, baby on one
hip, or trundled in a rusty wagon, sometimes two or three
more children trudging behind. Tom let them sleep in the
barn, which was more than most ranchers would do, and sent
them on their way with whatever the kitchen could spare. By
stretching everything thin, the Madrona managed to keep its
regular crew fed and most often paid.

They sold off Alexandra's horses and used the money to
buy equipment and seed to put half the pasture in celery and
onions and a field in strawberries. Sally toyed with the idea
of putting in orchards. Some days, when the farmhands were
overworked, she drove the tractor herself and sat up over the
farm books at night, juggling accounts and reading agricul-

tural treatises with a newly acquired pair of glasses on the end of her nose.

When the Madrona was still in the black at the end of a year, in 1932, she went to Germany.

Sally stared at herself in the mirror of the smallest, cheapest stateroom, wondering what Juergen would make of her. She had scrimped to buy the ticket and some new clothes. Every time she saw him, fashions seemed to have changed radically, and she always felt as if she looked like a woman dressed up as someone else. Skirts had gone down again, and waists back up. Sally had let her hair grow out to shoulder length and wore it in soft waves. Was she too old for that? Ought she, at forty-eight, to adopt a bun?

Oh, for goodness' sake, she thought ruefully, and went to lean over the rail on deck and peer through the early morning fog. Maybe it would be different for Juergen and her this time. Maybe Americans were not so universally despised in Germany anymore. In times this bad, what use was it to go on hating people? Maybe she would write to Tim and Mike and tell them she wasn't coming back, tell them that she had gotten the Madrona on its feet and they would have to help it stagger along from here on. If she was still in love with Juergen after twenty-four years, didn't she have a right to him?

Juergen would tell her that, she thought. Maybe this time she would listen.

"Oh, dear God, it really is you. Here. I can hold you." He held her so tightly she could hear his heart thudding in his chest. Her arms tightened around his ribs. Hold on. Just hold on to him. It was all still there. There was no getting around it, no finding someone else to love while this still existed. Robin had married long ago and had babies; he had sent her their pictures.

When she could bear to lift her head from the tobacco-scented wool of his overcoat and look up at him, she could see the joy in his face. It was enough to stagger her. Each time they were reunited she feared that Juergen might have stopped loving her so much, and each time it was still there.

"I took an apartment for you," he said. "So you won't have to put up with Mother and Crista."

Sally laughed. "Do they know I'm here?"

"Certainly. And they have strict instructions on how to behave. But you do not need to share a house with them." He smiled lovingly and touched the lines around her eyes. "There are some advantages to not being an ingenue anymore."

Sally sighed and snuggled her head against his shoulder. There would be more privacy in this apartment, too, she imagined.

"I may be going to Berlin soon," Juergen said as they walked along the platform. "If that happens, we will find you a nice place there." He smiled again. "If we are very lucky, Mother and Crista will refuse to move. They think Berlin is decadent and full of Jews."

"At least I'm not Jewish," Sally said with a chuckle.

Juergen's hand tightened on her arm. "Don't even joke about that."

She looked at him, puzzled, but he was hailing a taxi, his back to her.

He took her straight to the apartment he had rented, a little villa near the Ringstrasse—where he had once proposed they should live, Sally thought wistfully. They laughed, kissed, made love, went out for schnitzel and beer in a café where a man with a cornet played smoky jazz, and went home again. There they made love as if they were still twenty, and Juergen spent the night.

In the morning he dressed and went to the office, where he was involved somehow in regional government and politics. Sally didn't understand it well. Germany's government had undergone too many incarnations since the war for her to follow them. In the evening he was going to take her to call on Frau von Appen and Crista and to meet a few of his friends there. That was all the politics she thought she could manage.

In the end, however, she got an introduction to German politics at Frau von Appen's. No one talked of anything else.

"So, Juergen, why has Hitler turned down the vice chancellorship?" a man in evening dress and a monocle inquired. He had been introduced to Sally as Herr Witt.

"I have no idea," Juergen said dryly. "I am not in his confidence."

"He has made a mistake," Witt said. "Hindenburg didn't want to offer it. He won't get the chance again."

"Then he has outfoxed himself. It makes the balance better. We should be grateful."

"You don't support him?" Witt said.

Juergen opened his mouth and closed it again. When he finally spoke, he sounded to Sally as if he had been arranging his words. "I support a balance. There is no question that parliamentary government will have to be abolished. It has lost all control of the country and become useless. But I support a coalition in its stead. There is room for Hitler and his party within that."

"Mmm!" said Witt.

Juergen slid away from him and took Sally by the elbow. "Come and meet some more people." Frau von Appen had apparently invited whomever he had told her to, an odd mixture of politicians and personal friends, it seemed to Sally. They looked at her curiously—they had obviously heard about her from Frau von Appen—but no one was rude. They seemed to her obsessed with genealogy, and she recited her pedigree several times. A Bavarian great-great-grandmother on her mother's mother's side seemed a point in her favor. Talk always slid back to politics, but there was something strangely stilted about it at odd moments, as if a clamp would suddenly tighten on a conversation and someone would think better of what he was about to say. As usual, the men did all the talking about politics. The women talked about the men, each other's clothes, and whose husband was being given a post in Berlin.

"Why are you going to Berlin?" Sally asked Juergen as he drove her to the apartment.

"It's only a possibility," he said. "To be some sort of balance point, I suppose. The fellow who hitches all the horses together and tries to make them run as a team." He sighed, and when they reached the apartment he poured himself a glass of whiskey from the cabinet he had stocked. It was becoming obvious to Sally that he was expecting to spend most of his time in the apartment with her.

"Juergen, will everyone think I'm your mistress if I stay here alone?"

"Yes. Do you want me to go home to Mother so they won't?" He looked at her over his glass.

"No." She sat beside him on the sofa, and he cuddled her.

"Oh, my blissful darling, give up your horrible cabbages and stay here with me while I wrestle my dreadful horses." He lit a cigarette and leaned his head back, blowing smoke at the ceiling. "We have too many factions, left and right, too many freelance military, too much unrest and riot. We never managed to make democracy work, and it is going to go out with a bang if we are not careful."

"Who is this Hitler everyone was talking about? They all seemed to get *very* careful when his name came up. My German has improved, you know."

"Some people think he's Germany's future," Juergen said.

"Do you?"

"I will tell you a secret. I am afraid of him." He put his cigarette out. "And I don't want to talk about him. I want to make love to you. We are not so old as we thought."

Sharing a double bed with Juergen, curled together like spoons, his even breathing warm on her neck, was a luxury Sally had never had before. It could be like this always if she stayed. They could get married. It was too late for children probably, but they would have each other. And she was older now, old enough to laugh off Mother's and Crista's barbed comments. Cologne was depressed, but the whole world economy was depressed, tumbled over by the American stock market. She could always go home to visit, but with both her parents gone, that didn't seem so important. Tim and his wife came to Europe regularly anyway. Ships were faster now. . . . She drifted to sleep with Juergen's arms around her waist, his warm body against her back, and thought about what one wore to be married at the age of forty-eight.

In the morning she was less sure—dreamtime always felt more certain than reality—but it still seemed feasible. Watching Juergen button his shirt, his pale hair freshly slicked down, whistling under his breath, she was overwhelmed by the strength of love. It was a hellish force when you tried to go against it.

When Juergen left for his office, she went out to explore. There was little else to do. *I suppose I will have to make friends*, she thought, and she wondered how hard that would be. Surely there must be other people like Juergen, people who would like her.

The Wall Street crash had reverberated through Europe, but in Germany, weakened by punitive reparations payments and economically dependent on short-term loans from abroad—loans that were suddenly unavailable—the damage cut deeper. Unemployment had soared. The ragged men Sally passed in the street looked no different from the ones who had come to the Madrona's back door. Statements of protest and anger were scrawled on the walls, and she saw six or seven styles of uniforms—the "freelance military" Juergen had spoken of, she supposed. Each political party seemed to have its own, a notion that made her uneasy. She saw hanging from windows the hammer-and-sickle banner of the Communist party and the odd, crooked-armed cross that she learned from a newspaper article was the badge of Adolf Hitler's Nazi party. All the newspapers were full of the November elections, of the claims and counterclaims of Communists, Social Democrats, and Nazis in Parliament, and of the violent battles of their adherents in the streets.

Juergen came back from his office tense and white around the mouth, wanting to make love and talk of getting married. When she asked him about German politics, he shrugged and asked her if she had been to the Museum of Eastern Asiatic Art yet.

"It opened just after you were here last."

"Juergen, I am not a silly little woman with her head stuffed with fluff. If I am going to marry you, you will have to tell me things. I don't understand entirely from the newspapers."

Juergen sighed. "No, of course not. Maybe I don't want to tell you. But you deserve better. If we are not very careful, there may be civil war here. Hitler's thugs and the Communists' thugs and the people who want to blame all their misery on someone else fight each other in the streets, and honest citizens are afraid of them. It has to be brought under control. But you are not in danger. I wouldn't keep you here if you were. Nor Mother and Crista. There is no danger in Berlin, either, not for you. You mustn't worry. I'll take you there. I want you to see all of Germany."

He didn't appear to be holding anything back, but it wasn't an entirely satisfactory answer. Yet she cashed in her

return ticket and decided to wait a bit and see, through
Christmas anyway. She had never had a Christmas with Juergen. They would have to go to Mother's house, she supposed, but afterward they could be by themselves. She could
put up a tree, buy him presents. . . .

Only when he said they could get married on Christmas
Eve did she panic. "No, Juergen. I want to get married at
home. In America. That's important to me."

The newspapers were full of a speech by Hitler blaming
everything on the infiltration of Germany by Jews and other
undesirables, but not saying a word about Germany's having
started a war. "Not everyone thinks that way," Juergen said
uncomfortably when he saw her reading the speech, but
something about it made her skin crawl. No one she met at
the parties Juergen took her to seemed to disagree, at least
not out loud.

And then in December and January the government
came apart yet again, and suddenly Adolf Hitler was chancellor.

"Oh, Juergen, that horrible man." Sally read the news,
appalled.

"Hush. The other factions can keep him on a leash," he
said. "People are afraid. They want someone strong. The
common people believe in him."

Then in March Hitler managed to pass the Enabling
Law—which enabled him to pass any further law he wanted.
The first was to purge the civil service of Jews and political
opponents.

Juergen began to come home late, then sometimes not
at all. In the market the grocer gave Sally an odd look, and
his wife and the fishmonger whispered behind their hands. *I
have to marry him or leave*, Sally thought. She was foreign
and therefore subject to suspicion. She heard the words as a
kind of background mutter: *Foreign whore. Foreign Jewish
whore.*

In March a camp was opened in Dachau, near Munich.
The Cologne newspaper called it a "concentration camp" in
which "antisocial elements" were to be incarcerated and
made to work for the benefit of the state. Homosexuals were
rounded up and sent there, along with criminals, loosely defined, including political opponents of Hitler. The newspaper
was very proud of the camp. The new People's Community

of pure Germans did not include the deformed or defective, the mixed-blood mongrel, the Jews or the Gypsies. The country would purge itself of the "bacillus," the paper said.

"How long have you known about this?" Sally held the paper out to Juergen. She was furious to find that her hands were shaking. *Why am I frightened?*

"A month," he said. "It is a prison camp."

"For people who don't agree with your Hitler?"

"He is not *my* Hitler! Sally, please—"

"Juergen, I have to go home."

His eyes closed briefly. He stood, head down, so long that she assumed he was angry. When he finally looked at her, his face was bleak. "I know."

She put it off then, terrified that she wouldn't see him again. "I have to stay" was all he said to her pleas that he come with her. The May afternoon that he put her, finally, on a train for Paris, the German trade unions were replaced with the tame German Labor Front, and a bonfire of books by Jewish, left-wing, and other "un-German" authors went up in smoke.

Juergen held her as if he might change his mind and pull her back from the train. Then the whistle shrieked, and he pushed her through the clouds of steam and up the iron steps just before the conductor pulled them up. She leaned out the window and grabbed at his upraised hands. "Come with me! Get out of here!" she said. "How can you *stay* in a place like this?"

"You are talking about my country," Juergen said with an edge to his voice. They had quarreled, and she had cried all morning.

His country. His horrible country that had started a war and hadn't learned a thing from it. Sally's misery overflowed. "Then don't write to me again!" She pulled her hands in and slammed the window shut.

The train eased down the platform, picking up speed. She had always had the unfortunate tendency to hear things in the wheels rolling over the tracks. Now they said, *I could have stayed, I couldn't have stayed.*

"It's time you got home," Tom said, as if Sally had taken an extra week at the seashore. "You want to put in some hops, now we got Repeal?"

She looked across the valley, unable to decide.

"Hops makes money." He grinned. "Gonna be a big demand. Maybe we should have put in a distillery."

"Let's settle for hops." It didn't seem to matter, Sally was thinking. The Madrona had gotten along fine without her, for all her previous notions that a Holt had to be on the land. Holts had been on the land since 1840. Now she suspected that the land had nurtured them, rather than vice versa.

Tom leaned on a fence post, watching a jay on the next one, its head cocked at them. "Birds got it easy," he said, turning toward her. "You think things'll pick up some now we got Roosevelt in?"

Sally sighed and put her hands on her hips. "I hope so. Hooverville isn't going to disappear overnight, though, no matter how hot his New Deal is." At least Roosevelt wasn't looking for some hapless segment of the population to take the blame, to be responsible for the shantytowns of tin and cardboard boxes that edged every city in America. Except maybe the Republicans, but no one wanted to put them in jail.

"What do you think of the Communists?" Tom asked. "They claim they got the answer. Some of the boys been to their meetings, say they make sense."

"I don't think anybody knows what to do," she said sadly.

"Including your fella in Germany, huh?"

"I'm not writing to him anymore."

Juergen pulled his coat collar up around his neck against the snowfall, his hat low over his eyes, and immediately felt that he looked furtive. The fear of a hand on his shoulder, of a sudden shout from across the street, was overpowering, and he fought to control it. When he relaxed, the images flooded back, of the house in Berlin where Hitler was supposed to dine, the basement smelling of mold and cat pee, with its small grilled window giving way onto the sidewalk. The explosive had been fastened to the ceiling joists, just under where the head of the table would be in the dining room above. Hitler had gotten loose from the leash the old politicians thought they could hold him on, and now there was no way to stop him but one.

Juergen shivered as he stood in the shadows of the docks, his fingers cold through his gloves. He had with him only one bag, all he could take safely, he thought. One bag and himself. Mother and Crista had refused to come, had reviled him for endangering them and then refused to leave. It was that woman, they said. That American who had turned him against his own country.

"My country has turned on itself!" he had shouted.

"And you have turned on us!"

"No. You can still go with me. I bought passage for three."

But they wouldn't. Women like his mother and sister were the ones always in the right, he thought. Maybe the Germany that Adolf Hitler was building was for them.

All he knew was that he couldn't have a part in it. But the explosive hadn't gone off. It had been bad, or the men who had sold it to him had betrayed him. Juergen and the two others, watching from across the street, grew white-faced as Hitler came and went. Then the police came. The other two ran, Juergen didn't know where; they were politicians, not criminals, and didn't know how to hide.

He had gone back to Cologne, packed a bag, and bought tickets on a Rhine steamer going north to Holland. If the authorities were looking for him, they would watch the trains first. But even if they didn't catch him, didn't suspect him—even if he didn't end in the Dachau camp where the sign over the gate read ARBEIT MACHT FREI, work makes you free—he couldn't stay, not even if he was safe. He couldn't have a part in what was happening to his country. It came down to a matter of his soul.

He watched the snow fall into the dark river, lit beyond the docks only by the running lights of moving steamers. His boat didn't leave for an hour yet. What was his mother doing? Did he dare write to her? Send her money? Probably not, but Frau von Appen had money of her own and would do well enough. Better if she and his sister could denounce him and mean it. He supposed they probably did. Something slipped away from his shoulders with that thought, a kind of painful freedom resting on them instead.

A hand fell on his shoulder, and he whirled around in terror.

"Juergen! You old reprobate! What are you doing hanging out by the dock?"

Juergen made himself chuckle. "What are you?" he inquired with a leer.

"Waiting for Lorelei," Herr Witt said. "Haw!"

"I think I just saw her around that corner," Juergen murmured.

"What, am I in the way here?" Witt guffawed again, but he didn't go away. Juergen watched him with unease. Did he know? Had he been sent to find him, keep him until the police came?

"I thought you were in Berlin," Witt was saying. He rattled on. "I meant to tell you, I found an excellent new tobacconist. Some thieving Jew had the shop, but the new fellow's quite sound, has all the old Jew's stock at bargain prices. I'll take you round there tomorrow if—"

"I can't," Juergen said abruptly. "I was in Berlin, and I have to go back there tonight. I'm afraid I can't discuss it with you, but it's a matter of the utmost importance to the chancellor. You'll hear some pleasing news in a day or two, I expect, but matters are delicate just now. I don't wish to be rude, but it's important that I don't attract attention at the moment."

"Ah!" Witt looked impressed. He straightened his hat on his head and gave an odd impression of a salute. "Well, then! I'll be off." He lowered his voice. "Good luck."

When he had turned the corner, Juergen let his breath out in a soft rush of fear. Someone else who knew him might come along any moment. The steamer wouldn't sail now for forty-five minutes, but it was docked. He had been afraid to sit on board—too easily trapped—but now he thought he had to. He would be out of sight. He picked up his bag.

The cabin was small, not as palatial as on some of the Rhine steamers. From his porthole Juergen could see the dock, the splashes of yellow from the lamps, the fairylike strings of light along the bridges. Footfalls on the deck above and in the gangway outside sounded hollow, ominous. Distant shouting made him stiffen.

Juergen looked at his watch, looked out at the dock. He still had his overcoat on; the melted snow ran down his collar. On the dock police had materialized, as if from the dark air. He ran out of the cabin and up the steps to the deck, afraid of being cornered, and saw them marching down the gangway toward him, guns on their hips. The Dutch freighter carried few passengers. The deck was empty. Juergen flung himself under a lifeboat and waited while he heard brusque voices ask for the passenger list. At first the Dutch captain protested, but then he produced it.

Juergen held his breath. He had not bought the ticket in his own name, and the papers in his pocket didn't bear the name von Appen—some things politicians did know how to manage. But what if the man from whom he had procured them had turned him in? What if? What if? What if the whole world were hunting him now, ready to turn him in for being a traitor, a would-be assassin, an enemy of the state? *I fought for Germany,* he thought. *Now I am hiding under lifeboats. And I am old.* That was the worst of it. He had given his youth to a country that had turned into something he feared.

He heard the voices, and the Dutch captain's angry reply. Then the boots marched away again, hollow steps thudding on the gangplank. The captain went to the wheelhouse and gave the order to cast off. Juergen could feel the heavy engines thrumming under the deck, like muffled explosions —the sound the dynamite might have made if it had gone off. With profound relief, he came out from under the lifeboat as the steamer nosed into the current, sliding past the lights of Deutz on the opposite bank, under the Hänge-Brücke.

When he got to his cabin, Witt was in the armchair.

"I expect the chancellor will like my news even better than yours," Witt said. He looked at Juergen with something that resembled pity.

Juergen unbuttoned his overcoat. There was the gun, the one he had brought in case he wanted to shoot himself with it. If he were taken for questioning to Dachau, he would not survive it, and he might slip and tell them something. A gun was easier.

He pulled it from the folds of the overcoat and shot Witt with it.

No one ever came unannounced to the Madrona. The farm dogs would set up a ruckus, the geese would wake up and honk, and Tom would come from the foreman's cottage with his shotgun, just in case. Sally heard the cacophony through her sleep and got up to peer through the window. She could see the lights of a taxi turning in the oystershell circle in front of the house. She grabbed her wrapper and went to the door.

The wraithlike figure on the steps was bundled in an overcoat and wet with the light, misting rain that came down.

"I sent the taxi away," Juergen said. "If I can't come here, I don't have anywhere else to go anyway."

Sally stood silhouetted in the warm glow of the hall behind her, wondering if he would vanish if she touched him, or if she would fall if she tried to take a step. Behind Juergen, on the first step up to the porch, Tom looked at them thoughtfully and turned back to his cottage. "Shut up, you idiots," he said to the dogs.

She held the door wide, and Juergen stepped into the light, the single bag in his hand. "It may be too late," he said.

"What have you done?"

He told her. "Until we crossed the border into the Netherlands, I waited for Witt's ghost to come out from under the bed where I had put him and radio the police, and wondered if he had done it before I shot him. Later I knew the Dutch police would be looking for me when they found the body." He was still standing in the hallway and hadn't taken off his coat, as if he wasn't certain she would let him stay. There had been no letters between them since last May.

"Why didn't you cable me?"

"I was afraid you would tell me not to come."

"Because of what I said on the train?" A flicker of terror went through Sally. What if he hadn't come to her at all? "That was because you were going to stay in Germany! I couldn't face writing to you and not being able to be with you. But you're *here*!"

"I didn't come here because of you," he said quietly. "I came because I had to get out. I tried to stay and stop what is happening."

"You came to Portland for me. You could have stayed in New York."

"Yes, once I had left Germany, I came here because of you. But I didn't leave Germany because of you."

"Why are you so anxious to make sure I understand

that?" Sally demanded. "To be sure I know my place in your priorities?"

"No. Just because it was my country, and it matters to me that you know *me*. I can't come here under false pretenses."

"Do you want to be here?"

"Desperately." He held out his hands to her, and she took them.

"Then it doesn't matter how you got here." She moved closer and touched his face, patting him to make sure he was real. "If circumstances have cut you free, then you are here with a clear conscience, which you wouldn't be if you had left for me. I would hate for you to be here feeling miserable and guilty." She buried her face in his coat, inhaling the smell of rain and tobacco. Over it, faint and still horrible, lay the odor of gunpowder. She wrapped her arms around him tighter still. "How could I throw you away after this long? Do you think I'm a fool? Oh, Juergen, I'm so glad you're home."

XVI

Washington and Albuquerque

India Blackstone studied her wayward child. It was 1934, and David was fourteen now, tall and rangy and beginning to get broad in the shoulders. *Good heavens,* she thought every time she looked at him. He seemed so large and so self-sufficient. She had no idea what he was thinking most of the time.

"Have you finished your schoolwork?" she asked him. David had a bridle in his hand and was headed for the barn. "And be back by four with Taffy. I need to take the cart into town."

"Be back by four," David growled, mimicking her. "Why don't we get a car?"

"We'll get a car when we get some money." She was at the sink scrubbing carrots for dinner.

David reached around her and took one, biting into it. "You just sold a painting to some museum in Los Angeles. Isn't that money?" He smiled, wheedling. "Isn't that money?"

"It's money for you to go to college. And to buy you some clothes before the weather gets cold." She looked down at his feet. "You've outgrown your boots again. I don't know where you got feet that size."

"Probably from Dad's side," he said. "Anything you don't like about me always comes from there."

"Stop it. I'm not that bad." India chuckled. They could joke about such things now, at least most of the time. "Go on to wherever you're going. But please bring Taffy back on time." She made herself not ask where he was going.

"You sound like I'm taking him on a date," David said. "I might as well. No girl will go out with someone who drives a horse and cart."

"Half the boys in school don't have cars," India called after him, but he was already gone. "And you aren't old enough to drive anyhow!"

He seemed to be content in Taos, India thought. There was a girl, the daughter of a Princeton archaeology professor who brought his family every summer, but she wasn't here now. Local girls hadn't interested him much, but maybe that was changing. If India got a car, he'd want to drive it, drive girls around. In the country being underage didn't matter, since the farm boys drove their battered trucks from the time they were twelve. Did she want David driving around with girls? Not now, not yet. He was too volatile. Who knew what injudicious form his urge to do everything right now might take? David continued to resent Frank, even though he did spend time talking with him every time Frank was here. But should India take notice of their camaraderie, or if David found himself having too good a time with Frank, he would find a way to make the situation explode, to push Frank into a shouting match with him. He was not a malleable or comfortable child, and in many ways he remained a mystery to her. Only Eleanor seemed to have any influence on him, or at least she was the only one he never yelled at.

They were managing repairs to Eleanor's house, keeping up with the deterioration—barely—with labor from the pueblo and assistance from Frank when he was here. Frank had given up on watching the Wobblies' dying gasp and was working for John L. Lewis, the new leader of the United Mine Workers, who was trying to organize all the country's industrial laborers into the conglomerate that the IWW had envisioned but never managed to create. Lewis was self-educated, Frank said, and had read in their entirety the Bible, the *Iliad* and the *Odyssey*, Oswald Spengler, Shakespeare, Karl Marx, and Friedrich Engels.

The next time Frank came through Taos, the spring of 1935, it was just to get a rest from Lewis, he said. He put David to work with two women from the pueblo to learn how to mix adobe and later made him help replace the split roof beam. Surprisingly, after a few routine squawks of protest, David didn't object.

"The Young Communists say that every American ought to know how to build his own house," David informed him while they were working.

Frank looked thoughtful. "You hanging around with them?" He shoved a brace under the beam they were taking out.

"It makes sense to me," David said stubbornly. "We're in the mess we're in because not enough people are willing to work with their hands instead of sponging off the ones who *do* do the work, and holding them down. I've grown up some, you know. I don't want to go back to New York and be a banker like Dad anymore. It was capitalism that sucked him into what he was doing. And then he couldn't get out. He ended up dying because of capitalism."

"I can't argue with that," Frank said. "Here, hold this steady. I just think they've been a little too busy. The Young Communist League comes on like the DAR and the Girl Scouts. There's a lot more to their ideology than they're putting in their leaflets."

"Jesus Christ, Frank, people are starving."

"That doesn't change old Bolsheviks into two-hundred-percent Americans. Their first loyalty is still to the Soviets, and the Soviets are afraid they're going to have to fight Germany pretty soon, and they'd like America on their side. That's why they haven't mentioned revolution lately."

"You're a socialist yourself," David said indignantly.

"If you are under the impression that that's the same thing as a Soviet Communist, you'd better go read Marx again," Frank said. "I don't notice their state withering away, and I don't like dictators."

"Mother let me go stay with the Holts in Hollywood," David said. "For a whole month. I met a lot of people who think that the party can change things for the better."

"And a lot of people who like to hang around with movie stars and rich intellectuals while they make plans to make everybody equal." Frank saw David's stubborn expression and backed off a little. "Look, I'm a cynical old man. I don't trust anybody. Join the YCL if you want to. It won't do you any harm. Just keep your eyes open. Don't get so loyal to a cause that you can't see when you're being hornswoggled."

"Well, you've raised a revolutionary," Frank said later to India as they were washing the dinner dishes. "Jerry must be spinning in his grave."

"*I* did?" India inquired with raised eyebrows. "I'm not political, Frank, and I've never been. That was you. I told you you were an influence on him. It's just that neither of you will admit it."

"I didn't tell him to go join the Communists," Frank said, handing her a cup to dry. "I don't trust those bastards. They're a repressive regime that squashes people who don't toe the line. And don't tell me you aren't political," he added. "You've done posters for the CIO."

"That's art."

"You didn't charge for them. That's politics."

India was at the cupboard across the room. "Maybe I just like your Mr. Lewis," she said over her shoulder.

"Of course you like him. You like what he's accomplished. That's politics. You just like to pretend artists have a soul above all that."

She walked back to the sink. "Artists have to look out their souls don't get stolen. You might be interested to know that the President is asking people to consult with him on putting artists to work. Artists, writers, actors—instead of trying to turn them into bricklayers in PWA projects. I'm included."

Frank whistled. "Highfalutin company. Congratulations. And what's not political about that?"

"We'll see," India said dubiously. "I've got some ideas. We probably *all* have ideas, all different. You have no idea what working with artists is like."

"Neither does the President, I expect." Frank chuckled as he rinsed a plate.

"I met him once," India said. "At a party in New York, a long time ago, but he remembered me. I think he's an extraordinary man."

"You think he can pull us out of the hole? I've seen worse than you have, honey. I've seen people starving on the road in broken-down cars, farms gone to hell and dust, bulldozed out by the banks." He looked down into the dirty dishwater for a moment. "I saw a woman in the police station who had drowned her four-year-old kid. Said she couldn't feed him and couldn't bear to see him starve."

"My God," India whispered. She turned around and leaned against the sink. "At least Roosevelt's trying to help. He's set up programs. Hoover wouldn't do that."

"Poor old Hoover. They threw eggs at him when he campaigned."

"Poor old Hoover? I listened to you rave about that man for hours. You said he was a stupid, insensitive fat cat who didn't care if the poor all fell off the edge."

Frank was wiping the table. "So now I feel sorry for him. He's living proof of why this country needs socialism."

"They're calling Roosevelt a socialist," India said.

"They'll call him worse things if his programs work. Social Security is already making the press and prosperous citizens hysterical. They're comparing him to the Nazis. Or the Communists."

"Sally's told me what the Nazis are like," India said indignantly. "Imagine Juergen living there all that time, trying to fight them. And anyway, how can he be a Nazi and a Communist at the same time?"

Frank dried his hands and put his arms around her. "Figure out the American public, and we'll elect you president."

India went to Washington the next month determined to tell the President that the public had elected him to maintain all aspects of American life, even art. "People need roses besides bread!" she said with an angry intensity. "If we let the arts die while we try to revive the economy, what will we have to do afterward for pleasure?"

Roosevelt smiled. He was already convinced. He chomped happily on the end of his cigar and let India spew fire at the collection of men in blue suits who sat around the Oval Office. He had a lap robe over his knees. She hardly noticed that he was in a wheelchair.

"There is plenty that artists can do—they can paint murals in public buildings. They can record ancient folk art designs before they vanish. They can make sculpture for public parks. They can record local history. They can teach art to children. They can—"

"Thank you, Miss Blackstone, we know they can." Holger Cahill held up a hand. "We're convinced we need a

Federal Art Project. What we have here is a disagreement on how to run it."

"You've got to have an orderly system," another man said. "How do we know what these people are doing if we don't have them in a central work area? How do we monitor their progress? Now, a system of cubicles, such as I have proposed, would—"

"Turn out trash," India said abruptly. "Or they would all start to drink, or worse. This isn't an assembly line."

"Now, didn't I say?" Cahill said to the other man. He chuckled. "You listen to Miss Blackstone here."

"Do *you* drink, Miss Blackstone?" the other inquired with disapproval.

India began to feel as if she had inadvertently slid down a government rabbit hole. Holger Cahill was a tenant farmer's son from Minnesota. He had gone to the New School for Social Research and become a writer and then a museum curator. Now he was head of the new Federal Art Project. There were Federal Theater, Music, and Writers projects, too. India wondered if the musicians had to punch a time clock or the writers hand in six pages each day. She envisioned actors rehearsing in cubicles. The blue suits all wanted to run the arts program the way they ran the public works projects.

"We have called Miss Blackstone here," Cahill said with a wink at India that she thought the President caught, "to tell us how an artist works. Miss Blackstone has a notable reputation and is eminently qualified to give us insight." She suspected that Franklin Roosevelt had told him she was eminently qualified to give them a piece of her mind.

"This is a project for artists on relief," one of the committee protested. "If Miss Blackstone has a notable reputation, then she is not in need and therefore not qualified to—"

"You can't eat a notable reputation," India said snappishly. "I assure you I am as starving as the next woman."

"Very well." The committee member seemed satisfied now that she had admitted to her poverty. India looked at him with loathing. "Now then, we propose a pay scale higher than relief and lower than the prevailing outside wage, to encourage them to move on to independence as quickly as possible. The WPA requires ninety hours of work per month, clocked by timekeeper—"

"You'll wish you hadn't," India said. "They'll do something you'll hate if you do that."

"Gentlemen, I think you begin to see the problem." Cahill smiled at the committee.

"You can't just turn them loose," someone said plaintively. "They are unreliable."

In the end, after talking to India and half a dozen other artists and listening to detailed descriptions of their workdays, Holger Cahill decreed that an artist's creation should be proof of hours spent. No cubicles, he said firmly.

India went home to Taos and applied for relief and then for the Federal Art Project. A candidate had to be on relief first; that was a condition. She could feel her father's ghost blazing around her ears as she filled out the papers.

"Now they have you in a basket," Frank said, and she told him querulously to be quiet. In the last year she had sold only two paintings. Nor was she the only artist of national reputation to sign up. Jackson Pollock and a host of others couldn't eat paint, either.

At first she thought Eleanor would be horrified. To qualify for relief an applicant had to be investigated. Did she own any property? Have any savings? Insurance that could be cashed in? Relief investigators took her word for nothing. They asked the neighbors. They barged in to see how much food was in the icebox and to examine the clothes in her closets. David could go to work, couldn't he? they said. India endured the investigation with bad grace and gritted teeth, but Eleanor answered their questions placidly and didn't protest when they rummaged through her dresser drawers. "We have to put up with what we have to put up with," she said.

"I shouldn't have to put up with this!" India wrote in a blistering letter to President Roosevelt and to Holger Cahill, but not much came of it. Each state bureaucracy was in charge of determining its residents' eligibility. How it did so was up to the bureaucrats. And in the end she didn't qualify for relief anyway. David's college savings would have to be spent before she and Eleanor were eligible.

"No, damn it," India said. "I won't sacrifice David's education. But I want to work!"

"Well, of course you do," Eleanor agreed. "We need you

to, but not at the expense of that savings account." She looked wearily at India. "I'm sorry I'm so old."

India chuckled. "You sound as if you had done it on purpose. I'm no spring chicken myself. Now rest and pick the bad ones out of those beans—you can do that sitting down. I'm going to go pick the rest of them, and we'll can the lot of them tonight."

She didn't tell David they hadn't qualified, but he knew anyway and railed against the government, the state investigators, and the capitalist system.

"Stop it," India said. "When you're old enough to run the country, you can get elected and do it. But I can't stand having us both in a temper over this at the same time. It gives me a headache."

"He didn't even answer your letter," David said indignantly. "I don't see why you like him so much. What has he done for *us*?"

"So much for altruism," India commented cynically. "I thought you wanted to save the suffering masses?"

David glared at her and then, after struggling with it for a moment, gave a rueful laugh. "I want to go to college, too."

India gave him a wry smile and said, "I'm relieved."

And then, rather unexpectedly, she did get a letter, not from Franklin Roosevelt but from Eleanor. The First Lady had a pet project, and she had used her forceful nature to push for it. Under the Treasury Section of Fine Arts, the Public Buildings Administration reserved one percent of all construction budgets for public art. Artists submitted their designs anonymously, and juries selected the winners. Would Miss Blackstone like to submit? And would she care to sit on a jury for projects for which she had no intention of submitting? *"My husband says you have strong opinions,"* the First Lady added. *"I do not know whether we shall always agree, but I approve of that."*

Americans either adored or loathed Franklin Roosevelt, and even those who loved Franklin often hated Eleanor. She was like no First Lady the country had ever seen. She wasn't pretty, and she wasn't grandmotherly and retiring. She didn't know her place, and there was deep suspicion that she was far too smart. She wanted to give the country away to the Negroes. If a Roosevelt supporter didn't like something the

President had done, he could blame it on Eleanor. Everyone was happy with that except, presumably, the First Lady. India wondered why she hadn't told the country to go to hell yet.

All of Roosevelt's New Deal programs were controversial. The National Recovery Administration regulated wages and working hours and drew fire from businesses and union men both. It was either creeping socialism or business fascism, and that, said Frank, was how one could be a Communist and a Nazi at the same time; it all depended on the point of view of the observer. The Civilian Conservation Corps took two and a half million young men and paid them thirty dollars a month to plant trees, build reservoirs, and clear firebreaks. Not too many people could argue with that program, or with the Public Works Administration, which built the Lincoln Tunnel in New York, the Mall and National Zoo in Washington, a prison farm in Georgia, a municipal swimming pool in West Virginia, a mental hospital in California, and endless courthouses, bridges, and water systems. But the public flat out hated the Art Project. Paying artists, whom no one trusted, public money to paint things that nobody understood, were plainly subversive or lewd, or could be done better by every editor's five-year-old daughter—that was copy for tirades on editorial pages across the country and by Republicans in the Congress.

The Treasury Department built a federal courthouse in Albuquerque. India submitted a design for a mural and was assigned the central stairwell to decorate. Four other artists would do the lobby, the cafeteria, the gallery walls, and the main courtroom. She packed a bag and with some trepidation left David in Eleanor's care to finish his last year of high school.

Being in a community of artists again was exhilarating for India. She and the other four had rooms in a boardinghouse, and sometimes they would stay at the deserted courthouse to paint into the night with klieg lights set up on stands, just for the fun of it, because none of them really wanted to go home. Claire Pott, whom India knew from the first time she had stayed at Eleanor's house, had come to do the mural for the gallery that rose above the main courtroom, and they had a delighted reunion that lasted well into the night. Claire had married, and her husband had been injured in an industrial accident. What she could make painting kept him in a nursing home. "We didn't have children," she said. "Thank God."

Marty Dominguez, who was from Santa Fe, was doing the lobby; Dan Southern, an abstract expressionist, had been assigned the cafeteria, and Powell Sloan, the main courtroom. Powell worked with a flask of bourbon hidden under the dropcloth, and Dan smoked marijuana. Marty had two girlfriends in Albuquerque who didn't know about each other. All of this was zealously hidden from the project supervisors who came in every morning to record progress and reward the upright with a favorable report.

"Marty had a girl in here last night," Claire reported to India. "I don't know which one, but you could hear giggling in the cloakroom. Why do we protect those idiots when *we* behave ourselves?"

"Marty's young," India said tolerantly. "I'd misbehave, too, if I was."

"Do you think we're just past it?" Claire asked. "That's depressing. I wonder what I've done with my life, you know? Maybe I shouldn't have married."

"Do you love him?"

"I did," Claire said. "That's the worst of it. But he doesn't know me now."

Did anyone really know anyone else? India wondered. A woman might marry and get a Jerry. Or she might get someone like Claire's husband and have him end up not knowing her. Or she might wait half her life before her Juergen would come, finally. India brooded on that and added a wedding party to the scene in the stairwell, which depicted a terraced city, reminiscent of old cliff dwellings, rising up a mountainside. This one was modern, with boats on the river at the bottom, ragged dark-haired children doing handsprings in a schoolyard, a graveyard, and a factory sending white clouds of smoke into the sky. At least the bridal couple coming out of the Spanish church, the bride in a white mantilla, would always stay happy. India gave her Sally's face. As long as the courthouse was standing, there Sally would be, frozen in paint in a moment of perfect happiness.

Along the gallery, Claire was painting one of her luminous landscapes, which Dan Southern said was so restful it would put all the jurors to sleep. She retorted that it was all she could do to take a deep breath when he was working, for all the marijuana smoke, and no wonder his mural looked the way it did. In the main courtroom below, Powell Sloan was painting Justice with her scales, her skirts surrounded by the downtrodden of all colors.

The artists expected public criticism, of course; it was inevitable. Every citizen was a critic, particularly of scenes painted with public money, and the more opinionated inevitably wrote their congressmen. Most of the Treasury Section art—Dan Southern's was an exception—had been chosen to reflect the theme of the building and the triumphs of New Deal reform. It was in choosing their symbolism that the artists occasionally got in trouble.

Marty Dominguez was painting the "Heroes of Justice" in the lobby, where passersby could get an eyeful. He was copper-skinned, with a shock of thick black hair, a descendant of Indians and Spanish colonists, and Spanish was his first language. He had studied with Diego Rivera, and his murals were so vibrant they nearly jumped off the wall. The Heroes of Justice flanked a white-robed woman, presumably Justice herself, against a backdrop of New Mexico landscape —the towering Sangre de Cristo range and the blue of Sandia Mountains. Among the heroes were Abraham Lincoln and Thomas Jefferson, both in judicial robes. Opposite them, a group of muscular men were planting corn, the staple of New Mexico life and security, while Justice lifted her hand to them in acknowledgment.

Several people on the street were observing the project with interest one morning when Mr. Shelley, the project supervisor, came in with a tape measure—as he did every day—to see how much had been done.

"We get a flat commission," India said when he approached her work. "You don't have to do that. Go away."

"Imperative the building be opened on time," Mr. Shelley said, stepping around a ladder. He pointed at her mural. "Don't you think those children should look less neglected?"

"No."

"It makes it appear that Americans don't take care of their children."

"We don't," India said. "The idea is to remind people there's still more work to do."

"That's right," an indignant voice said. A woman who must have come through the front doors pushed her face up to Mr. Shelley's. "They stopped my relief check 'cause my brother-in-law sent me a ham. Said I had too much money. I got three kids and sixty-five cents in my pocketbook. What do you expect me to do now?"

"I'm sure the relief board can straighten it out," Mr. Shelley said. "That isn't my department, I'm afraid."

"While the government spends good money painting pictures to let everybody know we're poor!" the woman said. She glared at them both.

"This building is not open to the public yet," Mr. Shelley said firmly. Three or four more people were wandering around, looking at the walls, and others were looking in from the street.

"Hey! I know who that is!" A burly man in overalls who might have stepped out of Marty's mural pointed at the faces of the corn planters. "That's that Russian—Lenin what's-his-name!"

Mr. Shelley snapped his head around and peered at Marty's figures as he slowly walked toward them. "They do look vaguely familiar. Yes, that *is* Lenin, I'm almost sure." He turned away from the mural and addressed Marty. "These faces must be changed immediately."

"That's right," the woman with the ham said. "We don't want no Russians in our courthouse!"

"What else you got in here?" More people had come in, and they surged forward, smearing the wet paint by the doorway as they went. An interested crowd had gathered outside and were following them in, while Shelley tried to close the door and bolt it.

"I never! That mess in the cafeteria looks like dog vomit. Now, who would want to eat and look at that?"

"Who's that?" A man pointed a stubby finger at a factory worker in India's stairway city. "That's a black man. We ain't got any of those in Albuquerque."

"That doesn't mean they don't exist!" India snapped.

"Touch my paint and I'll knock you through the wall," Marty was announcing to a pair of local farmers.

"I have to ask you to leave," Mr. Shelley said, distressed. People were streaming through the doors again, which had been reopened by the good citizens inside. "Don't think you're going to get paid for this!" he snapped at Marty.

"The corn planters represent the seeds of social change," Marty said. "That was in my proposal."

"You didn't propose a bunch of foreigners and rabble-rousers," Shelley said.

"You weren't on the jury!" Marty cocked his fist at the farmers. "Get away from my work."

"She's got niggers in this one up here!" someone shouted from the stairs.

More people surged through the doors. Dan came out of the cafeteria to demand that someone run these people off and bumped headlong into the rest of the crowd going the other way. A siren in the distance didn't seem to disturb anyone. Claire Pott and Powell Sloan heard the noise and came to investigate, followed by their student assistants. The assistants made threatening noises at a trio of local boys, and in a moment they were swinging at them. India stood at the foot of the stairwell, trying to defend her work, while a woman screamed in her face about the unnatural mixing of the races. Three Indians in blankets and braids stood just outside the courthouse doors, watching but not participating. They had the attentive expression of theatergoers at an experimental performance.

"Don't touch that! It's wet!" India shoved a man in a denim jacket away from her mural.

"They're paying you with our money, ain't they? Well, lady, I figure that gives me the right to see what I'm payin' for. I see a bunch of Indians in there, too. How come you ain't got any white people?"

"There are plenty of white people," India said acidly. "They're the ones trying to boss everyone else around."

"Yeah, you're just like that woman. President tries to do a job helping the workingman, and you want to fill up the White House with Jews and niggers."

"Hey, look here!" Another man waved a broom in the air. "This oughta do the job!" He swiped it across the faces of the corn planters in the lobby.

"Hell, you couldn't tell the difference with that thing in the cafeteria!" Someone found a mop in the broom closet and ran down the hall.

India started pulling her scaffolding away so no one

could get at the upper levels, the only ones that were really wet. "Look out!" she called, and tipped it over the stair rail. The scaffolding exploded in a crash of splintering wood, and the invaders scattered.

Marty Dominguez wheeled his own scaffolding away and tipped it onto the bottom of the stairs for a barricade. A man fled over it from above with Powell Sloan in pursuit, brandishing a chair leg. A stout woman still clutching a shopping bag fought back, waving a mop.

"They got the right idea over in Germany, if you want to know my mind!"

"Trying to give the country away to foreigners! What about us back home?"

The sirens were louder. India saw a howling police car pull up in the street. The Indians who had been watching had vanished by the time half a dozen policemen came through the door blowing whistles. It was almost like the movies, she thought, watching Powell Sloan throw a bucket of plaster at a man in a white barber's jacket. Dan Southern had a paint sprayer. He aimed it and said, "Reach for the sky or I'll spray!" He seemed to be enjoying himself.

The woman who had had her relief check stopped for illicit ham climbed over the barricade on the stairs and stood just below India. "Brothers and sisters!" she shouted. "The Lord's given us a sign!"

Mr. Shelley tried to clamber after her, and India wondered whether to join the brawl—it was tempting—or hide until it blew over. The fear that someone would do something irreparable to her work kept her hovering on the stairs. Mr. Shelley grabbed the woman and tried to pull her back over the scaffolding barricade. Her knees hooked around a bar, and her rump wedged into the angle between upright and brace. India gave her a push to loosen her, and both collapsed under a policeman. The policeman straightened and grabbed India by the arm. "That's enough of that. You come along with me."

"Not her," Mr. Shelley said, his voice tight and furious. He pointed at the other woman. *"Her!"*

The Great Courthouse Riot made it into the morning paper, with photographs of the disputed artwork. Cleanup was progressing well, it said, and seven citizens had been charged with vandalism. However, the editors felt strongly that artwork purchased with public money should be held accountable. They had sent a reporter to inspect the lobby mural, and he had discovered along with Lenin the presence of Bill Haywood, Emma Goldman, Pancho Villa, and Karl Marx. Mr. Shelley ordered Marty to paint them out.

"The hell I will," Marty replied.

India came to his defense. "The jury approved this design. You can't come in here and censor it."

"Look at this!" Mr. Shelley held up the newspaper. The offending corn planters were pictured right next to the headlines about the war in Spain. India peered over his shoulder, ignoring the mural photo. Hitler was sending more ammunition and aircraft to the Nationalists in Spain. The Soviets were arming and advising the Republican People's Army. International Brigades were joining them. The town of Guernica had been nearly destroyed by air attack.

Shelley rattled the paper in India's face. "On the front page! We can't have this!"

Powell Sloan, looking over her shoulder, whistled at the photograph of the wreckage of civil war. "Hold that still, will you, Shelley?" He grabbed the pages and squinted at the type.

Shelley snatched the newspaper back and stuck it in his overcoat pocket. "Paint them out. Or you won't get paid!" he said to Marty Dominguez. Turning on his heel, he shouldered his way through the front doors.

"Are you going to do it?" India demanded.

"The hell he is!" Powell Sloan said. "We won't stand for this. Shelley said there were too many 'coloreds' in mine. That's just how he put it." He shook his head to indicate bemused humor. "Wanted me to lighten them up a bit."

"Of course we won't stand for it," Claire said. "Two of my students got hurt. I'm almost ready to put something *in* my design just so Shelley won't like it."

"Don't you do that now," Dan Southern said. "You got the only design that's gonna keep Shelley happy. He asked me if I couldn't make mine 'somewhat more representational.' I told him if he knew what it was a picture of, he wouldn't like it."

"He hasn't actually ordered the rest of us to make changes," India said. "He knows these designs were ap-

proved. I don't think he really has the authority to tell Marty
to."

Shelley came back the next day, though, and repeated
his orders. He had, he said, been to the jury members who
had approved Marty's design in the first place and received
their approval. No specific mention of foreign revolutionaries
had been made in the proposal.

The artists held an indignant meeting in the parlor of
their boardinghouse. Their credit was no longer good among
the more conservative citizens of Albuquerque, and the landlady asked them pointedly how long they were going to be
staying. She had her bridge club to think of, she said, and the
city Fine Arts Committee had been to see her.

"We're all of us almost done," Claire told her. After she
had left, Claire said to the others, "Are we going to have to
take a train out in the dead of night? I want my last check,
but I won't take it if they don't pay you," she told Marty.
Powell took a drink from his flask and raised it in salute to
Claire before he passed it to her.

"Ah, hell," Marty said. "I'm thinking about enlisting
anyway. Go to Spain and let Shelley go to hell."

"That doesn't mean you shouldn't get paid," India said.
"Are you really going to enlist?" Another war, this one not
even theirs. But Marty was young and had convictions.

"The Abraham Lincoln Brigade is still recruiting. If the
government won't step in and stop the fascists, private citizens still have the right to."

"Get Shelley drunk and sign him up," suggested Dan
Southern.

"Take him down to the railyard and put him in a boxcar," India said.

Claire giggled. "Bury him up to his neck and let the ants
eat him."

"Tar and feathers."

"There must be some way to get past him."

They brooded on the subject.

Mr. Shelley nodded approvingly at Marty's mural. The
corn planters showed blameless American faces to the public. The ribbon-cutting would be held the next day. All the
artists had finished and packed their bags. Marty Dominguez, unfortunately, would not be there, since he had indeed

enlisted and was scheduled to leave that night. Shelley had already presented him with his final check. Marty had complained with every brushstroke when he'd finally conceded that he had to repaint the faces, and Shelley appeared to be relieved that the artist would not be present for the ribbon-cutting. After all, he might say something inappropriate, and that would be most unfortunate. Mr. Shelley had even agreed, at Marty's request, to drive him to the train station that evening.

The other four stayed late, finishing details while the workmen mopped and waxed the red tile floors. "We'll lock up," India said when the building was cleaned, the ribbon in place. "You boys go get some sleep. It's nearly midnight."

"Yes, ma'am," they said. The artists ushered the workmen out solicitously and cut the lights. A Chinese screen borrowed from the judge's chambers slid into place before the lobby mural. The dim glow of a flashlight flicked on.

"It's cracking off already," India said with satisfaction as she examined Marty's painting.

The next morning Mr. Shelley discovered that the corn planters had regrown their original faces. Lenin was there, and Pancho Villa. But Karl Marx had unaccountably become Mr. Shelley, and now he was holding hands with Emma Goldman.

"I don't think I ever saw anything so wonderful in my life," India said. "He'll hire someone to paint it over again with paint that will stick, but at least Marty didn't have to change it. And he got paid! His wife's going to need that money, too."

Marty had been scared enough to marry one of his two girlfriends before he left, and now he was fighting in someone else's civil war, trying to save the world. They all shook their heads over him.

The world was getting ready to blow up again, India thought. All the earmarks were there.

She went back to the boardinghouse to collect her bags and found a telegram on her bed: David had finished high school on Friday and enlisted in the International Brigade on Saturday.

XVII

One Last Hurrah

India Blackstone was too late to catch up with David, and the recruiters she interrogated didn't care that he was only seventeen. Even Frank Blake told her to give up on it and let him go.

"It might be a good thing for Hitler to get his hand smacked for sticking it in other countries' business," Frank observed.

"Juergen says that's not enough to stop him," India said gloomily. "David's only seventeen, Frank. He doesn't have any sense."

"He won't at eighteen, either. I remember. And Juergen's probably right. Juergen was in the middle of it all. In which case, if David goes into our army as a veteran, he'll be a step ahead of the rest."

"*Our* army?" India dug furiously at the adobe floor with the end of her cane, making a little round hole. "Oh, not again!"

"You say it's inevitable—'according to Juergen'—and then you say, 'Oh, not again!' " Frank commented. "You don't sound as if you've thought this through."

"Things are just beginning to get better here. Roosevelt's programs are just starting to work. We can't fight a war now!"

"It might improve the economy," Frank said, ever the cynic.

Dear Mom,

Now that I know you can't catch up to me, I'll
try to tell you why I went and did it. If we don't put
some kind of stop to the fascists now, it will be too
late. England is trying to appease them, and trying
to appease them is like trying to appease an alliga-
tor. You can throw it somebody else for a while, but
then it's still going to want you. The International
Brigade is a tiny proportion of the Spanish forces.
These people believe in their government, but the
deserters from Franco's side (a lot of them are
Italians) tell stories of being forced to fight—and I
believe them. They're too damn lackadaisical to
have their hearts in it. It's beautiful country here,
where it hasn't been torn up by bombing at the
front. Olive trees everywhere, and most of them
haven't been picked because of the chaos. They fall
to the ground and rot, and we spend a lot of time
lying among them, turning all shades of purplish-
red. There are refugees everywhere, women and
children and old men, staggering down the bombed-
out roads. Half the children are scarred by shrap-
nel. I am much in demand because I can speak
Spanish, even New Mexico Spanish. Tell Frank I'm
glad he taught me to shoot. I've just been made a
group leader. Do you suppose you could send me
some chocolate? The English and the American bat-
talions are getting to know each other. And we have
a lot of IRA men with us—our best fighters. Yesterday I was in my first air raid. The bombs come
down with a whistling sound that drowns out the
airplane engine. And there is nothing you can do but
wait and see if they hit you. The fascists try to bomb
out the factories and bomb the most densely populated districts while they're at it. These people's
courage is remarkable. One thing we need is better
ambulances. The fascists are using incendiary bullets—I've seen men with their wounds burning—
and exploding bullets. Tell Pablo and Martin I'm
sorry I didn't stay for the graduation party. I wish
now I had. War has its humor, too. Our political
officer only has one arm. He took a bullet between

*the stump and the artificial arm. One of the
stretcher-bearers nearly fainted when the arm came
off in his hand.*

> *Give my love to Eleanor. I'll write again soon.*
> *Love,*
> *David*

That night India dreamed, for the first time in years, of
Ben. She painted him the next day, one last time, his face
superimposed on David's, star shells bursting behind him.
What did incendiary bullets look like? What did war look
like now? And what about the Japanese? Last year Japan had
invaded China and sunk a U.S. gunboat in Chinese waters.
She couldn't paint that because she couldn't imagine what it
looked like.

But she had plenty of material closer to home—*our own
war*, she thought. The stock market was sliding again, and it
looked as if the economic improvement was stalling. Last
year there had been sit-down strikes, and John Lewis's CIO
had won, but there had also been suffocating dust storms,
and people were still starving. Frank said that with a war
coming, industry would boom, but in the fields nothing had
changed since before the last war. The New Deal agricultural reforms paid their subsidies to the farmers, not to their
pickers, who still lived in huts made of boards and weeds.
They still had no permanent home, and therefore no vote, no
choice, no voice. The Communists and the Wobblies had
tried organizing them, and occasionally the workers had tried
organizing themselves with the backing of rebels in the ranks
of the officials of the Agricultural Adjustment Act. But the
rebels had been sent elsewhere, and the organization had
come apart. Discontented workers were more likely to be
debated with baseball bats and ax handles. In 1937, the year
before, the government had finally begun to construct camps
for the migrants, enough to house perhaps a tenth of them.
But the camps kept wages down: with a halfway decent place
to live, the reasoning went, the workers could subsist on
lower wages.

Frank argued with Lewis over the migrants. The CIO
couldn't overextend itself, Lewis said, and those people were
harder than hell to organize; they never lit anywhere more

than a month or so. "But have a shot at it if you want to," the
CIO boss said. "On your own."

"I've *been* on the road," Frank said to India and Eleanor
at the dinner table the next evening. "Industrial union men
haven't any idea what that's like."

"Looking for a new crusade at your age?" India inquired.

"I've done this one before," he said with a grin. "Remember?"

"There was a riot. You're too old for riots, Frank, you
damn fool," India said repressively. She knew he was going.

"You want something to paint, you come with me," he
said. And where had she heard that before? "Did you see
Dorothea Lange's photographs?"

"I saw them," Eleanor said. She looked at her hands,
twisted in her lap. She could hardly hold a spoon now.

India turned from her to Frank and said, "I couldn't
leave Eleanor. And I'm too old."

"That's why you should come. Before you dry up and
blow away."

"One last hurrah?" She looked amused.

"There's a little money in the bank," Eleanor said.
"Manuela from the pueblo would come and stay. And Mabel
and Dorothy Brett will look after me."

"You'd sell pictures," Frank said, wheedling.

"Why are you so determined to make me go?" India
demanded. She got up from the table and went to Eleanor's
shabby, soft leather sofa.

"If you paint these people you will give them a voice,"
Frank said.

"In art galleries?" India chuckled. "Dorothea Lange's
pictures are what you want. I'd have to take a camera, not an
easel. And Eleanor's already tried to teach me that. I just
don't have the knack."

"You never see anything straight on," Eleanor murmured.

"You're well known," Frank said stubbornly. "You have a
name people recognize." He looked at India peering at him
suspiciously from her seat. It was early spring, and a fine,
thin dust danced in the stream of light that shot like a projec-
tor's beam through the window behind her. It caught her
dark, gray-streaked hair and haloed it. Frank sighed and

looked down at his hands, then back at India. "Because I am old," he said. "Because I've gone all my life racketing after some cause or other, telling myself I was too busy and too important to sit still. To *stay* anywhere. With anyone. Because now I want you with me."

Eleanor looked thoughtfully from one of them to the other, then rose creakily. It took her a long time to get up these days. They watched her, Frank embarrassed, India blank-faced.

"You're a son of a bitch to ask," India said, when Eleanor had gone.

"I know," Frank said. "But you asked me why."

They left in mid-June to pick figs in California. It was *Frank's* last hurrah, India thought, some proof to himself that he wasn't really old, despite evidence to the contrary and his own admission. Or proof that he hadn't wasted his life, that what he had done had been worth doing, still needed doing.

Why she had come was, of course, another matter. Maybe because he had finally said he needed her, although she had spent her life stubbornly refusing to do things that men said they needed. There was no telling why she had come, she thought, or at least it was for reasons she wouldn't tell herself. She painted Frank several times, something she had rarely done before. Once she painted him nude, sitting on the edge of the bed, sewing a button on his shirt. The scars, the sagging skin, the thinning hair on his bent head caught at her heart in ways that the younger, muscular body never had.

And there were the migrant workers' children, who gave India more than enough reason to stay. They were ragged and dirty and, as often as not, too proud to be endearing. They might have been the offspring of the ragged children she had seen here twenty-six years ago. Their numbers had grown, swollen by small farmers foreclosed on and bulldozed out by the banks, tenant farmers blown out by the dust, Okies and Arkies out of work and looking for the fields of gold. The fields of gold were all somebody else's, though, and California didn't want them—except when it needed its crops picked.

There would be no schooling for youngsters such as these, either, no hope of a way out. The local schools didn't take transient children. They had no fixed address, school officials would say, and they would be a disruption in the classroom.

In late summer many migrant workers moved on, north to Oregon for the hops picking, and Frank and India went with them, now trying a different approach: They would organize a group of people instead of a place, which was populated with constantly shifting faces. Some of these hops pickers had been involved once in a successful strike, they told Frank. For a season, helped by the threat of rain, they had managed to get their wages raised. "But it don't last, you know. Next year the growers set the price down again."

A reporter for the Portland *Oregonian* came into the camps and, to India's outrage, photographed her and not the migrant children. To add to her fury, they referred to her as a "lady artist," as if only male artists were real ones. This time she and Frank didn't sleep in the camps—age and arthritis opted for a room in a cheap hotel—but India went every day with her easel and paints and incurred the wrath of the landowners who had seen her picture in the paper. Do-gooders were an unwelcome presence.

"You're an embarrassment," Sally said, laughing, when India and Frank went to the Madrona for a visit. "Anson Bender asked me if I wasn't related to you, and when I told him Frank was Aunt Cindy's son, he went off about how there'd been Holts and Blakes on the land since 1840, and now look what had come of raising your kids up loose."

"We pay our pickers a decent wage," Juergen said quietly. "That is what Anson Bender doesn't like."

India studied Juergen with curiosity. He had said "we," as if he were part of the Madrona. Of course he was, since he had married Sally, but there was an ownership in his voice that India found odd. Sally didn't seem to mind. Men were all that way, she said, most of them worse than Juergen. You could tell just by looking at her that she was happy, India thought. Some outer shell had dropped away, an old defense flaking into brittle shards, slivers at her feet now. And the hunted look that India had noticed at their wedding on both their faces was fading. It only came back now, India noted, when they listened to the evening news and heard that President Roosevelt had recalled the U.S. ambassador to Germany, and Germany had done likewise. But even with that

bit of grim news ringing in his ears, Juergen's face had lost
the tautness that had made India think of skin stretched too
tight by scarring, ready to split. He looked at Sally with a
kind of wonder while she did ordinary things like butter toast
or comb her hair. And when they looked at each other, something leaped up between them that was hotter than fire. A
body could warm his hands at them, India thought. She
sighed. Frank was talking about the hops pickers, waving his
arms. No one could warm his hands at Frank. He never
stayed still long enough.

"There may be a strike," India said to Sally. "That's
Frank's business. But if there is, someone will have to take
care of the children, and if they aren't in school, I don't know
what will happen to them."

"Have you heard from David?" Sally asked quietly.

"I get letters. He won't come home." India paused, then
said, "Now I need someone who's known here—a Holt—to
make an impression on these school boards. I'm going to go
to all the schools in these little towns where the hops fields
are—"

"You can't haul David home, so you'll educate these
migrant babies come hell or high water," Sally said astutely.

India was momentarily at a loss for words. "Maybe so,"
she finally said. "But it needs doing anyway. They're left
alone all day, or worse yet they're in the fields working, children of five and six."

"Not in our fields," Juergen said quietly, turning away
from Frank.

"In nearly everyone else's," Sally said. "Anson Bender
pays them half wages and says he turns a good profit. I'd like
to slap him."

"Then come with me," India said stubbornly. "And talk
the school boards into slapping him."

"From my lofty perch as an Old Oregon Family? All
right."

"Sally." Juergen looked concerned. "It could get bad.
You don't know what it could get like."

"I've got mine. I'm happy," Sally replied. "I owe God
one. And in any case I'm not going to lead a march. I'm going
to bring social pressure to bear. There are still some advantages to being a Holt in Oregon."

"You aren't a Holt anymore," Juergen said. "You're a von Appen. And they don't like me."

"For purposes such as these, once a Holt, always a Holt," Sally said, her smile radiating confidence and contentment.

"It's a mystery to me how you can lend your name to these people, Mrs. . . . von Appen." As always, Anson Bender pronounced her married name as if he thought it were an alias.

"This isn't in the country's best interest," Randall Meade said. "It disrupts production at a critical time."

"Maybe you haven't been here long enough to understand the way we farm," Sally commented. Meade had bought the farm that bordered the Madrona ten years ago. The other men gathered in Sally's parlor recognized her standing as Old Oregon, but they shook their heads at her.

"Times change, Sally," Warren Stull said. "Not like when you were a girl here. You been gone a long time."

"My father brought us up to feel a responsibility to our people," Sally said. "To treat them decently and take care of them. Are you telling me *that's* changed?"

"These aren't the kind of hands you're used to," Anson Bender observed. "These Okies and Mexicans, if you give 'em an inch, they'll take a mile. Rob you blind."

"A dollar a hundredweight is a disgraceful wage," Sally insisted. "Who's robbing whom? And hovels made out of cardboard!"

"Where they live isn't my business," Bender said.

"They won't take care of a place," Warren Stull stated. "I've seen it time after time. They live like animals, honey. They don't know any better."

"And I suppose that's why the schools were refusing to admit their children," Sally said. There was a tap at the door, and the cook came in with tea. At Sally's orders, she had added a brandy decanter to the tray. "Mr. Juergen say to tell you he be in close to dinnertime."

"Thank you," Sally said. She knew Juergen was staying away because these men distrusted him. The brandy might sweeten their natures, she hoped, or at the least dissolve a few of their prejudices.

"Mighty good scones, honey," Warren Stull said. "And

I've got nothing against these kids going to school. Might teach them better than their parents know."

"They can't go to school when their parents can't make enough money to buy them shoes," she protested.

"Look here, I've got a business to run, and kids of my own to support," Randall Meade said. 'You stick to educating those brats if you want to—you've done a good job there—but stay out of setting wages. You don't understand how it's done, and your husband doesn't either, being a foreigner."

"I was born here!" Sally snapped.

"Your brothers would understand me," Warren Stull said. He shook his head affectionately and poured some brandy in his tea. "Women have too soft a heart."

Randall Meade pushed back his chair. He hadn't been born here, and he didn't seem inclined to listen to the lady of the manor any longer. She was married to a German, after all. "You drop your wage," he said, standing up, "or you're going to make trouble for the rest of us." He jammed his hat on his head.

Anson Bender got up, too. "You folks don't want to antagonize the rest of the county. You got their dirty brats in school, and that cut my pickers by near a quarter. You leave it at that. Don't take it any further."

"Well, now, honey," Warren Stull said softly, "I could have told you."

Some of the children were going to school. Together, Sally and India had achieved that much. But even that had caused trouble. Some of the teachers, appalled at the condition of the migrant children, were calling for an investigation of the camps. When outsiders raised hell, the county didn't pay much attention, but when the teachers got up in arms, it was harder not to listen. The county sheriff had been by the camps on a perfunctory trip, which sent Anson Bender into an apoplectic rage. He threatened to punch Juergen in the mouth.

When Juergen went out to the fields now, he carried a rifle in the back of his truck.

It was going to be an early winter. Sniffing the air, everyone was sure of it. The Madrona crops were in. Pickers had gone to the the Madrona first because they paid better, and the hops pickers' camps there had concrete floors and running water. A threatened strike elsewhere had got the wage up to $1.30 a hundredweight, and Sally and Juergen were held to blame for that by the rest of the Willamette Valley. Then it rained, and the wage went to $1.50. Frank, with water streaming off his hat, got out his old Wobbly songbook and taught Randall Meade's camp to sing "Pie in the Sky."

The time had come to get a contract for the next year. Frank made the demand, and the growers professed to think about it. They thought until the last hops were picked on Randall Meade's place. It froze that night, unseasonably early, and then poured rain the next day. With his hops in the shed, Meade called the county sheriff to evict the pickers.

A deputy came and stood in the shelter of Meade's pickers' shacks and ordered everyone out. "Look smart, folks. Mr. Meade doesn't keep these dormitories for charity beds. Your work's done. Move on if you don't want to pay rent."

"My baby's got the croup!" a woman yelled.

"Where are we gonna go?"

"Can't get nowhere with the roads like this anyway."

"My wife's sick, too sick to move."

"We aren't the health service," the deputy responded.

Outraged, India telephoned Sally from the grocery store down the road, and Frank went looking for Meade. After he pounded fruitlessly on the farmhouse door, Meade's wife shouted orders to go away. Frank found Meade sitting, warm and dry, in the deputy's car.

"It's raining like hell!" Frank said through the window.

"Yep," Meade replied.

Sally and India pulled up in the Madrona's farm truck, its fenders splashed with mud. Sally got out in a huff and said, "I heard what you're doing, Randall Meade. And you claim to be a Christian!"

India climbed out, too, her cane sinking into the quagmire when she leaned on it. She pulled it out and waved it at Randall Meade. "Half these children are sick from your filthy conditions. But even your shacks are better than nothing. They are not going anywhere until the weather clears."

"You and your goddamn Communist friends and your goddamn German-lover get off my land!" Meade roared.

India clenched her cane.

The sheriff's deputy got out of his car and took her arm. "You'll have to leave now, ma'am," he said quietly.

"Like hell I will." India pulled away from him. "These people have rights!"

"Not to stay on this land."

"You better not try to move them," Frank said carefully. Pickers were beginning to gather behind him.

"My kids are sick, you son of a bitch!" one of them shouted.

It didn't take much more. They swarmed over the muddy ground carrying pieces of hops trellis or anything else that was handy. The deputy dived for his car and radio. Randall Meade seemed to shrink down in his seat.

"Get the hell out of here!" Frank said to India and Sally, but it was too late. The hops pickers swarmed over the ground, blocking the road. Meade locked himself in the deputy's car, but the hops pickers took it by the bumpers and rocked it. Then a stone smashed through the windshield.

"No! This isn't the way to do it. Just refuse to move. Don't attack them!" India shouted into the rain, but nobody was listening. Frank had known they wouldn't. A siren screamed down the farm road, and she saw six cars sending up waves of muddy water as they came. Deputies with rifles piled out. India tried to push her way through the crowd but was stopped when someone grabbed her arm and twisted it. She struck out blindly with her cane and felt the silver head smack into flesh. As she jerked away, another pair of arms caught her.

"You goddamn rabble-rouser, you're under arrest!"

Her second time in jail, India thought, and she was too old for it now. She sat dripping in a cell jammed with mud-stained migrant women, one of them with a howling baby. Sally sat beside her. That ought to stir up the Oregon papers, India thought. She had no idea where Frank was, but she supposed they had him, too. She had seen him fighting with a deputy. *Nothing has changed,* she thought wonderingly. *All that work and we haven't changed a thing.*

A matron came down the hall and unlocked the door. She eyed the women, then jerked a thumb at India and Sally. "You two. Out."

They followed her into a little room, where Juergen and

a dapper man in a herringbone suit were sitting. They rose. "Daniel Garrett," the man with Juergen said. "Mr. von Appen has retained me to represent you. You ladies look pretty bedraggled." He shook their hands.

Juergen took Sally's arm. "We've got you out on bail," he said.

Sally shivered in her wet clothes. "Juergen, where did you get the money?"

"I went to Warren Stull," he said. "And then to Randall Meade and threatened to sue him."

"Resourceful," Garrett said.

"And they *gave* it to you?"

Juergen smiled. "I pointed out that it would be embarrassing if they gave you a podium from which to castigate them."

"But that's just what we need!" India said.

Juergen ignored her with Continental politeness. Sally sneezed, and he gave her his handkerchief and rubbed her hands.

"I'm reasonably sure we can get the charge thrown out, Mrs. von Appen," Garrett said. "An innocent neighbor caught in unexpected events. Mr. Meade has decided not to press charges, thanks to your husband."

"But what about India?" Sally asked.

Garrett steepled his hands and sighed. "I'm afraid the judge was disinclined to hear from me on that subject. Mr. Meade *is* pressing charges against Miss Blackstone. The judge wouldn't even set bail, since you don't live in the county." He looked at India and spread his hands. "I fear I was unable to convince him."

This time India made the national news. The newspapers dug up the Blackstone Girl and ran her picture as well as India's, along with a picture of Sally as the model, which irritated Juergen. They traced the lurid high points of India's more recent career—her previous arrest in Salt Lake City, her leg wound during the war, her conference with President Roosevelt over the Federal Art Project, and her son's enlistment in the International Brigade in Spain.

The judge looked disapprovingly on the publicity and, as a Republican, even more disapprovingly on the President's letter requesting leniency. "I'm just a simple country judge," he said, prefacing his explanation of why not even the President of this great land could sway the impartial course of justice.

The district attorney held a finger to the winds of local sentiment and patriotism and charged her with criminal trespass and sabotage for an attempt to disrupt the food supply of the country. Daniel Garrett said that if the food supply of the country depended on beer, they were in sad shape. That got an appreciative quote in the newspapers but not much else. Garrett did his best. But the district attorney dug up David's Communist party membership as ominous evidence of the family's revolutionary tendencies, and India's acquaintance with Juergen, who was a German and therefore deeply suspect, as evidence of being in foreign pay. And she had hit a deputy in the face with her cane and knocked two teeth out. He exhibited them in court.

The judge said again that he was just a simple country judge but personally he thought it was a disgrace when the so-called intellectual elite of the country thought they were above the law. He fined India five hundred dollars and sentenced her to five years in prison.

"This is outrageous!" Sally said with tears streaming down her cheeks. Her own charge had been dismissed. "We'll appeal this. I can't believe they did this!" Frank, India learned, had gotten five years, too, and the same fine.

Five years. In five years she would be sixty-three. What would happen to David? And Eleanor?

Frank wrote her a contrite letter, miserably self-accusatory. India felt bewildered. She had Sally send the best of her paintings of the migrant children to the gallery in New York to pay the fines, and they sold immediately for more money than she would have believed.

"You're a cause célèbre," Sally said the day before they sent her to the Willamette Women's Facility.

I'm in prison, India thought. It seemed unbelievable to her, not an adventure as she once might have thought it. She knew too much now.

They issued her two gray cotton dresses and flat shoes. She rode in handcuffs on a train with a female guard. Where did they think she was going to run to? She wasn't Bonnie Parker. At Willamette they put her in a cell with a thin blond woman who said her name was Kate and to leave her the hell alone. "Watch your mouth," the guard said, whether to India or to Kate, India couldn't tell.

Prison life became a routine. The women rose when they were told to, cleaned the dining hall, and weeded the flower beds on the grounds. India longed to be assigned to the flower beds, which she found incongruous here. She yearned to put her fingers in the dirt and grow something. In the evening they were allowed to listen to the news on the radio in the day room, and there was a library. The life here wasn't brutal, not like the stories she had heard of men's prisons, but it was brutalizing. The women seemed to India to have been beaten and mangled by some power, rather than to be inherently rebellious. The more violent of them had either followed some man into crime or had killed or tried to kill some man. Kate, someone told her, had killed her lover, and the state had taken her kids.

"Why did she kill him?" India asked. Kate would never tell her, but Rosie, the prison gossip, knew all about it.

"Beat her once too often, I reckon," Rosie said. "Before she quit talking, she told me she had one like that once before; she swore she wouldn't ever take it from a man again."

Eleanor wrote to her, and Sally, and Daniel Garrett. David's letters were forwarded, and then India broke down and told him where she was, and he wrote to her directly. *Atta girl,* he said, and she broke into tears over it because she didn't think she had enough convictions left to require courage. Daniel Garrett wrote that they were working on an appeal; there was great popular sentiment for her release. Frank was appealing as well, Garrett said. He had been to see him. Frank's arthritis was worse, but he looked good, considering. India never heard from Frank, since prisoners were not allowed to write to each other.

She stared drearily out the day room window at fields that seemed to stretch to the horizon. If she wanted to, she could make a little money sewing. She had a sketch pad, but they wouldn't give her paints. She didn't know whether there was a specific regulation against that or if it was merely the caprice of the guards or perhaps the warden. She slept a lot. She made friends of a sort, but there was no one very much like herself to talk to. Rosie was a cheerful ignoramus with a third-grade education, in prison for writing bad checks.

Six months went by; the appeal process was stalled by the glut in the courts and by the possibility of something unspecified that might happen in the near future. When Daniel Garrett came for a visit, he claimed that something *would* happen any day now. Then he came again, grinning, with the news that the governor had commuted her sentence.

He chuckled. "I'm here to tell you, a whole lot of political arm-twisting went on."

Leave here? India felt as if she had been in a coma for six months and was about to wake up. "What about Frank?"

"Well, the governor isn't in such a hurry with him," Garrett said. "But I got the word that when he's served a full year, they'll think about it. His family's put a whole lot of pressure on. I guess he's the black sheep. They're embarrassed to have him in the pen at his age."

India laughed in spite of herself. Frank's nieces and nephews might find it an inconvenient connection.

Garrett patted her hand. "I'll let you know when they're going to spring you. I'll bring you some clothes."

The guard took her back to her cell, and India blurted her good fortune to Kate, then wished she hadn't. Kate just stared at her. In six months India had never been able to pry open that shell. Maybe there was nothing inside. Maybe whatever had been in Kate was squeezed out, battered to powder by her prison sentence and her missing children.

In two days Daniel Garrett came for her. In leaving the prison, India discovered that she was liked. Mildred, who had embezzled five thousand dollars from a bank, patted her on the arm and said, "Good luck, hon." Rosie gave her the thumbs-up sign and slipped a reefer into her pocket. What on earth was she going to do with that? India wondered. Maybe she'd smoke it.

"Brace up, Miss B.," Daniel Garrett said. "It appears you have a welcoming committee."

India stared at the crowd that pushed against the prison fence outside the main gates. The March air was sharp, and she pulled her coat around her shoulders and walked as briskly as she could, leaning on her cane. Garrett had brought it for her. They hadn't let her have her own in prison; she'd used a rubber-tipped one with which presumably she couldn't knock out anyone's teeth.

The crowd outside the gates was young and fairly shabby looking. "Viva Blackstone!" someone yelled, and they all took it up.

A guard let Garrett and India through the gates, and the crowd surged around them. India stared at them.

A bear-shaped boy grabbed her by the hand. "I saw your work in New York. I went all the way to Albuquerque to look at your mural."

"I saw the story *Life* did, but they didn't use your best work," a blond girl said, tucking her windblown hair under a wool cap. "Magazine editors don't know anything. Are you going to change your style now that you've been in prison? Will your work take a new direction?"

"Miss Blackstone, are you going to take students now?"

They were all artists, India realized with a kind of thud in her chest.

"Viva Blackstone!" they shouted again, encircling her.

"Miss Blackstone needs to rest before her trip home," Garrett said.

"Of course. We won't bother her." They followed India and Garrett to Garrett's car, parked in a lot with a motley collection of others around it. The young people piled three and four into cars or into the backs of trucks. India saw plates from New York and Illinois and California.

"We'll give you an honor guard!" one of the children shouted. They all looked like children to her, shabby, endearing children. They leaned out the car windows, waving and shouting "Viva India!"

A boy and a girl stood up in the back of a pickup, unfurled a banner, and hung it over the side of the bed: ART IS FREE! The truck lurched forward, the banner flapping in the wind.

"My God," India said. She looked at Garrett as he turned the key. "Where did they all come from?"

"You're famous," Garrett said happily. "You can probably even pay my fee. Most artists have to die to get this famous."

"My God," she said again.

Her entourage dispersed when Garrett turned the car into the Madrona gates at dusk, but at least half of them reappeared at the Portland station the next day. Sally had asked India to stay on, but she felt an unrelenting need to go home, to go where she belonged and see about Eleanor.

"I thought you might need a lap robe. I'm Sadie." The blond girl she had seen before tucked it around India's knees. "Can we get you anything else?"

There were four or five young people in the railroad car with her. "What on earth are you children doing?" she asked, amused. Most of them didn't look more than sixteen to her, but she supposed they were in their twenties.

"We're sitting at your feet," a boy said. He wore a jacket, workman's boots, and paint-stained blue jeans. "You're a pioneer in modern art. It's important to learn everything we can from you."

"Just because I've been in jail?" India asked him.

"You paint things that need to be said, in a way that goes beyond social realism," he explained.

"Are you cold, Miss Blackstone? I brought some tea." Sadie uncapped a bottle.

When the train stopped, they bought her sandwiches, in case she didn't feel like going to the dining car, and occupied all the adjacent seats, plying her with questions about art. When she got to know their faces, she realized that they changed at every stop, and she suspected that at least six of them were traveling on three tickets. The ones not in the car would be in a boxcar, she supposed, Sadie as well as the boys. *Frank offered to take me in a boxcar once,* she thought, and wished wistfully, from this perspective, that she had done it. But maybe that was just a desire to be Sadie and twenty again.

They followed her all the way to Taos, where, they said cheerfully, someone was meeting them; they could sleep in his truck.

She was going to have students, India realized. That would be amusing. Eleanor would like them.

Manuela from the pueblo was at Eleanor's when they got there. Eleanor looked so thin that India thought she could see through her, and it hit India for the first time how really old and frail Eleanor had become. She had a walker now, and she used it to get herself up and come to hug India, a folded newspaper under her arm.

"Such a *good* day," Eleanor said. "Have you seen the

paper? The war in Spain is over. The Nationalists have taken
Madrid. The International Brigades have already left, poor
boys. They won't like being beaten, but our boy will be
home."

Home. All of them.

"And this came for you." Eleanor pulled an airmail letter out of the folded paper. "I've been sitting here waiting to
give it to you. I couldn't stand not to open it. I didn't know
when you'd be home, and I thought maybe I could wire you
the news," she added sheepishly.

"It's all right. Of course you could open it." India un-
folded the paper from the blue envelope, neatly slit at the
top. Her agent in New York was pleased to announce the sale
of six of her paintings. *Six?* Four to influential collectors and
two to the Museum of Modern Art! India sat down on the old
leather sofa.

"And there's a young man who's wired three times and
even called long distance once," Eleanor said. "His name's
Leland Hopper. He wants to write your biography."

During India's first week home the art students gradually sifted themselves out until only two were determined to
study with her: Sadie and the bearlike boy, whose name was
Tom. The others drifted away finally, sending postcards from
places like Tucson, San Diego, and Shreveport. Tom and
Sadie were enormously impressed with the idea of David's
having been in the International Brigade. They waited ea-
gerly to meet him, sitting up late passionately discussing the
bungling of that war and the mistakes made by the Republican government and the Soviets.

India was overjoyed and relieved when David came
home in April and announced that he was going to get the
garden in shape. He inspected it even before he went in the
house.

"Someone's done some work here already, Mother," he
said suspiciously. "I know it wasn't you. That took heavy
digging."

Did he think she had replaced him, *could* replace him?
she wondered. "It was Tom and Sadie. I have students now.
I'm a grand pooh-bah."

David put his arms around her and buried his face in
her hair. "I'm glad you're all right," he said, holding on to

her tightly. It was the closest he was going to come to acknowledging that *he* might not have been all right. She wondered what stores of fears and angers he had, like the ones she kept in her own mental storeroom.

Leland Hopper arrived and interviewed India, further convincing her of her own antiquity. He didn't look much older than Sadie, David, or Tom, whom she could see through the veranda doors, shucking corn. But her students had assured her that Hopper, an art historian, was held in high regard in the academic world.

"What has your philosophy been?" he asked her.

India looked at him blankly and started to laugh.

In August of 1939 Stalin signed a pact with Hitler, and the American Communist movement collapsed, its ideological rug pulled out from under it.

David was furious and bitter when he heard the news. "This is what I went to Spain for? To be made a fool of?" His eyes unexpectedly filled with tears, and he slammed the door behind him. India could see him stalking across the yard to the barn.

"Poor David," Eleanor murmured. "I think it's as well we haven't bought that car yet. It's very hard to wreck yourself on a horse." She sighed. "Oh, dear, we're going to have to fight Hitler soon. I'm afraid that's obvious."

It was even more obvious on September first, when German tanks went into Poland. England and France declared war, and horrible rumors began to filter back about what was happening in Germany and the occupied countries. At the end of the month, Frank came home.

"Hey, jailbird." He put his hand under her chin and smiled down at her.

Out of the corner of her eye India saw David slide toward them. She turned toward him, held out a welcoming arm. David put his hand out. "Welcome back."

Frank shook it. "You, too."

"Eleanor says to come in and see her," David said. "She can't really get around. Mother's tame art students fetch and carry for her."

India ushered Frank into the house, feeling rather as if she were welcoming the prodigal. Her art students had awaited him with even more anticipation than they had accorded David, and Sadie ran up to take his bag and his hat.

"Manuela has dinner on the table," Eleanor said. "You still have your timing."

Frank chuckled. He helped her gently up from the sofa and handed her her walker. The table was set with Eleanor's best pottery, glazed a deep rich green with streaks of blue. India blinked in mild surprise. Eleanor hardly ever let anyone eat off it. A roast sat steaming in the center of the table, and Eleanor handed Frank the carving knife. He chuckled again, softly, just a small, pleased noise in his throat.

When they had sat down, Eleanor tapped her spoon on her plate. "This is an auspicious evening," she said gently. "Our wanderers have come home. And because of that, I have something that I want to tell you. India—"

"What is it, darling?"

"This may come as a great shock to the young people, but one does not live forever."

"Thank you," David said gravely. "I have managed to get that one down."

"Well, you did it the hard way, dear," Eleanor said. "In any case, *I* shall not live forever, and I have no one but you here. So I want you all to know that I am leaving this house to India in my will."

India looked wildly around the dining room as if it might suddenly change color or proportions while she looked. It stayed its solid self, adobe walls rosy in the late sun. "Oh, Eleanor!"

David had got up and was kissing Eleanor on the cheek, while India stared around her again in a sudden surge of almost complete happiness. If ever there had been a house that was home, this was it. She had retreated from all her troubles here, raised David here, truly learned to paint here. And now there was even a little money to put it right—and it was a blessing that Eleanor should see her house properly loved while she was still alive.

We'll have the roof mended, she thought. *I was going to anyway, but now . . . And Frank won't have to do the work, either; he's too old for that.* Suddenly she thought, *I must be a success. I have pictures in the Museum of Modern Art. A baby historian is writing my biography.* She looked wonderingly at Frank and David, at Eleanor and her students. *My, my, my.*

After dinner she took Frank into the garden to show him the young people's handiwork. She saw Tom and Sadie shaking out the tablecloth and laughing by the back door. "They think we're cute," she informed Frank.

"Lord," he said as they strolled along. "There's my comeuppance."

"They're very nice children. And very talented. They'll be known in a few more years." She sighed. "If the war doesn't get them. Frank, are we really going to have another war?"

"What do you think? Do you really need to ask *me* that?"

"No. I suppose I just keep hoping you'll say, 'Why, no,' and I'll believe you." She laughed quietly. "David will join up if there is one, you know. He's very angry."

Frank looked at her and raised his eyebrows. "You can't stop him."

"I know. We're all making bandages again, to send to Britain."

"Do you want to hear something funny?"

"Desperately."

"I had a wire and then a letter from the President."

India gasped. "Congratulating you on the commutation?"

"Nope. Offering me a job."

"*What?*"

"In the Department of Labor."

India gave a low hoot of laughter. "*You* work for the government? Will you take it?"

"I don't know," he said. "I'm thinking. John Lewis says that Roosevelt has let labor down, but I don't know. Maybe he's done everything he could. Things look more complicated the older I get. I'm thinking."

India slipped her hand into his. They walked past the garden, where the dry cornstalks rustled, down to the stream that burbled beyond it. "We still have a spare room," she said. "Even with the art babies here." She'd never felt like giving Frank a room in her house before, particularly not in the interior house that had been her way of sorting her life, but now . . .

"I'd be in Washington most of the time," he said.

He *was* going to take the job. India smiled. She laced her fingers through his. "You need a home, too."

They turned along the stream and back up the other side of the garden to the back of the house. The sun was just a red egg halfway down behind the mountains. "When I retire," Frank said quietly, "I'll put a truck garden in, there on the other side of the creek. I always wanted to be a farmer."

They propped themselves against the sun-heated house, soaking up the warmth of the adobe wall. Leland Hopper was coming again tomorrow to ask India what it was like to be a pioneer. She thought that she would tell him it was a lot of trouble. She chuckled suddenly and reached with her free hand into the pocket of her faded blue dress. She pulled out the reefer that Rosie had given her and handed it to Frank. "I kept this till you got here," she told him. "I don't know how to smoke it."

He looked at what was in her hand and burst into laughter, then kissed the top of her forehead and pulled a box of matches out of his pocket. They stood together, leaning against the warm adobe wall, the smoke drifting above their heads.

From Dana Fuller Ross

WAGONS WEST
THE FRONTIER TRILOGY

THE FIRST HOLTS. The incredible beginning of America's favorite pioneer saga

Dana Fuller Ross tells the early story of the Holts, men and women living through the most rugged era of American exploration, following the wide Missouri, crossing the high Rockies, and fighting for the future they claimed as theirs.

WESTWARD! _____ 29402-4 $5.50/$6.50 in Canada
In the fertile Ohio Valley, the brothers Clay and Jefferson strike out for a new territory of fierce violence and breathtaking wonders. The Holts will need all their fighting prowess to stay alive . . . and to found the pioneer family that will become an American legend.

EXPEDITION! _____ 29403-2 $5.50/$6.50 in Canada
In the heart of this majestic land, Clay and his Sioux wife lead a perilous expedition up the Yellowstone River while Jeff heads back east on a treacherous quest. With courage and spirit, the intrepid Holts fight to shape the destiny of a nation and to build an American dynasty.

OUTPOST! _____ 29400-8 $5.50/$6.50 in Canada
Clay heads to Canada to bring a longtime enemy to justice, while in far-off North Carolina, Jeff is stalked by a ruthless killer determined to destroy his family. As war cries fill the air, the Holts must fight once more for their home and the dynasty that will live forever in the pages of history.

THE AMERICAN CHRONICLES

by Robert Vaughan

*In this magnificent saga, award-winning author Robert
Vaughan tells the riveting story of America's golden age,
a century of achievement and adventure in which
a young nation ascends to world power.*

"The American Chronicles . . . [are] not only
historical fiction, but also romance, thriller,
travelogue, and fantasy." —*Entertainment Weekly*

From Dana Fuller Ross, the creator of WAGONS WEST

THE HOLTS: An American Dynasty

OREGON LEGACY _____ 28248-4 $5.50/$6.50 in Canada
An epic adventure emblazoned with the courage
and passion of a legendary family.

OKLAHOMA PRIDE _____ 28446-0 $5.50/$6.99 in Canada
America's passionate pioneer family heads for new adventure.

CAROLINA COURAGE _____ 28756-7 $5.99/$6.99 in Canada
In a violence-torn land hearts and minds catch fire
with an indomitable spirit.

CALIFORNIA GLORY _____ 28970-5 $5.99/$7.99 in Canada
Passion and pride sweep a great American family into anger from
an enemy outside . . . and desires within.

HAWAII HERITAGE _____ 29414-8 $5.50/$6.50 in Canada
The pioneer spirit lives on as an island is swept into bloody revolution.

SIERRA TRIUMPH _____ 29750-3 $5.50/$6.50 in Canada
A battle that goes beyond that of the sexes challenges the ideals
of a nation and one remarkable family.

YUKON JUSTICE _____ 29763-5 $5.99/$6.99 in Canada
As gold fever sweeps across the nation, a great migration north
begins to the Yukon Territory of Canada.

PACIFIC DESTINY _____ 56149-9 $5.99/$6.99 in Canada
Henry Blake—a U.S. government spy—undertakes
a dangerous secret mission.

HOMECOMING _____ 56150-2 $5.99/$6.99 in Canada
The promise of a new adventure draws Frank Blake toward New Mexico.

AWAKENING _____ 56904-X $5.99/$7.99 in Canada
The dawn of an age of discovery and danger.

Ask for these books at your local bookstore or use this page to order.

Please send me the books I have checked above. I am enclosing $_____ (add $2.50 to
cover postage and handling). Send check or money order, no cash or C.O.D.'s, please.

Name _____

Address _____

City/State/Zip _____

Send order to: Bantam Books, Dept. LE 12, 2451 S. Wolf Rd., Des Plaines, IL 60018
Allow four to six weeks for delivery.
Prices and availability subject to change without notice.   LE 12 11/95